Chaos Rising

CHAOS RISING

THE ERSTALLIUS CHRONICLES

VOLUME ONE

BY P. D. BLACKWELL

Chaos Rising: The Erstallius Chronicles, Volume One

Paperback 2nd Edition, Revised with Maps
First Edition entitled: Chaos Rising: A Clan Erstallius Chronicle
 The characters and events portrayed in this book are fictitious. Any similarity to real persons, living or dead, is coincidental and not intended by the author.

ISBN: 978-1-7366096-4-4

Cover design and all interior artwork by: P. D. Blackwell

Dedication

For all the dreamers who see beyond the veil.

CONTENTS

TERMINOLOGY OF THE ALLIANCE

ACCESS TUBE: Typical deck-to-deck transfer system for crew and passengers on board large space vessels. Various types: pneumatic or magnetic driven capsule systems; hollow micro gravity tubes with either internal rails or conveyor ramps.

AKU: An independent human clan from the Ja'bar river region on Kainogae. They settled GSW-183 (Ni'apinu) after a brief battle for freedom from Clan Tuma in 3360.

ALLIANCE: The Merchant Alliance of Great Clans (Established in 3365). The universal development syndicate created to **1.** control settlement and resource use of surveyed worlds, and **2.** ensure proper control and regulation of support structures.

ALSTEEL: Moldable steel (pliable above 323°C) used only for planet-bound construction. Made by melding carbon crystals with magnesium hydraduranide via the Herz-Gamble fusion process. Resistant to oxidation and common acids.

ATMOCON: Colloquial term for Atmosphere Conditioner. A device used in terraforming operations to alter existing atmospheres for human occupation.

CENOTAPH: A monument built to honor people whose remains are interred elsewhere or whose remains cannot be recovered.

CHAOS YEARS: The interval of time when the merchant clans were not unified by a central governing organization. From 3358 to 3365. Many clans took advantage of the economic and political turmoil and seized holdings belonging to the weaker houses. Fifteen merchant clans were dissolved during this time. Six clans rose to an overpowering prominence: Clan Cormed, Clan Dejoria, Clan Emlito, Clan Sabballi, Clan Sorrell, and Clan Vestlok. They spearheaded the movement that led to the formation of the Merchant Alliance of Great Clans.

CLANMAN: Idiomatic for a member of a clan's security forces.

COMM: **1.** A communication device. **2.** Intercom, an internal communication system.

COMCHANNEL: A communication frequency.

COMDRONE: A communication drone, used to relay messages through Hyperspace.

COMNET: 1. The network of communication pathways used by comdrones and/or direct link TAC emitters. **2.** The network created to access data from planet-bound colonies, often with access to off-world data storage centers via comdrones or TAC.

COMPAD: A portable communication device able to access the comnet.

COMPRESSION DRIVE: Main engine system used to propel space vessels through hyperspace. First developed in 2832 by Goddard Simkins during experiments with the less efficient Spatial Warp Generator technology.

COMM TRAFFIC: All messages relayed over communication frequencies and/or via comdrones.

DATA PAD: Portable computation and electronic storage device.

DISPLAY PAD: Portable imaging device used for creating and viewing two-dimensional data.

DESTROYER: Medium size military spacecraft. Average length is two hundred meters. Typical crew capacity: 120. Usually equipped with separate shuttle and/or cargo craft. Standard weapons, including, but not limited to: Plasma Burst Emitters (PBE); Phase Induction Torpedoes (PIT); Tactical Nuclear Mines (TNM); and Particle Disrupters (PD).

DPS: Department of Planetary Settlement. A branch of the Alliance's Commerce Department that has oversight of all settlement operations, which includes Terra-forming operations on holdings owned by Great Clans and/or under contract for development.

DREADNOUGHT: Large military spacecraft. The average length is four hundred meters. Typical crew capacity: 400. Usually equipped with separate shuttle, cargo, and attack craft. Standard weapons, including, but not limited to: Plasma Burst Emitters (PBE); Phase Induction Torpedoes (PIT); Tactical Nuclear Mines (TNM).

DURAPLEX: Glass made from duranide crystals (a product of durillium processing) infused at high temperature within the lattice structure of supaline quartz. Its finished form is usually tinted gray because of the duranide bonding and is an excellent barrier to ultra-violet and other high frequency radiation. High tensile strength (11,000 to 14,000 kilos per square centimeter at one centimeter thickness).

DURILLIUM: Metallic composite (symbol Dr) discovered (2807) by Seth Lorin. The chief source is from certain ores of nickel, sometimes associated with platinum. It does not react with oxygen at normal temperatures nor with common acids. Under certain conditions, most notably in its unprocessed state, it can severely alter surrounding EM emissions, often increasing levels beyond the normal dynamic range by amplifying all frequencies reflected. A primary metal used in Compression Drive coils and other power systems.

EM: Electromagnetic. Refers to radiated emissions of any frequency.

EMP: Electromagnetic Pulse. A brief, powerful wave of electromagnetic radiation.

EVAC LIFT: The main elevator used in underground mining for swift evacuation of large groups of miners. Various types: Hydraulic, pneumatic, or magnetic.

FRIGATE: Small military space vessel usually no longer than one hundred meters. Typical crew capacity: eighty-five. Usually equipped with the standard complement of weapons, including, but not limited to: Plasma Burst Emitters (PBE); Phase Induction Torpedoes (PIT); Tactical Nuclear Mines (TNM); and Particle Disrupters (PD).

FIRST REBELLION: Revolt against the Alliance (3498 - 3501) by independent clans led by Wolfram Sy. Caused by trade restrictions imposed by the Merchant Houses. After three years of feuding the rebels withdrew from Alliance controlled space.

GRAND CRUSADE: The revolt against Trans-humanist technologies from 3226 to 3315. GRAND is an acronym for Genetic, Robotic, and Nano-technology Development.

GLOWBALL: A small globe (usually 50 to 100 centimeters in diameter) filled with lumicrystals. Used for lighting small areas. Activation can be canceled by changing the direction of electronic flow within the sphere.

GPG: Graviton Polarity Generator. A gravity field emitter, sometimes (although incorrectly) referred to as an anti-gravity device when used to counter local gravity fields. Most common use for positive gravity emission is in vessels designed for interstellar transport.

GUILDMAN: Idiomatic for a member of the Guild of Free Traders.

GUILD OF FREE TRADERS: The organization was established after the First Rebellion to help keep the rebels united against further Alliance expansion into new territory.

HELIOSPHERE: 1. The spherical area around a star produced by the outflow of solar radiation that is used to define the boundary of the star's influence. **2.** The area inside the heliopause, where the stellar wind meets the radiation produced by other stars.

HOLDING: 1. A landed estate, usually encompassing the entire surface of a planet. **2.** The portion of land claimed by a Merchant House and secured by contract or deed. 3. Any property by which a Clan may receive benefit.

HOLOMITTER: The source of holographic projections used for large presentations where the ability to zoom in and out of the displayed data is necessary.

HOLOPAD: A portable holoscreen.

HOLOSCREEN: Holographic displays projected from a control console to present a variety of digital information, some of which can be live, interactive media.

HOMEWORLD: 1. Origin point; The planet from which any Clan originates. **2.** The planet on which a Clan has established its central base of operations; the capital settlement of a Clan.

HYPERSPACE: 1. Alternate space, compressed space. **2.** The dimensional warping of normal space. By manipulating hyperspace great distances may be traversed across normal space with minimal dilation effects. The Time Lapse Ratio (TLR), or difference between space-normal time (T) and hyperspace time (τ), depends on energy use and distance traveled but will not exceed the ratio of 1T to .33τ if warp energy is constant above 15.5ζ. Thus, the traveler in hyperspace will, on average, experience the passage of 7.92τ hours for every 24T hours experienced by planet-bound individuals. Average distance traveled in 24τ hours: 5 parsecs.

JAPS: Judge Advocate for Planetary Settlement. **1.** An investigator assigned by the Alliance of Great Clans, Office of Planetary Settlement, to oversee compliance with the Rules of Acquisition. **2.** The legal department under the Office of Planetary Settlement overseen by the Alliance of Great Clans.

KENTAO: A form of martial art. The term is derived from the ancient kuntao, or kuntau, which means, Way of the Fist. Kentao traces back to the oldest organized system of fighting among the Old Worlds, predating the colonial expansion from Terra Prime. Many techniques and weapons of kentao are also associated with ancient silat, and is believed to have been disseminated by the Sino-Iban clans and adopted by the Iban people. Though traditionally passed within the family, aspects of kentao have been identified as the underlying style of martial training for clanmen among the oldest clans.

KOTTREL SPHERE: 1. Composite, multi-element sphere used as a self-regulating, high-energy container at the heart of power generation systems first developed by Marcus Kottrel in 2896 during experimentation with gravity generators. **2.** The heart of ignition systems for Compression Drive engines built between 2997 and 3429 by the Mayfair-Courkos Transport Company, and other spacecraft manufacturers originating among the Old Worlds.

LSC: Life Support Control. The system that regulates the interior temperature and atmospheric composition inside any compartment used for human occupation. Especially pertaining to compartments on board space vessels and living quarters within eco-domes that are used on planets with environments hostile to humans.

MAGAR: Acronym for Magnetically Accelerated Rail used as the propulsion system for a variety of weapons issued by clan security forces. **1.** Magar-pistol: A miniature rail gun developed as a survival weapon for Alliance clanmen. A difficult weapon to detect with standard security scans due to its polymer frame and lack of metallic components. Able to accelerate standard issue projectiles within the 9-millimeter size limit to 400 mps in a vacuum. Actual speed of projectile is dependent upon density of atmosphere and type of ammunition used. Accuracy depends on the type of projectile. Effective planet-bound range about 40 meters. **2.** Magar-rifle: Standard issue for all infantry and special operations clanmen. Rail-length varies from 40 centimeters to 80 centimeters. The maximum projectile diameter is 20 millimeters. Effective planet-bound range is 350 meters. Projectile velocity ranges between 900 mps to 1500 mps in a vacuum.

MAG-JET: Magneto-turbine propulsion system used in a variety of planet-bound aircraft. Often incorporated as a back-up propulsion system in non-planet-bound shuttles for use within atmospheres. Developed in 2653 by H. Lawrence Heldra, the first working model was called SCOMIT (Super-Conducting Magnetic Induction Turbine).

MAG-FAN: Magneto-driven fan propulsion system used for light weight aircraft. Maximum load usually one thousand kilograms. Used for short range transfer of personnel and/or cargo.

MAD: Acronym for Mobile Articulated Drill. A device commonly used for ore extraction.

MERCHANT HOUSE: Any family or defined group (Clan) having reached the status of interstellar entrepreneur, with controlling interest in more than one holding.

MILITARY RANKS:

DIWA: Lowest ranking clanman among the Great Clans. Two levels: **1.** Diwa: Enlisted recruit, general beginning rank. **2.** Diwa-Major: A trained specialist, which can include engineering and other technical services, or combat specialties.

NARED: Non-commissioned officer among the Great Clans. Three levels: **1.** Nared: has oversight of a platoon of six clanmen.

2. Nared-of-the-Corp: Has oversight of a company (30 clanmen). **3.** Nared-Major: Has oversight of specialist disciplines among the clanmen, which includes engineering and other technical services, as well as special combat operations groups up to 30 clanmen.

SEGEN: A commissioned officer among the Great Clans. Three levels: **1.** Segen: Commands a company (30 clanmen). **2.** Segen-of-the-Corp: Commands 1 Unit (60 clanmen). **3.** Segen-Major: Commands specialist Units which includes engineering and other technical services, as well as special combat operations groups up to 60 clanmen.

DEGEN: A commissioned officer among the Great Clans. Three levels: **1.** Degen: Has oversight of a regiment (150 clanmen). **2.** Degen-of-the-Corp: Has oversight of a brigade (300 clanmen). **3.** Degen-Major: Commands specialist Regiments which includes engineering and other technical services, as well as special combat operations groups up to 120 clanmen.

JEGEN: A commissioned officer among the Great Clans. Three levels: **1.** Jegen: Commands a regiment (150 clanmen). **2.** Jegen-of-the-Corp: Commands a brigade (300 clanmen). **3.** Jegen-Major: Commands a division (1500 clanmen).

MERCHANT ALLIANCE OF GREAT CLANS: See Alliance.

OFF-WORLDER: Any person on a foreign world.

OLD WORLDS: The first planets settled by humans. All colonized worlds at the heart of the Alliance. The "heart" encompasses an imaginary sphere 6 parsecs in diameter, centered between Centauri Base and Terra Prime.

PARSEC: A standard astronomical unit of distance equal to 3.262 light-years. The standard parsec is a measurement from the Old Worlds era. It is based on how much Terra Prime's distance from its sun would subtend one second of arc. (< parallax + second2)

PLANET-BOUND: Anyone or anything on the surface of a planet.

PLANET-FALL: Descent to a planet's surface.

RELAY NET: See COMNET.

RULES OF ACQUISITION: The directives of propriety agreed upon by the founders of the Merchant Alliance pertaining to the settlement and oversight of newly acquired holdings.

SALIX: A tree with long flexible branches, narrow leaves, and catkins containing small flowers without petals. Several species are common among the Old Worlds and on several Alliance colonies. Salix - from the ancient Englo'ni designation for this type of flora and often transliterated in other languages.

SAPI: **1.** A derogatory term for a contract laborer who does manual work (informal). **2.** The lowest class level based on the Drupal caste system that originated on Centauri Base in 3152 and continues among some of the clans who trace their origins back to that Old World colony (Clan Vestlok, Clan Sabballi, and Clan Polinda).

SINCOS: Acronym for Supreme Interstellar Commerce Syndicate. (3156 to 3358) The first organization established to control interstellar trade.

STANDARD TIME: The system of time measurement developed in 2880 by The Council for the Unification of Time. Long before humans began colonizing space, they understood that time is relative to location. Every planet orbiting a star has unique properties that determine the duration of a day and the number of days that occur during one orbit of the parent star. Standard Time breaks down the elements of time measurement and unifies them for any planetary system so there exists agreement between colonies regarding the progression of time. This time matrix overlays local time to create consistency regarding date measurement and tracking.

STRAD: unit of measure first introduced on Kainogae c.3120. One strad equals two thousand meters.

TAC EMITTER: A transmitter designed to relay signals via Tachyon Assisted Communication. Frequency band width ranges between 4.5Ghz to 11.7Ghz. The higher the frequency the faster the transmission rate across distance.

TECH: Anyone assigned to perform periodic maintenance on various types of mechanical and/or electronic equipment.

TRANSCEIVER: Portable communication device.

TRANSPORT: The largest space vessel capable of planet-fall. Hauling capacity: 250 metric tons, including crew and passengers.

WORK POD: A mobile, inverse-gravity assisted device (usually basket shaped) used to lift workers and material to great heights. Used during all types of large-scale planet-bound construction.

ERUPTION

PART ONE

In the 160th year of the new Alliance, in the 3,525th year by our common reckoning, chaos reigned supreme. Hatred and ambition were the catalysts, time and space the crucible.

— From *Conversations at Kuliq'Quad*
By Petra Sitlyn

BEV COLLI: SAPI

Cold morning rain pelted Bev as she walked with her parents to the Labor Bureau office in the clan administration complex. It was the day after her fourteenth birthday, the day her life would change. Born into the lowest social caste on Pigrell, the homeworld of Clan Polinda, her future would be limited to a life of service to the clan. Her appearance before the Labor Bureau would tell her what her service would be for the next ten years.

"We are sapi," her mother often reminded her. "We serve the will of the high-born."

Bev followed a clan official into the meeting chamber and was directed to stand in front of the seated Labor Bureau Committee. The four men and five women were unknown to her, and she wondered how they could decide professions for someone they never met.

The old woman seated at the center of the group focused her attention on Bev. She saw a girl short of stature, but of natural beauty—smooth tawny skin, bright green eyes, and thick, shoulder-length crimson hair. "Remove your coat."

Bev slipped out of her heavy winter coat and held it at her side.

The old woman noted the toned muscle in the girl's exposed arms, the firm set of her shoulders, and the shapely curves of her body, beneath the bland cotton dress that was hemmed at mid-calf. "What is your name?"

"Bev Colli."

The old woman looked down and reviewed her data pad. "You are from Shengri City?"

"Yes."

"Your parents are Sanja and Merik?"

"Yes."

"We base your labor options on clan needs. Hopefully, you will find comfort in one of the professions chosen for you."

Hopefully, Bev thought. Her parents had warned her to choose one of the Bureau's selections, even if she found the options unbearable. The alternatives would be worse. Alternatives were always worse for a sapi.

"Review your options," the old woman said. She ignited a holoscreen on the wall behind her, above her head.

Bev watched as the screen displayed the luxurious apartments in the pleasure palace that serviced the clan hierarchy. The labor contract specifics rolled across the screen—they would train her in the art of massage and the intricacies of the pleasure arts. She would service the hierarchy in whatever capacity they required. The amount of the contract surprised her. "One million credits?"

"That's standard for all ten-year agreements," the old woman said.

The display on the holoscreen faded to an aerial view of undulating, rocky terrain, then dropped to ground level and focused on a cluster of domed structures beneath a star-filled sky. The contract specifics rolled across the screen. Bev would learn the art of ore extraction and work in the clan's durillium mine on Alpha Cephei Four.

Bev stifled a giggle. The difference between the two options couldn't have been more extreme. She shrugged aside her amusement and took the next few minutes to review the choices. Her mother had told her the Bureau often presented two different professions to steer the sapi toward the clan's preferred choice.

"The clan prefers that a sapi choose, rather than be told," her mother had said. "In choosing a path, one validates their freedom. When forced down a path, one validates their submission. In freedom, there is hope. In submission, there is only despair. The clan wants their sapi to have hope."

Bev recognized the labor the clan preferred. "I choose the second option."

The Labor Bureau Committee had not foreseen that outcome but stayed true to its principles and accepted Bev's decision.

Alpha Cephei Four will be my home for the next ten years, Bev thought. *Leaving the slums of Pigrell is a step in the right direction.* She glanced back at her parents and noticed her mother's thin smile. Seeing her mother's quiet approval bolstered her confidence. *Surviving in the mine will be hard, but I'll preserve my dignity.* She returned a brief smile to her mother, then turned from her parents as she was led away through a side door.

Her first duty after signing her contract was to get stained. Every contract laborer had to accept the stain; the symbol of Clan Polinda infused into their skin with a rust-colored dye that would brand them for the length of their contract. They could get the mark anywhere not covered by hair.

"Where do you want the mark?"

Bev looked at the tech who held the stain tool and pointed below her left eye.

A brief sting and the stain was set. It was a shallow serif that ran under her lower lid and split into two prongs that pointed toward her ear. The lower prong had a slight bend, like the prong on a pitchfork.

"Most sapi get the stain where it can't be seen unless they're naked," the tech said.

Bev smirked. "Why hide what's obvious?"

After a day of farewells with her family, the Labor Bureau transferred Bev and twenty other new recruits to a cargo ship waiting in orbit. Their journey to Alpha Cephei Four took ten hyper-days. Based on the ship's average speed, a month of days passed on Pigrell when Bev exited the ship and followed the other recruits into the mine complex.

Once the orientation meeting was over, Bev hurried with the other new recruits to the fitting room, where they each received an environment suit. The bulky garment provided minimal protection from the intense radiation that bombarded Alpha Cephei Four's airless surface but was adequate for the deep tunnels and access structures inside the rock. The snug helmet demanded all miners have their heads shaved. Bev was glad her head had a nice smooth contour; unlike other heads she saw. The bulky torso limited the range of her upper body movement, despite the loose fit around her hips, which chafed her skin within an hour of her first shift in the mine.

"Expect calluses from the constant rubbing," her trainer said after her first day. "To avoid blisters, use this." He offered Bev a small tube of ointment. "Apply it before each shift."

Bev took the tube. "Why didn't you tell me about this before I put on this suit?"

The trainer shrugged.

Bev could hear him chuckle under his breath as he walked away and left her in the orientation barracks.

By the end of her first week, the physical discomfort faded. She acclimated to the sparse living conditions and defined her personal space among the other miners. She was small for her age, but the kentao instruction from her parents enabled her to discourage the rapists, and she gained a cautious respect among the other miners.

"Smart sapi learn the martial art," her father had told her after her fourth birthday. "Smart sapi learn how to survive."

Her first year in the mine was spent as a bucketeer, transferring ore from the narrow tunnels to the transport carts waiting in the loading rooms. In the middle of her second year, she became a splitter and spent her twelve-hour shift ripping durillium ore from the rock with a pickax. She toiled for five years as a member of Splitter Crew Nine and marked the passage of time by how many environment suit adjustments she needed. She grew twenty-five centimeters during that time, which demanded seven suit adjustments, but the garment always felt too tight in the torso no matter how much adjusting was done.

At twenty years of age, she was still smaller than the other miners in her crew.

My size must be why I got the promotion, she thought. Fitting inside the cab of a Mobile Articulated Drill was difficult because of the bulky environment suit, she couldn't imagine anyone else in her crew fitting inside the cramped space.

After a week of drill training, she was on level 22, at the end of a new tunnel. She cut guide troughs around the ore veins to help loosen the precious metal for the splitters. She was now Mad Japer, the unofficial title given to those who drive mobile drills—a name taken from the vehicle manufacturer, Japerson Industrial, combined with the understanding anyone who became a drill-driver must be insane because of the demands put upon them.

Bev sat in her drill and punched up the coordinates for a pass along a narrow vein of the blue ore.

The drill bit bored silently into the rough rock wall to a depth of five centimeters, then pulled back half the distance to the surface, moved upward and gouged a three-centimeter-wide trough parallel to the ore vein. The cutting stopped when the articulated arm hit the limit of its reach.

Bev entered new commands. The drill pulled back, moved to the other side of the vein, and burrowed into the rock.

The only sensation Bev felt was the slight vibration that ran down the length of the articulated arm and into her cab. The only thing she heard was the sound of her rhythmic breathing inside her helmet as she watched the coordinate display screen on the control panel.

The drill reached the end of the laser-guided cut, and Bev punched in instructions for another pass to widen the trough.

An alarm shrieked, and the drill died.

Bev stiffened in the unexpected darkness, startled by the immediate stillness. She flicked on her helmet lamp and examined the master panel in the dim yellow light. Two breakers had tripped. She reset the circuits and the panel screens lit up. She checked the power flow monitor, then pushed the start button. A tiny spot on the rock face flashed red as the guide laser illuminated the rock.

The alarm shrieked again.

Bev pounded the dark control panel. “Eetah!”

She reached down by her left knee and pulled open the access hatch to the main bus relay, then paused as her foreman’s voice sounded in her headset.

“Colli, what’s happening?”

The calm inquiry cut through Bev’s anxiety. “Got a circuit problem.”

A heartbeat later the cab door swung open and Josh Gridle leaned inside. His helmet lamp brightened the small cabin. “Probably another E.M. pulse.”

“Yeah, I know.” Bev leaned back in her seat so Gridle could get a closer look at the dead panel.

Dead drills were common in the deeper tunnels. The reason was always an electromagnetic pulse. Durillium amplified electromagnetic emissions, but why that problem persisted was a mystery. The engineers debated and hypothesized, and the drills kept dying.

Splitter Crew Nine began circling around Bev’s inactive vehicle. They could not make quota if the drill was idle.

Bev tensed at the sound of the crew’s grumbling in her headset. Making the daily quota was mandatory, regardless of any delays. Disgruntled crews had caused the replacement of many mad japers they felt had been negligent. “Will it take long to fix?”

Gridle backed out of the cab. “I’ll get a tech. Take a break, Colli.”

An hour later, Bev relaxed against the tunnel wall, hidden in the shadow of her crippled vehicle. She avoided the hard light coming from the overhead lamps in the main tunnel so she could evade the angry glares from the splitters.

Not since her first few weeks in the mine had she felt so alone. Proving her worth in the mine wasn’t a one-time event, and she knew no matter how much respect she had earned during the last six years, if her drill could not be fixed the splitters would hold her responsible. Mad japers had to watch the energy buildup in the ore to avoid E.M. discharges. Because of that, Gridle would not prevent her from being removed. The longer they waited for the tech, the more that possibility crept toward reality.

Gridle paced in front of the inactive drill, furious about the delay. “Where’s that tech?” He turned toward Bev. “Colli, get your ass up and go find that tech.”

Bev had learned long ago not to argue when a foreman gave an order. She hurried toward the main tunnel but had no clue where to find a tech. She stopped and glanced back at her dead drill. "Gridle, I'll need to head up."

"Of course you will," Gridle said. "Do you see a tech down here?"

The idle splitters, maddened by the long break, jeered and hissed as Bev headed toward the evac lift.

Splitter Crew Seven had made quota and was jammed together on the lift.

Someone yelled, and Bev's comm channel crackled with static. She whirled to see the end of the tunnel beyond her drill crumble as a brilliant burst of cyan light broke through and engulfed the drill.

Bev turned from the cyan glare and fled for the evac lift as pandemonium shrieked in her headset—a jumble of voices, horrible cries, and screams of confusion.

The evac lift began rising toward the next level.

Bev ran faster, straining against the stiff joints in her suit. She lunged for the lift's undercarriage, grabbed a shock absorber strut, and held tight as the ascending platform lifted her into darkness. The noise in her helmet shifted to static. She glanced down.

Cyan light filled the bottom of the shaft.

"What happened?" she cried, thinking the miners on the lift might hear her, but all she heard was static.

The lift passed Level Twelve, and Bev readjusted her grip to swing out. If she stayed here, the lift would trap her when it stopped. She would be too far from the second level and blocked from Level One by the platform. She glanced down again. The cyan light was rising, but it was not the swift surge from an explosion. It was pacing the lift. The control behind the light's advance forced Bev's awareness to another level of fear.

"We're being attacked!"

She rushed past Level Ten and began to swing, building momentum for her exit.

She rushed past Level Eight.

Upon seeing the floor of Level Seven, she pulled hard, swung her body toward the opening in the rock and released her grip. Her plunge into darkness ended when her feet hit gritty soil and slipped. She fell backward and her backpack support frame slammed into her shoulders. She winced from the sting and scanned her life-support gauges on her chest pack.

No damage.

Her helmet lamp defined a large tunnel that faded to blackness in front of her. She pushed up and rushed into the abandoned passage, only to pause in confusion at an intersection of three tunnels. She put her helmet lamp on its brightest setting. Another lift was a kilometer away, but she could see no markings to identify which way to go. Tunnel Three headed east. *The lift will be there,* she thought. She glanced down at her life-support gauges. Her suit temperature was rising. She opened her coolant feed valve one-half turn and felt a sudden chill migrate from her back to her arms and legs.

The main shaft brightened.

Bev glanced back. The blazing surge of cyan light had reached Level Seven.

She opened her coolant feed valve as far as she could turn it and ran into tunnel Three. She ran until her temperature gauge crossed the red danger zone and a beep sounded in her helmet. Her suit temperature needed to drop before she could continue. The inner layer of her suit was damp from sweat and there was no way to vent the moisture. Her helmet visor fogged up, which turned on the anti-fog element embedded in the duraplex. That would add to the internal heat. She looked down the black tunnel—no cyan light. She leaned against the tunnel wall, dimmed her helmet light, closed her eyes, and let her body relax.

A few minutes passed, and she felt cool again along her spine. She also felt a vibration in the rock. It was a subtle sensation at first, then stronger, a rhythmic pounding that caused loose pebbles to spill down the wall.

She stepped away from the rock, fearful of what the vibrations implied. She reassessed her path. *The lift has to be close.* She checked her suit temp again and walked toward the eastern exit.

The ground rumbled beneath her feet.

She looked back and saw only blackness.

A few more steps and she was walking on a metal floor plate. She brightened her helmet light and saw the lift about fifty meters away.

She rode the lift as far as she could take it and stepped off into a circular maintenance tunnel lined with metal plates. The tunnel led to a large exit staging area. A closed oval hatch was in the eastern wall.

The handle on the hatch turned without resistance. She pushed hard on the closed door and it swung open in the vacuum, then rebounded back to block her exit. She pushed again with less force, shouldered her way through the hatchway, and stepped out onto the airless surface.

⟡ ⟡ ⟡

The mine complex exploded into the vacuum of the surface. Soundless flashes of cyan light ripped the domes and connecting tubes apart, flinging metal, bodies, and other debris over the dark terrain.

Bev collapsed as she reached a sun-lighted hilltop and lay on her side. She looked westward and squinted as her helmet visor adjusted to block out the intense glare from the setting sun. She shifted her eyes toward the valley below, fingered the control panel on her wrist to change the spectral sensitivity of her visor, and saw twisted remnants of the mine complex collapse into the shapeless black shadows cast by the western hills, and thick ribbons of luminous, cyan-colored plasma flow upward into the black sky.

She surveyed the gauges on her chest pack. The surface temperature of her suit was only 48 degrees Celsius in the sun thanks to the thermal reflectivity of the fabric, but it would get colder as Alpha Cephei Four turned the devastated mine deeper into night. Two-hundred and thirty hours would lapse before the torturous sun would reappear on the opposite horizon.

The temperature will drop 250 degrees below zero Celsius, she thought. *I'll freeze.*

She pushed up to a sitting position and focused on miners nearby who had escaped to the hilltop. She counted fifty-three. Most of them sat, but seven lay motionless on the rough ground. The comm traffic was filled with complaints about re-breather failures and circulation pump breakdowns.

A cloud of the luminous, cyan-colored plasma appeared above the hill and lit up the survivors with its light.

Bev fell into a state of wonder as she gazed up at the rolling eddies inside the plasma. The radiated heat forced her coolant pump to rumble to life, and a chill flowed over her limbs.

"Flee, you idiots! You'll be burned to ash!"

That warning sounded in Bev's headset, and she watched half of the stranded miners scramble away from the hot cloud. Those who remained on the hill looked up in silence at the churning ionized gas thirty meters above them.

The tactical display in Bev's visor showed the cloud was hot, 10,000 kelvins at its core, and yet the radiation from the cloud bombarding her suit was only 50 degrees hotter than the emissions hitting her from the sun. She glanced at the plasma still streaming out of the mine through melted foundations and collapsed surface structures.

It melts durillium girders like butter, but 10,000 kelvins thirty meters above my head and I'm not a pile of ash? "Anyone know what that is?"

After a long pause, a male voice sounded in Bev's headset, “It destroyed the mine.”

The cyan tendrils of energy above Bev undulated like electric discharges within the churning cloud, stabbing in multiple directions from what she perceived to be a tight collection of independent balls of energy.

That is so weird!

The rolling cloud of cyan-colored plasma vanished.

Bev gasped at the return of the stars.

She searched the airless sky and saw running lights on two Polinda frigates in low orbit. The ships approached the main body of the glowing plasma that continued to stream out of the mine. Strands from the plasma stream leaped toward the vessels, and there was a brilliant burst of white light.

Bev turned away from the intense flash that outshone the setting sun and curled into a fetal position. Surviving hardship had been the key to her success in the mine. She had learned to steel herself against the harshest circumstance. But now, as she scanned the cracked, fogged surface of her life-support gauges, the anxiety of the moment gripped her, and she felt a tear roll down her cheek.

CLAN ERSTALLIUS: OUTPOST

Arlud Reynaldo Erstallius was Regent of his clan's outpost on planet GSW-183. Regent was a position not eagerly sought, but humbly accepted at the request of his father, Armand, the High Regent of the Clan.

At twenty-six years of age, Arlud had received few endorsements for the job. His father's advisers had encouraged the selection of someone with more experience, with more years of service to the clan. Many among the inner circle believed the prime reason for Arlud's appointment was familial indulgence, but Armand Erstallius was not a fool. He had considered the other candidates, and after a thorough review, his son had been the only one he felt he could send.

Arlud relaxed on his pallet within the dark confinement of his large dome tent and recalled the protests uttered behind his father's back. The cadre was not obligated to agree, but rarely voiced contrary opinions once the High Regent had made a decision. The fervent gossip that filled the Great Hall the week before his departure had been disheartening. He never realized his abilities were considered with such low regard.

Success here will change that, he thought. And he knew his father's decision had been a personal one, despite statements to the contrary. It would mean the acceptance of his son as a valid member of the cadre.

My trial of manhood.

The settlement under construction on GSW-183 was only a landing field but was essential for the clan's continued expansion in the district. GSW-183 was the official Alliance designation for the second world in the PDN160 system and was named Ni'apinu by the first settlers. Arlud preferred Ni'apinu over the other identifiers. The word meant *secure abode* in the original Akün language and honored the Aku people.

The rugged simplicity of Ni'apinu appealed to Arlud's pioneer spirit, and the small number of personnel would avoid the bureaucratic maze prevalent at larger installations. An ideal situation. In two weeks, outpost construction would be completed. All the bustle and hurry to build this landing field would be replaced with the calm movement of structured administration. He looked forward to the slower pace.

The only obstacles to success were the natives. The Aku people had prevented Alliance settlement for over one-hundred and fifty years. Reputation had been their best deterrent. Clan Tuma had followed them here to reclaim them as their slaves, but Clan Tuma was sent limping back to Kainogae. The successful Aku rebellion had shocked all the Clans. Fifty years later, after four more attempts to planet-fall by Clan Tuma had failed, GSW-183 was declared a holding-complete of the Aku by the Department of Planetary Settlement. They had won and retained their freedom.

This Erstallius attempt to establish a foothold on GSW-183 had been easy. His father's advisers had encouraged this move, thinking the Aku no longer burned with the fire of their rebellion, and lacked the means to evict anyone who possessed a modern arsenal.

So far everything Arlud had witnessed about the Aku had proven his father's advisers to be correct, but he knew a thing done too easily can often conceal a more difficult truth. The threat of a confrontation seethed just below the surface of the native demeanor. During the first few weeks of outpost construction, they had kept themselves at a peaceful distance. Now that the outpost was nearing completion, threats of belligerence had begun and were increasing daily. Arlud hoped that Erstallius benevolence, not the flesh-searing deterrent of plasma burst emitters, would sway the natives to accept the outpost. Regardless of the means, he knew the protests would end. An Erstallius triumph here would be a reality. A reality not easily vanquished.

Voices drifted outside as a sudden surge of activity moved around the tent and a robust figure flung open the entry.

Arlud sat up on his pallet and ignited a glowball. The amber light revealed the dark, weathered face of Gustav Eahuda.

"Come in, Gus."

The old Degen-of-the-Corp entered the tent and pressed close with controlled urgency. "We've got trouble, lad."

Arlud paused as he reached for his boots. "What?"

"Polinda's mine on Alpha Cephei Four was attacked and destroyed."

Arlud frowned at that revelation. He was relieved the natives were not the cause of trouble, but knew the Alpha Cephei Four incident could be more devastating than any local uprising. Clan Polinda had been a constant prickling to the Erstallius. Alpha Cephei Four's destruction would only make that agitation worse. "When?"

“Fifteen days ago,” Eahuda said. “A Cormed envoy brought the news. He said they think it’s the work of the Guild. Apparently, some of Sy’s men were detected near there.”

“They blame Wolfram Sy for everything in this district.”

“The Guild has had many bouts with the Polindas. Odds are the locals are right.”

“Maybe,” Arlud said. “If our homeworld was less than two parsecs from Polinda, we’d also have more bouts with him.” He pulled on his boots, stomped both feet for a snug fit, then stood and grabbed his tunic. Arlud knew Wolfram Sy’s history—he had led the First Rebellion against the Alliance that resulted in the birth of the Guild of Free Traders, and it was true Sy had frequent skirmishes with Clan Polinda—but sacking an Alliance holding would be a fool’s endeavor. “The Guild’s prosperity comes from avoiding conflict. Why would Sy destroy an Alliance resource and force the wrath of all the clans in the district?”

Eahuda shrugged.

“Who’s the Cormed envoy?”

“Milos Fore, their Regional Director of Clan Affairs. He’ll be down in about twenty minutes.”

Clan Cormed was a strong Erstallius ally in this district. It had fifteen holdings-complete and twenty contract partnerships throughout Alliance territory. An important Cormed colony, Roth-513, was the first stop on the trade route from Alpha Cephei Four. Polinda’s sacking was also a threat to them.

Arlud buttoned his tunic. “How are the natives this morning?”

“Quiet. Too quiet, if you ask me.”

“Send their council a note about the envoy’s arrival. The usual protocols.”

“I fear they may bite off that hand of kindness one day soon. We’ve spotted more of them in the local woods. Things are stirring.”

“Until our hand is bitten off, I’ll always extend it. Get that note to their council.”

“Right, lad.” Eahuda turned, and with a swish of fabric, shouldered his way out of the tent.

Polinda’s mine has been destroyed.

Arlud was well aware of inter-clan feuding. His family had suffered many years to overcome past confrontations. Feuds killed, but never had a source of wealth been annihilated. A holding’s value was in its resources and the people trained to extract them. Whoever was responsible for Polinda’s loss had sparked a terrible current of aggression that would ripple across the district to the heart of the Alliance. He was glad two Erstallius frigates guarded the perimeter of this system. Then he wondered how much strength the Polinda colony had maintained, and he contemplated sending a request for reinforcements.

Milos Fore had not intended to planet-fall. He had three more colonies to reach with the news about Alpha Cephei Four. When he heard the son of the Erstallius patriarch was on the surface, he bowed to the demands of propriety. He did not like the delay, but who could argue with protocol? He walked with Arlud along the edge of the completed tarmac, under the angled shadows of the half-finished central tower, while a cold, gentle wind escorted their passage. Workers swarmed with purpose around them, hurrying to complete their construction assignments, and delivering furniture to the service buildings that flanked the tower.

"Only twenty-two survived," Milos said. "Less than half of those who had escaped to the surface."

Arlud glanced down at the fat little envoy in rumpled clothes. "Their struggle must've been severe."

Fore nodded. "A horrible place, Alpha Cephei Four. It has no atmosphere, you know." He shuddered at the thought.

Arlud pictured the destruction in his mind: The shattered pressure domes, the push out into the vacuum, the torture of lungs collapsing. "The survivors are sure they were attacked, but they can't identify the attacker?"

"They were hit so forcefully their first concern was to get out of the complex. None of them saw any vessels. One survivor—a young girl named Bev Colli—said the surge of energy that filled the lower tunnels was controlled. It wasn't a natural outburst. Unlike anything she'd ever seen down there, and she'd been there for six years. Had an unusual blue glow."

"She's certain it was controlled?"

"Yes. I've questioned her at length. She's aboard our frigate with five other survivors. We're taking them to U'galem."

"They couldn't identify their attacker, but you still suspect Wolfram Sy?"

"Of all potential villains, he is the nearest at hand, and the one who benefits most. Without Polinda's nagging armada in his way, he has open access to that part of the district."

"But Sy is alone, Mister Fore. Over the last twenty years, he has watched the Alliance advance around him, isolating him from the free trade regions he helped create. I doubt he would intentionally incite the combined aggression of all the Clans in this district. I read all the Intel reports about this district before I got here. Sy is not an animal. He doesn't strike out of desperation and fear."

"Not an animal? You suspect he's innocent?"

"There are many possibilities. We may have an opportunity here to begin a more peaceful relationship with Sy if we approach him with respect."

Fore chuckled. "Young man, have you had many dealings with Sy?"

"No."

"He's a pirate. He doesn't bargain with Alliance Clans."

"He's never had a reason before."

"You're right about that," Fore said.

Three local Clans, led by the Cormeds, had sent a combined force of eight frigates into the area between Roth-513 and Alpha Cephei Four to uncover any trace of the attacker. They were sweeping toward Wolfram Sy's fortress world, Al-phaq. Al-phaq was the fifth planet of Eta Cephei, roughly one point three parsecs from the Alpha Cephei system, and the closest inhabited world to the Polinda colony. If evidence was not found, they would blockade the planet and force Sy to respond. It was a valid effort, but one that Arlud knew could lead to chaos if forced out of control.

"Understand, Mister Fore, as my father made very clear at the last General Assembly, 'Clan Erstallius does not act out of terror and will not be a party to unwarranted retaliation.'" Arlud had never quoted his father before, but the words fit the situation, and they filled him with a greater sense of authority.

"When has aggression against a pirate been unwarranted?"

Arlud stopped walking. "Sy could help us. Hold back your forces and give him a chance to express himself without looking down the muzzle of a weapon."

Fore stopped and turned to face Arlud. "You're serious?"

"Yes."

Fore rubbed his fat chin. Arlud's attitude was typical of the moderate stance that had dominated his clan for generations. Their conviction that balance-in-all-things promoted fortunes beyond immediate expectations had helped them rebound from a disastrous past, but that philosophy would be hard-pressed against a murderous pirate like Wolfram Sy.

"Pirates don't bargain," Fore said. "We'd be wasting our time."

"Everyone is running on emotion. Allow tempers to calm a bit. A cool heart can see reason that a man enraged can't."

"Sy is a pirate. That's reason enough to force the blockade."

"You may be leading us into chaos, Mister Fore."

"On the contrary, Mister Erstallius, we're already there."

Arlud watched the envoy's shuttle rise off the tarmac. It was an old vessel, its olive-drab skin battered, looking like an ancient insect beaten by time and too many journeys. It banked north and disappeared into the gray clouds above the dark wall of trees that surrounded the outpost.

Gustav Eahuda walked over from the temporary encampment of tents. "The natives acknowledged your message about the envoy."

"What did they say?"

"Nothing specific. Their runner delivered a written reply that only acknowledged the receipt of your message."

"That's better than no reply at all." Without more direct communication, Arlud knew the gulf between his people and the natives would only get wider. "Remind me to take a transceiver to the native council the next time we meet."

"They wouldn't accept it the first time you offered—"

"Next time I'll leave it with them. It may spark some curiosity. We've got to start a meaningful dialog. Someone's bound to see the benefits, eventually."

"Or throw it in the river."

"You're such an optimist, Gus. What would we do without you?"

Eahuda smirked and turned to leave.

"Wait," Arlud said, his tone grim. "Start preparations to evacuate."

Eahuda could not believe his ears. "Evacuate? You've got to be joking."

"We're too vulnerable here. The possibility of an attack from Polinda increases by the minute."

The old Degen-of-the-Corp glanced around at all the activity. "That'll be a major setback. I don't think we should do that. You really believe we're a target?"

"When Farquar Polinda hears about Alpha Cephei Four, he'll come looking for blood. I'd rather face that from orbit."

"Isn't Sy more likely to attract Polinda's wrath? I thought the local clans—"

"Unless they find something to incriminate Sy, Polinda will head straight for us. He'll be relentless."

Eahuda knew meeting Polinda on an unequal front would be disastrous. Past confrontations between the Erstallius and Polinda forces had left both Clans limping for a safe retreat with high losses and few rewards. Confronting the Polindas always had dire implications. "I don't relish meeting Polinda on unequal terms either, lad. But we shouldn't abandon this place completely. We've got a responsibility to protect what we've established here. Move the admin personnel and the work crews, but leave a guard detachment to stand watch, otherwise the natives will have this place half demolished by the time we return."

"Then we'll re-build it."

Eahuda was bewildered by Arlud's sudden lack of insight. "Lad, think of all the—"

"We're leaving, Gus. That's final."

Eahuda rocked back on his heels as if restraining what he wanted to say.

"Look," Arlud said, his voice softer, "any detachment we leave here will be subject to a more aggressive assault by the natives, and we'll be leaving them open to an attack from Polinda's armada. If a battle is to be fought, I won't fight it on two fronts. I'd rather have the natives overrun this place than have Polinda demolish it from orbit. Part of our bargain with the Aku was to protect them from further Alliance intrusion. We'll do that, but we can't do it from here."

Eahuda took a deep breath as he pondered Arlud's words. The lad had made a good point. He hated to admit it, but it was a good point. And he was struck by the undeniable reality that here, standing in front of him, was no mere wet-behind-the-ears young pup. Standing in front of him was the Regent of GSW-183. "I'll inform the duty chiefs," Eahuda said. "We'll have everyone back in orbit by the end of the week."

"Let the work on the tower continue, so the framing gets done. Stop everything else and store all supplies and unused material inside the buildings and hangers. Leave nothing outside for the natives."

"What about the heavy equipment?"

"Store it in the maintenance hangar. There should be enough room. Make sure all the buildings are properly sealed. And make it very clear to the natives we'll be coming back."

"Right. Yes, sir." Eahuda turned away and strode toward the encampment of tents.

Arlud surveyed the outpost. Construction workers were busy on the command tower, fastening the last girders in place on the tenth floor. Support staff had begun unloading a bulging cargo shuttle near the east entrance. Maintenance workers maneuvered heavy equipment at the southern end of the field. Despite the hassles with the natives, Arlud knew in time this outpost would become an important addition to his clan's holdings. *If we can survive the storm of Polinda's wrath, this effort will not be in vain,* he thought. *But our surviving will not be easy.*

A major weakness in the Alliance was the delay due to distance. Messages between colonies were conveyed by comdrones through hyperspace, and transmitted via TAC emitters as the drones passed the planetary systems along their established routes. The communication pathways were constantly in use near the heart of the Alliance, but out here in the peripheral district, the lack of route access compounded problems, forced haphazard solutions, and often alienated holdings belonging to the same clan. The isolation had forced Milos Fore to use a frigate to deliver the news about Alpha Cephei Four, and it demanded the Erstallius rely on what was available locally for defense.

Arlud walked back to the encampment of tents. He knew there was strength in this outpost's isolation. The delay due to distance would give his people time to prepare for the expected assault. Farquar Polinda could not respond until he knew about Alpha Cephei Four, and the news would take another week to reach him. The time would also allow Arlud's request for help to reach his homeworld.

With luck, the outpost will still be here when the reinforcements arrive.

He reached his tent and noticed the workers at the cargo shuttle pause a moment as they received their new command.

The order to evacuate was a bitter surprise.

THE GUILD: PIRATE

The library held a modest collection of ancient bound volumes, all sorted and arranged on the shelves that lined the north wall. The floor was blanketed with a tapestry from U'galem, a handcrafted masterpiece of intricate detail and design. A long wooden table fronted the south wall. Two wing-backed chairs of polished leather stood in the center of the room.

Wolfram Sy stood at the library's west window and leaned against the sill. Through the pressure-sealed, triple-thick panes, he watched the sky shift to orange above the domes and spires of his sprawling keep. The sunset's fiery glow reflected off patches of ice that clung to the surface of each roof. Icicles stabbed the thin atmosphere from overhangs and ledges, glistening gold in the amber light.

This fortress had served him for twenty-three years, but life on this frigid, carbon dioxide shrouded planet had been difficult for his family. Their undaunted struggle against the environment had made this situation work, but Wolfram had always known this stronghold could not stand forever. The feud he had successfully waged with the local clans now threatened to devour everything he had accomplished here. A retreat from Al-phaq was inevitable.

The guild security minister, Eber Kurnes, entered the library, clutching a small folio under his right arm. He was bald, thin, dressed in dark clothes and moved with the hesitant stride of caution. One does not bother Wolfram Sy without such an attitude. He stopped at the end of the table and put down the folio. "Sir?"

Wolfram recognized the voice and said without turning: "Yes, Eber, what is it?"

"They have not been found, sir." His voice held the regret of failure and unsettled promises. "There has been no further evidence of their passage."

Wolfram tensed. He folded his hands behind his back and continued surveying his keep. His narrow ledge of tolerance was eroding fast. Einar Duballik's delay prompted visions of betrayal.

To counter Wolfram's silence, Kurnes added: "The Alliance has moved in a team of searchers on Alpha Cephei Four."

Wolfram hung his head. Why Polinda's colony had been sacked was a terrible mystery. "Have we been betrayed, Eber?"

"I think it not likely, sir. The Polinda incident appears to be unrelated to Duballik's disappearance."

Wolfram turned. His face was hard edged, with a furrowed brow and small dark eyes. "Who hit Polinda?"

"That has yet to be discovered, sir. One of our operatives stumbled upon unusual emissions. A very faint radiation of strange harmonics. It erupted at specific points along the orbit plane of Alpha Cephei and near the mined planet. No source for the eruptions has been found, but they are most likely related to the devastation. Odd hyperspace fluctuations coincide with each area of incidence."

Wolfram had flown over Alpha Cephei Four soon after he had settled Al-phaq. He remembered a dark, barren world, void of atmosphere, bombarded by the energetic outbursts of its massive sun. It was rich in the precious metal durillium. Polinda had made a fortune from his mine. He had developed a powerful armada to protect his interests there. Whoever had sacked him had overcome that power.

Wolfram scowled. "It must have been the Erstallius."

"No, sir. Armand Erstallius is ambitious, but he is no fool. To utterly destroy the holding of an Alliance clan would be a blatant disregard for propriety. It would be viewed as a threat and only isolate Clan Erstallius."

Wolfram recognized the truth in that. The Erstallius patriarch sought to rally the Great Clans together in true unity and throw off the veil of pseudo-partnership that now cloaked the Alliance. A most ambitious vision. Evicting Polinda would stifle opposition, remove seeds of insurrection. But total obliteration of a holding would not be tolerated and only result in ostracism.

"Then who is responsible?"

"We are searching, sir," Kurnes said. "The Alliance investigators have cordoned off the Alpha Cephei system. It is becoming increasingly difficult to continue our surveillance."

"Continue as best you can. I want to know their every move."

"Yes, sir."

Wolfram moved to one of the leather chairs and sat astride an arm. "What about Einar?"

"We are searching, sir."

"Find him!"

Kurnes fingered his folio. "We are searching."

Wolfram thought a moment, then: "Send a message to the Cormeds on Roth-513. Tell the regent there of our desire to resolve the mystery of the destroyed colony. Offer our support."

Kurnes was surprised at the request. "Sir?"

"We are going to be the focus of some furious people, Eber. Let's see if we can avoid any undue hostility."

"Yes, sir." Kurnes doubted extending the hand of kindness would prevent aggression against them but thought better of expressing such a view.

Wolfram folded his arms. "Well, go man. Do it!"

Kurnes nodded, picked up his folio, and hurried for the exit. As he turned into the corridor, he confronted a young woman dressed in a flowing gown of lumisilk. She was a porcelain beauty, skin as white as cream. Her eyes were bright green and set wide above a petite nose and generous mouth. Her dark hair was gathered high, and long curls framed her oval face. Kurnes stopped short to avoid a collision. "Pardon, lady."

"Eber," the young woman whispered. She cradled his arm to forestall his retreat. "Is he in a good mood?"

"Mood? Lady, there are many worries as of late." Kurnes removed the girl's hands from his arm. "Pardon, lady, but I must be off." He spun away and strode down the vaulted corridor.

The young woman peered through the entry into the library: Wolfram was at the window. She saw the hint of fatigue in him, the obvious signs of stress in his posture. She hesitated for a few heartbeats, then swept into the room, halting beside one of the wing-backed chairs. "Father?"

Wolfram stepped away from the window. "Shanna, what brings you here?"

"Mother sent me, Father. We'll be dining soon and she—we would very much like you to attend."

"My dear Shanna," Wolfram said. He came to her, held her hands, and kissed her forehead. "Affairs of state have necessitated my absence. Tell your mother I'll attend. I've been too long from both of you."

"Eber said there were many worries. I—"

"Don't trouble yourself with such things," Wolfram asserted. "It's just normal routine. A pirate's life is never peaceful."

"Oh, Father! Why do you insist on using such vulgar terms?"

"Because it's true, my dear. We are renegades. A thorn in the Alliance's side. An agitation that will not go away. We are free traders and that upsets many people."

"It's not fair, Father."

Wolfram chuckled. "You're right, my dear, it's not, but that's what gives us our power. They fear us as much as they detest us."

"Do you fear them?"

"It's always wise to know your own limitations."

Wolfram moved away and leaned against one of the chairs. "I've been thinking of a holiday. A trip off planet may do us all some good. Would you like that?"

The confining walls of the family keep had been the only world Shanna had ever known. *To step into open air and feel the caress of wind,* she thought. *What a sensation that would be! To stroll without fear of the poisonous gases that have confined us to this stronghold. How exhilarating!* "Oh, yes, Father. But where?"

"There are a few choice places outside the district I've been curious about for some time. I'll send your mother the specifics and let her decide. You should be able to leave at the end of the week. I'll join you when proper arrangements have been made and my absence won't unsettle things too much. It shouldn't be more than another week."

"Marvelous!"

"Yes," Wolfram said, and he smiled. "It'll be good to get away for a while."

Shanna rushed forward and kissed Wolfram's cheek. "I can't wait to tell Mother." She turned and hurried from the room.

Wolfram returned to the window. The orange light of dusk shifted to violet as the sun fell below the horizon. A fog settled over his keep and froze as it contacted the cold rooftops.

This place has been my haven, he thought. *I must not let it become my tomb.*

CLAN CORMED: JAVELIN

Einar Duballik was a grizzled old guildman. He had joined Wolfram Sy during the First Rebellion and had logged thousands of hours since then, overseeing Guild trade routes from Jai'raan to Oikía. He never imagined he would end up in a Cormed brig.

The detention cell was a cramped space, half a meter wider than the sleeping pad, with a sloped ceiling that allowed its occupant to stand erect only by the doorway. A constant chill circulated through a small vent up in the corner.

Einar had drifted into a fitful sleep but was jerked awake by the sudden scream of a klaxon as the frigate shuddered out of hyperspace.

A flat-nosed Cormed crewman peered through the small rectangular window in the door.

Einar sat up and rubbed his wrists. The impressions the shackles had left were deep and painful.

A young woman replaced Flat-nose behind the small window. Blue eyes below a wisp of auburn hair.

The Bitch, Einar thought. When the Cormed clanmen stormed aboard his freighter, she had been among them bellowing orders. She had demanded certain crew members be searched. Some of them had protested, and many heads had been bloodied before they were transferred to this brig. Einar had escaped a beating by not struggling. He braced himself for the woman's entrance.

Eve-Ann Corbas slid open the cell door. Her green jump suit was the uniform of Cormed Security, banded at the left shoulder with the rank marking of Prime Director. "Come with us."

Einar hesitated. He knew the evil this woman could commit.

Flat-nose swaggered into the cell, grabbed Einar, and yanked him up.

Jegen-of-the-Corp, Ethan Grant, waited in the *Javelin's* forward lounge. His black uniform was pressed and tailored, its precise creases typical of his strict sense of military deportment. He stood, contemplating the schematic rendering of the *Javelin* that hung on the starboard bulkhead. Three outer decks filled a long torus where standard gravity was maintained via embedded GPGs. Twelve inner decks, designed for access in the weaker gravity fields farther from the GPGs, hugged a central engineering section that ran the length of the vessel, and led to the compression drive engines at each end. Not the best design Grant had ever seen, but good enough for the mission at hand.

He had accepted this assignment without reservation, as would have any exemplary officer, but now he was not sure they were proceeding correctly. Fleet Command had ordered the seizure of any vessel not accompanying the Alliance armada. They had stumbled upon a Guild freighter, and her crew was now confined in the brig. Grant bristled at that thought. Keeping the Free Traders on board seemed contrary to the mission objective. He could see no legitimate reason for arresting the scoundrels. The armada was en route to Al-phaq to rid this district of Wolfram Sy and his band of cutthroats. The time taken to subdue and imprison the brigands could have cost the Alliance the advantage of surprise.

We should've blasted their bulkhead and left them to rot.

Eve-Ann Corbas entered the lounge. "Jegen?"

Grant turned as two clanmen entered behind Eve-Ann with the old trader between them. "Sit him down over there," he said, pointing to the long bench against the exterior bulkhead.

The clanmen hustled the old man across the lounge and forced him to sit.

Einar sat back against the soft bench and massaged his arm where Flat-nose had gripped him.

"Relax, Duballik," Grant said. "I understand you're a member of Wolfram Sy's inner circle of advisers."

Einar shot an insolent glance at Grant, then stared at the deck and continued to rub his bruised arm.

"I had not intended to question you," Grant said. "I normally find such trivialities a waste of my time. However, the situation has suddenly changed." He manipulated a dial on the wall. The lights dimmed and panels blocking a long window behind Einar slid open.

"We're very close to Al-phaq," Grant said. "Look."

Einar twisted to face the window and took in the view. They were cruising at sub-light speed through the black emptiness at the edge of the Eta Cephei system. The sun was just left of center, a distant orange glare. Alpha Cephei was at the upper right, its white radiance outshining every star but Eta Cephei. Another Cormed frigate came into view as it sped across the star field from the lower left.

Grant sat next to the window. "There are two frigates belonging to Clan Sabballi out there somewhere. They've disappeared. We've no contact at all. Their TAC emitters went silent an hour ago."

Einar stared back at Grant, maddened by his friendly demeanor. This bloodthirsty Cormed had imprisoned his crew and was en route to assault his comrades, yet he dared address him as if his purpose had no ill intent. "Don't expect me to mourn."

Grant nodded. "If you know anything that could help us unravel the mystery, you'd be wise to let us know. We're heading in toward Al-phaq, regardless of the obstacles. Any threat to us will also affect you."

"Is that supposed to frighten me?"

"We had the frigates on track twenty million kilometers out, fifteen degrees starboard, and they just vanished!"

Einar peered at the stars, and he realized the Cormeds had swung around to approach the system from the direction used least by Guild traders. It was a good choice, but one that could have led the Sabballi into Guild security forces. "Traders don't like to be crowded."

Director Corbas stepped toward Einar. "There has been no sign of confrontation. If they had dropped out of hyperspace, we would have detected them." She flicked a disdainful glance at Grant. "There is nothing."

Einar cracked a thin smile.

"This does not have to end in disaster for you or your comrades," Corbas said. "We are here because of Alpha Cephei Four. If Sy is innocent, we intend no hostilities."

Einar looked away from the bitch. "Your lies are transparent," he muttered. Then something outside diverted his attention.

About five degrees south of Alpha Cephei there was a rippling, like heat waves rising in the desert. The effect was about two degrees wide, an asymmetrical crinkling of space, undulating, moving.

A comm bell dinged, and a voice sounded via the intercom: "Degen-Major Turl here, Jegen. A disturbance has appeared six hundred kilometers out, advancing quickly."

A holoscreen ignited along the bulkhead to Grant's left that displayed the approaching anomaly.

"Evasive action," Grant ordered. "Let's keep our distance. Tell our sister ship to veer off and notify the rest of the armada."

"Aye, sir."

The window's protective panels began to close. Einar was seized by his two guards and pulled toward the lounge entrance.

The distortion filled the shrinking window, and the *Javelin* jerked hard astern as the strange effect enveloped the vessel. The stars outside the window became a meandering flux of spectral colors.

Warning klaxons blared throughout the ship.

Grant stepped back from the window, transfixed by the flow of colors. As the vertical panels reached the point of near closure, brilliant white light burst through the opening—a shaft of energy that hit Grant head on. He fell to the deck, shielding his face with his hands.

The panels closed and the sliver of light winked out.

Corbas rushed to Grant's side. She smelled the stench of burned flesh and hesitated before gripping the Jegen's shoulders.

Grant moved his hands to reveal charred flesh and bloody pools where his eyes had been. He tried to speak, but his injuries prevented it.

Urged on by his guards, Einar moved out into the corridor and was hit by an intense rush of heat.

Heat upon heat upon heat.

Einar collapsed. Pain contorted his body, and he felt himself floating in a frightening blackness.

The frigate trembled under the strain of the crippling heat.

Heat upon heat upon heat...

CLAN CORMED: SURVIVORS

Jegen Zebulan Farvic, commander of the Cormed frigate, *Iron Spear,* sat under the restraint of his seat harness, looking at the holoscreen above his course-plotting pedestal. The five operations personnel surrounding him focused on their stations.

Farvic targeted the *Javelin* in the holoscreen. His hard features belied his unease as he watched Ethan Grant's ship disappear inside a ball of brilliant white light.

There was a brief pause of astonishment by the entire command crew.

The ball of light around the *Javelin* dimmed and morphed back into the rippling distortion. It left the *Javelin* and rushed after the *Iron Spear*.

The Helmsman looked into his imaging scope. "It's after us now, sir."

"Full power to the engines," Farvic ordered.

The frigate shuddered as it lunged into hyperspace.

"Fifty kilometers and advancing," the helmsman said.

Farvic looked into the holoscreen. The undulating shape pressed closer. "Evasive maneuvers, Helmsman. Get it off our tail!"

The frigate shook again, then jerked hard to port as the surging effect slammed against her starboard plating.

"We're completely enveloped," the helmsman announced.

The holoscreen presented a swirl of colors that flared white.

A klaxon shrieked its warning.

An automatic verbal warning activated, a soft contralto spoken with emotionless programmed efficiency: "Interior temperature fifty-three centigrade and rising."

"Turn that alarm off and kill the voice," Farvic ordered. He focused on his plotting cubicle. Large beads of sweat formed on his forehead.

"Interior temperature sixty-five centigrade and rising."

"Kill that warning," Farvic demanded. "Energize all PBE's. Set—"

"It's gone!"

Farvic glanced at the helmsman, unbuckled his harness and pushed himself toward the weapons station. Their target had disappeared. "I want full scans. Tell me what's out there."

The crewman at the sensor station checked his data. "It's gone," he said. "Space normal, Jegen. We are no longer in hyperspace."

The intercom buzzed for attention.

Farvic tripped the talk switch on the weapons console intercom. "Farvic here."

"Sir, Degen Plucket in Engineering. We've lost compression drive. The plasma injectors are fused. That damn thing burned through the hull into both the aft and forward drive coils."

Farvic turned and scanned the schematic of the *Iron Spear* on the engineering station ready board. The diagram displayed the damage relayed by Plucket. He shook his head in disbelief. "How many people did we lose?"

"Not sure. We need to—"

"Do you have a repair estimate yet?"

"Too soon. We need to assess the exterior damage and repair the hull breech before we can do anything else."

"Keep me posted."

"Aye, sir. Plucket out."

"Send a distress call," Farvic ordered. He wiped his brow and felt cooler air flow into the command center from the floor vents. "Contact the *Javelin*." He returned to his couch and centered the *Javelin* on his view screen. Her hull plating was buckled and blackened. Gas seeped from her aft engineering section.

"No response from *Javelin*," the comm officer reported. "Our TAC emitter is damaged. Can't send the distress call."

"Send drones," Farvic ordered. "Target four optimum directions." He moved to one of the sensor stations and hovered next to the operator. "What have we got on the *Javelin*?"

"Hull breach," the crewman said. "Loss of atmosphere in engineering and central decks. Twenty-one live crewmen concentrated in the torus. Ten crewmen in the debris streaming from the hull breach."

Farvic twisted to look across the room. "Helmsman, can we dock with her?"

"It'll take a while, sir. We have limited maneuvering ability right now. Until we repair the damage, we—"

"How long?"

The helmsman shrugged in his harness. "Three hours, maybe two, if we can nail a precise alignment. The venting is causing the *Javelin* to spin on all three axes, and she is moving away from us."

Farvic moved back to his command chair and tripped an intercom switch.

"Shuttle Bay," the duty officer responded.

"This is Farvic. I want two teams headed for the *Javelin* in fifteen minutes."

"Aye, sir."

Farvic settled back into his command chair and secured his harness. There were survivors on the *Javelin*. He hoped they would last long enough for rescue. He hoped he would last long enough to track down whoever did this.

Einar Duballik floated in smothering blackness.

No pain.

No sound.

Only darkness, and an overwhelming fear that erupted in a silent scream.

Hissing static rose, then faded back to silence.

Einar's panic flowed into quiet confusion. He struggled in his numbness to find something solid in the darkness. His limbs tingled, then hurt as feeling crept back. Both legs twitched from the ache, and he felt a restraining presence, like many hands gripping his body. He fought against the confinement and the nauseating sensation of tumbling backward. Then he saw the cavern—a dark, twisting tunnel that seemed to go on forever. The grip on his body tightened, and he rushed through the cavern.

A strange woman, her dark face twisted in agony, rushed up before him. He jerked to avoid a collision, but she was a dream and dissolved before impact.

The cavern faded to blackness.

Fear returned and in the sudden stillness, Einar felt the rapid throbbing of his own heartbeat and his thoughts drifted to his last moments on board the frigate.

Pain and terrible heat.

He tried to speak, but something pressed against his mouth.

A sudden shift in motion sent him tumbling. He endured the pressing darkness, his body now rigid in a restraining presence. His mind wandered between the agony of pain and the numbing terror of black seclusion. Then, shattering the darkness, the woman came back again, screaming.

A spot of white light appeared on the internal bulkhead of the *Javelin*'s outer torus, then grew, moved into the dark corridor, and illuminated a body floating outside the closed doorway to the ship's forward lounge.

Two members of the *Iron Spear*'s rescue team, clad in white environment suits, advanced toward three floating bodies—two clanmen and one civilian. Equipment bags attached to their waist belts trailed behind them as they moved through the corridor. Small position thrusters in their suits pushed them to the unconscious men without the need to rebound off the bulkhead.

"This one's alive," the first rescuer said. He rolled the civilian's body over so he could see the face. "One of the guildmen." He patted the old man's face. "Unconscious."

The other rescuer ignored the dead crewmen, reached the guildman's body and pulled out a blue respirator from his equipment bag. As he secured the device's small air tank to the body, by wrapping straps around the upper chest and arms, his companion placed the respirator's mask over the old man's mouth and nose. They then secured his lower arms and legs with more straps, pulled a silver body bag over him, and sealed it. They watched the man through the small window over his face as the bag inflated into a firm cocoon.

"Right," the first rescuer said. "Let's go."

The two rescuers pulled the cocoon along with them as they retreated through the corridor, their lights now illuminating the way back to the exit.

Another team of rescuers advanced deeper into the dark corridor to retrieve the dead crewmen.

Pallis Nin brushed back his long blond hair and gazed out the view port. He enjoyed space travel. As an envoy for Clan Cormed, he had made many journeys. This current trip had been the most troublesome. The damaged *Javelin* was five hundred meters away, flanked by the teams of rescue shuttles ferrying people and supplies to the *Iron Spear*. Alpha Cephei was to the extreme left edge of his view limit, moving downward as the *Iron*

Spear rotated to keep alignment with the *Javelin*. He turned and pressed against the duraplex, searching for the sun of Roth-513, a medium yellow star in the opposite direction from the brilliant shine of Alpha Cephei.

"They won't get any closer," a ragged voice said.

Nin pushed away from the window and turned toward the voice.

Jegen Zebulan Farvic entered the conference room and sat down at the oval table. His staff officers followed him. Degen Plucket, the sinewy chief engineer, sat to Farvic's right. Jarred Molska, the aged, gray-haired physician, took the seat next to Plucket. Grom Anen, the youthful, square jawed First Officer, sat at Farvic's left.

"Sit down, Mister Nin," Farvic said.

Nin eased into the seat across from Farvic.

"This is the situation," Farvic said. He pushed a button on the table and a holomap of the area surrounding his ship floated above the table. "It's not to scale, but it will give you a good idea of our predicament."

Two blue icons representing both Cormed frigates drifted amid nine yellow dots, most of which were concentrated to the port side and aft. A red line connected four of the dots and came close to the frigate icons.

"We're about half a parsec from the district trade route," Farvic said. "Repairs are underway, but it doesn't look good. Our only hope of rescue may rest in the chance someone picks up our beacon from one of our comdrones."

"We have sent out four drones," Anen said. "They will reach Alliance assets, but that will take at least two standard weeks.

Nin leaned forward. "What do we do in the meantime?"

"Stand guard as best we can," Farvic said. "We are still very close to the Eta Cephei system and the Guild homeworld."

Nin was confused. "Why do we not leave?"

"Supplies," Plucket explained. "We need to strip the *Javelin* of everything we can use. She's heavily damaged, but we can get spare parts, extra food stuffs for extended isolation, and the torpedoes should not be left on a derelict ship."

Nin sat back. "You expect us to be stranded more than two weeks?"

Farvic nodded. "One standard month, at least."

"One month?"

Plucket leaned toward the befuddled envoy. "Standard time is very slow, Mister Nin, compared to Hyper-time."

Farvic leaned back. "If we can't repair the compression drive, we could be out here a very long time. We're too far from the trade route for standard

EM frequencies and our TAC emitter is damaged and may not be repairable, even with equipment from the *Javelin*."

"What about the remaining ships in the armada?"

"They were running silent to avoid early detection and did not have contact with us at the time the attack happened. They have no way of knowing where we are. From their perspective, we have vanished—just like the Sabballi ships."

Nin stood and went back to the view port. The stars seemed to pull at him. A dizzying experience. "What happened to the *Javelin*?"

"Same thing that happened to us," Farvic said, "only more intense."

Nin turned and faced the Jegen. "The same fate suffered by the two Sabballi vessels?"

"Probably."

"What was that thing, Jegen?"

Farvic stared at a spot on the table in front of him. Neither he nor his crew had experienced anything close to what had happened. "We're not sure yet," he said. "We're still examining the sensor input."

Nin scanned the officers. They all looked lost. He turned back to the window. "A new weapon developed by Sy and his pirates."

"I doubt it," Farvic said.

"It wasn't a natural phenomenon. I understand it pursued us."

"Yes."

"It had to be Sy," Nin said. "Who else could it have been? Sy and Polinda have been clashing for years because they are so close to each other, just a little more than a parsec away. Polinda's mine was sacked. Then we are attacked on the outskirts of Sy's territory. It must be Sy."

"That would seem to be the logical conclusion," Farvic said, "but highly unlikely."

Nin slid back into his seat and folded his hands on the table. "Why?"

Farvic leaned forward. "Technology, Mister Nin."

That statement pushed Nin back in his chair, forcing him onto a train of thought he had not expected. Technology implied many things. His mind whirled with the unstated implications. The GRAND Crusades of the past century had forced the study and development of devices, machines, and applied techniques into a tight control system, overseen now by the five highest ranking Clans. The GRAND Crusades did not wipe out development entirely, as was the intended goal. They only restricted development, and reshaped how it was deployed. Clan Cormed was among the current overseers. Their colony on Roth-513 was the preeminent source for all micro bionic and robotic systems. Wolfram Sy was a user of those systems, not a developer. The Free Traders partook from the technological table provided by the Alliance, as did most of the Clans and all the independent colonies within Alliance reach. While a few independents had surged ahead of the regulated distribution system, they were the exception. The odds were against that happening among the Free Traders.

Nin leaned forward. "But it could be possible."

"Unlikely," Plucket said.

The Envoy refused to accept that.

"Sy is still a threat," Farvic said. "Of that, you can be sure. But this attack is not his doing."

Nin leaned back and brushed aside his long blond hair. "Why did we not suffer like the *Javelin*?"

"I don't know," Farvic said.

"Very odd."

"We considered contacting Sy," Farvic said, "since we have a guildman on board. But, knowing Sy, he'd take advantage, and we would end up in a worse condition."

Nin folded his arms across his chest. This conversation was beginning to bore him. "There is nothing else we can do?"

Plucket leaned toward the envoy. "We considered, and then rejected, an option that might speed up our rescue. Once the *Javelin* is stripped and all survivors have been evacuated, we could back away and shoot a torpedo at her. That would send up a big signal, like sending up a flare at sea. But unfortunately, that might also attract Sy's attention, and we want to avoid that."

Nin sat up straight, hands folded in his lap. "How many from the *Javelin* survived?"

"Twenty-one," Doctor Molska said. "Her First Officer, two junior grade officers, and eighteen enlisted crewmen." He frowned and flicked a glance at Jegen Farvic. "Twenty-two if you count the guildman."

Nin stood and went back to the window. He had heard all he cared to hear. He leaned against the duraplex and shifted his focus to the swarm of stars surrounding the crippled *Javelin*. Space was a lonely place, dark, and unforgiving. Those aspects of reality had always been there, just out of the way, behind the curtain of routine, blocked by more important matters, shrouded by the ease that came with the modern convenience called compression drive. Technology had its benefits. Now he knew firsthand it also had its dangers.

◆◆◆

Einar Duballik felt the tug of acceleration and the nauseating force of sudden weight.

Gravity.

Without warning, he found himself on a hard surface, still covered in darkness, muffled by something over his mouth, and secured by the constant pressure against his body.

Then the pressure released, and he felt straps around his body. He spoke through the mask over his mouth: "Why am I tied up?"

A basso voice answered: "Safety precaution. Had to bring you over in a body bag."

And then the mask was off.

The old pirate squirmed to free himself. "Body bag!"

"Hold on," the basso voice insisted. "I need to get you out of these bindings."

"Why can't I see?"

"You can't see?"

Realization whirled in Einar's mind. The flash of light that had burned Grant had also affected him. "I'm blind!"

The bindings were gone.

Einar sprang up and brought his hands to his face.

"Whoa," the deep voice cautioned. "Not so fast. You might fall off the exam table."

"Exam table?"

"You're in the infirmary. On the *Iron Spear*. We rescued you from the *Javelin*."

"I can't see!"

"Yes, I'll have the doctor come look at you. Stay put. I'll be right back."

Einar wept. "I'm Blind!"

"Hello?"

The tenor voice came from behind Einar, but he did not move. He wiped the tears from his dead eyes.

"Hello?"

The voice was next to him now and a firm hand clasped his right shoulder.

Einar stiffened and forced back his tears.

"It's all right," the voice said, trying to soothe the old man. "You're safe."

The hand patted Einar's shoulder.

"The bastards blinded me," Einar said. The hand left his shoulder, and he listened to the scuffle of footsteps as the man moved in front of him.

"I'm Degen Turl from the *Javelin*. Let me take a look."

Turl held Einar's head with both hands and examined his eyes. The hands were big but the touch gentle.

"No visible damage," Turl said, and he withdrew his hands. "It may be temporary."

"I'll be the judge of that," Doctor Molska said. He nudged Turl out of the way and placed a hand on the top of Einar's head. "Don't move. I need to look into your eyes." He raised a small hand tool, leaned forward and peered through the device into the damaged right eye, and then the left eye. "Hmm."

Einar protested: "What?"

The doctor released his grip on Einar's head and stood straight. "Your retinas have been burned. Nothing I can do about that here. How did it happen?"

"When we were attacked. Your Jegen had opened the view port in the lounge. There was a bright flash. The Jegen got the worst of it."

"My Jegen?"

"He means Ethan Grant," Turl said.

"Oh," Molska said. "What's your name?

The old trader wiped his face dry. "Einar Duballik."

"Grant is dead," Turl said. "Only twenty-two survived."

"And the red-haired bitch?" Einar asked.

Turl frowned at that remark. "You mean Director Corbas?"

"Yeah, the bitch."

"Dead," Turl said. "The heat killed her."

"You're one of Sy's men," Molska said. "My Jegen will want to put you in the brig soon. I'll try to convince him to keep you here."

Einar did not expect compassion from a Cormed. "Thank you."

Molska faced Turl. "Since you're here, Degen, help him to that chair. I'll see about getting you some food." The doctor turned with a smile and was gone.

Turl grabbed Einar's arm. "Hop down."

Einar slid off the table to stand on the metal deck. "You were on the *Javelin*?"

"Yes," Turl said.

"Are you injured too?"

"No. It's standard procedure to examine all survivors in case something is missed. I couldn't join the crew until cleared by the doctor."

"Who attacked us?"

"I don't know."

"Bloody thugs!"

Arm in arm, Degen Turl led Einar from the cold exam table to one of the cushioned chairs in the adjacent room.

CLAN ERSTALLIUS: FLIGHT

Arlud Erstallius strolled to the edge of the tarmac, escorted by two of his guards. The field was quiet. The rush to make the final departure before sundown had emptied the outpost of all builders and mechanics. A skeleton crew of security guards and a few engineers remained. Arlud fastened his long gray coat and shifted his gaze to the storm approaching from the East. Curtains of rain draped the forested hills in the distance. An obscured sun sent beams of light through holes in the dark clouds.

He knew his decision to leave was correct, but that had not made it easier to bear. This retreat had dug a deep well of regret within him. He turned and surveyed the work his people had accomplished. Frame construction had been finished on the central tower and the service buildings had been completed. The temporary encampment of tents had been removed and the construction supplies for the personnel quarters had been hauled back into orbit. The worst thing about this whole affair had been watching his people work hard for something they might never see again. He promised himself they would receive extra compensation for their effort.

Gustav Eahuda came out of the service entrance, flanked by another guard. Their blue long coats billowed in the wind as they crossed the tarmac to join Arlud.

"Our shuttles should be here any minute," Eahuda said.

"Good. Any sign of the natives?"

"Not yet, lad."

Arlud expected a large crowd would arrive to witness this last Erstallius departure. The natives were elated. They had put more observers in the surrounding hills when outpost activity had shifted three days ago from unloading cargo to sending supplies and personnel back up to the transports in orbit. A message from the native council arrived soon after the first departures, asking about the sudden change in procedure.

Arlud's reply had been brief: "Settlement has been postponed."

The native response had wished a safe farewell.

Arlud glanced around again. "Everyone set to leave?"

Eahuda nodded. "Yes, sir."

"We lose track of anyone?"

"All names counted and verified. The last engineering team is waiting inside the service entrance."

Arlud turned his back against the wind. He knew a confrontation with Polinda would be severe. The Polindas did nothing piecemeal. They would come armed for an annihilation. "As soon as we're in orbit, I want central command moved to a position near the fifth planet, to draw attention away from Ni'apinu as much as possible."

Eahuda nodded agreement, then glanced behind him at the sudden approach of footsteps. "They're here, lad."

An old native had sauntered up behind them. He was called Nujo, the elder who had once voiced his displeasure about the Erstallius presence with detailed descriptions of how the intruders would be emasculated if they stayed.

Arlud took in at a glance the leather sandals, the loose-fitting woolen trousers, the tunic made of animal hide, the dark, seamed face with an aquiline nose, the long gray scalp lock gathered by leather ties at crown and left shoulder. These people did not look like the kind who could defeat Clan Tuma, and yet they had, five times.

"L'dyém dü sebüqu," Nujo said. His voice was a hoarse whisper and flavored with the rhythmic modulation of his language.

Arlud started forward, then balked as Nujo spat at his feet.

Eahuda moved in front of the old native as the other guard took up a defensive position beside Arlud.

Nujo sneered at the off-worlders and retreated toward the main entrance, where five other natives waited.

"Crusty old bastard," Eahuda said.

Arlud stepped around Eahuda, amazed at Nujo's bravado. He looked down at the spittle on the ground. The old man's act of defiance was fueled by genuine hatred—a demonstration for the other natives now entering the field. The ruling council would use this departure to rally their people together, reinforcing the conviction that they had won, that they had pushed the Erstallius off planet and saved their world from Alliance intrusion. It was a lie, but a perfect opportunity to strengthen their unity and shore up their pride. They would be even more difficult to deal with when the Polinda situation was settled.

The roar of descending shuttles diverted attention skyward.

The lead vessel made a tight turn over the outpost as the pilot aimed her aft end toward the waiting men and landed about thirty paces away. The other shuttle landed near the service buildings inside an orange parking circle painted on the tarmac. Both vessels sat like squat, six-legged insects. Their short wings remained extended from their protective sheaths because they would stay here just long enough for the remaining clanmen to board. The rear hatch swung down on the nearest shuttle and became the boarding ramp. A crewman leaned out the entry and waved for Arlud and his guards to enter.

Arlud ignored the crewman's gesture and began walking toward the growing crowd of natives by the main entrance.

Eahuda rushed up behind Arlud. "What are you doing, lad?"

Arlud gave Eahuda a quick glance. "Relax, Gus. This is necessary."

Eahuda took a position to Arlud's right and matched his pace while the other guard fell into position on Arlud's left flank. They walked straight for Nujo and stopped five paces from him.

The old man stood his ground without flinching. A small group of natives formed a wall of curiosity behind him.

"Ousdá rauhr, sij yêbu," Arlud said.

Nujo folded his arms across his chest. He was surprised the Erstallius could speak Akün but did his best to hide his reaction. He let out a long breath, indicating he was not only bored, but was also distraught after hearing that Arlud would continue in the common language of the Alliance.

"My Akün is not what it should be," Arlud said. "I wish nothing misunderstood."

A younger male native next to Nujo whispered the translation of Arlud's words into the elder's ear. That was unnecessary, but Nujo liked the deception it presented. "Yahaj," he said.

Arlud smiled. "Clan Erstallius respects your people. Your struggle against Clan Tuma has brought renown to the Aku. Your successful battle for freedom is legendary among the Clans. But as great as that victory was, it will not deter the Clans from Ni'apinu forever. In the years since your great victory, the Clans have advanced around you. You are an island amid powers who would rip Ni'apinu from you if they knew what we now know."

Nujo returned a blank stare as the interpreter finished his translation.

Arlud paused for a response, but Nujo stood silent.

"My clan needs this landing field," Arlud said. "We need a secure foothold in this district. This outpost will help ensure your people keep their freedom."

Nujo still did not react to Arlud's words. He had heard all this before at the Council Hall in Ji'dess the day these off-worlders arrived. These words meant nothing to him.

"We understand your reluctance to trust us," Arlud said. "We also understand that you are no longer capable of defending this world like your ancestors. Your years here have weakened your defenses. We are leaving because we have pledged our lives to protect you. An enemy is coming. We must confront him before he has a chance to planet-fall."

Arlud dropped to one knee but kept his gaze on Nujo. He placed his right hand over his heart. "You have my solemn promise we will not return until this threat is vanquished."

Nujo nudged the young interpreter away and took a step toward Arlud. "The enemy comes," he said, "because you are here."

Arlud stood and presented another smile because of Nujo's switch to the common tongue. "The enemy would still come if we were not here."

Nujo scowled. "What has caused you to think you are our protectors? We did not ask you to be here."

"When the strong help the weak," Arlud said, "it is a blessing for those in need. You need us."

"That," Nujo said, "is yet to be proven."

"You have no ships in orbit. No satellites. While your settlements range for thousands of kilometers in this region, we could have landed on the other side of this world, on another continent, and you would never have known we were here. In the years to come, will you awaken one day to find yourselves surrounded by foreign settlements? Ni'apinu will no longer be yours if that happens. It will not happen because we honor your claim to this world. Your people won this right through blood and strife. We will help you preserve what you have built here. We are your allies, not your enemies."

Arlud reached into his coat and knelt down again. He withdrew a small, rectangular, metallic object and placed it on the tarmac. "I leave this for you," he said as he stood. "It's a transceiver. Once we return, you can contact me anytime, about anything."

Nujo stared down at the off-worlder's device and clasped his hands behind his back. The boy regent had surmised he would not take the device from his foreign hand, so had left it on the ground. *He knows something of our culture, Nujo* thought. *That won't help him.*

Arlud turned and led his guards back toward the waiting shuttle.

"Nice try, lad," Eahuda whispered as they walked against a cooler breeze. "I'll wager he'll leave it on the ground."

"Someone will pick it up," Arlud said in a hushed tone that matched Eahuda's. "One step at a time, Gus. One little step at a time. They may not believe our words. Maybe they will believe our actions."

The rain was getting closer, and the breeze had become more forceful as the three men reached the shuttle's boarding ramp. Arlud stopped and surveyed the outpost one last time. The remaining engineers were filing into the shuttle by the service buildings. More natives were gathering by the main entrance to the outpost. He caught sight of Nujo watching him from the place he had left him. They stared at each other for a few heartbeats, then the old man bent forward and spat on the ground.

Arlud dropped onto one of the starboard seats. He secured himself in the safety harness and relaxed. This shuttle was designed for troop and cargo transport, so the seats faced inward, five to each side. An empty cargo rack ran down the center of the compartment.

Two long coat clad engineers bounded inside and took seats on the port side next to their Senior Commander.

Gustav Eahuda sealed the rear hatch, blocking out the thunderous rumble of the approaching storm. He sat between Arlud and his guard. "We've quite an audience out there."

"A peaceful nudge," Arlud said. He looked through the cargo rack. The two engineers flanked their Senior Commander. Nared-Major Petra Sitlyn was on the Commander's left. She had proven her worth many times. Nared Drake Tomson sat to the Commander's right. He was the youngest of the engineering group, spirited and smart. The Senior Commander was Gustav's sub-Degen, Gene Crowel, an effective, detail-oriented organizer, and a man who could hold his own in any physical contest. They were the Crew Managers who had worked through the night to ensure this departure happened on time. They looked exhausted. Arlud's father had often reminded him such diligence could not be bought. "Their loyalty is a response to the loyalty we demonstrate toward all who serve our clan," his father had said. "Loyalty begets allegiance." Arlud promised himself never to forget that.

The shuttle lifted under the droning impetus of her engines and arched upward.

Arlud peered through the cockpit windows. Gray mist obscured their passage as they sped through the storm clouds.

"Sit back and relax," the copilot said. "We'll dock with the frigate in about twenty minutes."

They broke through the clouds into bright blue daylight.

Something jarred the shuttle with a hollow thud.

Interior lights flickered, and the engines went silent.

The shuttle pitched downward, and the rush of descent pressed everyone toward the rear of the cabin—safety harnesses kept them all from crashing into the rear bulkhead.

The pilot fought to regain control as they plunged into the clouds.

"What happened?" Arlud yelled.

"Something hit us and killed the electrics," the pilot yelled back. He reached under the control console and yanked back a lever.

Overhead, there was a scraping of metal as the wings fanned farther out of the shuttle's back.

They pitched deeper into the storm, buffeted by thundering turbulence.

The pilot fought to level the craft. "We're now a heavy glider."

The copilot checked the panel above his head. "All engine systems are dead."

Everyone aboard braced as the shuttle swayed and bobbed from the storm winds.

Arlud watched the swirling gray clouds through the cockpit windows. "Can we return to the field?"

"No, sir," the copilot said. "We've come too far and we're descending too fast."

"Need to find somewhere to land," the pilot said. He turned the craft in a wide arc, brought the nose into the wind, and dove deeper into the clouds.

Rain spattered the windows in the shaded light of the storm.

They glided lower and forest became visible as the clouds thinned.

The shuttle rasped against treetops.

They lurched amid snapping sounds and the jerk of breaking branches.

A screech of ripping metal filled the cabin as impacts sheared off the wings and the craft rolled. Her starboard landing struts furrowed the ground.

The concussion of final impact toppled two trees that smashed the port hull.

◈◈◈

Arlud woke to the faint spatter of rain and the scent of evergreen. His head throbbed above his left eye. He raised a hand and felt a hard roughness at his hairline.

Dried blood.

He opened his eyes. A dead arm floated in his vision. It reached through the weapons rack hanging above his head. It belonged to the Senior Commander, who had suffered the full impact of the crash. His body was pinned between the cargo rack and the shattered hull, dried blood spattered everywhere around him and on Arlud.

The shuttle's turned on her side.

Arlud glanced to his right. A felled tree had bashed through the shuttle's skin, and he noticed a boot jutting out from under the trunk, the toe pointing upward.

One of the engineers.

Arlud looked to his left. The cockpit was smashed. He could not see the pilots. Protruding foliage prevented a clear view.

The guard on his left was dead, pinned in his seat by the edge of the cargo rack, held in place by a large tree limb.

Gus was at my side and the seat is untouched. He must have survived.

Arlud took a deep breath and tried to slide out of his seat. A hammer blow of pain forced him back.

He felt his head again.

This will take some time.

Gustav Eahuda leaned his head through the escape hatch in the ceiling above the port boarding ramp, which was now a vertical opening two meters from Arlud, just beyond the tree limb that had pushed the cargo rack into the guard. Eahuda's long coat was rain-soaked, his black hair dripping. "You're awake," he said. "How do you feel?"

"Awful."

"Rest easy. We're setting up a shelter out here. We'll help you out as soon as we're finished."

"You and who else?"

"Nared-Major Sitlyn."

"The pilots?"

"No," Eahuda said. "Rest easy, lad. We're almost finished." He turned and moved out of view.

Arlud closed his eyes. He listened to the rain drumming against the battered hull, and he found it difficult to ignore the terrible pounding in his head.

⟡⟡⟡

Arlud drifted back from unconsciousness. He felt his body. He was lying on his back on a firm support, covered with a heavy blanket from his chest down.

He opened his eyes to darkness.

The memory of his transfer to this shelter came to him in bits and pieces. A vague recollection of something distant. Almost surreal.

There was movement at his feet. A dark, hulking shape rustled the fabric of the enclosure.

Arlud asked in an undertone: "Who's there?"

The figure leaned to the left and ignited a small glowing ball. Under the globe's dim amber light, Arlud recognized Nared-Major Sitlyn. She shifted to a more comfortable position and rubbed a slim hand through her sand-colored hair. "It's just me, sir. How do you feel?"

Arlud pondered his condition. He felt a dull pressure above his left eye. "Fine," he said. "I feel fine."

"Good. The Degen should be back soon. He's gone down to the wreckage to get some equipment."

"How long was I unconscious?"

"About three hours."

I'm lucky to be alive, Arlud thought, and the vision of crushed bodies flashed through his memory. "Were you injured?"

"Bruised hip. Nothing serious."

"What about Degen Eahuda?"

Sitlyn presented a small cup. "He cracked some ribs. Thirsty?"

Arlud accepted the water and sipped it as he looked around the tan colored shelter. They were inside a partially erected dome tent that formed an irregular oval with just enough headroom to sit up. "Why the cramped quarters?"

"The support poles were damaged by the crushed bulkhead. We rigged this inside a thicket. The shuttle's about two hundred meters downhill."

"Who hit us?"

Sitlyn shrugged. "After the dust settled, the Degen and I scrambled out of the wreckage and saw what looked like plasma bursts to the north. The whole sky was red in that direction. Must be nothing left of the outpost."

"Did you see any attack craft?"

Sitlyn shook her head. "Just the plasma bursts."

Arlud laid his head back down and balanced the cup on his chest. Frustration overwhelmed him. *The outpost was hit. That means the orbital defenses collapsed.*

At the sound of snapping twigs and rustling branches, Sitlyn placed a hand on her pistol and turned to face the sealed entry.

A voice sounded outside the tent: "Mission accomplished."

Sitlyn relaxed and pulled open the fabric doorway.

A heavy pack landed at Arlud's feet.

Gustav Eahuda crawled into the tent and sealed the fabric door. His black hair was still wet from the rain, and his exhaustion showed in the ponderous way he opened the pack. He looked at Arlud. "How's your head?"

"Fine."

Eahuda pulled a small rectangular device from the pack and examined it. "This may quicken the healing."

Arlud raised his head, then lowered it to ease the pain. "Do you know how to use that?"

"These things are idiot proof," Eahuda said. He leaned over, placed the unit on Arlud's forehead, and pushed the start button. "How's that?"

Arlud felt an immediate vibration and the dull pressure faded. "It works."

"Good," Eahuda said. He turned back to the pack. "And now for your hip, Sitlyn." He withdrew a larger device that had straps attached. "Lower your trousers and secure this over the bruise."

Sitlyn complied and buckled one strap around her thigh and the other around her waist. She turned it on and went numb from hip to groin. "How long will this take?"

"By morning, you'll be much better," Eahuda said as he tossed a blanket over the engineer's lower body.

Sitlyn reclined on her side, keeping her injured hip off the ground.

Arlud asked: "How could this happen?"

"We got lazy, lad."

"I thought Polinda was in his home district. How did he get here so fast?"

Eahuda shrugged and stretched out in front of the entrance with his head at Arlud's feet. He winced from the sting of injury. "The surviving Polinda ships from Alpha Cephei may have had orders to attack us if anything happened to them. Polinda is always looking for an excuse to hit us."

"He is persistent," Arlud agreed.

"Then again, that fat envoy from the Cormeds was already inside our defenses. It could've been him."

"The Cormeds are our ally."

"You refused to help them. Maybe he was offended and took advantage of the situation. Any damage here could always be blamed on a Polinda retaliation."

"The Cormeds wouldn't do that. They need our friendship as much as we need theirs."

Eahuda folded an arm behind his head. "Only speculation. The Polinda incident has put everyone on edge. Something was bound to happen."

Sitlyn gestured for Arlud to return the cup. "It could've been the same ones who hit Polinda," she said, and she took the cup from Arlud's outstretched hand.

Arlud agreed. "Now that is also possible."

Sitlyn screwed the empty cup onto the mouth of the water bottle. "What do we do now?"

"Rest," Eahuda said. "Can't do much in the dark. We'll heal a bit and set out at first light for the nearest peak and get our bearings."

"Bearings for what?" Arlud asked.

Eahuda threw a puzzled look at his young Regent. "For the outpost. The only way we're getting off this planet is by contacting our fleet. We need a transceiver with enough power to reach orbit."

"But the field was attacked."

"It may take some time to dig through the rubble, but we're sure to find one. There's five comm stations on the ground floor alone."

"Those stations weren't connected to the power grid," Sitlyn said. "That was scheduled for next week. The engineers took their portable setup with them in the other shuttle." She shifted her position a bit. "The power grid is probably smashed from the assault."

Eahuda pondered that hard reality. "We've got a lot of work ahead of us."

"What about enemy troops?" Arlud asked. "They could be all over the place."

Eahuda nodded. "We must be careful."

Slanting shafts of warm morning light cut through cold shadow, and the forest glistened from the wet the long rain had left as the three survivors made their ascent. The squawk and chatter of birds fluttered around, concealing the noise of their passage.

Gustav Eahuda reached the jagged rocks at the summit and pulled an obscuring branch out of the way. The land fell away into a deep, forested valley split by a winding river. Beyond the valley, a forested mesa dominated the horizon, and the half-finished central tower of the Erstallius outpost stood above the trees. "Didn't expect to see that."

Arlud brushed beside Eahuda. The cut on his forehead was scabbed over, and he still had the medpad on his forehead to help reduce the pounding when he leaned over. "It doesn't look damaged."

Sitlyn climbed atop the rock cluster to look over the surrounding brush. She focused her field glass on the tower and examined the neighboring buildings and portions of the tarmac. "There's damage along the edge of the exposed framing and scorch marks on the tarmac. I can't see the entire field, but it looks like that's the extent of the damage."

Eahuda reached up and took the field glass from Sitlyn to do his own magnified inspection. He scanned the forest to the south of the outpost. "There," he said, pointing to a large black area in the treetops. "Scorched woodland, with a few small craters."

Arlud sighted along Eahuda's finger and noticed the burned, cratered treetops on the southern slope of the mesa. "What's over there?"

"Bad targeting," Eahuda said. "That means they were not close. Probably fired from orbit and the storm interfered with the trajectory."

Arlud surveyed the surrounding country. "No troops anywhere."

Sitlyn backed down off the rocks. "Do you think it's safe to go over there?"

"Whether it is or isn't doesn't really matter," Arlud said. "We can't stay here."

"Yeah, we have little choice," Eahuda said. He gave the field glass back to Sitlyn. "We need to contact the fleet."

Sitlyn examined the valley through the field glass. "It'll take a full day to get over there if we can find a place to cross that river." She focused once again on the outpost. "No bodies."

Eahuda glanced at the engineer. "What?"

"No bodies, sir. There were at least one hundred natives down there when we took off in the shuttle."

"They would've fled when the attack began," Arlud said. He stepped down onto a narrow path leading into the valley. "Let's get over there."

Sitlyn brushed past Eahuda and followed Arlud down the path.

Eahuda left his vantage point, and the branch whipped back to its normal position.

BEV COLLI: U'GALEM

The dream began with the darkness Bev Colli had seen too many times.

Not again, she thought, as the blackness enveloped her.

The dream had intruded into her sleep cycle after her rescue from the surface of Alpha Cephei Four and repeated every time she slept during the journey to U'galem. She could not divert the outcome, no matter how hard she tried. The blackness dissolved into a rock tunnel where a woman lay half buried, screaming.

The heartbreaking cry forced Bev awake and the dream faded.

She sat up in her bunk and took a few moments to regain her senses. The dream had her in a grip she could not break, and the meaning behind it remained a mystery.

By the time she was notified to board the shuttle for planet-fall, the dream's overwhelming depression had faded, and she felt invigorated by this first step toward freedom. Her light brown skin was scrubbed clean of the muck and smell from the mine, and she was determined to never experience that again. Her once shaved head was now capped with a short growth of crimson hair that held the flowered scent from the shampoo she had found in her cabin shower stall. She wore one of the blue jumpsuits the Cormeds had given the survivors. The white canvas shoes were so light she barely felt them on her feet. She huddled in her shuttle seat, arms hugging her knees, and peered out the cabin window.

Twenty minutes after leaving the Cormed frigate, the shuttle entered the U'galem atmosphere and was cruising at high altitude toward the city of Kythria, in the southern hemisphere. The port city was on the coast of the eastern sea and had the largest population of any urban center on the planet. Kythria was the vacation home of Clan Dejoria's High Regent, the location of clan embassies, and the local hub for interstellar commerce.

"Magnificent," Bev said to herself.

The distant hills were bathed in the golden light of the rising sun. The towers and pinnacles of the city sparkled in the low angle light.

Bev remembered the bleakness of Shengri City on Pigrell. *That slum was nothing like this wonderful metropolis.* She smiled. Despite her doubts, she knew this place might hold the key to her future. A future without allegiance to Clan Polinda.

The shuttle drew closer to Kythria and banked over the southern suburbs, toward the space port that hugged the coast just outside the city limits.

Bev was mesmerized by the coming and going of vessels above hundreds of landing pads that followed the shoreline and spread out across a thousand acres of land. Ships of all sizes were here—luxury liners, massive cargo transports, and the smaller aircraft used for planet-bound excursions.

Where do all these ships go?

As the shuttle moved into the landing path, a young female attendant passed by Bev's row of seats. "Seat belt," she said, "we are on approach to land."

Bev smiled in response to the young woman, then sat up in her seat and latched her safety harness across her lap. She glanced out the window again. The buildings were getting bigger as the shuttle dropped toward the landing pad. She decided then that no matter what happened here, she would never allow Clan Polinda to put her back in that horrible mine.

Bev fell in line with the five other survivors and walked down the shuttle's loading ramp into warm air that held the smell of salt and the light mist of morning. The other survivors were men—they wore the blue jumpsuits and white shoes provided by the Cormeds, and they averaged about a half meter taller than Bev.

Milos Fore, the short and pudgy Cormed envoy, met the miners on the embarking platform. He was accompanied by two Cormed security officers in gray long coats.

"Welcome," Fore said. "I hope you are all doing well. If you could, please follow these men. They will take you to the lodging we have prepared for you at our embassy. You will stay there until Clan Polinda can send someone with your reassignments."

Bev shouldered her way to the front of the group of miners. "What reassignments?"

Fore shot Bev a quizzical glance. "I know you have suffered a major disaster, but you are still under contract with Clan Polinda. We must honor that arrangement."

Bev scanned the two large men with Milos. "Are we prisoners?"

"No, no, no," Fore assured. "If you have any objection to this arrangement, you can always get an arbitrator for your contract. We recommend that you stay on embassy grounds for your own protection."

A miner at the back of the group asked: "Why do we need protection?"

"Like all large cities," Fore said, "Kythria has its share of criminals. Staying on embassy grounds will also protect you from unauthorized Polinda aggression. It is important that they adhere to Alliance protocols. By leaving the embassy, you will abandon clan protections."

A few of the men chuckled.

Fore found that reaction odd. He smiled. "We are just adhering to protocol," he explained, and then gestured for the group to follow the security officers.

The miners were led off the embarking platform, to a long, blue passenger van that had the winged torch crest of Clan Cormed painted on the side.

An embassy van, Bev thought, as she clambered inside with the men. She sat in the back row by the window, purposely separating herself from the men, who made no attempt to sit near her. *They remember my kentao. My reputation is embedded in their brains.* She smirked and looked out the window.

As they left the space port and passed through the city, she enjoyed how different Kythria was from Shengri City—how clean the streets were kept, and how few pedestrians could be seen along the walkways. And then she remembered it was early morning.

Most everyone is still asleep, she thought, and she wondered how long a day was on U'galem. *I have much to learn about this place.*

The lodging at the embassy was sparse. Just a large gray room filled with cots and a row of lockers, with a narrow strip of windows near the ceiling. Two doors blocked access to other rooms beyond the back wall.

Bev was disappointed when she entered the room. "You have got to be joking," she said to herself, but the men nearby heard her and snickered. They found it to be adequate, and that made Bev even more unsettled. Lack of privacy in the mine was expected, but not here on U'galem.

Bev stormed out of the room. The two men who had escorted them from the landing pad were gone. She charged down the tiled hallway until she came up behind a tall woman dressed in a gray skirted suit. "I want my own room."

The older woman turned around to face Bev. She had ebony skin and large brown eyes that sparkled in the hall light. "Pardon?"

"I want my own room," Bev repeated. "I shouldn't have to stay with the men."

The older woman recognized the tattoo under Bev's left eye and realized what had happened. "Oh," she said, and she extended her right hand in greeting. "Hello, my name is Karisa Marsh."

Bev glanced down at the woman's hand, then up at her dark face. There was cheerfulness behind those big brown eyes. Bev felt out of place and a little embarrassed. "Hello," she said. She gripped the woman's hand just long enough to feel sweat on her own palm. "I'm Bev Colli."

"Yes," Marsh said. "You're one of the Polinda miners. Nice to meet you. Follow me."

Bev fell in step behind Marsh, who led her to another room farther down the hallway.

"This is your room," Marsh said. "I'm a clerk here at the embassy. If you need anything else, just ask for me at the front desk. I am usually available during the day."

Bev smiled. "Thank you."

"You're welcome, my dear," Marsh said, and she turned to leave.

"Wait," Bev said. "How long is a day on U'galem?"

Marsh stopped and looked back at the young survivor. "One point two standard. How long were you in the mine?"

"Six years."

"Well, you'll adapt to the length of the day. After a few weeks, you won't even think about it." She smiled, then turned and headed for the lobby.

Bev watched Marsh retreat for a few heartbeats, then entered her room. It had the same gray walls as the men's room. The same cots, the same lockers, and the same windows. *Good enough,* she thought. There was a lavatory through one door in the back wall and a shower stall through the adjacent doorway. The only locker she found open contained towels, another jumpsuit, a mirror, and a small compad.

She grabbed the pad and sat on the edge of the nearest cot. After fumbling through the controls, she figured out how to access the comnet and brought up a map of Kythria to pinpoint her location.

The Cormed embassy sat on fifteen acres west of the central business district. This building was in the south-eastern quadrant of the compound and was labeled East Residence Hall. There was a central garden, a gymnasium, a Western Residence Hall, a cafeteria, and a building labeled Consulate, which was the largest structure and filled the entire northern quadrant of the property.

Bev zoomed out the map display on her pad. Other clans also had embassies nearby. She counted ten, but Clan Polinda was not listed.

Perfect, she thought. Without a local presence, Polinda will get bogged down in official protocols before they can get anywhere near the survivors from the mine. *That should give me a little more time to carry out my plan and escape their grip for good.*

After the mid-day meal, when the consulate staff had returned to their offices, Bev came down to the East Residence Hall lobby. She approached the receptionist at the front desk. "Can you please tell Karisa Marsh I need to see her?"

As the receptionist complied with her request, Bev sat on one of the gray upholstered chairs along the wall. She pulled out her compad and continued her search for her labor contract. An hour passed without success. If she could not find the contract, her plan might fail.

Disappointed, Bev looked up from her compad and leaned back in the chair. She had tried to take a nap before lunch but was forced awake by the same repetitive dream that put her in a dark, twisting tunnel where a woman lay half buried in rock, screaming. The shriek woke her every time she heard it. She tilted her head back against the wall, closed her eyes, and took a deep breath. She exhaled and let her body relax.

"Hello, Bev," a soft voice said.

Bev opened her eyes to see Karisa Marsh's dark face smiling down at her. "Hi," she replied with a brief smile, and sat up straight.

Marsh sat in the chair next to Bev. "Everything all right?"

Bev nodded. "Almost."

"How can I help you?"

"I can't find my labor contract."

"You don't have a copy?"

"Lost it in the mine."

Marsh straightened at that remark. She had no grasp of how horrible Bev's experience had been, but she should have realized everything had been lost. She cursed herself for not seeing the obvious. "Well," she said, "maybe I can help you find it. Where was the contract ratified?"

"In Shengri City."

"Where is that?"

"Pigrell."

Marsh flinched. "Pigrell? Not here on U'galem?"

"On Pigrell, the Polinda homeworld."

"You are not from U'galem?"

"No," Bev said. "I thought I could find my contract in the local Labor database. Doesn't the Labor Bureau link all contracts by the Alliance comnet?"

"Not all of them," Marsh said. She sat back and contemplated the implications of what Bev had just said.

Bev leaned forward. "What's wrong?"

"Normal protocol should have sent you with the group of survivors from Pigrell, back to Pigrell. You should not have come here. It is standard procedure to return contracted labor back to their port of origin. It is a legal issue, regulated by Alliance decree."

"What does that mean?"

Marsh took a moment to consider Bev's question, then: "Well, it will take longer to get a copy of your contract. And there may be ramifications regarding your re-assignment. Polinda could disavow you completely. You could be left on your own with nothing."

Perfect, Bev thought. That was the reason she had come to U'galem. She would regret losing her promised wealth, but if she could gain her freedom that easily, she would take it.

"However," Marsh cautioned, "Polinda might take another path. One that would be most unpleasant for you."

"What path?"

"Some clans send retrievers to collect what they are due."

That was a threat Bev had not considered. "The Polindas would not go through all that trouble for me," she said. "The clan has more important things to worry about."

"Yes," Marsh agreed, "but it has happened."

Bev pondered the possibilities. A retriever was unlikely in her case, but she also knew if Polinda did not disavow her, avoiding the possibility of a retriever would rest on whether she could get a copy of her contract. "I need an arbitrator. Do you know where I can get a good one?"

"Yes," Marsh said, "you definitely need an arbitrator. Let me make some calls. Wait here." She stood and walked over to the receptionist.

Bev smiled to herself and let her body relax in the chair. *Step one accomplished,* she thought. The first step is always the hardest when you have no idea where to begin. The first step in her plan was finding the right person to help her. It had taken her almost a year in the mine before she could trust anyone. Karisa Marsh had made the search here on U'galem far easier than she had envisioned. The sliver of doubt that had troubled her during the voyage from Alpha Cephei Four was now gone for good. When Karisa came back and handed her directions to an arbitrator, step two of her plan was complete. Now all she needed was to get her contract into the arbitrator's hands.

Before Bev left the residence hall lobby, she composed a message to her prospective arbitrator. His name was Ozwald Rugeri.

"He is the best prospect among the negotiators I have worked with in the past," Marsh said.

Bev hoped he would accept her case but was prepared to widen her search if needed.

After sending the message, Bev walked over to the garden at the center of the embassy compound. She was a little apprehensive at first, not having been in open air, surrounded by plants, birds, and insects, in over six years.

"Mind the yellow and black flying insects," Marsh had warned her. "They sting when upset but will usually leave you alone if you don't bother them."

Bev almost changed her mind after that warning but could not resist the sensation that awaited her. She stepped through the arched doorway onto the paved walkway that led to the large octagon-shaped fountain at the center of the garden. She sat on the bench that protruded from the fountain's outer rim, closed her eyes, and focused on the smells and sounds of nature.

A light breeze carried scents she had not experienced on Pigrell. Birds chirped and fluttered amid the Lilies, Buttercups, Verbascum, Pimpernels, Mallows, Blue Gems, and Roseweed. Faint buzzing caused her to stiffen, and she opened her eyes, dreading the sight of yellow and black. She relaxed, seeing the insects were busy moving from flower to flower.

I've never seen so many different flowers in one place, she thought, and decided to stay until sunset.

Her compad buzzed. The message was from Ozwald Rugeri.

> "Greetings, Bev Colli.
> I have reviewed the details of your case. Please stop by my office tomorrow. I have scheduled you between 10 and 11. Please be prompt. O. Rugeri."

Below the text was a map to Rugeri's office. It was only a kilometer from the embassy.

I can walk there.

Rugeri had also attached a note of intent, indicating his assignment as the arbitrator for her case against Clan Polinda. That would enable her to leave the embassy grounds and allow her to return without argument from the guards.

She held her compad in her lap, closed her eyes again, and enjoyed the sounds and fragrance of the garden until the sun dropped below the horizon.

The next morning, Bev left the Cormed embassy with enough time to reach Ozwald Rugeri's office, walking at a leisurely pace. The pedestrian traffic was sparse along the busy boulevard. She was overwhelmed by the size of the buildings and walked an entire block before she noticed the odd looks from the people she passed.

The gawking must be due to these clothes, she thought. *Blue jumpsuits with white shoes must be out of style.*

She believed the Cormeds had given the survivors what people on U'galem usually wore, but as she continued down the boulevard, she wondered if the jumpsuit was intentional, to make their guests easier to find if they left the embassy.

She shrugged off the reactions and kept her attention on the path in front of her.

One block from where she needed to make a left turn, two men came around the corner and headed in her direction. The man on Bev's left had dark curly hair and the other man had spiky blond hair. They were both dressed for the warm day, wearing mid-length pants and short-sleeved pullover shirts. When they saw Bev, they nudged each other and pointed in her direction.

It's got to be the clothes.

As the men came closer, they began taunting. The blond man said, "Hey cutie, where have you been all my life?" His dark-haired companion stepped in line with Bev to block her advance and said with arms open wide: "Where you going beautiful?"

Bev stepped sideways toward the street to avoid the men.

Both men moved to block her path.

Bev moved toward the buildings.

Both men formed a wall across the walkway and forced Bev to stop.

"Let me pass," Bev said.

"Love that crimson hair," the blond man said. "Is that natural?" He reached out to touch Bev's hair.

Bev shifted her stance, reached up with both hands and placed a quick thumb lock on the man's outstretched hand, then spun and thrust her heel into his groin.

The blond man fell in a fetal position to the pavement with a quiet groan.

The other man lunged, reaching with both hands for Bev's shoulders.

Bev whirled to face the attacker and thrust her arms inside his, driving her fingers toward his throat.

The man leaned away from the strike.

Bev gripped his biceps so he could not retreat, stepped forward, and rammed a knee into his groin. As the man buckled, she pushed his arms away and jabbed her right fist into his throat.

The man dropped to the ground, choking.

Once satisfied the men were done, Bev continued down the walkway, leaving the assailants whimpering on the pavement. She turned left at the end of the block and headed for the office building where Ozwald Rugeri waited.

The office was on the third floor. It was a modest workplace separated from the main corridor by a transparent doorway with the title, OZWALD RUGERI A.E., etched in white.

Bev entered the small lobby and was greeted by a young woman with straight brown hair, wearing a dark green skirt suit. "Hi," the woman said. "Your name?"

"Bev Colli."

"Oh, yes," the woman said. She brushed her hair back and tapped her silver ear comm. "Bev Colli is here." After a brief pause, she said, "You can go in." She gestured to the open doorway next to her desk.

Ozwald Rugeri sat behind his desk, shuffling papers. He was a middle-aged man of thin stature with a bald head. The suit he wore had a drip stain on the left lapel. He looked up as Bev entered his office. "Hello," he said. He set the stack of paper aside and stood. "Ozwald Rugeri, at your service."

Bev smiled. "Hi." It surprised her to find Ozwald was her height, and by the look of him, close to her same weight.

"Have a seat," Rugeri said.

The chair was stiff, but Bev ignored that. "Karisa Marsh said you could help me."

"Yes," Rugeri said, as he sat in his chair. "You've complicated the process a little by not going to Pigrell, but that can be overcome."

"What do I need to do?"

"Nothing at this point. What I need to do is find your contract. That may take a day or two, but it will be found. Once I have that, I'll have a better idea of what you need to do."

Bev leaned forward. "All I want is to be free of that contract."

"I understand."

"There's a clause in it that nullifies the agreement if Clan Polinda does not fulfill their responsibilities. Providing adequate safety for all sapi is their responsibility. They failed, so the contract should be easily voided."

"You read the contract?"

"Yeah."

Rugeri sat back. "Huh!" He leaned forward and cupped his hands on his desk. "You'd be surprised how many of my clients don't read what they sign."

"What do you want for your services?"

Rugeri sat up straight. "I like your directness. My fee is ten percent of any monetary settlement, or one-thousand credits if only a legal settlement."

"My contract was for ten years, with a payout of one million credits. I fulfilled six years, so that should give me six-hundred thousand with the rest of the contract voided, minus Polinda's usual taxes."

"Well," Rugeri said, "that is a lot." He sat back. "If Polinda disavows you, you'll get nothing. I am sure they will press for that."

"It's your job to make sure they don't."

Rugeri nodded.

"I'll be fine if all I get is a canceled contract," Bev admitted, "but if you can secure my payment, I will give you half."

"That's unnecessary. I do not rob my clients. I set my fees at a reasonable rate."

"That is my offer to you," Bev said. "Call it an incentive. If I get nothing, you won't get paid because I have nothing."

Rugeri considered Bev's offer, and her honesty. The smart choice would avoid her case—she could not pay, and the odds were not in her favor. However, he could use the extra credits, and based on what he knew of Polinda contracts, what Bev had said was most likely legitimate. That favored a big reward if the proper arguments were made, and the correct process was followed. "Fine," he said. "I'll do what I can."

"So, we are agreed?"

"Yes."

"Then draw up the papers and I'll sign them."

"You are sure about this?"

"Yes, if you are sure about no payment until the settlement."

"Agreed."

Bev relaxed. Her goal was almost accomplished. "Then I have a favor to ask."

Rugeri sat back and gripped the arms of his chair.

"I need credits," Bev said. "We arrived here with nothing. I would like to get out of this jumpsuit into real clothes. And the embassy is limited in the personal items they supply. We are only temporary guests."

Rugeri stared back at Bev and pondered her future. *She's lost everything. Probably never had much to begin with in her life. Anyone signing on to work in a Polinda mine had to be desperate.* "I'll have my assistant open an account for you at our local bank. I'll deposit a modest sum to cover your expenses during the negotiations. Hopefully, we can have this all wrapped up in about two weeks."

"Thank you," Bev said.

"Understand, Miss Colli, those expenses will come out of your settlement."

"I understand. Thank you."

"See my assistant before you leave. She'll give you all the information and have our contract ready for you to sign."

Bev stood and walked to the doorway. She stopped at the threshold and looked back at Rugeri. "Thank you."

"You are welcome," Rugeri said. "I'll contact you as soon as I have your Polinda contract."

CLAN ERSTALLIUS: NI'APINU

Kudu was a robust young man from the city of Ji'dess, the closest Aku village to the Erstallius landing field. He was not yet beyond the year of acceptance, which was evident by the leather braids that bound his black scalp lock at crown and left shoulder. He trudged through the forest, wading through the thick underbrush, sporting a small backpack and a belt with bulging pouches at each hip. The Aku council had sent him and five others to search the crashed Erstallius shuttle for survivors.

The path the doomed shuttle had taken through the trees was visible for kilometers in every direction. Kudu advanced uphill through the thick forest and entered the path of shattered omèu trees that would lead him to the wreckage. The damage to the trees was most severe near the beginning of the track where the shuttle had hit the treetops at the greatest speed. Each omèu the vessel struck slowed the approach, shearing off bits of a wing here, a strut over there, branches everywhere. As Kudu neared what remained of the fuselage, it was obvious the shock of final impact had done the most damage to the shuttle. The larger tree trunks stood defiant against the mangled metal fuselage, half buried in plowed up undergrowth and broken branches.

About ten meters from the wreckage, Kudu noticed human tracks around the escape hatch, which meant there were survivors. As he drew nearer, he also recognized klâwpa tracks, which meant the small carnivorous scavengers had been feeding on the dead inside the smashed cabin. The human tracks led him around the wreckage, up a hill to a thicket, and into a collapsed tent. He examined the debris left inside the abandoned shelter, then continued following the human tracks up the hill to a rock outcropping near the summit.

Kudu climbed atop the rock cluster and spied the central tower of the Erstallius outpost. The metal framework jutted above the trees on the forested mesa north of the intervening river gorge.

That's where they will go, he thought. He pulled a hand-sized scanner out of his left hip pouch. He held the device in front of his face and watched the small screen as he aimed the scanner toward the eastern horizon, where Yoslyn Valley began, and panned it across his field of view to the west, where the Sequleg Mountains formed the valley's western border. He adjusted the settings and let the scanner analyze the data it had collected.

A few moments later, the small rectangular screen displayed potential signatures of human activity.

Kudu selected one of the data points and aimed the scanner in that direction, halfway across the forested valley, near the river. He took another scan. Heat from three bodies displayed on the small screen. They were at rest at the edge of the river. He touched the metallic ring around his neck and pinched the relay switch. "I have them," he said, his voice calm, with no apparent enthusiasm for his discovery. "Three survivors on the southern edge of the river, about five strads west of the bridge. Move in."

A man's voice replied through the receiver in Kudu's left ear: "We are on our way."

Arlud Erstallius sat on a stone outcropping at the river's edge as Petra Sitlyn washed the dried blood off his head wound. The gash had closed with the aid of the medpad, and the bump was smaller, but pain persisted when he leaned over too fast. Sitlyn's light scrubbing was within his tolerance level, but his patience had ended. "Enough," he said, and brushed her hand away.

Sitlyn resisted. "I'm not done."

"Yes, you are," Arlud said. He blocked her arm as she tried to continue. "Enough."

Sitlyn acquiesced. "Yes, sir."

Arlud lowered his arm, stood and surveyed the rushing river. The broad, open riverbank continued upstream for at least five-hundred meters where the river turned out of sight. Downstream there was only a narrow, rocky bank that fell almost vertically into the surging water. He turned and headed toward the line of the omèu trees about thirty meters away, where Gustav Eahuda sat, resting against one of the broad tree trunks. Arlud stopped at Eahuda's feet and asked: "How are we crossing that river, Gus?"

The old Degen stirred from his rest and leaned away from the tree. "I remember seeing a bridge somewhere in this valley. We just need to find it."

Sitlyn strolled up and stood beside Arlud. "We have two choices. East or West. Which way will it be?"

Arlud turned to answer, but was stifled by the sight of a small, winged aircraft above the trees. It was a light blue vessel, soaring with no perceptible sound, with short, broad wings that reminded Arlud of a butterfly. Two smaller airfoils were angled under the larger wings. All four structures pivoted to guide the yaw and pitch of flight.

Eahuda stood as the craft banked over the river. "Who's that?"

Sitlyn drew her pistol as Arlud ushered her farther beneath the trees.

Two more winged aircraft flew overhead. One pitched downward and dropped toward the river, her four wings tilted back and cupped like sails to catch the wind, slowing the near vertical landing so the craft touched down onto the rocky bank with no forward speed.

Just like a bird, Arlud thought.

The fabric wings relaxed, and revealed the pilot standing behind the controls, atop the small twin nacelle sled that supported the engine housing and wing pivot assemblies. He wore a helmet with a clear eye shield and a mouth filter.

Four more aircraft soared overhead and banked into a circular glide path above the river.

Arlud motioned Sitlyn to holster her pistol.

The engineer obeyed the command and stood with Arlud and Eahuda as the pilot approached from the landed aircraft. He was a young man, clothed in a thick woolen tunic and pants, with boots covered by leather leggings that stopped just below his knees. He raised his eye shield, then detached the mouth filter and let it dangle from his helmet. "L'dyém," he said in his quiet basso. "We have found you."

The brush became noisy with the swish and bustle of movement as four Aku men stepped from their concealed positions in the surrounding undergrowth.

Eahuda spun toward the commotion and cursed himself for not hearing the natives approach. He relaxed a bit when he noticed none of the men had weapons. He turned back to face the pilot. "What do you want?"

"We want you to come with us," the pilot said. "We have been sent to find you and bring you to Ji'dess."

Arlud took a step forward. "Who sent you?"

"The council," the pilot said. He placed his right hand over his heart. "I am Salus, Ni'desiah."

Arlud translated to himself: *Ni'desiah: Leader of Twenty, Commander of the Watch. A low rank, but one that demands respect.* He found it intriguing that the Aku used their ancient military designations without the uniforms. Salus led the flyers in the air and the men standing around them. Arlud took another step forward. "If we do not wish to go with you—"

"That would be a mistake."

Arlud did not detect a threat in the pilot's words. Salus had only stated a fact. "Do you know who we are?"

"Yes."

"Then you must know we need to get to our outpost."

The young pilot thought a moment, then: "No, you do not. There is nothing there for you. You should come with us."

Two more aircraft landed along the riverbank.

The pilot turned and gestured toward the other flyers. "Those ciâfey can each take one of you. I will take the one who remains."

Arlud surveyed the natives. They were calm and appeared weaponless, but there was determination in all their expressions. They needed to do this to fulfill an obligation. "What's in Ji'dess?"

"Come with us and see for yourself," the pilot said. He displayed a brief smile, then turned and gestured again toward his aircraft.

Arlud felt the hypocrite by resisting this offer. He had tried to forge a better relationship with the natives, and this was the perfect opportunity to form a deeper bond. He let himself relax, releasing all the tension he had built up inside, and followed the young pilot to his aircraft.

Arlud took his station behind Salus and leaned back into the passenger seat. The form-fitting restraint supported his weight and held his hips in place with his body in a half-squat position. Once secure in the seat, he pushed his feet into the cushioned leather loops on the metal deck. Mounting this open-air vehicle was both exhilarating and foreboding. Among the Clans, only stunt flyers braved the open winds. He asked Salus: "Why do you fly exposed like this?"

The pilot shot back a quizzical glance. "Why not?"

That answer was all Arlud needed to hear. This mode of flight was a regular part of the Aku experience. He pulled on the goggles Salus had given him, then gripped the hand railings at each side of the seat.

Salus motioned for Arlud to hold on tight.

A quiet hum erupted from the two nacelles. The four wings flexed upward, then dropped in one powerful downbeat, and the aircraft was two meters off the rocky ground. In one quick motion, the pilot banked to the left, readjusted the wings, and engaged the thrusters. The aircraft rushed over the river, rising above the tree line.

Arlud had not expected that. The force of the pivot and lunge shot a sting of pain through his forehead. He lowered his head to relieve the hurt and gripped the hand-railings as the craft sped eastward, following the river.

Eahuda and Sitlyn soon appeared to Arlud's right, both clenching the restraints behind their pilots. Sitlyn grinned at him. Eahuda frowned. Two more aircraft flew at Arlud's left. The pilot had called these aircraft "ciâfey," which meant "soaring wing" in the Akün language and soar they did. Their passage was almost silent, save for the faint hum of the engines. These were low altitude flyers, meant for short duration flights. After a few minutes, Arlud relaxed, letting his body flow with the yaw and pitch of the vehicle, awed by the skill Salus displayed as they cut through the wind and flew over the Yarward Bridge.

Gus's bridge, Arlud thought. He chuckled to himself. *We would have gone in the wrong direction.*

The wood and stone bridge spanned the wide river, connecting dirt roads that snaked north and south through the forest.

Leaving the bridge behind, the soaring wings continued eastward. They turned north after reaching Lake Yoslyn and flew over the rolling hills separating the valley from the coastal plain.

Arlud felt the air thicken with humidity as they dropped altitude and flew nearer to the coast. He looked ahead and saw the haze-shrouded buildings of Ji'dess. The small rectangular and circular structures stood amid salix trees, bordered on the nearer side by the green furrowed fields of the coastal plain. Beyond the buildings, he spied double-masted boats clustered in the calm waters of the harbor east of the village.

The Aku had proved to be more complicated than Arlud expected. They were fierce warriors when the chains of slavery needed breaking, humble agrarians when life needed living. They had a good life here on Ni'apinu. He understood their desire to keep this world from unwanted intrusion. Based on the pilot's demeanor, he was optimistic about this situation, but caution tempered his enthusiasm. What lay ahead in Ji'dess could prove to be a benefit for everyone, or a resounding defeat for Clan Erstallius.

Nujo waited on the wooden porch of the Council Hall. He watched the off-worlders advance up the narrow, grass lined trail from the ciâfey staging area. They looked worn out, and each of them moved with obvious signs of injury. He had expected worse. Based on Kudu's report, it was a miracle anyone had survived the crash. He backed toward the hall entrance, turned and made a hand gesture to someone inside the building.

The off-worlders stopped about a meter short of the porch.

Salus walked past them, up the steps, and met Nujo in front of the doorway. The young pilot exchanged a few words with the elder, then stepped aside.

Nujo moved to the edge of the porch. "When the strong help the weak," he said, "it is a blessing for those in need. You need us."

"Yes," Arlud said, not missing the irony in Nujo's statement. *I said the same thing to him at the landing field.*

Nujo reached into his pant pocket and pulled out the small, metallic transceiver Arlud had left on the tarmac. "Interesting," he said. "Similar to what we use. You should not leave these laying on the ground." He tossed the device toward the young Erstallius.

Arlud caught the transceiver with both hands. Scratch marks along the edge meant the natives had pried it open.

"It still works," Nujo said. "I would rather talk face-to-face. We have much to discuss."

Another elder stepped out onto the porch behind Nujo. He wore the typical woolen trousers and leather boots, but his linen shirt was embellished with intricate blue stitching around the collar and cuffs. His long gray scalp lock was banded at crown and left shoulder with gold rings.

Nujo stepped aside. "This is Paaq. He is our Bi'au."

Arlud bowed his head. The Bi'au was the central figure of Aku government who mediated all disputes. "We are honored."

"And we did not expect to be attacked," Paaq said. His voice was a smooth tenor, full but quiet. He moved next to Nujo. "Young Erstallius, the three of you are lucky to be alive."

Arlud nodded.

Paaq rubbed his bulbous nose. "A horrible mess, this Polinda affair. What do you plan on doing about it?"

"How do you know about Polinda?"

Paaq flashed a brief smile. "You are not alone, young Erstallius." He gestured to his left, down the dirt path that led to a cluster of buildings standing among trees about fifty meters away. "Salus will show you."

The pilot led the three off-worlders down the narrow trail, past two small dwellings, into a stand of salix trees. Beyond the wood they entered a dirt field scraped clean and hard pressed that surrounded a large structure skinned with metal siding. Arlud estimated the height of the large building at fifteen meters, the width at twenty. A curved roof and no windows on the near side, with two rectangular metal doors blocking an entry ten meters square, told him this was a storage building.

"We found more than you," Salus said. He gripped the left door latch and pulled hard, sliding the door open.

Arlud peered through the opening and saw the back end of an Erstallius shuttle. The six-legged vehicle dominated the center of the interior space, illuminated by overhead lamps and the filtered light from painted windows high in the side walls of the building. Two men squatted at mid fuselage, examining the ruptured skin. To the right of the shuttle, four men sat on benches to either side of a long table. They were Erstallius clanmen. Their blue uniforms unmistakable in the interior light.

Our Engineers, Arlud thought. He stepped into the room, followed by Eahuda and Petra.

The old Degen snapped erect. "Stand for your Regent!"

The men at the table turned toward Eahuda's commanding voice and stood at attention. The two men at the shuttle dropped their tools and also stood erect. That quick jump to formality ended as the clanmen rushed forward and surrounded the three survivors with hugs and handshakes.

"We thought you dead," the bald clanman said. He was Winstone Bittle, Nared-Major in charge of Engineering Crew Gamma.

"Fate was kind," Arlud said. "How did you come here?"

"Before we cleared the tower, a plasma ball grazed our port side." He gestured to the rip in the shuttle's skin. "We were able to land on the tarmac. Fortunately, the rest of the salvo was off target. The outpost suffered a few bruises, but the forest took the brunt of the assault. Polinda killed many trees."

A few of the men chuckled.

"They never broke atmosphere," Bittle said. "Once the assault was over, the natives appeared and suggested we come here. The shuttle can fly. She just can't reach orbit with that damage."

"We saw the burned trees," Eahuda said. "You're sure it was Polinda?"

"Absolutely," Bittle said. "We contacted the fleet after we landed. Three Polinda destroyers had entered the system, and one was in orbit. Then we lost contact."

Arlud pondered the implications. Lost contact and no surface landings meant both sides had suffered. "How are your repairs coming?"

"Good," Bittle said. "The natives have been very helpful."

Salus walked up behind the Erstallius group and said, "In case you are hungry." He gestured to the line of women now bringing food to the table.

"Thank you," Arlud told the young pilot. "Tell your elders we are overwhelmed by your kindness."

Salus nodded acceptance of Arlud's compliment. He lingered until all the food had been delivered, then left with the women.

After the meal of pristal-berries and meat that tasted like chicken, the engineers continued their repair work. Sitlyn joined the men at the shuttle. Eahuda took the medpad from Sitlyn, strapped it over his ribs, and reclined in a hammock hung between two support beams along the west wall—his bruised ribs and the journey here had worn him down—he needed to sleep. Arlud stayed at the table, lowered his head onto his arms, and drifted into sleep.

"Did you enjoy the meal, young Erstallius?"

Arlud looked up from his slumber to see Paaq standing on the other side of the table. Salus and Nujo stood a few paces behind the elder, to his left.

The old man gestured to the bench. "May I sit?"

Arlud nodded and sat up straighter. He glanced around to get a sense of the time. The engineers were still working on the shuttle. Gus was still in the hammock. Sunlight still illuminated the painted windows.

"I was impressed by your sincerity," Paaq said, as he straddled the flat bench and sat. "Nujo told me what you said before you left your landing field. Solemn promises can be difficult to keep."

"Yes," Arlud said. "More difficult than I had planned."

Paaq swung his other leg over the bench, leaned forward, and clasped his old hands on the table. "You were presumptuous, young Erstallius. We understand your motive is genuine. Did you not understand my people would reject your words?"

"We knew it would take time before you would trust us. We hoped that would not take too long. Patience is a virtue."

Paaq sat up straight. He could see the young Erstallius was being forthright, and that was encouraging. "The Aku have been very patient."

"Yes, you have," Arlud said, "and for that I am grateful."

Paaq crossed his arms on the table. "We monitored the battle as best we could. Your people sacrificed themselves to stop the destroyer in orbit. The outlying conflict appears to have also ended in a stalemate. The battle had no victors, and based on the telemetry, there were no survivors."

Arlud stared at the table. The weight of that defeat pushed his head back down on his arms.

"Your people upheld your promise at the cost of their lives," Paaq said. "We owe them our lives. And now the Aku must act."

Arlud raised up on hearing that statement.

"The Council debated all night," Paaq said. "We need your help."

Arlud shook off that idea. "How can we help you? We've been rendered powerless."

"Your knowledge," Paaq said, and he gestured toward the shuttle.

Arlud turned and glanced at the engineers repairing the shuttle's port side. Petra's upper body was inside a service tube in the center of all the damage, her feet dangled between two engineers who were repairing a conduit cluster in the exposed hull above her legs. The other clanmen were in various places around the aircraft, all focused on their repair tasks.

"Your people have knowledge we need," Paaq said.

"You want to repair your old ships."

Paaq was pleased with Arlud's keen insight. "We must repair them."

"How can you use a spacecraft for seventy years and not know how to repair it?"

"Seventy years is a long time for any technology. Systems break down. Some parts are not replaceable. We have the engineering schematics, but without all the working parts they are useless. It has been over eighty years since the last transport left orbit and was placed in storage. We have done what we can, but that has not been good enough. Perhaps if Seelay were still alive, our situation would be different."

Arlud had read about Seelay. He was the rebel leader who breached the Tuma compound on Kainogae, in the city of Dong'ra, that led to the confiscation of five transport ships and destroyed the local clan forces. He directed alteration of the transports and turned them into warships. They became more powerful and had weapons none of the clans had seen. One year later, the Aku left Kainogae with sixty ships and over fifty thousand people. When Seelay died, most of his knowledge went with him. "You are fortunate your rebellion is widely known among the Clans."

"Yes," Paaq said. "A good reputation is priceless."

Arlud gestured to the damaged shuttle. "This operation is nothing compared to what you hope we can do."

Paaq nodded. "To do nothing ensures defeat."

"Then we will do what we can," Arlud said, "but I will not make any promises."

Paaq grinned and reached out to seal the accord with a handshake.

Arlud gripped the old man's hand, sealing a relationship with the Aku not experienced by an Alliance clan in over two hundred years.

THE GUILD: RESCUE

The freighter shuddered.

Shanna Sy woke to the rattle, flicked on her bedside lamp, and focused on the faint rhythmic drone of the engines.

Space travel was new to her. Everything outside the family keep on Alphaq was new to her.

The freighter shuddered again.

Her briefing about what to expect during this journey should have prepared her for such happenings, but the reality of the experience set her nerves on edge. She reached over and pressed the comm button next to the lamp.

A deep male voice answered: "Yes, lady?"

"Is everything all right?"

"Yes, lady. Sorry to have awakened you."

"Are we at Wald-415?"

"No, lady. We've just met a disabled Cormed frigate. We may be delayed a few hours while we assess the situation."

"Oh, my! Is anyone hurt?"

"They appear to have engine problems. We'll keep you informed."

"Thank you," Shanna said. She rolled onto her back. Her dark curls flowed over the pillow. She folded her arms behind her head.

A Cormed frigate.

She had heard her father mention the Cormeds on various occasions. They were not his favorite people. She wondered how they could have let their ship break down. Space was such a lonely place. Why would anyone abandon proper maintenance and risk being stranded? She turned on her side and curled into a fetal position. She was confident her captain would do everything in his power to secure the situation and still deliver her and her mother to their destination within the desired time. She closed her eyes, and the rhythmic throbbing of the ship's engines lulled her back to sleep.

⬥⬥⬥

Fifteen hours after first contact, the Guild freighter maneuvered within six meters of the disabled Cormed ship and latched on to her hull. A pressurized gangway was extended to allow the Cormed crew to leave their disabled ship.

A crippled vessel was a prime quarry for the Guild, but this time no treasure would be seized, no cargo would be unloaded, no manifests would be checked for valuable commodities. Some things are more precious than material gain, and Captain Erlis Pardee was not ignorant of priorities. After learning of the onslaught that had damaged the frigates, his initial considerations of wealth gave way to thoughts of survival and weapons capabilities.

Repairs to the damaged frigate could not be made outside a maintenance dock, and towing was not possible. The compression field generated by Pardee's ship would not envelop the *Iron Spear*, and she would be ripped apart the moment hyperdrive was achieved.

Captain Pardee plotted a course for GSW-183. The new Erstallius settlement on the Aku homeworld was closer than any other colony. The detour necessary to reach the world was a minor one and would delay their arrival at Wald-415 by only two days and seventeen hours. The Cormed crew would debark at the new port and find passage home through Alliance channels.

Madame Wellen Tallilia Sy accepted the news of the course change: "Their welfare is more important than our holiday sojourn. They may be Alliance, but they are still human and very much in need."

Captain Pardee was impressed by her selfless attitude. "I will lessen the delay, if possible," he said, standing at ease at the threshold to Madame Sy's cabin.

"I appreciate that, Captain," Wellen said. "Do what you must."

"Thank you, Madame," Pardee said. He tipped his head as he backed into the corridor, and the door to Madame Sy's cabin slid shut.

As wife to the most prominent renegade inside Alliance territory, Wellen was no stranger to altered plans and sudden problems. The events that had led Wolfram Sy to Al-phaq had been fierce and bloody, with danger lurking at every turn.

"A pirate's life is never peaceful," Wolfram had often said.

So right you are, my dearest, Wellen thought. She swept across her cabin, skirts swishing, then covering the low settee as she settled at one corner and pressed the comm button for Shanna's cabin.

"Yes?" Shanna answered.

"It's Mother, Dear. Captain Pardee will change our course. We'll be taking the Cormed people to an Alliance world. We'll arrive at Wald-415 a few days late."

"Oh. Father may be there when we arrive then."

"Yes, dear, he may."

"Mother, did Captain Pardee say anything more about what happened to the frigate?"

Wellen hesitated, recalling Pardee's cautious words about a strange force and its awesome threat. "No need to worry about that," she said. "Captain Pardee assured me the danger is far away now."

"I hope so, Mother."

"Dear, why don't you join me for dinner? Afterward, I'll challenge you to a game of Stratagem."

"That would be nice, Mother," Shanna said, knowing the diversion would soothe her nerves.

Degen Duncun Turl of the Cormed frigate *Javelin*, escorted the blind Einar Duballik through the weightless gangway to the Guild freighter. They reached the ship's portal, and a robust guard blocked their passage, forcing Turl to separate from Einar.

Einar protested when Turl's grip left his arm. "What? Where are you, Commander?"

"We'll take you the rest of the way," the guard said.

Einar erupted: "You will not!" He pushed away the guard's hand from his arm. "Degen Turl will escort me!"

The guard hesitated.

Einar was defiant. "Do you know who I am?"

"Yes, sir," the guard said. "Captain Pardee ordered—"

"Degen Turl will escort me!" Einar reached out for Turl. "Grab my arm, Degen."

Turl moved in and held Einar's left arm.

Einar pushed forward. "Move aside sentry!"

The guard acquiesced. "Fine. Your quarters are on deck 3. Cabin 12."

Turl guided Einar into the ship and led him down the segmented access corridor to the transfer room, where they could enter the simulated gravity environment of the ship's outer decks. The gravity there was heavier than on Cormed ships, and he found walking tiresome.

Einar adapted to the heavier gravity with ease and sensed from the rough motion of his guide that something was wrong. "You all right, Degen?"

"Seems I've gained a little weight."

Einar and Turl had bonded during the days after the attack, sharing stories that led to Einar's descriptions of the odd dreams he began having after the assault. Before their transfer from the *Iron Spear*, Turl had sent a priority request to Captain Pardee about Einar, and insisted he meet with them.

Captain Pardee came to Einar's cabin as soon as he heard the old guildman was aboard. They shared a welcoming hug. "Good to have you here, old friend."

Einar patted Pardee's back and sat down.

Pardee reacted to Einar's blindness with a brief tinge of silent regret, then acknowledged the Cormed officer. "Degen."

Turl nodded.

Pardee settled into the chair across from Einar, next to Turl's seat. "So," he said, "what news do you have?"

Einar leaned back in his cushioned chair. "You have the Cormed report about the attack?"

Pardee nodded. "Haven't gone over all the details yet. I'll be meeting with Farvic after we're done."

"You must understand," Einar said, "the Alliance sent eight frigates to blockade Al-phaq because of the Polinda incident. My ship was boarded by Cormed security. They suspected Wolfram was behind the Polinda mine attack. After the Cormeds were attacked, that belief faded." Einar leaned forward. "What hit us was not a natural event. It changed course to pursue us."

Pardee leaned forward. "A new rebellion among the clans?"

"Not sure," Einar said. "After the attack on the *Javelin*, I had intense visions. Like lucid dreams. I believe whoever attacked us is behind those nightmares."

Pardee rocked back against the cushion and folded his hands in his lap. He was bemused by that last revelation but knew Einar to be a serious man. "Lucid dreams?"

"They are some of the most intense dreams I have ever had—so real."

Turl faced Pardee. "Einar was not the only one to experience odd dreams. Three clanmen had the same experience."

Pardee was now intrigued. "Exactly the same?"

"Yes," Einar said.

"We don't know what the dreams mean," Turl said, "but whoever is behind the attacks is also behind the dreams. They have a technology beyond anything we possess."

"Whoever or whatever," Einar said.

Pardee faced Einar. "Whatever?"

"Could be aliens," Einar said. "If not aliens, then it's a clan of which we know nothing about, with a technology beyond our ability. We all know how the idea of aliens faded the more man spread among the stars, but there are a lot of stars out there."

"Aliens," Pardee muttered, "that would be the discovery of the millennium."

"Yes, it would," Einar said.

Pardee frowned. "The restrictions fostered by the GRAND Crusade have been crumbling for decades. A renegade clan is more likely the cause."

"Yes," Turl agreed. "The simplest explanation is usually the correct one in cases like this. Whoever hit us, probably hit the Polinda mine. Polinda has many enemies."

Pardee wondered: "But why cause the survivors to have dreams? What are the dreams about?"

"A woman in a cave," Turl said.

Pardee flinched. "A woman in a cave?"

"A burning woman," Einar said. "She's not in the Polinda mines. This woman is not wearing an environment suit. She is in a cave, a rock tunnel, screaming in agony."

"And how is she connected to attacks on a mine and Alliance frigates?"

"The dreams began after the attack," Einar said. "They are connected. No doubt about it. Why they are connected is what we need to find out."

Pardee considered everything Einar and Turl had said. "Does Farvic know about this?"

"We've kept this to ourselves for now," Turl said. "I want more time to reason this out before going to Farvic."

"Farvic could site you with treason if he knew you were talking to me first."

Turl nodded at that possibility.

"And what about your clanmen?"

"They understand the need for silence," Turl said. "They've a reputation to maintain. On the surface, this dream thing sounds crazy, unless you've experienced it. All three of them came to me independently when I prompted all the survivors from the *Javelin* to inform me of any unusual aftereffects. They have not spoken of this among themselves."

Pardee understood the cultural issues among crewmen. Gossip could destroy morale and a clanman's carrier. "Have you experienced these dreams, Degen?"

"No, but I believe Einar and my crew do not fantasize. Four independent witnesses seal the truth of it for me."

Pardee nodded. "And me."

"The woman is the key," Einar said.

"That would seem to be the intent of it," Pardee said. "Tell me, Degen, why speak to me about this?"

"Einar and I have had many conversations during the past few days. He tells me you are an honorable man. We are told by our teachers and superiors not to trust each other. That may be warranted, but I believed Einar's sentiment that you would handle this information properly. Farvic would disregard it. He is a good Jegen but has a very closed mind toward anything that does not agree with his world view. He would be an obstacle in our search to understand this."

"I see," Pardee said. He understood the implications Einar and Turl were suggesting. An unknown enemy had struck an Alliance colony and forced adjoining clans into battle mode. More attacks could propel the clans into civil war. The Alliance could crumble. "Well, I suggest you continue to analyze all the data you have. We need to question all the survivors again who have experienced these dreams and place them under medical surveillance. If we can collect data while they are having these dreams, we might discover more about who the instigators are. Somewhere inside all that is an explanation."

"I agree," Turl said.

"I'll speak with doctor Molska about monitoring your clanmen."

"And me," Einar said.

Pardee nodded. "And you, old friend."

Captain Pardee watched the replay of the attack from his seat in the forward lounge. On the holoscreen to his right, the undulating shape engulfed the *Javelin*.

"Notice the brief flare," Jegen Farvic said, pointing to the odd shape on the monitor. He sat across the table from Pardee, bracketed by two armed guards standing behind his chair.

On the screen, the edge of the disturbance flashed yellow, and the entire shape burst into white fire.

"We recorded a temperature of 9,350 kelvins," Farvic said.

On screen, the white fire faded to its original rippling distortion and rushed forward, growing larger as it approached the fleeing *Iron Spear*.

Pardee was surprised by the obvious intent behind the distortion's movement. "It changed course."

Jegen Farvic nodded as he watched the monitor. "It's controlled. It has a purpose."

Pardee turned toward Farvic as the monitor winked out.

"It pursued us," Farvic said. "We could do nothing to stop it."

"You never found the missing Sabballi vessels?"

"No."

"Why would it destroy three ships but only immobilize you?"

"I don't know," Farvic said. "I'm thankful but have no answer."

The intercom buzzed for attention.

"Pardee here."

"Captain," a male voice said, "we've picked up a very weak, narrow band distress beacon. It's from the PDN160 system."

"GSW-183," Farvic said. He returned his gaze to the monitor as the recording of the attack replayed. "That's almost directly in line from where we were to Alpha Cephei Four."

Pardee shot a quizzical look at Farvic. "You think that thing hit the Erstallius colony?"

"The course is in line."

"That's where we're taking you, so I guess we'll find out for sure."

"You can't take us there. If the destruction on Alpha Cephei Four is typical, all we'll find is rubble."

"Someone sent the beacon."

"Detour to another place, Pardee, or your ship may end up like mine."

"Suggestion noted," Pardee said. "I am thankful you saved Einar Duballik. I understand your original motive for approaching Al-phaq, and I have disregarded my personal feelings about that. My choice of destination, however, will be based on what's best to fulfill my obligations. GSW-183 is the closest world with an Alliance presence, and since it's a small outpost, making orbit should be easy. Less security to harass us."

Farvic rose to protest but fell into the grip of the guards.

Pardee flashed a hand signal, and the guards escorted Farvic from the room. He faced the intercom. "Can we return a message, Comm?"

"Yes, but we'll be there before it arrives."

"Continue silent monitoring."

Pardee looked at the replay of the attack on the monitor. The evidence was mounting. The Alliance frigates met whatever destroyed the mine on Alpha Cephei Four, and no matter where it came from, it was a threat to everyone in the district.

Despite their strained relations, Pardee knew saving the Cormeds had been the proper thing to do but allowing them to stay aboard would only irritate old rivalries. He had to unload them as soon as possible to avoid a serious confrontation. That danger lurked just beneath the surface of the Cormed officer's demeanor.

Pardee punched another comm button. "This is Pardee. Release the *Iron Spear* and set course for GSW-183."

"Aye, sir."

A few minutes passed, and the Guild freighter rumbled into hyperspace.

Pardee hit the comm button again. "Pardee here. What's our ETA at current speed?"

After a brief pause the crewman said: "Thirty-seven hours, sir."

"Do your best to cut that time in half."

"Aye, sir."

The freighter shuddered as the compression drive increased by a factor of two.

Pallis Nin pulled his way along the central access corridor toward the cargo bay where the Cormed crewmen had been billeted. The cramped space forced them to bunk in the microgravity wherever they could find room between the shipping containers already stored there. It was not as comfortable as desired, but at least they were alive. At least the pirates had displayed some humanity by not leaving them to rot on their disabled ship. Nin reached the rear section and eased up between two netted containers where Jegen Farvic had secured enough room to confer with his first officer, away from the probing eyes and ears of their hosts.

"He insists on continuing to GSW-183," Farvic said.

Nin pushed himself alongside Grom Anen, not knowing the reason Farvic had summoned him here.

"Nin," Farvic said, "it's about time you got here."

"I'm not that familiar with low gravity, Jegen. Sorry. I was in sick bay, the last of our group to be cleared."

"We have learned that Madame Sy is on board," Farvic said. "We need you to entreat her for us."

"Why?"

"Pardee refuses to change course. He will drop us off on a dead world, Mister Nin."

"A dead world?"

"The thing that hit us has been to GSW-183. This ship received a distress call when I was reviewing the attack with Pardee."

"Then it can't be a dead world."

"Oh, there will be survivors," Farvic said. "We're a good example of that. But if I'm right, and it's the same thing that hit Alpha Cephei Four, the colony there will be destroyed. We'll be stranded on that planet just as we were on our frigate. That is not acceptable."

"What do you want me to say to the lady?"

"You're a diplomat. It's your job to sway opinion, to cloak deceitful motive with smooth words. Tell her of our displeasure. Give her an impression of the disaster that will result from her Captain's stubborn refusal to agree to our needs. Urge her to persuade Pardee to change course."

"What disaster?"

"Blood will spill, Mister Nin, and most of it will be Guild blood."

"How do you plan on doing that?"

Grom Anen reached under his tunic and pulled out his small magar-pistol. "We have these."

Nin flinched at the sight of the weapon.

"These magars are designed to avoid detection," Anen said. "They're standard issue survival weapons."

Nin focused on the magar-pistol. A circular, ten-centimeter-long magnetic rail was set into a rectangular receiver that housed a five-shot magazine and the electronics that flung the projectiles along the short rail. The stubby grip housed the micro power supply and allowed a firm hold on the small weapon.

"Their range is limited," Farvic said, "but they can do enough damage in these close quarters."

Nin could see no way out of Farvic's intent. "I can't threaten Lady Sy."

"This is no threat, Mister Nin. It is a promise."

The two Cormed officers stared at Nin with the same determined look. He felt pressed in under their scrutiny. An underlying viciousness seethed behind the Jegen's dark eyes—a hidden ferocity Nin had never seen before. There would be bloodletting on this ship for certain if Pardee refused to listen.

BEV COLLI: FREEDOM

Bev leaned close to the mirror and, using a small brush, painted a dusty beige compound under her left eye. With one stroke, her rust-colored tattoo was hidden under the obvious swath of what Karisa Marsh called makeup.

Bev frowned. "It looks horrible."

"You need to blend it in," Marsh said. She hovered behind Bev, guiding her young friend's first foray into the world of cosmetics. "Use your fingers."

After a few gentle rubs with her index finger, the coloration matched her own skin, and the tattoo was gone.

Bev smiled. "This is great!"

"It's not permanent," Marsh said. "You must apply it daily."

Bev examined the small round jar of the compound. *I'll be buying this about every four weeks,* she thought. It was worth it. The Polinda mark would last another four years before decomposing. For her plan to succeed, she had to hide any link to Clan Polinda for as long as possible.

Bev turned to Marsh. "Thank you. This is just what I needed."

Later that morning, Marsh took an embassy car and drove Bev to a clothing store. The shopping spree was brief. Bev went in, chose two sets of blue pants, three pullover shirts, one blue, one gray, and one green, and a pair of black, slip-on shoes. The entire process took just over twenty minutes.

Marsh was amazed how fast Bev had chosen her outfit. "Are you sure these are what you want?"

"Yes," Bev said. She thought Marsh's question was strange. "Why? Should I have picked something else?"

"No," Marsh said. "Most women I know take more time to choose."

"Then they must not know what they want."

Marsh smiled.

Once back in the car, Bev pointed out the window. "Can we stop by that tech store over there?"

"Why?"

"I want to get another compad. The one I found in my locker keeps freezing up."

"Oh," Marsh said. "You should have told me about that. We would have given you another one."

"That's OK. I'd like to pick one out for myself."

Marsh veered toward the tech store.

Once back in her room, Bev used her old compad to check the remaining credit amount in her account.

1,662 credits. Rugeri has been more than generous.

She now had the most important decision to make about her future. Either stay at the embassy and let the legal battle proceed or disappear into a new identity. She had planned to disappear, having no faith the system would help her, but that was before she met Marsh and Rugeri. She could never see them again if she disappeared. Running away might void any legal advantage and would place her new friends in an undeserved position of concern for her welfare. She searched the comnet for answers to her legal position. After about twenty minutes of searching, she found the answer:

> "Contract disputes may proceed without the appearance of the contracted laborer, provided one of the following stipulations are met:
>
> "1. The contracted laborer has signed over all authority to a third party.
>
> "2. The contracted laborer, after initiating legal proceedings, is prohibited from appearance because of physical or mental limitations, or other natural causes beyond the contracted laborer's ability to overcome."

Clan Polinda could not be trusted. Six years in the mine had taught Bev that harsh reality. She knew the only sure way of protecting herself was to disappear.

Her mind made up, she activated her new compad, navigated to a list of legal forms, and filled out a *Transfer of Authority* document. She saved the form and then searched for a local listing of help wanted notices. That search took over an hour and revealed two possibilities.

Satisfied her plan could still work, she turned off her compad and laid out her new clothes on the cot. She stripped off her jumpsuit, pulled on both pairs of new pants and rolled up the cuffs to mid-calf. The material was thin enough, so the result was not too bulky in appearance. All three pullover shirts fit with a similar result. She then stepped back into her jumpsuit, and the other garments were hidden from view. Her new slip-on shoes bent flat and slipped into one of her side pockets. She checked her appearance in the mirror. A little thicker, but nothing out of the ordinary. Trying to leave the embassy with a backpack or satchel would draw suspicion. This way, no one would suspect she was leaving for good. She pocketed the small make-up kit, then grabbed a hand towel and brushed off her white shoes. Content with her appearance, she wrapped the old compad in the towel and placed it on the shelf in her locker.

They won't be tracking me with that anymore.

She dropped her new compad in her jumpsuit pocket and headed for the embassy's rear gate.

The warehouse was full of activity. Manned cargo lifts transferred containers along the rows of metal shelves that filled the center of the building. Robo-lifts shuttled small crates and pallets stacked with boxes around the perimeter.

Bev estimated the five-tiered shelves were ten meters high.

"You done?"

Bev looked at the obese warehouse manager and handed him her labor information form. "All filled out."

The old man glanced over the information, then sized up Bev from head to toe. "You ever work in a warehouse before?"

"No," she said, with no sense of an apology. "I worked in a mine for six years. I was a mad japer."

The manager raised an eyebrow. "A what?"

"A mad—" Bev searched her memory for the local term. "A driver. I controlled a mobile drill."

"Well, we ain't got any of those here, just forklifts and work pods."

"Then the danger should be minimal."

The old man smiled at Bev's bravado. "You look like you can handle yourself. Be here tomorrow. Seven sharp."

Three blocks from the warehouse, she found an apartment. A small, furnished one-room flat with a balcony that overlooked the industrial district north of Kythria's space port. Once settled in her new quarters, she took her new compad and sent Rugeri her Transfer of Authority form along with a brief note stating her fear of Polinda reprisal, ending with the request, "Please honor my need for anonymity."

Rugeri did not write back.

Bev went to bed that night wondering if he had dumped her case. That was a risk she had to take. If he had dumped her, then she was better off without him. Lack of loyalty like that could put her back in a Polinda mine.

She curled up in bed and listened to the sounds of the city. Production never stopped in this industrial neighborhood. The clangs and thuds reminded her of the mine—sounds familiar and easy to ignore. The periodic rush of aircraft overhead was more intrusive.

Now I know why the rent for this flat is so low.

The roaring shuttles passed to the south, toward the spaceport, every thirty minutes. She covered her head with her pillow to muffle the sound.

After midnight, the air traffic faded, and she drifted into sleep.

The dream came as usual: a rock tunnel, twisting through dark strata toward a dying woman half buried in the rock, screaming. This time, Bev withstood the agony of that nightmare and the scene changed. She was thrust into a new perspective above the woman, looking through the tunnel toward a pinpoint of light. She rushed toward the light and flew out of the tunnel over sandstone terrain under gray clouds that flashed with lightning. Cracks of thunder revolved around her as she sped through the clouds and was surrounded by the silent expanse of stars.

The quick change in location startled her.

She rolled over and was floating high above dark, rocky ground. It was a turbulent terrain, pock-marked with craters. She moved toward the surface, sensing movement by the ground's slow advance. Her path drifted to the left and then rushed toward rugged hills surrounding a flat plain. The landscape became more detailed as she drew closer, and she realized she was heading toward the mine. The surface buildings surrounding the landing terminal and the habitat structures above the basement complex were half hidden in shadow.

Then the explosions began. The mine was ripped apart from below, spewing cyan-colored plasma. Debris was flung over the surrounding plain, crashed into the outlying buildings and cratered the gray terrain.

Her course shifted again, and she headed to the hills east of the surface buildings where she saw the survivors clustered along the hilltop. Her motion drifted from the center of the group to a lone miner, laying face up a few meters from the rest of the survivors. The soil-stained environment suit looked lifeless, but as she drew closer, Bev could see the blinking light on the chest pack.

She rushed forward, stopping inches away from the helmet, and saw her own face staring back at her behind the frost-rimmed face plate.

A blinding light erased the vision.

Bev sprang awake with a gasp. The apprehension she had felt lying in the dirt on that cold, airless planet chilled her to the bone.

She laid back down and focused on the dream. This was the first time her perspective changed. And she knew the cause of the destruction at the mine was not intentional. That was a crazy thought, but deep inside her, she knew it was true. The realization flooded her mind, and she understood the deeper implication no one had recognized.

That blue cloud was alive.

"This is bigger than I remember," Bev said, as she stepped through the doorway into the main storage area of the warehouse.

"What you saw yesterday was only an annex building," the foreman said. He was a grimy fellow who chewed on something in his mouth, but never swallowed.

Bev took a step back from the foreman. He smelled of garlic and something rank she could not identify. To disguise her olfactory displeasure, she surveyed the warehouse.

This main storage area covered twenty-two hundred square meters, with a ceiling twenty meters high. Three rows of support pylons segmented the space into four sections, each filled with eight-tiered metal shelves, similar to the ones Bev had seen in the other building, but twice as high, and filled with crates.

The foreman gave Bev a tour that lasted about thirty minutes, then handed her a small data pad. "Your first duty will be inventory control," he said. "This screen will tell you which section needs counting." He pointed to the graphic display on the pad. "You enter the crate serial numbers here."

Bev took the pad and reviewed the screen.

"When you're done, come see me," the foreman said. Then he turned and shuffled toward the doorway to his office.

Bev watched the foreman's large back recede and was glad his smell went with him. She stifled an urge to call out a question. All the answers she needed were on the pad he had given her. She reviewed the screen info again and headed toward row five, section two.

The deeper into the row she went, the ambient light grew dimmer. The overhead lamps were so high the floor level near the center of the row was enveloped in shadow. Her inventory pad glowed and told her she had reached section two.

Bev looked up.

Eight tiers of gray metal crates, all bearing the red stencil **TLO** and a serial number sticker at the bottom left corner.

Bev looked around for a work pod.

A tall man wearing a gray coverall turned into the row. "What you looking for?"

Bev spun around to face the man. He had a large nose that reminded her of someone she knew in the mine, but his hair was an oily brown and curled behind his ears, so the resemblance was minimal. "Work pod," she said.

"What are you doing?"

"Inventory."

"Don't need a work pod for inventory," the man said. He moved to the nearest shelf and opened a small panel on the vertical strut, revealing a two-prong electronic port. "Just touch this with your pad and it will count all the crates in each section."

"Oh, the foreman didn't show me that."

"That old fart hasn't done inventory in thirty years," the man said. He stepped toward Bev. "I'm Josh. I drive a forklift."

Bev flinched at hearing the man's name. The memory of Josh Gridle jumped to the forefront of her mind. "I'm Karisa," she said. Taking her friend's name was necessary to keep her true identity hidden.

"Well, Karisa," Josh said, "let me know if you need anything. And welcome to Kasimir Storage."

He turned with a smile and headed toward his waiting forklift.

Bev looked down at her pad, pushed the memory of Josh Gridle from her thoughts, and scrolled through the storage list.

"Five hundred crates."

She focused her attention on the task at hand and began checking serial numbers. Keeping busy was the best thing she could do. She lost herself in her work and was glad she had disappeared.

CLAN ERSTALLIUS: TREK

Two days after arriving in Ji'dess, Arlud walked with Winstone Bittle around the repaired shuttle as the Nared-Major relayed the details of the repair work.

"She's all patched up," Bittle said. He stopped at mid-fuselage and pointed to the new hull panels left of the center strut assembly. "All the internal circuits have been re-worked, thanks to the material the natives supplied us, but we still need to pressure check everything and re-charge the LSC. To do that properly, we need to get back to the field."

Arlud nodded that he understood. "And once that's done, we'll be able to make orbit?"

"Yes, sir."

"Good," Arlud said. "I trust the native assessment about what happened up there, but we need our own eyes in orbit."

"We should have all the final checks done tomorrow morning once we get to the field."

"Excellent, Chief," Arlud said, as he squatted to view the underbelly of the shuttle. New plates covered half of the airframe.

"That was mostly scorch damage," Bittle said.

Arlud stood. "Your crew did a fine job."

"Yes, sir."

"I'd like Sitlyn to oversee the final checks."

Bittle drew back at that statement. "She's a construction engineer."

"You're the best mechanic we have. I need you to come with us to examine the Aku ships."

"This is a working shuttle," Bittle said. "She can be up in orbit by tomorrow. Those Aku ships have been mothballed for decades. Might take a year to get one of them up and running. I believe I can be of better service here."

Arlud appreciated Bittle's resolve. The crew chief preferred to see every assignment through to the end. "Pressure tests are simple enough for your crew to handle without you. I need your expertise with me."

Bittle nodded acceptance, but Arlud saw the disappointment in the Nared-Major's eyes.

"Relax, Winny," Arlud said as he moved forward and patted the engineer on the arm. "Petra will see your crew do a fine job. You've already overseen the most difficult repairs. What's left is the easy part."

"Yes, sir."

"And besides," Arlud said. "I know the engineer in you is dying to see those old ships."

Bittle relaxed his posture and flashed a brief grin. "True enough. I'll make sure Sitlyn has all the specs and understands the process." He nodded to Arlud, then turned and headed for the clanmen grouped outside the warehouse entrance.

Arlud knew Bittle was correct. The Aku transports were ancient. It might take parts from ten ships to repair one, and they had the ships stored in groups of four at six different locations. *A year to repair one ship might be a fool's assessment,* he thought. *It could take much longer.*

Arlud followed Gustav Eahuda along the narrow dirt trail that wound through a stand of salix trees. Both men lugged backpacks stuffed with supplies they would need on their journey. Behind Arlud, Winstone Bittle trudged, weighed down by his own bulging backpack, followed by Dirk Siegers and Haden Pyle, two young clan engineers who also carried packs filled with tools and testing equipment.

The men strode out of the trees, past two wooden dwellings where three children frolicked, and two women stooped in a garden. Arlud watched the carefree children as he passed their homes and contemplated their innocence. They had known no other place. They had a wonderful life here, simple and secure.

The children stopped their energetic play and returned Arlud's quizzical stare. One of the little boys rushed to stand by his mother in the garden and waved a cautious greeting at the passing clanmen. The mother reached over, held the boy's hand and mouthed a brief, but forceful, instruction. The boy dropped his head and turned away.

They still don't trust us, Arlud thought.

The two women ushered the children out of the garden into the adjacent building, and Arlud's attention drifted upward to the clouds beyond the hills to the northwest. A gray wall that would dump more rain on Ji'dess. He shifted his attention back to the trail.

The dirt path snaked into a small meadow and led the clanmen to where Salus waited with five grounded ciâfey and four other pilots.

Salus rushed forward and guided Arlud to his aircraft, while the other pilots paired up with the remaining Erstallius clanman.

"You can stow your pack here," Salus said. He pointed to the space behind the passenger station.

Arlud dumped his pack between the nacelles and secured it to the seat struts with the available straps.

"We should miss the rain," Salus said. "We'll fly southeast over the coastal plain to the Wassúa Caphága and stop for a break in Squa Paln. Then we'll fly down the valley to Kuliq'Quad. Should take us about four hours to reach the Mánu."

Arlud translated to himself: *Wassúa Caphága, Valley of Streams.*

The valley was a wide depression, four hundred kilometers long, between the forested Umelk Mountains to the north and the jagged scarps of the Dekeg Mountains to the south. A waterway meandered west to east through the valley and flowed into the marshlands east of the tiny village called Squa Paln. Tributaries flowing from both mountain ranges sliced through the grasslands surrounding Squa Paln and cut shallow canyons into the foothills that dominated the eastern boundary of the valley. One map Arlud reviewed before coming here displayed over two hundred rivulets seeping from the ranges. These soaring wings would be the fastest way to traverse that terrain.

Kuliq'Quad, Place of Safety.

Kuliq'Quad was the first Aku settlement on Ni'apinu. Kuliq'Quad Basin was in the Dekeg Mountains near the eastern edge of the Wassúa Caphága, and now one of the six locations where they kept their disabled ships.

Mánu.

Arlud had never heard that word before. "The Mánu?"

"Mánu," Salus said. "Where we store the ships. Old Akün never had that word."

That last remark was a comment about Arlud's attempt to learn the native language and reminded him of how much he did not know about the current dialect. What he had studied to prepare for this assignment could never prepare him for how much the language had changed from the more ancient form. "Language is fluid and always changing," his instructor had warned. "Learn the basics, but always be ready for that which you cannot prepare."

Arlud mounted the ciâfey's passenger station. "What does mánu mean?"

Salus pulled on his helmet and took his station behind the flight controls. "Where we store the ships," he said. "You'll see." He signaled Arlud to put on his goggles, then started the aircraft's engines.

Arlud adjusted his goggles, secured his feet under the straps on the metal deck, and clenched the hand railings.

Salus flexed the ciâfey's wings upward and adjusted the two small underwings for takeoff. He pinched the metal ring around his neck and spoke to the other pilots: "Ous'awi. Gif sey'pey ju." Satisfied everyone was ready, he took the controls and with a quick downbeat of the wings, the ciâfey leaped off the ground. He engaged the thrusters, and the aircraft sped forward over the surrounding trees, toward the furrowed fields of the coastal plain.

Arlud glanced back. The other flyers followed, forming a single line trailing to the right at sixty degrees. Not a precise formation, but one that told him the pilots had experience. He returned his gaze forward and relaxed into his seat. They were two hundred meters above the ground and rising. The furrowed fields of the coastal plain retreated beneath them with an occasional wave from local farmers.

How much these people have confirmed the myths about them to be wrong, Arlud thought. *Salus is taking me from a simple agrarian paradise of dirt and plants to a world of forged metal and blistering energies.* He wondered how the Aku had balanced those two lives so successfully.

The soaring wings turned away from the coast as they passed over the last of the grasslands and flew parallel to the hills that fronted the forested ridges of the Umelk Mountains.

Arlud's thoughts drifted to the Erstallius fleet. He knew when the reinforcements arrived, the clanmen would expect this business with the Aku to be delegated to a lower priority. Retaliating against Polinda would be the primary concern. He promised himself to resist that urge. *The safety of Ni'apinu from this point onward will be a joint venture.* And he realized, as soon as he had that thought, the real reason his father had chosen him over the other candidates. *Only the son of the Erstallius Patriarch could break through the boundaries of clan priorities and fuse both efforts into one. As the son, I best represent the father. No other man could fill that role. They may be Erstallius clanmen, but I am Erstallius. No other man could speak with the same authority.*

Arlud pondered the wisdom his father had displayed, despite the ridicule from the cadre. "Stand," his father had said. "Stand firm, while those around you bleat their warnings of coming catastrophe. Stand firm in your truth and you will not fail. But first, make sure your truth is right."

Arlud smiled to himself. For the first time in three days, his head was free of pain. He closed his eyes and let his body relax as the wind rippled his attire.

CLAN CORMED: REBELLION

Wellen Tallilia Sy leaned forward. "You must have been terrified."

Pallis Nin rubbed his forehead as he recalled the attack. "Yes," he said, his voice crackling from the strain. "Thought we'd not survive."

Wellen lifted her cup from the tea service and sat forward on her settee, her blue eyes intent on the Cormed envoy and his obvious unease. Allowing him to join her for morning tea was a gesture she felt might help ease tensions between their peoples. It was unprecedented.

"And that," Nin said, "is why I've come to you. If your Captain Pardee continues for GSW-183, we may not survive."

Wellen sipped her tea.

"I implore you to advise your captain," Nin pleaded. "If that thing is still out there, we are doomed. If it is gone, you will put my people down on a dead world with little hope of being rescued."

This was not the conversation Wellen had expected, and she thought: *The rescued complains to the rescuer: I don't like this, rescue me another way.* She understood the horror this envoy had witnessed fueled his fear. *Fear is the breakdown of logic, the weed that strangles reason.*

"It is Captain Pardee's primary concern to deliver my daughter and I to our intended destination. If he feels it is safe to go to the Erstallius holding—"

"Madame, it attacked us without warning. Safety is uncertain."

Wellen put down her teacup. She sympathized with Nin's mindset, but alongside her empathy it gratified her seeing this scared little man, this nauseous representative of an Alliance Clan, was now forced to plead. *A cruel joy,* she thought.

"You interrupt me with the same callousness you showed when you commandeered our freighter. Do you hold all Free Traders with the same contempt?"

Nin wilted under the weight of that attack and slumped back in his chair. "This is no time to bleed old wounds. We are both in danger!"

"We have saved your people. Would you have done the same for us?"

"We will not accept abandonment."

"You are not in a position to dictate terms," Wellen said. "You commandeered our freighter and imprisoned her crew. Einar tells me you intended to blockade Al-phaq."

Nin nodded. "That was a legitimate reaction under the circumstances."

"Yes," Wellen said. "Especially when all problems in this district are caused by Sy and his Pirates. Is that not what the clans believe?"

"If we run into the thing that attacked us, it could mean the end to us all."

"I understand the threat of which you speak."

Nin leaned forward and sighed, relieved Madame Sy saw the importance of his argument.

"I understand ex-slaves settled GSW-183," Wellen said. "I am sure your people will also survive. Gratitude is the usual response when one is rescued."

"A distress beacon is not an encouraging sign," Nin said, hoping to kindle empathy. "The mighty Aku may have defeated Clan Tuma, but they sent a distress beacon!"

Wellen folded her hands in her lap. "An Erstallius ship sent the beacon. Where would you have us take you?"

"U'galem."

"That would take us too far off our original course. Captain Pardee will not be willing."

"Then you condemn us."

"A judgment expressed toward *Clan* Sy for many years by your Alliance associates."

Nin stood, not missing Wellen's stress on the term *clan*. That was a direct assault. It was a reminder of Wolfram's honorable roots and how he had been betrayed and forced to rebel against the Alliance. He realized this argument was useless. "We will not accept abandonment," he repeated, then turned and left the cabin.

Wellen watched the envoy retreat until the guard in the corridor shut her cabin door. She poured herself more tea, remembering Wolfram's admonition: *Never help an enemy.* She was glad the nervous little man had left. *How could I have been so naïve?* Helping the Cormed people from their crippled frigate was not a regret. It was an action that had arisen from her inherent duty to help anyone in distress, but the denial she had just voiced brought her a deeper satisfaction. She grinned and sipped her tea.

❖ ❖ ❖

An Erstallius frigate appeared on the holoscreen. Orbiting the blue gas giant of the PDN160 system, the ship's silhouette followed the path of the planet's fourth moon.

"No response, sir," the comm officer said.

Captain Pardee relaxed in his seat. "Ease us in, helmsman. One quarter thrusters."

"Aye, sir."

"Magnify view," Pardee said.

The hull of the frigate was charred, pock-marked with blast craters, and displayed no running lights. The aft section was engulfed in a halo of debris.

"Still no response, sir," the comm officer said.

The engineer at the sensor station pushed away from his console. "She's dead, Captain."

"That looks like rail gun damage," Pardee noticed. "Find their enemy."

The helmsman entered a course that brought them into a wider orbit of the blue gas giant and put them on the other side of the Erstallius frigate.

"There, Captain," the sensor engineer said. "Just past the fourth moon. About ten degrees east of the limb."

The holoscreen displayed the image of a dark and battered Polinda destroyer emitting a curved tail of debris as she spun on her vertical axis.

"No response from the destroyer," the comm officer said.

The sensor engineer reviewed the scan results. "She's dead too."

"Stalemate," Pardee said. "Plant a beacon, helmsman, then push on to GSW-183 at full speed."

"Aye, sir."

Pardee pushed a comm button.

"Security," the chief in command responded.

"This is Pardee. Send a team to escort Jegen Farvic and the Cormed envoy to the forward lounge."

"Aye, Captain."

Jegen Farvic and Pallis Nin were held in the lounge for an hour before Pardee joined them.

"We've analyzed all the evidence," Pardee said. He sat at the table in the lounge across from his two guests. "It appears Clan Polinda attacked the Erstallius." He dimmed the lights in the room and activated a wall display that presented imagery and graphs showing the dead ships orbiting the gas giant. "This is where the distress beacon originated. The dead Erstallius ship."

"Maybe Polinda came to aid Erstallius," Farvic said.

Pardee chuckled. "Unlikely. They've been feuding for years." He stood and touched a wall switch that opened the window shutters.

Farvic and Nin turned in their seats to see another Polinda destroyer spinning about a thousand meters away, with an Erstallius frigate jammed into her aft engineering section. The debris halo contained chunks of bulkhead from both ships and dead bodies from both crews.

"The desperate end of a desperate battle," Pardee said. "There were no victors here."

Farvic and Nin both stood and moved to the window to examine the entangled ships.

"We are in high orbit of GSW-183," Pardee said. "A twenty-thousand-kilometer orbit. We can detect only minor damage on the surface. Looks like the fighting ended here." He moved to the doorway. "Enjoy your stay on the surface, Gentlemen. We'll begin taking you down once we've achieved a closer orbit."

Pardee left the lounge and two security guards joined Farvic and Nin.

Shanna Sy picked up her stratagem cubes, expecting another game after breakfast. Stratagem had done much to steady her nerves during this long and sometimes startling voyage. They had entered a close orbit of the Alliance world, and she was looking forward to viewing the planet from the forward lounge. She tripped the palm-lock for her cabin door, pulled it open, and stepped over the threshold into the muzzle of a magar-pistol. Her stratagem cubes dropped to the deck as she backed from the doorway, but two Cormed clanmen grabbed her arms and pulled her into the corridor. She stumbled over her unconscious guard lying on the deck plates. The sudden shift of her body weight helped her twist an arm free, and she struck the clanman holding her in the face.

The clanmen subdued Shanna's rebellion and pulled her down the narrow corridor toward a crew access tube, where they joined five more Cormed clanmen.

Shanna squirmed under the restraint and blurted: "Why are you doing this?"

Her abductors shoved her face-first against the bulkhead and bound her wrists behind her back with thin wire.

Grom Anen shouldered through the surrounding clanmen. He grabbed Shanna's hair, yanked her head around, and shoved a cloth gag into her mouth. He gazed into her frightened eyes—pools of green-blue, rimmed with white, wet with tears. "Desperate men do desperate deeds."

Shanna turned her head from Anen's acrid smell as he tied the gag behind her neck.

A magar projectile hit the clanman who had tied Shanna's wrists, passed through his torso and struck the bulkhead with a loud thump. Blood flowed from the clanman's torso as he slid to the floor.

Shanna was pulled out of view of the four attacking guildmen, and the Cormeds returned fire. The firefight ended after a brief exchange, leaving the four guildmen dead, and two Cormeds dead.

"Watch that corridor," Anen ordered his crouching soldiers. He faced Shanna, tied a blindfold over her eyes, then flicked a hand signal to the two men who held her.

Shanna was pulled into the crew access tube.

The crack of a magar-pistol pulled Anen's focus back to his clanmen, and he saw the corridor was empty. "What happened?"

"Lady Sy came out of her cabin," the Nared-Major said. "She ran into the stairwell down there." He pointed to the stair alcove half-way down the corridor on the left side. "Diwa Jono took a shot."

Anen faced Jono. "Did you hit her?"

"In the leg, I think," Jono said.

"Idiot! You could have killed her!" Anen grabbed Jono's pistol and handed it to the Nared-Major. He glanced at his dead men. "Get their weapons," he said, then led his team away from the access tube, toward an adjacent corridor and the ladder that led to deck Three.

Duncun Turl turned into the corridor on deck three and was confronted by a band of twelve Cormed clanmen armed with magar-pistols and short daggers. "What's going on?"

The clanmen parted and allowed Turl to advance once they recognized the patch on his shoulder that identified him as a crewman from the *Javelin*.

Grom Anen stood defiantly at the center of the armed group, in front of an open cabin hatchway, engaged in a heated conversation with someone inside the cabin.

Turl shouldered past the peripheral clanmen. "What's happening?"

Anen turned toward Turl. "I wondered how long it would take before you showed up!"

Turl reached the cabin door and saw Einar slumped on his couch with hands bound. He faced Anen. "What are you doing?"

"Taking a hostage."

"Hostage?"

"We're taking the ship," Anen said. "We control the mid-deck aft of the gravity furnace, the entire shuttle bay and cargo bay, and the aft engine pod. We intend to force Pardee out of orbit."

"What!? Why?"

"We will not be left on GSW-183."

Two clanmen grabbed Einar's arms and lifted him off the couch.

Turl pressed close to Anen. He was a half a meter taller than the square jawed Degen from the *Iron Spear*. "You are a fool."

"We have leverage Pardee cannot ignore."

"All Pardee needs to do is vent the atmosphere," Turl said. "We'll be dead in minutes."

"We thought of that," Anen said. "We have Sy's daughter. We almost had her mother, but she scurried off after we fought her guards."

Turl stepped backward and blocked the cabin entrance. "Then you are a fool. You've threatened Sy's family. He'll track you down, no matter how long it takes."

Anen stepped toward Turl. "And you are a traitor! Did you think we would not find out? How long have you been conspiring with this pirate behind our backs?"

"There's been no conspiring. We both survived the attack on the *Javelin*. We've been sharing ideas and searching for answers."

"Then why were we not told? Is it normal for a Cormed officer to befriend a pirate?"

"There is nothing of importance here. He is a blind old man, searching for answers. The same answers we seek."

Anen pressed close to Turl. "You are a traitor!"

Turl felt a hard blow to the back of his head. He collapsed against the door frame as a boot drove into his diaphragm. The constricting pain forced him to bend over, and he fell to the deck. His arms were pulled behind his back, and he felt the sting of thin wire tighten around his wrists.

Two clanmen dragged Turl into the corridor and stood over him.

Einar was pushed out of his cabin.

"You lost," Anen said to Turl. "Traitors always lose." He aimed his magar-pistol and pulled the trigger. The crack of the projectile leaving the muzzle was followed by the thud of penetration as it burrowed into Turl's forehead and blew out the back of his skull.

Einar groaned and lunged for Anen.

Two clanmen pulled Einar back and held him against the bulkhead.

"So," Anen said. "Feeling regret for your fallen comrade?"

Einar squirmed to free himself. "If I could see you'd be dead!"

"Yes," Anen said, and he aimed his magar-pistol at Einar's head. "But you can't see, and I've changed my mind."

Einar spit toward Anen's voice.

Anen pulled the trigger.

Two cargo shuttles and one personnel carrier were in line facing the bay doors, held in place by docking clamps. Cormed clanmen floated guard with magar-pistols in hand. Four guildmen, hands bound behind their backs with hoods over their heads, were lined up against the starboard bulkhead.

The Cormeds pulled Shanna through the micro-gravity of the bay to the personnel carrier, pushed her inside the unlighted cabin, and strapped her into a seat. A clanman untied her gag and pulled it from her mouth. "Breathe easy," he said, "but don't get out of this seat. You'll regret it." He turned and followed the other clanman out of the carrier.

The hatch closed with a hollow thud and the cabin went black.

Shanna gulped a breath of stale air and tried to work her hands free. The micro-gravity amplified her movement. A fiery sting shot up her arms. She forced herself to calm and braced her body by pushing her feet against the seat in front of her. Her wrists burned from the wire, and she felt a warm wetness where it had cut into her flesh.

The hatch swung open, filling the cabin with ambient light from the shuttle bay.

The four bound guildmen tumbled through the hatchway as the Cormed clanmen pushed them into the carrier.

The hatch slammed shut, and the cabin returned to blackness.

One guildman fumed: "Damn that Pardee!"

Another guildman agreed: "Never should've helped them!"

"If I know Pardee," a husky voice muttered, "he'll not let them get away with this. Help me get my hands untied!"

There was a shuffle of movement as the men gathered in the weightless environment to loosen each other's bindings and remove their blindfolds.

Shanna blurted. "Where's my mother!? What's happening!?"

The men fell silent for a heartbeat, then continued their frantic maneuvering to free their hands.

"Hurry," the husky voice said.

Moments later, a guildman groped through the darkness and settled into the seat next to Shanna. "The Cormeds have taken half the ship, lady. I believe Madame is with Pardee."

"Oh, I feared she was dead."

The carrier jerked.

"They're forcing us off," the husky voice said. He was in the cockpit trying to power up the carrier's systems. "The bay doors just opened. Damn! Someone get in here and help me!"

There was a swish of movement, and the overhead lights filled the cabin with warm light.

"I'm Ross Cordova," the man next to Shanna said, and he touched her shoulder. "I'll take your blindfold off."

Shanna raised her head and let Cordova remove the cloth. Her reddened eyes were swelled with tears.

"Now your hands," Cordova said.

The old guildman was bigger than Shanna had sensed in the dark. His grizzled hair reminded her of her grandfather, and she remembered seeing him outside her mother's cabin. "You're assigned to my mother's guard."

"We are guards assigned to your family," Cordova said. "We were on our rest period when the shooting began." He released Shanna's seat straps so she could lean forward, then he reached down and held her bloody wrist.

"Prepare yourself. This may hurt."

Shanna winced at the burning tug, and then the wire was off. She wrapped her bleeding wrist in her skirt. The uncertainty of her mother's safety drowned her thoughts in sorrow, and she bowed her head and wept. "What are we to do?"

Cordova patted her arm. "Stand firm, lady. We'll survive this."

THE GUILD: DESCENT

The personnel carrier drifted away from Erlis Pardee's freighter.

Shanna Sy shifted position on her seat and peered out her porthole at the Alliance world. It was a beautiful planet, and so different from Al-phaq. Blue seas sparkled. Dark, river-worn land presented the mottled green of forests and grasslands, obscured beneath patches of cloud and the white pinwheel of a major storm front.

The husky-voiced guildman floated out of the carrier's cockpit. He was bald, with a thick, black mustache. Dried blood stained his wrists and shirt sleeves. "The main engine's dead," he said. "The bastards put us in a disabled carrier!" He moved to a starboard porthole and pressed against the duraplex. "Where are they going?"

The dark-faced guildman sitting across the aisle from Shanna peered out the window next to his seat. "If I know Pardee, he's giving us distance."

Shanna glanced at the worried guildman. "Who are you, and what do you mean by that?"

"He's Donté," Cordova said. "He's crewed with Pardee for ten years. He thinks Pardee is moving away to keep us safe."

"Safe from what?"

Cordova exchanged a knowing glance with Donté—if losing his ship to the Cormeds could not be prevented, Pardee would blow it up without the slightest hesitation. He looked at Shanna. "Safe from the Cormeds."

"So Pardee pushed us off his ship in this broken shuttle?"

"Most likely. The Cormeds needed hostages to keep them safe and used this shuttle for a prison because it is not flight ready. Pardee outsmarted them by forcing us off his ship. We can't use the main engine, but we have other options."

"So now Pardee can defeat them?"

Cordova nodded.

"Everyone strap in," the bald pilot said, and he returned to the cockpit.

"That's Bern Pryce," Cordova told Shanna. "He's a good pilot."

"What's happening?"

Cordova reached over and reconnected Shanna's safety harness. "We're going to planet-fall."

"Without the engine?"

"Bern is a good pilot. He and Harlon will get us through planet-fall safely."

Shanna leaned sideways to see the back of Harlon's blond head in the cockpit. "How?"

"We can use the plasma thrusters to start descent," Cordova said. "When we hit atmosphere, we can switch over to the mag-jets. This carrier's top notch. We'll be fine."

"But what about my mother?"

"We can't stay in orbit and wait to find out. Life support is offline." Cordova gestured to the LSC panel at the front of the cabin. "We've only enough air for about an hour."

Shanna stared at her blood-stained wrist and wept.

The personnel carrier jerked as it glided through turbulence. The mag-jets had refused to start. The men in the cockpit searched for the system fault as the craft plunged deeper into atmosphere.

Shanna clenched the arms of her seat. She forced herself to avoid the view outside her porthole. The rushing stream of condensed air only made her more anxious. Weak from the pull of gravity, she laid back in her seat and stared at the ceiling. She tried to calm herself, but each jolt of turbulence pushed her pulse higher. Cordova had tried to reassure her when they began planet-fall, but the first fiery blast of atmospheric friction had ripped all hope from her.

We are going to die!

The carrier dipped to the right as the pilot turned the craft in a wide arc to help reduce speed.

Shanna closed her eyes. The press of the G-force made her grip the arms of her seat tighter.

Another jerk and a faint whining screamed all around the cabin.

"I love you, Mother," Shanna muttered, expecting death at any moment.

The whine increased and shifted to a hollow roar.

The carrier pitched upward, banked left, and leveled.

"We're fine, lady," Cegla said.

Shanna opened her eyes.

"Finally got those mag-jets working," Cordova said. "You can relax now."

Shanna gulped a breath and looked out her porthole. Far below, beneath patches of cloud, a land green and wet with rivers.

Bern Pryce announced over the carrier's intercom, "Everyone look at your monitors."

Cordova withdrew a monitor from the arm of his seat, switched it on, then leaned over and helped Shanna adjust her monitor. The display was a topographic representation of the terrain below them. On the lower left side was a yellow arrow marked Port. In the center and toward the upper right were clusters of yellow dots. The center cluster was large and stationary. The other cluster was small and moving, surrounded by pulsating red rings.

Bern Pryce said, "There's more activity down there than I thought there'd be. I'll swing around and bring us to the landing field. We're about a thousand strads away. Haven't picked up any comm traffic. Hopefully, they'll let us land with no protest."

The carrier banked to the left as Pryce swung the craft around to approach the landing field.

Shanna watched the terrain shift on her monitor with the carrier's movement. "What are these dots?"

"People or large animals," Cordova said. "Those red rings represent some kind of energy emissions. Probably vehicles of some sort. They're moving at a quick rate over rough terrain."

"Alliance people?"

"Or natives."

The Aku, Shanna thought. "Are the natives peaceful? I've heard horrible stories about them."

"The Erstallius wouldn't have come here if the Aku were belligerent," Cordova said, and he hoped that was true.

The moving dots went off the edge of the screen as the carrier flew closer to the landing field.

Shanna pointed to the cluster of dots that remained. "Is that a village?"

"Could be," Cordova guessed. "It's near a river."

"Why do they fade in and out?"

"The scanner has a narrow beam width. As we move, the forest or the terrain blocks the returning signals."

The carrier banked right, and the dots on the monitor winked out.

"The terrain got in the way," Cordova said.

Shanna peered out her porthole. White clouds spread out to the horizon, bathed in the bright light of the sun. She hoped whoever waited beneath the cloud cover would recognize their plight and lend support to save her mother.

Petra Sitlyn stood a few meters inside the repair hangar at the Erstallius landing field. Far enough inside the open doorway to avoid the drizzle that had been falling all morning. She and her crew of three engineers had arrived from Ji'dess after sunrise and had finished the shuttle's pressure tests in about three hours. She was now monitoring the LSC refill at the aft end of the shuttle and was looking forward to getting back into orbit.

> "This is carrier, Ajax-One-Four-Three, requesting an emergency landing. On route one-seven-eight magnetic."

The husky voice came over the shuttle's activated comm system, which had been turned on to monitor standard port communication frequencies for potential traffic.

The Erstallius pilot, Jens Orr, bounded out of the shuttle and rushed to the refill station. "We're being hailed, Nared-Major."

"I heard," Sitlyn said. She checked the transfer gauges and noticed the refill still had a few liters before completion. She lifted her transceiver. "Sitlyn to tower."

The engineer stationed as a lookout on the fifth floor of the unfinished central tower responded: "Bril here."

"We have a vessel on approach," Sitlyn said. "Can you see anything coming in from the south?"

"No. Rain clouds in every direction."

> "This is carrier, Ajax-One-Four-Three, requesting an emergency landing. On route one-seven-eight magnetic."

Sitlyn turned to Jens Orr. "Set the rear guns. Do not respond to the call."

The pilot nodded and rushed back into the shuttle.

Sitlyn reviewed the refill gauges as the engineer named Danik rushed into the hangar, dripping from the light rain. "I heard the comm," he said. "What should we do?"

Sitlyn gestured to the hangar doors. "Close that far side. It'll hide us from their view if they come in from the south. They won't see us until they are almost landed."

Danik nodded and hurried over to shut the door.

The refill completed and Sitlyn released the hoses, stowed them on the LSC supply cart and grabbed the steering handle.

The southern hangar door slid to its closed position, and Danik rushed over to help Sitlyn pull the refill cart away from the shuttle.

Sitlyn asked, "Did you get the generators up?"

"No. Not enough reserve power."

The shuttle's rear guns protruded from their stowed position with a thud that echoed inside the hangar.

> "This is Ajax-One-Four-Three, requesting an emergency landing. Please respond. We are on approach one-seven-eight magnetic, ten minutes out. This is Ajax-One-Four-Three requesting an emergency landing."

Sitlyn climbed into the shuttle's crew cabin, followed by Danik. She spoke into her transceiver: "Sitlyn to tower. What do you see, Bril?"

Bril scanned the southern sky with his field glass. "Nothing yet."

"Keep looking."

> "This is Ajax-One-Four-Three, requesting an emergency landing. We are on approach one-seven-eight magnetic."

Orr turned around from his station at the rear guns. "All set here."

Sitlyn nodded to the pilot, then scanned the shuttle's comm system. She hesitated out of fear. If this was a Polinda trick, they would be outgunned for sure. If they could hide until the last moment and get the first shot, they might have a chance.

"Traffic acquired," Bril muttered. "I got them, Nared-Major."

Sitlyn raised her transceiver. "What are they?"

"They're heading straight for us. Can't make out any markings because of the direct approach. Looks like an old Zavos series carrier."

> "This is Ajax-One-Four-Three, requesting an emergency landing. Please respond. We are on approach one-seven-eight magnetic, five minutes out. This is Ajax-One-Four-Three requesting an emergency landing."

Sitlyn spoke into her transceiver: "Get back to the hanger, Bril."

"Aye, Nared-major."

Sitlyn focused on the shuttle's comm system as Orr and Danik waited for her to make a decision.

Through the open hatch, they could now hear the faint hollow roar of mag-jets above the spatter of rain.

Shanna pressed against her porthole and watched the Erstallius outpost grow larger as the carrier dropped toward the wet tarmac. "Where are they?"

Cordova scanned the buildings as the carrier neared the landing area. "They must've left because of the Polinda attack."

The mag-jets roared as the carrier stopped its forward momentum and dropped amid a swirling mist as her landing thrusters heated the wet tarmac.

Once secure on the ground, Pryce killed the engines and leaned back in the pilot seat. Sitlyn's voice sounded in his headphones:

> "Erstallius Control to Ajax-One-Four-Three. We have you in our sights. Any provocative action and you will be destroyed. You will exit the carrier on the port side, in single file, and proceed to the orange circle on the tarmac. If you do not comply, we will open fire. You have five minutes to exit the carrier."

Pryce peered out the cockpit windows. "Where are they?"

Harlon leaned forward and adjusted the rear-view monitor. "They're in the hangar behind us. Military shuttle. Her rear guns are pointed at us."

Pryce shifted to view the monitor image, then pushed the comm button. "This is Ajax-One-Four-Three. We will comply."

Pryce removed his headset, unbuckled his harness, and led Harlon out of the cockpit. He paused at the port hatch. "Follow me, single file, and we'll be fine. They're a bit jumpy."

Shanna pushed off her seat and lined up with the others at the hatchway.

A cold, rainy gust greeted them as the hatchway swung down.

Shanna had never been in open air before—and never in the rain. Apprehensive about such a new experience, and a little frightened by the odd stillness of the outpost, she allowed the men to exit first.

Cordova halted, fearing Shanna would stay inside. He motioned for her to move ahead of him. "You'll be OK. I'll be right behind you."

Shanna hugged herself. Terrible uncertainty was closing in on her from every side. An impenetrable barrier she felt would suffocate her. She had faith in these guildmen. These men had more knowledge about these things than she ever would, but that didn't make the moment feel any better. She rubbed her injured wrist and stepped into the chill rain.

We never should have left Al-phaq.

PETRA SITLYN: BLOOD STAINS

Petra Sitlyn advanced across the tarmac, resting her right hand on the butt of her holstered pistol. Because the carrier's crew and passengers had complied with her request, she did not expect problems. But there is always a place for caution. The drizzle had turned into a light rain that pelted her back as she headed for a position between the new arrivals and the entrance to the central tower.

Danik crossed the tarmac holding his standard issue magar-rifle and rushed up the steps into the carrier's port entry.

Sitlyn kept her gaze on the strangers as she moved in front of them. Four men and a young woman. The men huddled around the girl, as if protecting her from more than the rain. Then Sitlyn saw their blood-stained sleeves. She stopped upon seeing red blotches on the woman's dress. She raised her transceiver. "Bril, we need the med kit."

Danik appeared in the carrier's port entry and flashed a hand signal—the carrier was empty.

Sitlyn tightened her hand around the butt of her holstered pistol as she scanned the blood stains. "What happened to you people?"

The gray-haired man standing next to the young woman took a step forward. "We were bound with wire," he said, and he displayed his wrists. "Just a few scratches."

Sitlyn was taken aback by the old man's quick dismissal of the injuries. "What happened?"

The young woman erupted: "Can we please get out of this rain!?"

The old man put a bloodied arm around the woman's shoulders and tried to calm her.

Bril rushed up to Sitlyn with the med kit.

"This way," Sitlyn said. She relaxed her grip on her pistol, turned, and guided the injured group into the ground floor lobby of the central tower.

Two hours after the carrier's arrival, Sitlyn sat with the guildmen in the central tower's lobby. They had arranged four of the upholstered chairs in a semi-circle facing the duraplex wall that gave them a wide-angle view of the rainstorm. Shanna Sy sat sullen between Bern Pryce, the bald, mustached pilot, and Ross Cordova, the grizzled old trader who was the obvious leader of the group. Donté Cegla and Harlon Sater sat on the floor a few meters away from the assembled chairs with their backs against the duraplex wall.

Sitlyn sat on the edge of the chair a few meters from Pryce, toward the entrance. She had learned all their names, and after their wounds had been cleaned and bandaged, they told her about the destroyed Cormed frigates, and the resulting chaos on Pardee's ship. In response, she told them how the Aku had helped her clanmen after the Polinda attack.

Cordova was surprised by the favorable tale about the Aku. "So the natives are not savage killers, as legend tells us?"

"I'm sure they can be," Sitlyn said. "There is a time for killing, and a time for saving."

"We need to save my mother," Shanna said.

Sitlyn switched her attention to the frazzled young woman. "Many people need to be saved. Including all of us. Polinda will come back."

Cordova leaned toward Sitlyn. "You know that for certain?"

Sitlyn nodded. "Our fleet reported three Polinda destroyers had entered this system. The Aku telemetry supports that info. You found only two destroyers. That means the third ship is hiding at the edge of the system, or she retreated to seek help. Polinda will be back."

Pryce agreed. "That old bastard won't stop until he has pounded this place to dust. A very vindictive fellow."

"Fortunately, we have the Aku to help us," Sitlyn said. "And our own reinforcements should arrive in about two weeks."

Pryce stroked his mustache. "Will the Erstallius help us fight the Cormeds?"

"The Cormeds are allies of Clan Erstallius," Sitlyn said.

Shanna sat up straight. "A scoundrel is a scoundrel, no matter his affiliation. Some allies make great enemies."

Sitlyn found that bit of insight intriguing. "Did your father tell you that?"

"If he did, would that change the truth of it?"

"No," Sitlyn said with a slight grin. "It would mean your father is a wise man."

Pryce chuckled. "Wolfram would love to hear that coming from you."

Shanna displayed a thin smile, but the positive feeling Sitlyn's remark instilled in her faded and she drifted back to a more sullen mood. The threat to her mother was too great to allow any hint of happiness.

Pryce also returned to a serious demeanor. "Will you help us?"

Sitlyn sat back in her seat. "Any officer who makes decisions like Farvic made should suffer the consequences. I agree with Lady Sy, but his actions do not void the Erstallius relationship with Clan Cormed."

Shanna groaned. "Will your clan help rescue my mother?"

"That is not my decision to make."

Shanna slumped in her chair. "The glue that holds the Alliance together must be strong to ignore such villainy."

"Clan Erstallius has no quarrel with the Guild of Free Traders," Sitlyn said. "We haven't been in this district long enough to have had any dealings with you. If we had settled Roth-513 instead of the Cormeds, our relationship might be different, but as it now stands, my Regent tried to convince the Cormeds to turn back from their plot to blockade Al-phaq."

That revelation pulled Harlon into the conversation. "Then Erstallius help is a possibility?"

Sitlyn looked over at the reclining trader. "Yes, but that is not my decision to make."

Cordova cleared his throat. "I would like to meet this regent of yours. He sounds like a reasonable man."

Sitlyn leaned forward and rested her forearms on her knees. All the chaos that had occurred over the last few days whirled in her mind, and she wondered how these events were affecting the other districts. A new rebellion among the Clans was a possibility, fueled by mistrust and a lack of answers. She felt lost amid all the uncertainty. "My regent is investigating solutions," she said. "He is working with the Aku."

Cordova leaned back in his chair. An alliance with the Aku would change the political power structure in the district. Having a favorable relationship with the Erstallius might help pull the Guild out of the weak position it now occupied and prevent complete evacuation from Alliance controlled space. "Can we meet with your Regent?"

Sitlyn knew she could not make the decisions that needed to be made. Her rank lacked the authority to do anything beyond her assigned command. "Yes," she said. "I can take you to him." She stood, moved to the window, and watched the rain. The wind was creating small waves of water along the skin of the Guild transport. "Based on your description, it will take days, possibly weeks, to repair your carrier. We can take you in our shuttle."

Cordova rushed up and joined Sitlyn at the window. "We are indebted to you."

"I make no promises."

Cordova nodded that he understood. "You give us an opportunity. We can ask for nothing more."

Sitlyn scanned the sky. The black storm clouds were drifting toward the southwest. "Looks like this rain may last all day. No worries though." She turned and faced the entire group. "We'll get the shuttle prepped. Be ready to leave in an hour."

NI'APINU: KULIQ'QUAD

Arlud tightened his grip on the hand railings as Salus steered his ciâfey toward the landing area.

The flight from Ji'dess had taken about four hours, just as Salus had predicted. After leaving the tiny village of Squa Paln, where they had taken on more supplies, the flat grasslands and furrowed fields of the eastern valley morphed into rocky foothills dotted with salix trees and stunted oméu.

Arlud leaned to his left for a better view of their destination.

The ciâfey landing field was a flat, rectangular patch of brown soil, hard-pressed and scraped smooth, encircled by small wooden bungalows, set amid the rugged hills that abutted the granite scarps of the Dekeg Mountains.

Arlud recalled Eahuda's report about the Aku after the first Erstallius ground survey: *They've kept their impact on this world equal to their needs.* The austere appearance of the ciâfey landing site reinforced that analysis. *Utilitarian to the extreme.*

The soaring wings glided toward the patch of dirt and settled to the ground under the halting effects of cupped wings and the brief, hollow roar of inverse thrust.

Arlud stepped off the ciâfey onto the hard soil, pulled off his goggles, and arched his back to stretch his muscles. He noticed a narrow gorge beyond the surrounding bungalows that split the southern hills—the beginning of a passage through the towering granite scarps. Kuliq'Quad lay at the other end of that ravine. "Why stop here?"

Salus faced Arlud from his pilot station and detached his mouth filter. "Flyers are not allowed over the basin. We'll take ground transport in from here. Help me unload these packs."

Twenty minutes later, the clanmen, with help from the Aku pilots, had moved all their supply packs to the edge of the dirt road on the other side of the bungalows. They waited for ground transport under the watchful eyes of the small Aku security team, who guarded the road at the mouth of the gorge about fifty meters away.

Arlud surveyed the small roadblock. Two wooden beams, supported by triangular metal braces, filled the space between two wooden booths on each side of the road. Both of the guardhouses were manned, and a third guard loitered behind the horizontal blockade. All three guards shouldered long-barrel projectile weapons that reminded Arlud of magar-rifles.

A tan colored ground car rumbled into view from behind a bungalow and turned toward the waiting men. The vehicle rolled on six tires made of metal mesh. The driver sat in an open turret positioned at the front left. Behind the driver were two bench seats set within separate passenger wells. At the rear of the vehicle, the body had been formed into a shallow depression for cargo.

Arlud noticed the wear on the car's metal skin. Battered and beaten. Such an obvious disregard for regular maintenance did not portend well regarding the transports they sought to repair. "She could use a coat of paint."

"Paint doesn't last long out here," Salus said. "The metal won't rust. Paint is just a cosmetic. We've more important things to focus on."

The driver stopped the vehicle next to the waiting men, and Arlud noticed a long gash in the metal outside the rear cargo area. "What caused that?"

Salus leaned sideways to view the gray scratch. "Nothing you need to be concerned about."

The cargo was loaded, then Arlud, Eahuda, and Salus sat in the rear seats. Bittle, Sieger, and Pyle took the front seats.

The car rumbled to life, and the driver guided them through the security check point and into the gorge. The narrow road hugged the eastern wall of the ravine and followed the meandering curve of the stream flowing from the granite scarps.

Arlud peered over the edge of the road. About twenty meters below the carved highway, patches of brush grew beside a shallow stream. The western face of the gorge rose at a steep angle, with folds and fissures that mirrored the shape of the eastern slope. The ravine looked more like a massive crack in the rock than a gully. The folds in the granite were too sharp to be the product of water erosion. "Was there a quake here?"

Salus nodded. "The basin is the remnant of an impact crater."

Arlud looked up. The rock faces of the gorge had risen to about three hundred meters. He was awed by the thought of the terrible force that had shattered the rock and formed this terrain.

The car slowed as the driver steered the vehicle as close to the granite slope as possible, stopped, and turned off the engine. He rotated his drive turret to face his passengers. "There's a security team coming," he said in the common tongue of the Alliance. "We need to share the road."

A few moments later, an Aku soldier walked around the bend in the road about fifty meters ahead of the ground car. He held the same weapon the blockade guards carried, wore a small pack, and sported a wide-brimmed hat.

"This would be the Road Patrol," Salus said. "Do not look into their eyes. And keep your hands inside the vehicle."

Eahuda shot a quizzical glance at Salus. "Keep our hands inside? Don't look in their eyes?"

Salus gestured toward the advancing patrol.

Eahuda recoiled as a large sipá padded around the bend behind the soldier. The animal had the grey fur typical of his breed, and the large shoulder hump and thick neck of a male. "Whoa!"

Salus leaned forward to get Eahuda's attention. "Do as I said, and the patrol will pass us by."

Arlud estimated the sipá's walking height at two meters from paw to the top of the head. "I didn't know you had bears here! That beast is huge!"

Salus leaned close to Arlud. "One transport Seelay commandeered had a cargo of sipá cubs bound for Glasel-221. He kept them, and a breeding program was begun about a year after arriving here."

Arlud watched as another sipá followed two more soldiers around the bend. "They're domesticated?"

"Trained would be a better description," Salus said. "They can still be dangerous if mistreated or surprised. These are the tenth generation. Very intelligent."

The first sipá stopped, rose on his hind legs, and sniffed the air.

Salus leaned back in the seat. "Average length is just over four meters, and they can run like the wind."

The sipá dropped to all four feet and continued lumbering toward the ground car.

Eahuda had noticed the pride in Salus' voice. "I understand their sense of smell is more sensitive than in canines. Good choice for a foot patrol."

"Yes, and their size is more intimidating than a dog's."

The patrol point man waved a greeting as he passed the ground car. Behind him, the sipá huffed and pushed against the car with his right front paw, forcing the metal body to rock back. The Erstallius passengers rose from their seats.

Salus grabbed Arlud's arm. "Sit down! He's just telling us to share the road."

Arlud fell back into his seat and wrinkled his nose. The musky odor was unwelcome. "Smells like wet grass mixed with urine."

Salus grinned. "If you smell that in the wild, look for a big tree to climb."

The driver chuckled.

Back in their seats, the Erstallius clanmen watched the last sipá brush by the ground car as he followed the other two soldiers down the road.

The driver engaged the car's engine. "The road should be open the rest of the way," he said. He rotated his turret forward, and the car continued toward the basin.

Two kilometers later, the ravine widened as the road veered left, hugging the slope, and revealed the western edge of the basin.

"Our first settlement," Salus said. He pointed to the ancient rock buildings clustered along the base of the rim wall. "You can see Seelay's memorial on the small hill, beyond the old village."

Arlud scanned the scene. A small obelisk stood at the apex of the hill, surrounded by a circular colonnade that was capped with a narrow roof. "Is that his grave?"

"Yes," Salus said, "His family rest there too. You should visit before you leave. There is a stone inscription, created by Seelay's own hand, attached to the obelisk. All our children are required to memorize it."

Arlud nodded at Salus' recommendation. *They have made a god out of the man,* he thought. That was to be expected, considering what Seelay had done for his people. "He was a great man."

Salus grinned at Arlud's admission.

The gorge widened and the modern village of Kuliq'Quad became visible to the ground car's occupants. White-walled houses, capped with steep blue roofs, were grouped in rings that radiated from a central park with a kidney-shaped lake.

Arlud was impressed by the layout of the village. "How many people live here?"

"About five hundred," Salus said. "Those who live here are responsible for the security and maintenance of the Mánu." He pointed to the eastern end of the basin that had come into view.

Arlud shifted his gaze to the Mánu. About a kilometer from the eastern rim wall, four spherical transports dominated the basin. They were grouped together, one at each corner of the square tarmac, 50 meters apart. Standing 74 meters high, each ship was covered by a blue canvas tarp held in place by four tapered, wooden posts that rose to 35 meters in a gentle arc away from the ships. Eight Y-shaped antenna arrays protruded from the center ridge of each ship, evenly spaced, with the bottom prongs twice as long as the two upper prongs. Four retractable landing struts, partly hidden by their curved bay doors, held each sphere three meters above the tarmac.

"You see them as we keep them," Salus said. "We have kept these ships in pristine condition as best we could."

Arlud leaned forward and patted Bittle on the shoulder. "What do you think, Whinny?"

Bittle twisted in his seat to face Arlud. "They look like Mayfair-Courkos ships from the early thirty-fourth century. Impressive, but I'm more interested in the guts. Being clean and shiny on the outside won't get them off the ground."

Arlud leaned back in his seat. Bittle had a way of stating reality that left him feeling uncertain.

"Think positive, lad," Eahuda said. "We're one step closer than we were three days ago."

Arlud nodded to Eahuda's encouragement and kept his eyes on the ships as the ground car turned south with the road and began the descent into the basin.

Arlud stood with Salus and Gustav Eahuda in the shade of the tented transport at the southwest corner of the Mánu. Winstone Bittle and the other Erstallius engineers had spent the last three hours examining the dead transports and were expected to disembark from this last vessel at any moment.

A light breeze rippled the tarp covering the massive vessel as an old Aku engineer pushed a waist high cart filled with analysis equipment toward Arlud's position.

"His name is Grénu," Salus said. "He's been overseeing the Mánu for thirty years."

The old man's gray scalp lock reached his waist and was bound by five silver rings.

A sign of great authority, Arlud thought.

Grénu stopped in front of Salus and angled the cart so Arlud could see the flat display screen on top. "L'dyém," he said in his quiet tenor. He pulled Salus toward him and exchanged a brief whisper. Salus nodded and the old engineer turned his attention to the equipment.

Salus faced Arlud. "Grénu has not spoken the Sij Yébu for many years. I will translate for him."

Arlud nodded approval.

The old Aku engineer revealed a schematic of a Mayfair-Courkos transport ship on the cart display screen and began speaking in hushed Akün.

Salus translated: "Your engineer will need to download his findings into my equipment."

Arlud nodded. "As agreed."

Grénu pointed to the display image, and Salus continued translating: "This is the ship we have in Kuliq'Quad. They were cargo transports, designed to haul two-hundred and fifty metric tons from surface to orbit, and then through hyperspace to faraway destinations. You can see here the large volume of cargo space surrounding the central core of the vessel."

Arlud moved in closer to the monitor for a better view.

Grénu replaced the diagram with another view, but this time, the cargo space was smaller.

Salus explained: "This is what Seelay did. Notice half the cargo volume is now filled with objects."

Arlud recognized a few of the markings on the new image. "Weapons," he said. "Seelay turned these transports into warships."

"They were designed for the rigors of space flight," Salus said. "Seelay reinforced their durability for combat. They were almost indestructible."

"The man was a genius," Eahuda said. "Clan Tuma probably never knew what hit them."

"But now," Salus said, "they sit under tents."

"We will do our best to revive them," Arlud said.

The old engineer smiled. He clasped his hands together and bowed to Arlud. "Oswu il'alnu."

"I leave you to your duty," Salus translated.

Duty? That word jerked Arlud onto another mental path. The Aku saw this as an Erstallius imperative. A demand that could not be avoided because of his proclamation to Nujo. He only had himself to blame for that, but he also knew it was the right thing to do. That made the responsibility easier to accept, despite the difficulties that lay ahead.

An aft access hatch slid open on the adjacent transport, causing a bell to chime until a circular elevator dropped through the opening to the tarmac.

Winstone Bittle stepped out of the elevator and walked up to Arlud. "We're done," he said. "Sieger and Pyle are packing the equipment." He moved to Grénu's cart and pulled a data pad out of his left coat pocket. He fingered the pad's interface and began the analysis download.

Arlud moved closer to Bittle. "What did you find?"

Bittle gestured to Grénu for permission to use his equipment.

The old Aku engineer backed away from the cart.

Bittle focused the display on the central core of the ship. "This is the main problem." He pointed to a circle in the diagram labeled G.F. in Englo'ni script. "The Kottrel Sphere's internal surface is corroded. Same problem on all four ships, to varying degrees."

Eahuda knew nothing about compression drive engines. "What's *G.F.* mean?"

"Gravity Furnace," Bittle said. "It's the central core of the compression drive's power system. Over time, this always happens. The core is usually replaced before it gets this bad."

Arlud did not like the implications. "Can we fix it?"

"There's another problem," Bittle said. "Some conduit fuses are burned out. They will need to be replaced before we try to power up the engine. The Aku probably had some spares when they first arrived here, but they could not manufacture replacements. You need durillium for that." He adjusted the schematic to show a close-up view of a rectangular conduit fuse. "These last many years, but like the Kottrel Sphere, they don't last forever."

Arlud pressed for an answer. "Can we fix it?"

Bittle thought a moment, then: "We can retool fuses we have in stock at the landing field. The sphere will need the corrosion removed, and then we must apply a coat of a durillium composite called Duranide-X. We should have a few containers of that in storage at the field. It will take sixteen days minimum if we have complete access to all four ships. Four days for coating and fuse replacement for each ship."

Eahuda sensed Bittle's apprehension. "But?"

"Coating is only a temporary fix for the sphere, and not one-hundred percent stable. We should be able to reach orbit and use the plasma weapons within a limited range, but only for a short time. The instability will eventually cause the system to fail again."

Bittle dove into a detailed explanation of the engineering specifics necessary to accomplish their goal and how to make it happen.

With Arlud and Eahuda focused on the engineer's explanation, Salus took the opportunity and broke from the group to engage Grénu in a private conversation.

The distant rippling of the tarp filled the uneasy silence when the conversations ended.

Salus approached Arlud with obvious hesitation. "Grénu has agreed to allow your engineers the access they need. Our only request is that, once your reinforcements arrive, the Kottrel Spheres will be replaced with new ones."

Arlud glanced at Bittle for an answer. The chief engineer's expression indicated he did not wish to commit to that request, but after a quick mental assessment, he smirked and nodded affirmatively.

Arlud disregarded Bittle's half-hearted response and extended his hand to Salus. "It shall be done."

A warning horn blared across the basin.

Salus turned, and after a quick scan of the basin, jogged toward the open area between the tented ships.

The maintenance crews around the other transports scrambled toward the service buildings along the eastern edge of the tarmac.

Arlud followed Salus to the open area, with Eahuda close behind him. They stood by the Aku pilot and followed his gaze northward. Arlud saw nothing. "What are we looking for?"

Another horn blast filled the air.

Along the basin's southwestern rim, camouflage covers moved to reveal three rail gun installations. The turrets rotated north and aimed at the sky.

A double horn blast sounded, and a squadron of ciâfey took flight from the eastern rim toward the northern gorge.

Salus took a deep breath. "We have an intruder."

Arlud noticed the soaring wings had rail guns mounted in front of the pilots. He was impressed by the quick response, then his heart sank when he saw the intruder fly over the northern rim.

PETRA SITLYN: COMRADES

Jens Orr piloted the Erstallius shuttle southeast over the Wassúa Caphága, guided by two transponder signals. If the repetitive pings were genuine, they would fly straight to the Erstallius Regent. The signals emanated from the same mountainous area for the past hour. *A good sign we're on the correct course,* he thought.

Petra Sitlyn sat in the copilot seat, monitoring the emergency communication frequency via the headset. All she heard was static.

In the main compartment, the guildmen filled the seats that faced inward along the bulkhead. They had been a quiet bunch since leaving the landing field. Now that they were out of the rain, Sitlyn thought their spirits would improve. She twisted in her seat and saw only sullen attitudes. Wolfram's daughter slumped between the old trader named Cordova, and the bald, black mustached pilot called Pryce. *She's a panic attack waiting to happen.* She feared the littlest thing would push the girl into a mental breakdown. And Danik's obvious interest in Shanna's female form wasn't helping the situation. Her comrades had already cautioned him twice about getting too close.

Sitlyn shifted her gaze to Danik and Bril. They sat at the rear of the cabin in the fold-down seats that faced the cockpit.

Danik had his head down to avoid any visual contact with Shanna. The second warning from Shanna's companions had been laced with sincere menace. The threat did its work. He forced himself to detach from his sexual urgings, but she was only two meters away, and her presence tugged at him like a magnet.

Bril caught Sitlyn's eye, and he flashed a brief grin. He found the growing tension between Danik and the guildmen amusing.

Sitlyn returned a brief smile, then swiveled back to the instrument console. She knew her decision to take these people to see the Regent had been rash, and might lead to a stern reprimand, but there was too much at stake to ignore their plight. *Arlud must see that,* she thought. Deep inside, beyond all the politics and clan priorities, she knew the Erstallius were sensitive to those in need. Any negative repercussions she might have created for herself were meaningless compared to the good that might be done.

Jens Orr banked the shuttle south, following the transponder signals that flashed on his NAV console. He checked the altitude and began a slow descent. "We'll be there in a few minutes."

Sitlyn glanced out the cockpit window to see rolling hills rush by, replaced by jagged granite slopes. Visibility was to the horizon, and she could see the limb of the approaching basin split by a gorge to her right. "Interesting terrain."

Orr half-heard her comment. "What?"

"That looks like an impact crater."

Orr shrugged and kept his gaze forward.

Something jarred the shuttle.

Sitlyn saw an explosion off their starboard bow. A small white puff of smoke. "Shell burst!"

The Tactical Action Console came to life, displaying six approaching aircraft and three ground targets along the basin rim.

Another shell burst jerked the shuttle.

"Warning shots," Orr said.

Sitlyn watched the tactical console. The six aircraft formed an arc in front of them. She looked out the cockpit window. "Where are they?"

Orr pulled back the forward thrust and began a flat descent toward the basin. "They're above us."

One of the ground-based weapons fired, and the projectile roared past the cockpit and exploded behind the shuttle.

Orr banked hard to starboard, away from the explosive turbulence, and the shuttle dropped below the basin rim.

The six ciâfey swarmed around the shuttle, holding their distance at fifty meters.

"Huh," Orr muttered. He chuckled at the bravado behind the Aku assault.

Sitlyn watched the soaring wings glide around them. "They've got rail guns."

"They seem content with forcing us down," Orr said.

Sitlyn scanned the transponder pings on the NAV console. "Arlud's probably behind that decision. They never hit us, just warned us."

"Yeah," Orr said. "It was a perfect maneuver."

Sitlyn twisted in her seat. "Everyone OK back there?"

Everyone nodded except Shanna. She had her head buried in the old trader's shoulder, and Cordova held her tight.

The turbulence had forced Danik out of his self-imposed stupor. "Should we extend the guns?"

"No," Sitlyn said. "We'll be fine."

The shuttle touched down amid a swirl of dust on a level patch of ground near the northern rim wall, and Jens killed the engines.

Sitlyn looked out the cockpit window and realized the Aku intent. "They're protecting their ships." She gestured for the shuttle passengers to come forward. "Come see."

Cordova remained seated with Shanna. Cegla slumped in his seat, relieved they were on the ground. Danik and Bril rushed forward, followed by Pryce and Harlon. They peered out the cockpit window at the tented, spherical transports silhouetted against the eastern granite wall of the basin.

The ciâfey squadron dropped out of the sky with wings tilted back and cupped like sails to catch the wind. They aligned themselves to face the intruder and settled in a circle around the shuttle with rail guns aimed at her hull.

Orr scrutinized the Aku aircraft. "What do we do now?"

Pryce leaned against the back of Sitlyn's seat and peered out the window. "I'm staying here," he said. "Look!"

Beyond the grounded ciâfey, five gray sipá galloped toward the shuttle, each carrying an Aku rider armed with a rifle.

Sitlyn re-set the comm frequency and sent a message she hoped Arlud would receive.

CLAN ERSTALLIUS: ALLIES

Arlud stood with Bittle, Eahuda, and Salus on the tarmac, in the open area between the four tented transports, and watched the shuttle drop out of the sky near the basin's northern wall. The ciáfey squadron fluttered around the shuttle like moths attracted to a flame and, once on the ground, formed a defensive circle around the shuttle.

Grénu agreed to honor Arlud's wishes and had rushed away to order the squadron to avoid damaging the approaching aircraft.

One more action putting us deeper in debt to these people, Arlud thought. Most Alliance Clans would see that as a weakness. Arlud knew it bound them closer to the Aku, and in time would make his clan stronger. "Honor your debts," his father had said, "and your good name will bring honor to you."

Arlud heard a bleep from his transceiver and pulled it out of his coat pocket. He scanned the caller's identity and walked away to take the call under the shade of the nearby transport.

"I'll get us a car," Salus said to Eahuda. He pinched the ring around his neck and spoke in hushed Akün as he walked a few paces away toward the western edge of the tarmac.

Eahuda turned and kept his eyes on Arlud.

Arlud pocketed his transceiver and stood with his back to Bittle and Eahuda for a moment, then turned and rejoined them. "Petra," he said. "She's got guildmen with her. Wolfram Sy's daughter."

Eahuda flinched at that revelation. "Wolfram's daughter? Why didn't she call us before trying to land here?"

"She thought I would make her stay at the landing field."

Eahuda pressed his lips together in anger. "She's damn lucky the Aku honored your request."

Bittle frowned but held back his opinion of the Nared-Major's actions.

"Her focus is narrow," Arlud said, "but her intentions are good."

A ground car drove onto the tarmac and stopped a few meters away.

Salus jumped in the car and called out: "We should get over there."

Arlud turned to Bittle. "Stay here, Winny. Help Sieger and Pyle finish packing the equipment and start sketching out a plan for the repair work. We'll send a car for you once this mess is resolved."

Bittle tipped his head. "Aye, sir."

Fifteen minutes later, the ground car left the dirt road from the Mánu, crossed a brief span of rocky terrain, and stopped behind the circle of ciâfey surrounding the Erstallius shuttle.

Sipá cavalry stood inside the ring of ciâfey with soldiers dismounted, grouped ten meters from the shuttle's starboard exit.

"They'll never come out with those beasts standing there," Salus said. He left the ground car and headed for the soldier in charge of the cavalry.

Arlud stayed in the car with Eahuda and the driver. They had no problem waiting for the cavalry to retreat. No matter how well trained they seemed to be, they were still bears.

Bears trained to fight, Arlud thought. *If we had been able to achieve this centuries ago, history might have been very different.* He leaned close to Eahuda and whispered: "Cavalry like that could change the future."

"You read my mind, lad."

Salus exchanged a few words with the commanding soldier, and the cavalrymen mounted their sipá and retreated to the west.

At a gesture from Salus, Arlud left the ground car and headed for the shuttle, with Eahuda following close behind him. He passed the line of ciâfey and noticed the pilots were more relaxed after the cavalry retreat.

Two more ground cars rumbled across the rocky terrain and stopped behind the ciâfey perimeter. They were filled with old Aku men. Grénu was among them.

Arlud raised his transceiver. "Get out here, Petra."

The shuttle's starboard hatch swung open and Sitlyn rushed down the steps. She stood at attention in front of Arlud. "Nared-Major, Sitlyn at your service, sir."

Arlud was startled by Sitlyn's formal stance. He never demanded such behavior, and that gave it more impact. It was her way of saying, "I know I screwed up, but I still honor you."

"Relax, Petra," Arlud said. "Is the shuttle ready for orbit?"

Sitlyn didn't expect that question. "Uh, yes, sir."

"Good. Job well done."

"Thank you, sir."

"You have guildmen with you."

"Yes, sir."

"You put their lives in jeopardy by coming here without authorization."

"I didn't expect the Aku response."

"The Aku are very protective of this place, but what concerns me most has nothing to do with the Aku. You lacked faith in me, Nared-Major, and that is my foremost regret."

Sitlyn dropped her gaze, and her posture went limp. "That won't happen again."

"What's done is done. I know your motive was to help. Moving forward, let's discuss things before taking any action."

Sitlyn straightened her stance. "Yes, sir."

"Now, take me to the guildmen."

Sitlyn nodded and led Arlud up the entry into the shuttle's passenger compartment.

Ross Cordova urged Shanna to move her head from his shoulder. She sat up straight but kept her eyes downcast and folded her hands in her lap.

Arlud noticed the blood-stained clothes. He touched Sitlyn's arm and shot her a questioning glance.

"They've been cared for," Sitlyn said. "This is Ross Cordova."

The old trader stood. "I wish to see your regent."

"I am Regent," Arlud said.

Ross chuckled. "You expect me to believe that?"

Arlud wasn't surprised by the reaction. He found it all too familiar.

Sitlyn stepped between the two men. "Ross Cordova, meet Arlud Reynaldo Erstallius, Regent of all clan holdings on GSW-183."

Ross mentally flinched but kept his outward appearance impassive. He reviewed Arlud from head to toe like a fighter sizing up an opponent. "Younger than I expected. You are Armand's son!"

Arlud nodded.

Eahuda entered the shuttle and planted himself at Arlud's left side.

"My guard commander," Arlud said. "Gustav Eahuda."

Eahuda stood unmovable, a rock-solid deterrent against aggression.

Ross sensed the fighter in Eahuda. He took a step back and gestured to Shanna. "Regent Erstallius, meet Shanna Sy, daughter of Wolfram Sy, Heir to Al-phaq, and all Guild holdings."

Arlud looked down at the young woman. She was a porcelain beauty, now blood-stained and dirty. Her green eyes were reddened, her dark hair a mop of limp curls. *She's probably never looked this bad in her life,* he thought, imagining her proper upbringing and the catered days she must have experienced in Wolfram's keep. He felt a tinge of sadness for her and wondered what put her in this condition. "What happened to you people?"

Cordova spent the next few minutes outlining the attack on the Cormeds, the rescue, and the rebellion aboard Pardee's ship.

Arlud's mind whirled. *Chaos increasing.* He looked down at Shanna. "I promise you, Lady Sy, you will be safe here."

Shanna stiffened and looked up at Arlud. "Really?"

"Yes."

"How will my being safe help my mother? Will you help us fight the Cormeds?"

"There are many battles to be fought. Our primary concern is Polinda, but we will do what we can to help you."

Shanna flashed a thin smile that vanished as she began to weep. She dropped her head into her hands, and Bern Pryce reached over from his seat to console her.

Cordova moved close to Arlud and said in an undertone: "She's been through a lot. May we continue outside?"

Arlud agreed and turned for the exit.

Salus and Grénu were waiting near the boarding ramp as Arlud appeared in the hatchway. Salus carried a magar-rifle.

Arlud paused. "What's this?"

"The elders do not want the intruders in Kuliq'Quad," Salus said. "They are not to leave the shuttle."

Arlud leaned against the airframe and sighed. The ciâfey line still had guns aimed and ready. He shook his head in disgust, turned and spoke a few words to those inside the shuttle, then proceeded down the boarding ramp and stood face to face with Salus. "These people are no threat to you,"

Salus looked determined, clutching his rifle. "You said you would protect us from further intrusion."

Arlud forced himself to relax. "The crew of this shuttle are the ones you helped in Ji'dess."

"Yes," Salus said, "but the passengers are intruders who came down in their own carrier to your landing field."

Arlud underestimated how fast news could spread among the Aku. "Yes, they did, but they had no other choice. They were put inside the carrier, bound and blindfolded, and forced off their freighter. They reached the surface with the main engines damaged and no life support. They're lucky to have survived."

Salus translated Arlud's explanation to Grénu.

Arlud continued: "They rescued the surviving crews of two damaged Cormed frigates, who later turned on them and tried to commandeer the

Guild ship. These people are victims of the Alliance. A crime to which you can relate."

Salus exchanged words with Grénu, then said: "What proof do you have of this?"

"Have your techs examine their carrier."

Salus pinched the ring around his neck. "Lief, sieg naru."

"Their freighter is probably still in orbit somewhere," Arlud said. "Finding her will verify the story and help us track the vessel for future intervention. I have promised to help these people reclaim their ship."

"You promise many things," Salus said.

"Many things need doing."

Twilight fell over Kuliq'Quad basin, cloaking the Erstallius shuttle in deep shadow.

Winstone Bittle pulled the starboard hatch shut and gave the pilot a thumb-up signal.

Jens Orr powered up the shuttle's engines.

A few minutes later, Arlud Erstallius settled next to Gustav Eahuda in their ground car's rear seat, and watched the shuttle rise amid a swirl of dust, then disappear over the basin's northern rim. She would return in about four hours, filled with equipment needed for the transport repair.

"We lost five hours, lad."

Arlud acknowledged Eahuda's comment with a nod and leaned back in the seat. "It's a cultural thing."

After four hours of debate, the Aku elders agreed to allow the guildmen to leave the shuttle. They were taken to the village and housed in a large dwelling in the outer ring of residences near the main road to the Mánu.

Eahuda sighed. "That culture needs to change if we ever hope to succeed before Polinda comes back. We only have so much time."

"Our integrity is intact. They found the freighter and the carrier's damage was confirmed. I expect no more setbacks."

Eahuda buttoned his coat against the chill air. "I hope you're right."

The ground car lunged forward as the driver headed across the rocky terrain toward the dirt road that would take them to the village.

"This friendship is new to all of us," Arlud said. "The Aku have been isolated for a long time. There are bound to be bumps along the way."

Eahuda knew that, and he didn't like it. "There's a lot at stake here, lad."

"We'll be fine."

"Can we trust them?"

Arlud pondered the implications of trust and how it affected every decision. "We have our motivations, and the Aku have their motivations. They are understandably suspicious. That will fade over time, and our relationship will become stronger. Our trust in each other will strengthen naturally."

Eahuda understood that was the expected result of bonding but was leery of the Aku willingness to accept off-world help as a permanent reality. "Independence is a thing not easily relinquished, lad."

"Then keep an eye on them, Gus. I trust you to keep me informed of any suspicious actions."

Eahuda chuckled. "Right."

By the time the ground car pulled up to the dwelling assigned to the off-worlders, twilight had faded into night, and the car's headlights threw a circle of illumination across the face of the white courtyard walls.

Petra Sitlyn stepped through the wooden entry gate and held it open.

Arlud and Eahuda exited the car. The driver waited until they had passed through the open gate, then pulled back and turned, removing the illumination from the entry.

Sitlyn lighted the path with a hand-held glowball and guided Arlud and Eahuda into the single floor dwelling. Once inside, she crossed the darkened entry, entered the dim light from the ceiling panel in the dining room, and turned on a display pad laying on the wooden table. She gestured to Arlud and Eahuda. "Here's the schematic Bittle made." She rotated the pad so Arlud could read it.

Graphic representations of the four transports dominated the view. Each ship was shown in different stages of preparation.

"Transport one has been prepped," Sitlyn said, "as you can see from the white color of the system icons. Sieger and Pyle showed the Aku engineers what to do, and as you can see, they have the other ships in different stages of prep. By the time Bittle gets back, they should all be ready for the coating."

"Good job," Arlud said.

"Bittle set this schematic to auto update on the hour so you can follow our progress."

"Excellent."

"Now, if you will excuse me, I need to get some rest. Salus will be here at sunrise to take me to the Mánu."

"Thank you, Petra."

Sitlyn retreated toward the entry, then stopped and turned around. "Our rooms are down the hall to the right. The traders are to the left. There's food in the pantry."

"Thank you," Arlud said.

Sitlyn turned and disappeared down the hall, her glowball lighting her way.

"With your permission, lad," Eahuda said.

"See you in the morning, Gus."

Eahuda nodded and headed toward the dark hall. He pulled a glowball out of his coat pocket to light his way.

Arlud pulled out a chair and sat. He leaned forward with his arms on the table, rested his head in his right hand, and closed his eyes. He needed to sleep but decided to review the engineering schematic Bittle had left to get more familiar with the system details.

Then he heard breathing. A low rhythmic sound from someone behind him.

In one smooth motion, Arlud sprang to his feet and whirled toward the sound, pulling his chair to one side, ready to use it as a weapon.

"Oh!" the figure lurking in the darkened hall exclaimed. "Sorry, I did not mean to startle you."

The voice was a soft contralto, and Arlud recognized it. "Lady Sy." He relaxed his grip on the chair.

Shanna stepped into the dim light of the dining room. She wore Aku clothing. A floor length woolen dress that covered her arms and revealed the toes of her sandaled feet. Her oval face was scrubbed clean, and her thick brown hair was still damp from being washed. "I can't sleep," she said. "I was hoping they had some tea in the pantry."

Arlud gestured for her to pass.

Shanna crossed the stone floor and entered the pantry adjacent to the dining room.

Arlud noticed her form was perfect. She strolled with the grace of a trained dancer, and he felt the tug of sexual attraction. He forced his thoughts back to Bittle's schematic and sat at the table.

Shanna searched the cupboards for tea. "My father never mentioned your clan. Are you a low-ranking family?"

Arlud leaned back in his chair. "We are new to this district. Our roots go back to the SINCOS era."

Shanna paused her search. "Petra said you tried to stop the Alliance plot to blockade Al-phaq."

Arlud nodded. "A Cormed envoy brought us the news about the Polinda mine. He was a very determined fellow."

Shanna returned to her search. "My father warned me once to avoid GSW-183 at all costs. He said the Aku are murderous savages."

"That view is held by most of the clans in this district."

"And yet we are still alive."

"Some reputations endure even though the people change. Reputations are best earned through experience, not acquired because of gossip."

Shanna paused again and looked at Arlud. "And all guildmen are pirates."

Arlud was amused by the young woman's implication. "Rebels are always viewed in a negative light by those who resist them."

"You imply we are Rebels?"

"Your father withdrew from the Alliance and formed the Guild as a response to trade restrictions imposed by the ruling clans. He rebelled."

"And what gives the Alliance the right to restrict anyone?"

Arlud leaned forward and rested his arms on the table. Shanna was digging for an argument. *Must be her way of dealing with her sadness,* he thought. *I'll not take her bait.* "That is a very good question."

Shanna leaned back against the cupboard. Her surprise was evident on her face.

"Lady Sy," Arlud said in a conciliatory tone, "I do not have answers for all the universe's problems, but I do have answers for our immediate situation."

"And what would they be?"

"Our shuttle will make orbit tomorrow and do a reconnaissance flight to Pardee's freighter. Once we know her condition, we'll be able to plan a rescue if that's necessary."

Shanna turned away to hide a sudden rush of tears. "Oh, that's wonderful!"

Arlud remained silent to allow Shanna time to compose herself.

"Thank you," Shanna said.

Arlud nodded. "The Aku have agreed to help us repair your carrier."

"How long will that take?"

"Maybe a few weeks. Their transports are the primary concern because of the threat from Polinda. We need to make sure they are ready as soon as possible."

"My father has nothing good to say about Farquar Polinda or his clan."

"A common view."

"Did your clan attack him?"

"No. His destroyers attacked us because of blind hatred, fueled by an ancient conflict that happened before my father was born."

"Who attacked him?"

"We don't know. The Cormeds sent an investigation team to the mine as soon as they heard of the attack. Clan Sabballi joined them a few days later. Neither clan could determine who was at fault."

"So they accused my father."

"Yes."

Shanna resumed her search and found a jar that looked like tea. She opened the lid and sniffed the aroma. "Can you read this label?"

Arlud examined the Akün letters from his seat. "Looks like, *Ahkhé*. I'm not familiar with that."

Shanna frowned. She shrugged and placed a small portion of the crushed plant into a cup and added water.

Arlud noticed her new bandages. "Are your wrists healing?"

"Oh, yes," Shanna said. "They don't sting anymore." She searched the counter. "How do I heat this?"

Arlud scanned the pantry. "On the shelf, over there." He pointed to the open shelves above the counter.

Shanna withdrew the heating pad from the shelf and placed it on the counter. "Would you like some?"

"No."

Shanna set her cup on the heating pad and noticed the immediate red glow, so knew nothing else needed to be done. "Could Polinda have attacked himself?"

"Why would he do that?"

"Well, he is not very popular. One way to gain more power is to create a disaster and then take advantage of the chaos. A mine disaster would be a great way to convince the clans to allow him to destroy his suspected enemies."

Arlud sat back. This young woman was no brainless, spoiled socialite. "We've considered that and have not ruled out the possibility."

Shanna smiled. Her cup was steaming, so she picked it up to taste. The bitterness made her scrunch her face. She put down the cup and spit in the adjacent sink. "Eeouw! That's awful."

Arlud smirked. "I guess it's not tea."

Shanna dumped the hot drink, refilled the cup with pure water, rinsed her mouth, and spit again. "If we will be here long, we need to get a translator." She filled the cup with water again and sat down at the table across from Arlud.

"I'll ask Salus to change the labels," Arlud said.

Shanna caressed her cup, wondering what to ask next, then: "If Polinda was attacked by someone else, who could it be?"

"Probably the same force that attacked the Cormeds."

"Then perhaps we should join with this unknown attacker. Cormeds are horrible people!"

Arlud forced back a quick response to that comment. Shanna was speaking from emotion and he sensed the wrong reply would send her into a rage. He let silence fill the room for a few heartbeats, then: "The mine investigation was not handled well. The survivors were questioned once and then released. They should have been secured for a more thorough interrogation. Most of them were taken to Pigrell, the Polinda homeworld, so they are beyond reach. Others were taken to U'galem, which should allow us an opportunity to find them without too much trouble."

"And why should we do that?"

"When you are attacked, things happen quick. It can take multiple reviews to fine tune the exact sequence of events. Everyone remembers events from their own perspective and that can cloud reality."

Shanna lowered her head and recalled her capture by the Cormed clanmen. *Things do move very fast.* "The Cormeds rushed the investigation?"

"Yes. I'm sure they were pressured to complete it as fast as possible, knowing how Polinda might react."

"And blaming my father was a quick resolution that would be agreeable to the Alliance, and especially Polinda."

"Yes."

"Then why did Polinda attack you?"

"He has his own priorities."

Shanna took a moment and reviewed everything Arlud had said. Her mind reeled with the terrible realization that her world would never be the same. "Why U'galem?"

"Alliance law mandates that when a holding fails, for any reason, all contract labor must be returned to the same world where they were recruited."

"Oh."

"Some survivors on U'galem may have been re-claimed by Polinda and transferred to other holdings by now. I'm hoping most of them are still on-planet."

"You intend to start your own investigation?"

"Someone has to do it."

"If they've already formed a conclusion, what difference will it make?"

"Their conclusion was wrong. Polinda was attacked, then Alliance frigates were hit. Until we know who is responsible for starting this mess, the clans will split into factions as they begin to fortify against their competitors. It will be similar to the breakdown after the fall of SINCOS, but this time it will be worse."

"How?"

"When SINCOS dissolved, there was still a remnant of political control governing the old worlds. The old worlds are now only a small part of our colonized universe. Remove the oversight of the Alliance and many worlds will be left on their own. Battles for trade routes will slow down supply deliveries. The struggles between the Guild and the Alliance will pale in comparison to the chaos that could ensue."

"Oh."

Arlud recognized he had upset Lady Sy. "We have time to prevent a total breakdown. I'm sorry if I—"

"No need to apologize," Shanna said. "I understand."

Arlud focused on Bittle's schematic. He could feel Shanna's eyes on him and felt uneasy under her scrutiny. *She's an attractive force,* he thought, *and that is a distraction I cannot allow myself right now.*

Shanna took a sip from her cup of water. "When will you leave for U'galem?"

"Once Ni'apinu is secure."

"Ni'apinu? That's the Aku name for GSW-183?"

"Yes."

"What does it mean?"

"Secure abode."

"Oh," Shanna said. "I hope that's true."

"We're doing our best to make sure it is."

Shanna let Arlud's words flow through her. She had never expected to meet someone like him from an Alliance Clan. He was a delightful surprise, and she found him very attractive. She noticed the tiredness in his eyes and wondered if he spent all his energy doing things that mattered to others, or only to himself. "Thank you for helping us."

"We do what we can."

Shanna emptied her glass and rose from her chair.

Arlud watched her move to the sink and when she turned to place the glass on the countertop her profile burned into his memory. Her physique was perfect—the most attractive woman he had ever seen. He felt his face flush.

Shanna veered within a half meter of Arlud's chair. "Good night," she said, as she walked past him and headed for the darkened hall.

Arlud turned to watch her retreat. "Good night."

Eahuda came out of the shadows from the other side of the entry. "You should get some sleep. lad."

"Spying on me again, Gus?"

"I'm your guard. I watch you always."

Arlud picked up Bittle's schematic and walked toward the old Degen. "We both need some sleep."

Eahuda grabbed Arlud's arm to stop his advance, and said in a whisper, "Careful, lad, she's Wolfram's daughter."

Arlud patted the old Degen's shoulder. "You worry too much. Get some sleep."

Eahuda let Arlud continue toward the guest rooms, then turned at a rustling in the dark hall across the entry.

Ross Cordova stepped into the light from the dining room and threw the old Degen a casual salute.

Eahuda returned the gesture and retreated to his guest room.

ALPHA CEPHEI FOUR: EVIDENCE

Artemis Parker was a Segen in the Sabballi security forces, and a judge advocate assigned to the Department of Planetary Settlement. The Alpha Cephei Four incident was his first assignment.

Alpha Cephei Four's long night had slowed the initial investigation and had caused the Officer-in-Charge to overlook what Parker saw as an obvious source for evidence: the perimeter cameras. The cameras recorded all activity around the mine, but the commander had insisted once the power conduits had been cut, the cameras would have frozen beyond repair, and any evidence lost forever.

With Alpha Cephei now low over the eastern horizon, Parker braved the searing radiation long enough to retrieve one camera. Clad in a bulky, white environment suit, he advanced across gray rocks along a narrow ridge line. Behind him, Nared-Major Tylo Singh matched his quick pace. Singh had been the only investigation team member brave enough to join him.

"You'll get toasted out there," the other team members had insisted. "It's not worth the effort."

Parker knew they had enough time. As long as they made it back to the team habitat in two hours, they would be fine. He stopped and glanced back. "How you doing, Tylo?"

"I'm still here."

Above the two men, the central bulge of the milky way split the star filled sky. In the valley below them, most of the destroyed Polinda mine lay silent under the long black shadows of early morning. The western edge of the shattered complex was the only area illuminated by the sun. Towering arc lights planted by the investigation team pushed back the black around the main excavation area on the south side of the complex.

Parker resumed his advance toward their goal. "My pad says it's another fifty meters to the spot."

"We should have done this days ago," Singh said.

"Yep."

Although Parker expected success, he also knew their chances of finding intact data dropped with each passing hour. The Officer-in-Charge had approved this operation only four hours earlier. Parker sensed that had been done only to prove him wrong. He paused upon seeing a small gray cylinder protruding from the dark soil a few meters away.

"There it is."

Both men crouched around the object. The cylinder was half a meter in height, with a vertical window in the side facing the valley. A label stenciled on top of the cylinder read, "Cam-17."

After a few minutes of work, they had the cover removed and Parker detached the small, insulated camera from the support bracket.

Singh opened a sample bag and held it out in front of him.

Parker placed the camera in the bag, then turned and surveyed the black valley below him. "If the on-board memory is still active, we should get a perfect view." And then his attention was diverted westward.

A white fireball rose above the black horizon and streaked into the star filled sky.

"Look!"

Both men watched the white fire descend toward the mine.

"It's a transport," Singh said.

The white blaze brightened the dark ground at the new landing area north of the mine. The large spherical transport settled to the surface amid a cloud of dust, and the bright blaze beneath it vanished.

Both men watched more ships pass overhead, outlined by their external lights as they blocked the stars behind them.

"They look like destroyers," Singh said. "I count ten!"

"Twelve," Parker said. "Look!"

Over the black horizon, two ships twice the size of the others blocked the stars as they sped after the smaller ships.

"Dreadnoughts," Parker said, as he looked up at the passing silhouettes. "Low orbit. Ten kilometers, maybe less." He gestured for Singh to start the trek back to their surface transport. "Let's get moving."

Singh stood, secured the sample bag to his waist belt, and retreated along the ridge line. "Are they who I think they are?"

"Yep," Parker said, as he followed Singh. "The Polindas have arrived."

An hour after his transport had landed on Alpha Cephei Four, Farquar Polinda secured himself in his darkened ready room and activated the communication console. The narrow control panel curved around his chair, a collection of knobs, dials and switches that gave him access to vast banks of data stored aboard ship, and all sources of information within reach of the local communication network.

He flipped two switches, and a curved array of holoscreens appeared, floating above the console. A glowing, colorful display of input from twelve different sources.

The Officer-in-Charge was due to give his report about the progress of the investigation. Farquar was not expecting any groundbreaking revelations. He had no concern about what the evidence declared, or the questions it did not answer. All that mattered to him was the loss of his mine, because that meant loss of income. He had already decided who was to blame.

The officer's oval face appeared on a screen to Farquar's right. He enlarged the live image, moved it to the prominent central position, and listened to the opening statements that excused the lack of progress because of the difficulties digging through the ruins deep in the mine. As the Officer-in-Charge droned on, Farquar's attention shifted to other reports as new info populated the other screens. From this one station he could monitor the status of his transport, the status of the other ships in his fleet, all communications sent and received, known locations of clan forces, and other reports of less importance but of personal interest, like a paper posted by the Kainogae School about a new strain of wheat.

Farquar's interests were many. Behind all the distractions, losing his mine was paramount in his thoughts. He just disliked lengthy explanations. He wanted answers, not boring monologues that only complicated and delayed the final point.

Then the Officer-in-Charge said: "We have a recording from the suit camera of a miner who witnessed the first eruption."

The center screen displayed the recording.

Farquar watched as Josh Gridle turned toward the camera and said, "Colli, get your ass up and go find that tech."

The suit camera swung to the right and revealed the raw rock of the tunnel wall, and then a small group of miners twenty meters away, entering the evac lift.

The camera motion stopped, and a contralto voice said, "Gridle, I'll need to head up."

"Of course you will," Gridle said. "Do you see a tech down here?"

Static began interfering with the recording as the camera moved closer to the evac lift.

Screams erupted, and the camera swung back around to show Gridle engulfed in a ball of light.

The static increased, and the screen went black.

The Officer-in-Charge appeared once again on the holoscreen. "This is the only recording we have," he said. "The survivors were questioned and were as mystified as we are. No absolute cause has been identified."

Farquar leaned forward and pressed a comm button. "Tell me, Degen," he said in his deep basso, "how did this sapi survive?" He pushed more buttons on his console and an image of Bev Colli appeared on one of the smaller adjacent screens.

"Sheer luck," the Officer-in-Charge said. "The miners you saw entering the lift reached the assembly area on Level Three. All but two died."

"Where are these survivors now?"

"They have been returned to their home ports."

Farquar fingered his console again and enlarged the information about Bev Colli. "This report indicates this sapi was taken to U'galem. How was this possible?"

"I don't understand the significance."

"We recruited her on Pigrell."

"Oh," the officer said, and his gaze shifted downward. That revelation had not been expected. He raised his eyes and said, "All labor records were destroyed in the mine. We assumed each survivor told us the truth about their origins. Why would they lie?"

"Indeed, Degen. Why would they?"

Farquar leaned forward and cut off the live transmission, then pulled up the data file on all the miners who had survived. Of all the survivors, only Bev Colli had lied about her home port. And she had been present at the first eruption, moving her drill into perfect position for the attack. *Sabotage?* Farquar wondered. *Why else would a sapi lie?*

He reviewed Bev Colli's records. *Find a lie and you find the guilty one,* he thought. He knew one lie wasn't enough proof to convict the sapi of sabotage, but it was enough to call for her retrieval. He relished the possibility of questioning her himself.

He called up a new screen and sent a priority command to his resource director that said, "All contract labor evacuated from mining complex thirty-seven are to be retrieved for placement evaluations." He added the seals and signature that would rush the request through the Alliance bureaucracy.

One of the smaller screens to Farquar's right flashed red and jumped to the center position. The red glow faded to reveal a square jawed Segen-

Major. "We just received confirmation," the Segen-Major said. "The destroyer *Tonor Dara* was the lone survivor of a clash with the Erstallius at GSW-183. She has just crossed into this system and will be in orbit within the hour. She has hull damage and is only twenty percent battle ready. Her commander reports the *Kuna Tane* and the *Caldera Meese* were lost at GSW-183. They responded per Fleet Command Order dating 3520.8.5 instructing all Polinda forces to respond against Clan Erstallius should any attack be suffered by us. We will provide updates about *Tonor Dara's* status as they become available."

The Segen-Major's screen flashed red and was replaced by an updated listing of all the Polinda ships in orbit.

As Farquar read through the list, contemplating a retaliatory strike against the Erstallius, a small screen to his left displayed the crest of the Judge Advocate for Planetary Settlement. He turned to focus on this new screen.

A head and shoulders view of Artemis Parker replaced the image of the JAPS crest, and Farquar moved the screen to the center location and activated the sound.

Parker was saying, ". . . these cameras are susceptible to extreme cold, but we retrieved a recording of the events near the latter stages of eruption."

The scene changed to display the recovered data.

The wide-angle view showed the surface complex in the late afternoon sun. A still scene of gray hills surrounding a valley with cylindrical, domed buildings protruding through the black shadows cast across the valley from the jagged western rim. A time stamp at the bottom right read: "25.4.5.19.0075."

Cyan light erupted out of the black shadows and the western buildings split open. Debris showered the area as the complex crumbled.

Static filled the holoscreen for a few moments, then faded to display a new scene with a time stamp: "25.4.5.20.0362."

What remained of the surface buildings was bathed in cyan light. Glowing cyan clouds streamed upward into the vacuum, rising toward the stars—a twisting flow of energy.

Then, to Farquar's amazement, one of the cyan clouds descended back toward the surface and floated above a group of survivors on one of the eastern hills.

The cloud hovered over the dying miners, illuminating them with cold light.

Then the cloud vanished in an eye blink.

Farquar sat back in his chair, dumbfounded.

Artemis Parker filled the screen again and said, "We are analyzing the blue energy, but I do not expect many answers from that data. Taken by itself, the recording shows the mine was destroyed from the inside, and based on what transpired on the surface, that destruction was intelligently directed. We will send a more detailed report once our investigation of this data is complete."

The JAPS crest replaced Parker's face on the holoscreen.

Farquar leaned forward and turned off all the screens. He leaned back in his chair and sat still in the dark, his mind whirling with this new data.

Sabotage for sure, he thought, and he felt a brief pang of helplessness at the revelation someone had accomplished such a feat. He clenched his fists and pounded the arms of his chair.

During his journey to Alpha Cephei Four he had learned of the Alliance effort to blockade Al-phaq but had dismissed Wolfram Sy's hand in the catastrophe. Despite their disagreements, he knew Wolfram was no fool. But the Erstallius rogues were well versed in subterfuge. Now that they had entered this district and had partnered with the Aku scum, they were a more immediate threat than they had ever been. GSW-183 was only a little over six parsecs away.

It would have been a little thing for Armand to have coerced a sapi to help ignite demolition, Farquar thought. *Damn them all!*

He sat forward in his chair and fingered his control console.

A single holoscreen appeared, and he typed a message for his Fleet Commander that said, "Jegen Marlow, please begin operations planning for a direct assault on GSW-183. Our aim will be to annihilate all Erstallius forces as swiftly as possible. There must be no survivors."

Farquar paused a moment and contemplated possible Aku involvement, then added: "We shall consider the Aku in league with the Erstallius. Our goal will be to eradicate all resistance. Plan your campaign accordingly. We will begin as soon as our forces can be mustered and set into action."

Farquar sent the message and leaned back in his chair.

Damn them all!

THE GUILD: CONTACT

The day after arriving in Kuliq'Quad, Shanna Sy sat at the dining table in the Aku dwelling and watched a video stream on the display pad she had propped up against a water pitcher. The video was from the forward port camera on board the Erstallius shuttle en route to Erlis Pardee's freighter.

Jens Orr piloted the shuttle. Bern Pryce, Harlon Sater, and Donté Cegla had agreed to join him in this attempt to connect with Pardee's ship.

Shanna's safety was secure in Kuliq'Quad and Ross Cordova agreed to stay behind as her sole guardian while the others helped Orr.

The Guild freighter dropped into view at the upper right corner of the display pad, half-lit by the sun, rotating amid a field of stars.

Shanna gasped. "Oh, there it is!"

Cordova leaned forward at Shanna's left side to get a better view. "Aye, she's still intact. That's a good sign." He grinned and patted Shanna's shoulder.

Petra Sitlyn smiled at the sight of the freighter. She pulled out a chair and sat at Shanna's right. "They'll be cautious. This may take some time."

Jens Orr's voice sounded from the display pad, the emotionless tone of a trained pilot:

"One hundred meters . . . we have matched rotation . . . closing at one meter per second . . . slowing to docking speed."

The view shifted as the shuttle maneuvered to approach the freighter's shuttle bay.

"They have vented," Orr said. "We are at full stop awaiting more analysis."

Shanna looked to Cordova. "What does that mean?"

"It means some Cormeds are floating in space."

Shanna returned her attention to the display pad. "Good."

The view shifted to reveal the open shuttle bay doors and the dark interior.

"They have powered down," Orr said. "Wait—Bern has just confirmed the freighter is hot."

Shanna was puzzled. "Hot?"

"The power generators are still working," Sitlyn said.

A search light from the shuttle panned across the interior of the open bay. Two cargo shuttles were still locked in the grip of docking clamps, but the other three clamps were empty, and the hatch that led deeper into the ship was open to the vacuum.

"Bern is sending a hail," Orr said.

"No one else left," Cordova said. "The two shuttles are still there."

Shanna gripped the edge of the table. "Please be alive," she muttered to herself.

The scene on the display remained unchanged and silent over the next few minutes as the shuttle crew waited for a response to their hail.

"No response," Orr said. "We are resending on all frequencies."

Cordova moved away toward the pantry. He didn't like the implications no response implied and forced himself to remain quiet.

Shanna turned at Cordova's retreat. She sensed concern from his posture. She lowered her head as regret began surging inside her.

"Look," Sitlyn said. "The hatchway."

Inside the shuttle bay, the search light illuminated the closing hatchway.

Cordova returned to peer over Shanna's shoulder. "That's it," he said. "They're alive!"

"Signal received," Orr said.

Erlis Pardee's voice sounded over the video: "This is freighter One-Nine-Seven out of Al-phaq. You are granted access to our shuttle bay. We are pressurizing the access corridors for your entry. Please wait for the amber light to dock. Once docked, wait for the green light before you disembark."

The shuttle bay brightened as the internal lights came on and red lights glowed above the three empty docking clamps.

"Be advised," Pardee said, "we've had some passenger problems, but have confined the unruly bunch on deck Three. We are working to restore all systems."

Shanna was ecstatic. "Can I talk to them?"

"We're not set up for that," Sitlyn said. "We can only receive."

"Be advised," Orr said, "Shanna Sy is well."

Pardee responded: "Thank you. Please relate that Wellen Sy is fine. We have control."

"Your Regent should be here," Shanna said. "This is wonderful!"

"He had other matters to attend to," Sitlyn said. "I'm sure he will be thrilled."

Shanna faced Sitlyn. "I did not expect your help, Petra. The Alliance has always been disagreeable. Most clans would gladly see us dead."

"A few would gladly see Clan Erstallius dead," Sitlyn admitted. "The Alliance was founded to regulate settlement and trade. All other affairs are handled by each clan independently. Some seek self-advantage in all things. Clan Erstallius has always sought to achieve mutual advantage in everything. You should judge each clan on its own merit."

Shanna nodded. "Yes, I see that now." She returned her attention to the display pad. "I hope it doesn't take too long before we can rejoin Pardee and be on our way."

"The Aku engineers are very good. I would expect your carrier to be ready by the end of the week. In the meantime, we'll work on getting the Cormeds off your freighter."

Cordova huffed. "I'd be happy if we just vented all of them."

Sitlyn understood the old trader's attitude and would have agreed with his sentiment under different circumstances. *Clan priorities must always override personal feelings.* "We have an obligation to see they are safely removed," she said. "They won't bother you anymore."

CLAN ERSTALLIUS: BURIAL

Arlud Erstallius tossed the last shovel of dirt onto the grave and used the flat side of the scoop to pound the loose pile flat. He stood back, leaned against the shovel handle, and wiped his brow with his sleeve. "All done."

Clouds had moved in, blocking the late afternoon sun, bringing a coolness to the air that refreshed him after the sweaty work. He and Gustav Eahuda had spent the last two hours digging, and then refilling, the last resting place for the pilots and engineers lost in the shuttle crash. The Aku had retrieved the crushed and half-eaten bodies from the crash site and brought them here to the Erstallius outpost. The single grave was just beyond the northern edge of the landing field, inside the perimeter fence.

Gustav Eahuda stood on the other side of the grave, holding his shovel against his left shoulder the way he'd hold a rifle for a parade march. "They were good lads."

Arlud looked across the field. "Here comes Danik."

Eahuda turned to watch the small utility car approach, with Danik behind the steering wheel. The car pulled a trailer with a work pod harnessed inside the cargo bed.

Danik stopped the car alongside the grave, then climbed inside the trailer to remove the straps that secured the work pod.

Arlud and Eahuda moved to the rear of the trailer to examine the thick rectangular gravestone held in the work pod's articulated claws. The Erstallius clan seal was etched near the top of the smooth granite face. Below the seal, an inscription read: "Virtue increases honor," in Englo'ni, which was the motto of Clan Erstallius. Below that, the carved names of those who had died were listed in order of rank:

DEGEN-OF-THE-CORP GENE CROWEL.
SEGEN-MAJOR LERU KIN.
SEGEN HUGO VAN.
NARED-MAJOR DRAKE TOMSON.
NARED, JON IRON WARD.

Below the names another inscription read:

THEY SERVED OUR CLAN WITH HONOR.
THESE MEN ERSTALLIUS WILL ALWAYS REMEMBER.
160.4.23 - A.E.

"Bril did a good job on this," Arlud said.

"Yes, he did, sir," Danik said. He dropped into the work pod.

Arlud and Eahuda backed away as Danik activated the pod's GPG and rose out of the trailer with the heavy stone held in the pod's grip.

Danik guided the work pod over the grave and hovered there while he set the large stone in the hole Eahuda had dug. He held the stone steady while Arlud and Eahuda filled in the gaps around the granite slab with dirt. They packed the hole and stood back as Danik released the claws. The stone protruded from the ground one meter.

Arlud moved in to check the firmness of the placement. He pushed the stone with his hand. "That's good. It's solid."

Satisfied that the work was done, Danik returned the work pod to the trailer, then drove back toward the maintenance hangar on the far side of the tarmac.

Arlud leaned on his shovel and paused a moment to reflect on those who had died. "They were brave men. They deserved better."

"They were faithful clanmen," Eahuda said. "No better reputation than that."

Arlud nodded. "But they deserved better."

"Success here will justify their loss."

Arlud frowned at that statement. Too often he had heard similar words meant to validate the unjustifiable. "Nothing will justify their loss. Life is a onetime event. You can't take it back or justify a bad ending."

Eahuda scowled at Arlud's rejection of his sentiment. "Bad ending?"

"I failed them, Gus. Every death is a regret, but deaths like these men suffered only bring shame to the clan, and to me."

"You did nothing wrong. You did what needed—"

Arlud raised a hand and silenced Eahuda with the gesture. "You'll not convince me otherwise. Those who died fighting, they died with honor. They sacrificed their lives for us, for the Aku, for Ni'apinu. There is nothing greater we can give to each other. These men died because of my negligence. They are my burden."

Eahuda recognized the futility of trying to talk Arlud out of his self-imposed guilt. "Losing clanmen, for any reason, is one part of command I have never enjoyed. You never get used to it, but you can learn to live with it."

"This will be our memorial area," Arlud said. "We need to create something to honor those who died in orbit. Something simple, but something all who come here will see as they approach the field. I want this gravestone to be at the center."

"Great idea, lad."

"Are you a spiritual man, Gus?"

"I prefer to focus on the here and now."

"Three-thousand years ago, many people believed we live on in another dimension at the whim of our creator."

"Never enough proof of that for me."

"Other people believed we return to dust, and that's the end of our existence."

"A more logical deduction."

Arlud rested his shovel on his right shoulder. "One thing is certain. The dead live on in our memories. We will build them a memorial. They will not be forgotten." He had nothing more to say about the deceased, so he turned toward the tarmac. "We're done here."

Eahuda nodded, and followed Arlud across the tarmac, past a group of parked ciâfey, toward the main hangar.

As they approached the building, Arlud focused on the Aku engineers working on the Guild carrier outside the hangar. Their help had surpassed all his expectations. He wondered if they would have been as accommodating had he seen the need to restore their dead transports before Clan Polinda attacked. Their help may have changed the outcome of the battle and prevented the shuttle crash.

Bril came out of the hangar and waved.

Arlud and Eahuda met the engineer outside the open doorway.

"Our shuttle's docked with the Guild freighter," Bril said. "Pardee should start transferring to a closer orbit in a few hours."

"That's great," Arlud said as he handed Bril his shovel. "Is the comm still open?"

"Yes, but they left the shuttle a few minutes ago to meet with Pardee."

Bril gestured to the display pad on the workbench along the hangar's north wall, then took Eahuda's shovel and veered away toward the tool crib against the back wall of the hangar.

Arlud and Eahuda walked over to the display pad. The shuttle's cockpit camera was pointed toward the vacant pilot seat and looked out the side window, past two empty docking clamps, with the doors to the freighter's interior passageway centered in the camera's field of view.

"We need to set up a direct comm with Pardee," Arlud said.

"Orr should have the channel specifics once he returns to the shuttle," Eahuda said. "Pardee may call us directly after their meeting."

"How do you change this display to show Winny's schematic?"

Eahuda reached over and touched the upper left corner of the pad. The scene changed to the engineering schematic that showed the progress of the transport repair work. Transport One was seventy-eight percent complete, with only the Kottrel Sphere left to finish. Transports Two and Three were at forty percent and transport Four was at twenty percent.

"Wow," Arlud said. "They're getting this done faster than I thought possible."

"The coating will take the most time to complete, but you're right, lad. They may have the first transport up by tomorrow."

"How much duranide did Winny say we will have left once these ships are ready to go?"

"That depends on how the coating progresses. Maybe enough for one or two more. But the fuses are another issue. Bittle said we may have just enough for these four."

Arlud withdrew his transceiver from his pant pocket. "There might me more fuses and duranide in the battle wreckage."

"That'll be dangerous, lad. Lot of debris there."

Arlud nodded as he punched up the code to hail Bittle.

"The traders who left with Orr will most likely stay with Pardee," Eahuda said. "Orr won't be able to retrieve what we need by himself."

"We have time. If Winny thinks it's worth the effort, once the traders are back on course, I'll send Orr up with Danik and Bril to retrieve as much as they can."

CLAN CORMED: ENVOY

The Aku engineers worked through the night to repair the Guild carrier, and the Erstallius clanmen spent the evening arranging quarters inside the central tower for the Cormeds. By morning, all preparations were completed and a contingent of forty Aku soldiers arrived at the outpost to help with security.

Two Guild shuttles landed after breakfast, each leaving fifteen Cormeds at the outpost before launching back into orbit. An hour later, a shuttle returned to the surface with the last sixteen Cormeds on board.

Pallis Nin stepped into the shuttle's open hatchway and noticed the men grouped along the edge of the tarmac a few meters east of the main tower. Three blue-uniformed Erstallius clanmen, one wearing a headset and holding a compad, an Aku soldier, wearing a tan uniform that was less formal than the typical Alliance deportment and presented a combat-ready appearance, and a slim young man clad in a gray long coat.

A three-meter-wide path to the tower's entrance was defined by two rows of Aku soldiers standing at attention with magar-rifles at their sides.

The Erstallius joined with the Aku, Nin thought, and that realization forced caution to surface, and he stalled at the hatchway's threshold. Even though the Aku presence appeared to be nothing more than typical ceremonial respect for another clan, he felt an underlying dread with so many soldiers guarding the path.

Nin's immobile stance brought immediate consternation from the other passengers. Pressed from behind, he jerked into motion, bounded down the entry ramp, and proceeded at a leisurely pace between the lines of Aku soldiers. The other fifteen Cormed clanmen followed him down the ramp single file, a silent procession of beleaguered survivors.

Gustav Eahuda leaned next to Arlud. "There he is. The short one in front with long blond hair."

Arlud spied the man. He was the only Cormed who did not wear the black clan uniform. "The envoy," Arlud said to Salus.

At a gesture from Salus, two Aku soldiers broke the line, stopped the envoy and escorted him to a few paces in front of Gustav Eahuda.

Eahuda asked: "You are the envoy for Clan Cormed?"

Nin stood straight and looked at the old degen. "Yes. I am Pallis Nin, Special Envoy for Clan Cormed. Thank you for allowing us to disembark." He glanced over at the Aku soldiers as they began dispersing toward the central tower once the last Cormed clanman entered the building. "May I meet with your regent?"

"I am Regent," Arlud said.

Nin shifted his gaze to Arlud and raised an eyebrow. "Forgive my surprise. I was expecting someone older."

"Most people do."

"You are Armand's son?"

Arlud tipped his head. "Arlud Reynaldo Erstallius, Regent of GSW-183, and Protector of Ni'apinu."

Nin moved to stand before Arlud.

"Your people will be housed here a few days," Arlud said. "I expect they will be civil. Belligerence will not be tolerated."

Nin bowed. "You will have no problems from us."

"Our fleet is scheduled to arrive in a few days. We will arrange passage for you to Roth-513 after they arrive."

"Thank you."

Nin stepped forward and extended his right hand.

Arlud stopped an auto response to feint left, away from the advance, when he saw no threat in the movement. He reached out and clasped the envoy's hand.

Nin tightened his grip and said in hushed tones: "Now you have all the information you need."

He withdrew his hand and retreated toward the building.

Arlud flicked a hand signal to the Aku soldiers that allowed Nin to leave. They turned and followed the envoy toward the tower.

Eahuda was puzzled. "What did he mean by that?"

Arlud looked down at his palm and showed Eahuda what Nin had given him—a small blue memory chip the size of a thumbnail.

Eahuda twisted to watch the envoy disappear into the building.

"Here, Gus," Arlud said. "Take this and find out what's on it."

The old degen focused on Arlud's outstretched hand and accepted the chip. "Right." He turned and headed for the open hangar.

Arlud pondered what Nin had done. *A clandestine transfer of data.* That told him there were divisions among the Cormeds. The need for stealth exposed fear of something, or someone. By Nin's own admission, the data would reveal all he needed to know.

"I would like a guard posted at all times," Arlud said to Salus.

Salus nodded. "My soldiers will stay until they are no longer necessary."

The hatchway on the Guild shuttle swung shut. The aircraft rumbled to life, rose off the tarmac, and banked toward the dark wall of trees to the south.

"We have one more incoming from orbit," Danik said. He stood at Arlud's right side, wearing the headset and holding a compad at chest height. He fingered the pad as he analyzed the data stream. "Our shuttle."

Arlud did not expect that. "Orr was supposed to pick up Shanna and Cordova at Kuliq'Quad."

Danik nodded. "Yeah, he was." He sent Orr a text hail and asked why he had changed course.

Orr replied via a secure channel.

"He's got Erlis Pardee on board," Danik said.

"The Guild captain?"

Danik nodded. "He requested a private meeting with you."

Arlud was surprised by that revelation, and he was thrown into a mental whirlwind of possibilities. *To leave his ship portends a terrible necessity.* "What's their E.T.A.?"

Danik reviewed the data on his pad. "About fourteen minutes."

"OK," Arlud said. "Have him escorted to the hangar. In the meantime, I'll see what Gus has discovered on Nin's chip." He stepped away from the group toward the hangar. "Bril, you come with me."

Bril fell into step behind Arlud and followed him across the tarmac.

By the time Arlud and Bril had reached Eahuda inside the hangar, the old degen had reviewed the info from Nin's chip and had the most incriminating data open on the display pad.

Arlud asked, "What've we got, Gus?"

Eahuda pointed to the open video. "Cormed killing Cormed." He set the video in motion and the recording of Grom Anen shooting Duncun Turl played within a small window on the pad.

"They accused him of treason," Eahuda said. "There are other clips of beatings of clanmen who disagreed with Farvic's decision to take Pardee's ship. He had his own rebellion to subdue. That slowed their progress, and before they could take control of any major system, Pardee vented the cargo bay. The surrounding corridors and compartments were then open to the vacuum. Of the one hundred and six Cormeds rescued, only forty-six survived the purge."

"Farvic was a fool," Arlud said.

Eahuda nodded agreement. "He thought if he had Shanna, Pardee would not vent the cargo bay out of fear of killing her. But according to this info, Pardee knew Shanna had been placed in the damaged carrier in the shuttle bay. It was Pardee who had the carrier forced off his ship."

"Pardee did that?"

"Remote release of the docking clamps, hatch open without decompression, and the carrier was blown out. That saved the girl's life."

"And it removed the only advantage Farvic had."

"Grom Anen is still alive," Eahuda said. "I think Nin wants us to arrest him."

"How many command officers survived?"

"According to this, just Anen, and the chief medical, Jarred Molska."

Arlud turned away from the display pad. "We have enough problems. We don't need this added complication." He took a few steps toward the open hangar door and watched the shuttle approach over the tree line to the east.

"We can ignore it," Eahuda said. "It's a Cormed issue. Let them deal with it when they return to Roth-513."

"Nin will expect action," Arlud said, and he faced Eahuda. "The Alliance charter demands a response. It's a legal issue between clans."

Eahuda had not read the official charter in decades, but he remembered something about clan response when criminal activity was perpetrated by clanmen in the jurisdiction of another clan. "Can't we let the arbitrators debate it? Besides, the crime was not committed here. It happened on board a Guild ship, and last I heard, the Guild is not an Alliance clan."

"It happened in our territory," Arlud said. "PDN160 is our territory now. That includes the entire system. That's the way the arbitrators will view it."

"Damn the arbitrators."

The hollow roar of the approaching shuttle diverted Arlud's attention outside the hangar. The vessel had entered the landing path and was out of sight above the tarmac. Arlud walked to the hangar doorway and spied the shuttle hovering about one hundred meters up, rotating to align with the ground markers. As the vessel began her final descent, Arlud turned toward Eahuda. "After I hear what Pardee has to say, I'll decide what to do about the Cormeds."

CLAN ERSTALLIUS: UNEXPECTED

Danik and Eahuda stood guard outside the hangar doorway with two guildmen who came with Erlis Pardee in the Erstallius shuttle. Arlud and Pardee sat on stools next to the workbench, with the display pad within reach for data retrieval and analysis.

Arlud watched while the recording of the attacks on the *Javelin* and *Iron Spear* played on the display pad.

Pardee sat with his back to the replay. He had seen it many times and found the activity outside the hangar more interesting.

The Erstallius shuttle rumbled to life, rose a few meters off the tarmac, and turned to align her nose to the southeast. With a sudden thud, she rushed upward and disappeared into low-hanging clouds.

"That's Orr," Arlud said. "He's going to Kuliq'Quad to get Lady Sy and Cordova."

Pardee turned and saw the replay had ended. He gestured to the display pad. "Well, what do you make of it?"

"No one knows what that was?"

"Correct. Whatever it is, we have nothing that can stop it."

"Then why did it stop?"

"The data doesn't tell us much, but I believe it stopped because it saw a different path."

Arlud drew back at that statement. "What?"

"There's intelligence behind it. That much should be obvious. I think it stopped because it either realized it didn't need to continue, or it realized it had made a mistake."

Arlud leaned forward on his stool. "And you know this because?"

"It stopped, and that's evidence there was a decision made that spared the *Iron Spear*."

"A decision by whom?"

"Degen Turl thought it was aliens. Einar Duballik felt it was a new breed of human. The other survivors lean toward Einar's opinion, but no one really knows."

"Aliens?"

"Because of the dreams."

"Dreams?"

"Einar survived the initial assault and began experiencing very detailed dreams about a dying woman trapped in a cave."

"That connection is a bit of a stretch, don't you think?"

"My first impression," Pardee admitted. "And then I learned the same dream was had by three of the *Javelin*'s crew. A dream is probably not the best way to describe it. Our brains are visual computers. We see mental images when we think about things we have experienced. The images we see are based on our individual perspective. We can improve our memories by creating a mental image filing system in our minds—a technique taught at many Alliance schools."

Arlud nodded, remembering his own training.

"So," Pardee continued, "instead of dreams, think of a mental image transfer. Somehow, four survivors on the *Javelin* all began seeing the same mental images after the attack." He reached over to the display pad and activated another data file. "Look at this."

On screen, the file opened to reveal a collection of four brain wave scans stacked one above the other. Blue lines punctuated with red markers against a white background.

"These are scans from the four who reported having the unusual dreams," Pardee said. "Fortunately, we got this info before the Cormeds tried to take my ship. All these men are dead now."

Arlud leaned toward the display. He had not been trained to read this data, but it was easy to see something unusual was recorded. The markers identified intervening wave patterns for the entire length of each scan. "I take it these waves are not normally seen?"

"Correct," Pardee said. "They indicate a wave that interrupted normal brain wave frequencies. My physician believes these patterns are influenced by an outside source."

"And the dream sequence was the same for each person?"

"Einar told me he saw a little more information each time he had the experience—as if each dream advanced a preset storyline. The interviews with the Cormed crewmen showed the same was true for them. You can review all that info. It's here in this file."

"If we accept this scenario as true, how is a woman dying while trapped in a cave connected to the attack on Alliance frigates?"

Pardee shrugged. "I have no idea—it's more complicated than that. Somehow, the Polinda mine disaster is related to this."

"How?"

"The unknown attacker. The frigates were attacked on the rim of the PDN198 system, just a little more than a parsec from Alpha Cephei Four. Based on the info we got from the Cormeds, a force similar to what hit the frigates tore through the mine like hot metal through butter."

Arlud's mind whirled with possibilities, and a new concern flooded his thoughts. "If that's true, then we've much more to fear than Polinda."

"Yes, much more."

"What do you suggest we do?"

"As an Alliance member, you can get access to the Polinda investigation. What they've uncovered should help us understand what we need to do."

"That won't happen. You saw for yourself the wreckage of our last meeting with Polinda forces. We expect they'll be coming back."

"Polinda must be forced to acknowledge your innocence."

Arlud chuckled. "Yes, he should, but nothing will deter him. We'll get nowhere near Alpha Cephei Four without a major battle."

"Send him a drone with the information I've brought you."

"We can do that, but I doubt it will stay his course."

"Every clan in this district needs to know about this. Polinda will back down once he recognizes the real threat."

"Under different circumstances, I would agree with you, but time is not on our side. If a drone is sent to all the clans in this district, it will take at least a month to get a response from everyone, and by then Polinda will have already attacked us again. I expect him to arrive sometime next week."

Pardee swiveled toward the display pad. "Then your fleet will need to stop him." He opened a file on the pad that presented a three-dimensional graphic of the local Alliance district, with the location of the attack against the Cormed ships marked with a small red sphere. "Look at this," he said. "Here is Alpha Cephei Four. Here is where the *Javelin* was destroyed. If the path continues true, the next attack could happen anywhere along this line."

A blue line appeared, beginning at Alpha Cephei Four, that pierced the red sphere and continued unobstructed through the district.

Arlud noticed the blue line went past Ni'apinu toward U'galem. He stood and paced a few steps toward the back wall of the hangar. If that line marked the true path, Ni'apinu could face attacks from both Polinda and the unknown assailant. And then he remembered what Milos Fore had told him. He faced Pardee and said: "Survivors."

"Survivors?"

Arlud straddled the stool again. "A Cormed envoy stopped here to deliver the news about the mine disaster. He had survivors from the mine on his ship. He was taking them to U'galem."

Pardee saw the implication. "The attacker is following the survivors?"

"Possibly," Arlud said. "If you're correct about the mine and the mental images, then one or more of the survivors could have formed a lasting connection with the attacker, and the attacker is following them to keep the connection. Are you sure this path is correct?"

"No, I'm not sure," Pardee admitted. "Until they appear again, it's the best guess."

"If they're following the mine survivors, and the dreams pass more information each time they occur—"

Pardee sat up straight. "Then those survivors may know more about what's going on and why."

Arlud nodded and noticed a sudden spark of hope in Pardee's expression. This Free Trader had surprised him. He had expected outrage from the man, not calm reflection. "I had visions of you coming down here screaming about the Cormeds. I did not expect this."

Pardee leaned back against the workbench. "The Cormed situation is over. No use dwelling on the past. What's done is done."

"I'm not so sure I could toss aside my anger that easily."

Pardee shrugged. "I've learned to focus. Besides, this situation threatens everyone. The Cormed incident was just a minor scuffle by comparison."

Arlud looked at the map on the display pad. He was leaning toward Degen Turl's opinion. This attacker was more alien than human. The facts contradicted normal human logic and strategy. There was no human technology that could transfer insurgents beneath the surface of a planet. There was no human technology that could both hide from sensors and burn through the hull of an Alliance warship. "We need to find the mine survivors. After our fleet arrives, I'll send a ship to U'galem."

"Good," Pardee said. "Spread the word about this any way you can, as quickly as you can."

"And what are your plans?"

"I'll take Shanna and her mother to their intended destination. Wolfram will meet us there."

That statement from Pardee revealed the unspoken possibility that Al-Phaq had been abandoned, and Arlud wondered: *Has Wolfram fled?* He sat upright on his stool. "Wolfram Sy is a man of great insight. I would like to meet him one day."

"He will enjoy meeting you. You helped save his daughter."

With that acknowledgment, Arlud reached over to the pad and closed Pardee's map. "I need to show you something," he said, and he activated the data from Pallis Nin's chip.

By early afternoon, the temperature dropped ten degrees and gray clouds filled the sky above the landing field. A light breeze greeted Shanna Sy and Ross Cordova as they disembarked from the Erstallius shuttle, bundled in light brown long-coats and klâwpa-skin boots given to them by their Aku hosts.

Shanna step off the exit ramp and voiced her displeasure: "Why did he put us down so far from the carrier?"

They were at the extreme southwest edge of the landing field. The Guild carrier was parked one hundred meters away, outside the open hangar.

Cordova brushed alongside Shanna and placed his arm on her back as they walked from the shuttle. "All landing fields have rules about traffic. Where to land and where to launch. It's a safety thing."

"Then why did we land closer to the hangar last time?"

"Because the tarmac was empty, and we had no direction from flight control. We set down at Bern's whim."

"Oh." Shanna frowned. The air was cold against her face, and the threat of rain made her uneasy—she still felt vulnerable in the open. The thought of the enclosed comfort inside the distant carrier caused her to quicken her pace.

Cordova separated from Shanna and advanced a step in front of her, an old habit that belied his training as a personal guard. "There's Pardee."

"Where?"

"There, standing next to the Erstallius Regent, by the boarding ramp."

Shanna looked past Cordova's broad shoulders and spied Pardee. The old trader stood a head taller than the Erstallius Regent. Both men were draped in gray long-coats. Shanna flashed a brief grin. "Wonderful," she said to herself. As she and Cordova walked past the cluster of ciâfey parked in the center of the tarmac, she noticed the Aku guards standing watch outside the central tower. "Is that where the Cormeds are being kept?"

"Probably," Cordova said. "No need to concern yourself with that."

Ten paces from the carrier's port side boarding ramp, Shanna burst into a wide grin, rushed past Cordova, and stopped in front of Pardee. "I am so glad to see you!"

Pardee extended his hands in a wide greeting, then brought them together in front of his waist. "You're safe now," he said. "Time to get you back on board."

Shanna reached forward and cradled Pardee's hands for a moment, then pulled away and clasped her hands together at her chest. "How is Mother?"

"Madame Sy is fine. She misses you."

Cordova moved to Shanna's side. "Time to board, lady."

"Now that we're here, don't rush me."

Cordova backed a step and nodded once in obedience to Shanna's mild reproof.

"And here you are," Shanna said, as she stepped sideways to stand in front of Arlud. "Erstallius Regent, a friend of the Aku, and the comrade of pirates!"

Arlud was surprised by that description, and it left him speechless.

"Didn't they tell you?" Shanna asked in a lilting tone. "Free Traders are pirates, just ask my father."

Pardee flashed a stern look at Cordova, then: "Lady, the Erstallius—"

"I know," Shanna said in her soft contralto. She reached out and held Arlud's head in her hands, leaned forward, and kissed his cheek.

Arlud stiffened against the unsolicited gesture, then relaxed as the young woman's lips left his cheek and her hands left his head with a soft caress. He felt his face flush.

Shanna stepped back with a wide grin. "You surprised me, Arlud Reynaldo Erstallius. I will not forget all that you have done for us. My Father will enjoy hearing the tale of how an Alliance clan sided with pirates."

Arlud cleared his throat and found his voice. "Not pirates," he said. "Free Traders."

Shanna nodded with a smile, then turned and walked up the carrier's entry ramp.

"My apologies," Pardee said. "I did not expect that attitude from her. She is usually much more reserved."

"Not a problem."

Cordova moved forward and paused in front of Arlud. "I think she favors you. Are you prepared for that?"

Before Arlud could answer, Cordova turned with a grin and followed Shanna into the carrier.

Arlud faced Pardee. "What did he mean by that?"

"That girl has kissed no one, except her father and mother, until now."

Arlud disregarded any implied infatuation. "She's been through a lot. I'm glad she appreciates what we've done here. Your respect for us has also not gone unnoticed. I hope Wolfram will recognize not all clans view the Guild as a den of pirates."

"Everyone stands on their own merit in our universe," Pardee said. "You, Erstallius, stand very well." He pulled a transceiver out of his coat pocket and brought it to his lips. "Do it now."

The rear cargo ramp opened on the carrier and settled to the tarmac.

Arlud raised his transceiver. "We're ready, Bril."

Bril drove one of the small utility cars onto the tarmac from behind the main tower. He pulled a trailer that appeared empty from a distance, but as he neared the carrier, Arlud could see a blue tarp covering the lumpy contents.

"Pull up to the rear ramp," Arlud said, as he gestured to Bril. He pocketed his transceiver and walked back toward the ramp, followed by Pardee.

"They will be surprised," Pardee said.

"Yes, they'll have a rude awakening."

Bril maneuvered the car and stopped when the back end of the trailer faced the loading ramp.

Two guildmen scrambled down the boarding ramp and pulled the tarp in the trailer aside, revealing three Cormed clanmen. The Cormeds lay side by side, bound, gagged, and unconscious. The thick gray rope that secured their feet also restrained their hands to their waists. The large leather gags that covered their mouths cupped their chins and prevented jaw movement.

Pardee stopped alongside the trailer and viewed the sedated clanmen. He turned to his comrades. "Make sure Shanna doesn't see them."

Both guildmen nodded at Pardee's command and lifted the first Cormed out of the trailer and hauled him up the ramp.

Arlud examined the two men remaining in the trailer. "Are you sure this is necessary?"

"Absolutely," Pardee said. "I am taking no chances with these scoundrels."

Arlud had agreed to allow Pardee to take Grom Anen and the other two remaining supporters of Farvic's revolt as a courtesy to the Cormed envoy. Pallis Nin was worried Anen would stir up more trouble if he stayed with the other survivors.

This removes my hand in the matter, Arlud thought, *and gives Pardee the opportunity to retaliate in full for the crimes Farvic and his followers committed on his ship*. Deep in his heart he knew it was the correct thing to do, even though Eahuda had protested.

"It's vigilante justice," Eahuda had said. "You're giving the criminal over to the victim for trial. Pardee will just vent them. Where's the justice in that?"

"Where's the justice for the men Farvic killed?" Arlud had responded. "Where's the justice for the innocent guildmen who died? Farvic took Pardee's hospitality and spit it back in his face. Would any clan look favorably upon such a despicable deed?"

Eahuda acquiesced to Arlud's logic. Anen and his two supporters were criminals and had to be punished.

The second sedated Cormed was hauled into the carrier.

"Wolfram will see this as a gift," Pardee said. "You have brought much favor upon yourself this day."

"This deed satisfies the needs of many. It had to be done."

Pardee stepped forward and extended his right hand.

Arlud clenched Pardee's hand with a tight grip.

"You're a good man, Erstallius," Pardee said. "I am very glad we could talk. I hope you fare well against Polinda."

"May your journey be swift."

Pardee withdrew his hand as the two guildmen lifted the last Cormed out of the trailer. "I believe Cordova may be right," he said, as he turned toward the ramp. "Shanna favors you." He grinned and followed the guildmen into the carrier.

Arlud stood on the tenth floor of the central tower and surveyed the landscape through the unfinished windows. He contemplated Cordova's assertion that Shanna was infatuated with him, and the memory of her kiss washed over him. *She's definitely alluring,* he thought. *Danik had been attracted to her like a fly to sugar.* That quality made her more intriguing, but he knew deep inside she was not the girl for him. *Her infatuation will fade with distance and time, but I must tread carefully if I see her again.*

He dropped his gaze to the landing field.

The Guild carrier had left more than an hour ago. The tarmac was deserted save for the small cluster of ciâfey parked inside the central landing circle. The shuttle was secure inside the maintenance hangar and was going through a quick system check before leaving again for Kuliq'Quad. From his vantage point, Arlud could see the forested hills to the south where his shuttle had crashed, and beyond that dark undulating barrier, the rocky scarps of the Dekeg mountains formed a jagged, snow-capped line along the horizon.

There is so much here on Ni'apinu, he thought. *A pristine, natural environment ready to explore.* He wondered how many settlements the Aku had built out of this wilderness. The smaller villages were built in harmony with the land and were very difficult to detect from orbit.

As he surveyed the surrounding landscape, he could not help wondering if the Aku friendship with his clan would be short-lived. He found it difficult to believe the Aku would betray his trust, but Gus had questioned their sincerity, and that had created a nagging doubt that called out from the depths of his mind: *When they no longer need us, will they evict us?*

Arlud's transceiver beeped for attention. He raised the small rectangular device to his lips. "Yes?"

"Bittle here, sir, with an update."

"Winny, I was hoping to hear from you. Everything going well?"

"Yes, sir. Transport One is complete and will begin system checks ASAP. If everything goes well, she should be flight certified by tomorrow. Transport Two is midway through coating. Transport Three has just begun coating. Transport Four will finish coating in two days."

"That's good news. Good job."

"Thank you, sir. We're doing our best."

"What do you think about sending up the shuttle to retrieve duranide and fuses from the wreckage?"

"I analyzed the data Pardee sent us, and it is possible, but it will be too risky using the shuttle. To do it properly, we would need to clear the debris and that would take weeks, even with the proper equipment. Orr and his crew would be in constant danger."

"I'd like you to plot the most accessible course through the wreckage, with target points for each cache of material. Once Orr has had time to review that, I'll let him make the final decision."

"Sir, Orr is a good pilot, but the time we have limits what we can safely do."

"I understand, Winny. Plot the course and get it to me as soon as possible."

Bittle hesitated to respond as he thought of options.

"Winny?"

"Yes, sir," the old engineer replied. "I should have that to you by morning. Complicated calculations."

"Thank you," Arlud said. He ended his connection with Bittle and dropped his transceiver into his coat pocket. Winny was always *safety first,* but they needed to take chances if they were to even the odds against Polinda. If Orr had an issue with the plan, Arlud would honor his decision, but he hoped the pilot's bravery would override caution.

The Erstallius shuttle arrived at Kuliq'Quad before the sun had crept above the eastern rim of the basin. Jens Orr landed the small craft on the northern side of the Mánu, a few meters from the edge of the tarmac. The Erstallius clanmen disembarked into the gray shadow of the granite rim wall, bundled against the chill air.

The first change Arlud noticed as he exited the shuttle was the open sky above the transports. The blue tarps had been removed, and their support beams sagged outward from the lack of tension. As he neared Transport Two, he noticed more activity around the other ships, and hazard warning blocks set up in a ring enclosing the landing pads of Transport One.

Grénu and Winstone Bittle met Arlud and his crew beside the port landing pad of Transport Two, and Bittle pulled Arlud aside for a private conversation.

"Transport Two's primary weapon has a malfunction," Bittle said, "and it will take weeks to determine what's causing the failure due to the complexity of the system. I'm not sure how it works."

"Are the Aku hiding details from you?"

Bittle shook his head. "No, that's not it. The Aku don't even know how the damn thing works."

"That's not good. What about schematics, diagrams, instructions?"

"That part of the manual seems to be missing. Seelay designed those weapons and apparently kept most of the inner workings to himself. They're connected to the main drive, but how the energy is directed internally is problematic. We need to place the primary weapons on our potential hazard list. I won't feel safe using them until we can resolve the issues with Transport Two."

"But they're working correctly on Transport One?"

"They seem to check out, but we won't test fire them until we're in orbit. And I really don't want to do that until we know more about them."

"We don't have the time to be extra careful."

"I know, sir, but—"

Arlud raised a hand to silence Bittle. "I understand your concerns. We'll move forward with no primary weapon on Transport Two. I assume the secondaries are working?"

"Yes, they check out fine. But they weren't designed for modern combat. They're magars designed to defend against small, one or two-man attack craft. Against one of Polinda's destroyers, they'll be no more effective than throwing a rock against an alsteel plate."

Arlud envisioned the crater that would form in a moldable steel plate if hit by a high-speed projectile. The impact concussion would rebound through the material and result in a depression surrounded by concentric ridges, like the pattern formed in water when hit by a stone. The primary weapons would be the only effective offense against Polinda. "I'll take responsibility if anything happens in orbit when we test the primary on Transport One. It must be done. If Grénu wants to halt testing, then so be it. It will be his call. Otherwise, plan on it."

"Yes, sir."

Bittle felt deflated by Arlud's decision. He never enjoyed ignoring safety procedures. He understood the reasons, but still did not like it. He reached into his coat and pulled out a rectangular memory chip. "This is for Orr."

Arlud signaled Orr to join him, and Bittle passed the young pilot the chip.

"Review all the approach vectors," Bittle said. "You'll see how constrained your course will need to be, and remember, the course is based on data that is constantly changing."

"I'll honor whatever decision you make," Arlud said.

An hour later, Orr, Danik, and Bril put on their pale blue environment suits, and left in the shuttle for the entangled wreckage of the Erstallius frigate and Polinda destroyer orbiting twenty-thousand kilometers from the surface. Their journey took two hours to reach the outer rim of debris, more time than a normal trip of that distance because Orr needed to track the real time positions of the material in the debris cloud.

"We should be able to reach this location," Orr said, as he pointed to a course icon on his plotting screen in the cockpit.

Bril looked intently at the position marker. It was twenty meters off the intact starboard hull of the frigate that protruded from the destroyer. Most of the rubble there were fragments smaller than a meter, mixed with fine dust particles.

"Getting there will be tricky," Bril said. He pointed to the many jagged sections of hull plating that rotated in small orbits around each other and continued to collide with smaller shrapnel from the initial impact.

"It's doable," Orr said.

Bril sat back on his couch. "You're the pilot."

"No fancy stuff," Danik said from the rear gun station. "Just get us there in one piece."

Orr turned around to face Danik. "No worries. Just keep an eye out for large incoming."

Danik nodded. Using the guns to blast large debris would make the situation worse, so he had readjusted the rails to throw projectiles at a lower-than-normal speed. With the right amount of energy, the projectiles would push incoming threats to the shuttle into different orbits without shattering them into smaller pieces or accelerating them to dangerous speeds.

Orr guided the shuttle into the debris cloud and thirty minutes later, after a few bumps and dings, and one encounter with the dead body of an Erstallius clanman, he brought the small craft within five meters of the wreck's starboard hull, matching speed and rotation to hold a position near an intact airlock.

Bril and Danik pushed out into the expanse and floated free through the cloud of dust particles and entered the wreckage through the airlock.

"We're in," Bril said.

Orr watched the transmission of Bril's suit camera on the display screen in the cockpit. "I see it. Good hunting."

As Bril and Danik searched the wreckage for fuses and duranide, Orr monitored the area for debris threats and sent update transmissions to the surface every fifteen minutes. An hour into the search, a comdrone signal interrupted his routine. The bleep from the TAC receiver caused him to switch frequencies and focus on the new transmission.

> "Alert . . . Alert . . . Alert."

Orr switched to his headset.

> "This is Guild Freighter One-Nine-Seven. Armada detected approaching GSW-183 from AC4, heading 2.43.48 by 15.02.34."
>
> "Alert . . . Alert . . . Alert."
>
> "This is Guild Freighter One-Nine-Seven. Armada detected approaching GSW-183 from AC4, heading 2.43.48 by 15.02.34."

The message continued to repeat.

Orr tracked the drone as it swung in an arc past his position and headed out of the system toward the expected direction of the Erstallius reinforcement fleet. He switched to the remote sensor pallet and focused on the heading stated in the message.

"Damn!"

Arlud gathered with Bittle and Eahuda inside one of the service buildings on the eastern edge of the Mánu. They moved into a meeting room that had a small round table at its center, rimmed with stiff wooden chairs. The north wall had single page paper documents written in Akün pinned to a large wooden board. A waist high shelf ran along the east wall and supported testing equipment used by the plasma containment engineers.

Arlud pulled out a chair. "Do the others know where to meet us?"

Eahuda nodded.

Bittle paced along the wall opposite the doorway. Arlud sat on the chair as Sitlyn, Sieger, and Pyle walked into the room. "Polinda has arrived," he said. "Much earlier than I expected."

"Earlier than any of us expected," Eahuda said.

Bittle withdrew his display pad, placed it on the table, and gestured to those standing to gather around to view the evidence.

The static-filled image of two dreadnoughts was undeniable.

"So here we stand," Arlud said. "With no fleet to protect us, and only one transport able to defend us."

"Two transports," Bittle said.

Arlud shot his chief engineer a quizzical glance.

"By the time Polinda reaches us," Bittle explained, "we will have two of the transports in orbit."

"Gnats against lions," Eahuda said.

"Careful," Arlud retorted, "don't let the natives hear you say that."

"I live in reality, lad. What are we going to do?"

Arlud stood. None of his clanmen saw success in this moment. He needed to pull them together. He needed to stifle their doubt and calm their fear.

"Polinda is being cautious," Bittle said.

All eyes in the room focused on the old engineer.

Bittle continued his assessment: "He's approached this system and detected the wreckage, but he can find no Erstallius armada, and no massive Aku deployments. The Aku reputation alone will cause him to tread lightly at first. He'll scan the system and devise his best attack plan, but he won't rush forward until he's certain his opposition is at a disadvantage."

"And discovering how weak we are," Eahuda said, "will take time."

Arlud folded his arms across his chest. "How much time?"

"Maybe twelve hours if we're lucky," Bittle said.

Arlud grinned. "We create our own luck. When you're outnumbered, the best defense is to run away."

Sitlyn moved closer to Arlud. "How are we going to do that, sir?"

"We won't," Arlud said. "I will."

Eahuda scoffed at that statement. "What?"

"We've more than just ourselves to think about. We've pledged to protect Ni'apinu, and I see only one way to do that under the circumstances."

Bittle scowled. "By running away?"

"Exactly," Arlud said. He saw confusion in everyone's eyes, and now that he had them focused on the same idea, he explained his plan: "Polinda is here to retaliate. To finish what his clanmen failed to do a few weeks ago. He is here to destroy Clan Erstallius. On GSW-183, I above everyone else represent Clan Erstallius. I am Erstallius. I will be the decoy that leads him away from this system."

Eahuda could not keep his sarcasm in check. "And just how do you plan on doing that?"

"Transport Two."

"Madness," Eahuda said in an undertone, but loud enough so Arlud could hear him.

"That madness will pull Polinda away from here," Arlud said. "I'll need the Aku to agree, but it is the only option. If I can get most of Polinda's force to follow me, the Aku may have a chance against the ships that remain."

"If Polinda leaves a dreadnought in orbit," Bittle said, "the Aku fight won't last long."

"Facing one dreadnought is better than facing two."

Sitlyn stepped toward Arlud. "Where would you go?"

"I'll lead him into a fleet."

"He'll see that," Eahuda said. "He won't take that bait."

"He'd follow me into the sun if he thought that would destroy me forever. Polinda runs on revenge and greed. His greed will see the advantage in keeping Ni'apinu safe if he feels he can claim it for his own.

His revenge will feed the chase. He will rush after me knowing his superior force can easily defeat me."

Bittle stepped between Pyle and Sitlyn to face Arlud. "And defeat you he will, if he catches you."

"Then I will have to make sure he doesn't."

"I don't see it," Sitlyn said. "I agree with Eahuda. He'll see a trap."

"He may," Arlud said, "if he doesn't believe what he sees first."

Sitlyn placed her hands on her hips. "What does he see first?"

"Clan Cormed in charge of our outpost."

There was a brief silence as everyone pondered that revelation.

"The Cormeds," Eahuda said. "That's brilliant!"

"Mister Nin may hesitate to partake in such a ruse," Arlud said, "but he'll eventually agree to the subterfuge. If Polinda attacks us, the Cormeds will suffer too."

Bittle liked the plan. "If the Erstallius are not here, then Polinda has no reason to attack."

"But he knows we came here," Arlud said. "My departure will cause him to believe our defeat at the hands of his clanmen forced us to transfer the outpost to the Cormeds."

"Then he'll follow you," Bittle said. "Like a lion hunting prey."

"Yes," Arlud said, "and Ni'apinu and everyone on it will be safe."

CLAN POLINDA: TYRANT

The Command Intelligence Center on board the Polinda dreadnought *Venka Kinall* was a terraced, circular pit with three levels. The floor of the pit housed the hologram emitter that projected three-dimensional maps used to plot ship positions and devise combat strategy. The glowing hologram now displayed the PDN160 system, both the primary sun and her smaller companion, all eight planets, and their larger moons. The bottom terrace held stations manned by systems control personnel. Fleet officers sat at stations around the second terrace, where they analyzed incoming sensor data. The top terrace was reserved for fleet commanders and clan regents in charge of operations, but on this day only Farquar Polinda occupied a command station.

Farquar always kept himself and his command personnel separated; a habit instilled in him during his youth. Separation removed the threat of favoritism and kept his commanders on the same level beneath him. No one had special access. Everyone needed to perform their duties well to assure the patriarch's favor.

Under the cool light from the holomap, Farquar reviewed his armada's encroachment of the PDN160 system. The *Venka Kinall* had crossed the heliosphere two hours ago with two destroyers and two frigates. They had just crossed the orbit of the blue gas giant and were about two hours out from GSW-183 at their current speed. Three destroyers had taken positions five million kilometers above GSW-183 to guard the northern flank. Two destroyers and three frigates were on course to reach their way point four million kilometers south of GSW-183. The dreadnought *Nero Leru* was on the opposite side of the system, just inside the heliosphere, with two destroyers and a frigate to block a retreat toward the Erstallius homeworld.

We have them surrounded, Farquar thought, and a malicious grin formed on his face.

The only cause for concern had been the comdrone that had flown through the system from an unknown source. Farquar analyzed the drone's sweeping path projected in the map. If the drone had transmitted a message, it had been a directional signal that was not detected by his armada. They had tried to plot the drone's path of origin, but whoever sent it was too far away to detect.

The only Erstallius ships detected were the wrecks from the previous battle. That was an odd situation that forced the Polinda commanders to urge caution, but Farquar saw it as an invitation to proceed at a swifter pace.

"I understand your concern," Farquar said. He turned to face the image of Jegen Marlow on the small holoscreen to his right.

Jegen Marlow's round face filled the screen. He had puffy gray eyes and receding black hair. "Then you agree to send in the frigates first?"

"We will attack full force," Farquar said. "No hesitation. All destroyers are to proceed to targets at my command."

Jegen Marlow's face did not reveal his dislike of that order. He tipped his head. "Yes, sir. I will send word to all commanders."

Farquar sat back as Marlow's image winked out, and he took in the luminous beauty of the map floating in the pit. The Erstallius showed no sign of being on alert, and he thought: *This campaign will be over quickly—a surprise Armand will never forget.*

The TAC receiver on Farquar's comm panel bleeped for attention. He hit the switch that activated another holoscreen in front of his seat.

The image of Pallis Nin formed on the new screen. His long blond hair was pulled back behind his shoulders, and he carried a slight smile. "Greetings from Clan Cormed," he said. "Welcome to GSW-183. Our landing field is closed until further notice. If you need to enter orbit for repairs, please submit your request using our standard Port Service form, which you can find included in this transmission." The Seal of Clan Cormed replaced Nin's image, a fiery, golden torch with white wings floating above a dark gray circle upon a silver shield.

Farquar chuckled and pushed a comm button to hail Jegen Marlow.

Marlow's image reappeared on the screen to Farquar's right. "Yes, sir?"

"What is this Cormed rubbish?"

"We traced the transmission to GSW-183. It's prerecorded. The announcer is Pallis Nin, special envoy for Clan Cormed."

"Ridiculous! Does Erstallius really expect me to believe Cormed is in charge here? Reply via TAC for a live chat. There is no longer any need for stealth."

"Yes, sir," Marlow said, and his holoscreen image blinked off.

Farquar wondered how long his armada's presence had been known. Each ship had proceeded to their assigned positions, and stealth had been maintained. *I've underestimated Erstallius capabilities.*

The live connection took a few minutes to secure, and Marlow appeared again with the frequency information. "Set your TAC channel to 78.93, sir. Nin is live."

Farquar entered the numbers and Nin appeared on the screen in front of him, this time wearing less formal clothing, and his hair was draped over both shoulders.

"Mister Nin," Farquar said. "Please explain how Clan Cormed now rules on GSW-183."

"Mister Polinda," Nin said. "You routed the Erstallius. Surely you have detected the wreckage. If you have come here to make sure the Erstallius were defeated, I can assure you they were. Your assault left only nine survivors."

"Nine?" Farquar rubbed his left cheek. "If there was one Erstallius survivor on GSW-183, it would still be an Erstallius holding."

"Because of post battle circumstances, the regent transferred control of the system to us. He felt that was best since our support systems are much closer and would allow the holding to remain under Alliance control."

"The regent?"

"Yes," Nin said. "Arlud Erstallius."

"Arlud?" Farquar restrained his excitement.

"He left with the remaining Erstallius about an hour ago. You just missed him."

Farquar scowled. "We detected no ship leaving the system."

"You destroyed their frigates. The Aku lent him a transport."

"Aku?"

Nin nodded. "Small ship. Easy to miss if you're not expecting—"

Nin's voice and image faded behind a sudden flood of static.

Farquar glanced at Marlow on the other screen. "What is this?"

"I've sent you some gifts," a garbled voice said from the static filled holoscreen. "You should receive them at any moment."

Farquar leaned forward. "What?"

"Sir," Jegen Marlow said, "we have been hit by two magar projectiles."

"What?"

"They struck our forward port sensor housing. Only minor damage."

The static on the holoscreen faded and a new face became visible.

"You haven't won yet," Arlud said.

Farquar glared at the holoscreen. "Arlud Erstallius!"

"You putrid pile of refuse," Arlud said. "You haven't seen the last of me or my clan."

Arlud's face dissolved, and the screen went black.

"We have him, sir," Marlow said. "Positive track of his ship's ident transponder. He's headed toward the *Nero Leru*, just as you predicted."

Farquar watched the holomap update with the position of Arlud's transport. With his route home blocked by the *Nero Leru*, the young Erstallius will be hard pressed to find an effective escape route. "Leave two frigates to enter orbit of GSW-183. Send a command: all other ships to converge on the Erstallius. I want him taken alive."

NI'APINU: STRATEGY

Arlud Erstallius clutched the hand railing that circled the chart pedestal in the center of the main control room on board Transport Two. Above the concave housing that held the holomitter, a spherical map displayed the positions of the Polinda armada within the PDN160 system.

"They've taken the bait," Arlud said.

Gustav Eahuda stood next to Arlud, awestruck that Polinda would commit the bulk of his forces to chase one man. "I never thought he'd do it."

"Witness and remember," Arlud said. "This demonstrates his hatred not just for me, but for our entire clan."

Salus stood on the other side of the pedestal, examining the ship positions. "At their current speed, the dreadnought group moving in from the rim will be at the drone's position in less than thirty minutes."

"They'll wait there for Polinda to arrive," Arlud said.

Narèndu, the transport's commanding officer, stood next to Salus. He was a tall, middle-aged man with a black scalp lock bound by two brass rings, and deep-set eyes that sparkled in the light from the holomap. He reviewed the Polinda ship positions and looked at Arlud through the map.

"That was a great ruse," Narèndu said, "but what will keep him interested once he discovers he's been fooled by the fake ident transponder?"

"Another volley will get his attention and cause him to change course to come after us."

"Even sipá tire of the same old tricks."

Arlud nodded at the commanding officer's remark. "Polinda hates being fooled, especially by an Erstallius. Our trick will only intensify his anger. He'll lunge after us committed to our destruction. We must keep our distance. Failure to do so will mean our deaths."

"He won't catch us," Narèndu said.

Arlud liked the pride in Narèndu's response. It exposed the trust he had in his ship and his crew.

"The volley is set and ready to go," Salus said.

Because of the distance across the system, the fire solution for the magar-canons was arrived at with much speculation. If Polinda's course did not hold true, a single shot might bypass him by kilometers. Ten projectiles would be fired with a wide, but specific, dispersal pattern, increasing the odds a ship in the armada would be hit.

"I'd like to see the plot," Arlud said.

Narèndu activated the plotting simulator, and Transport Two appeared in the holomap near the edge of the system, about ninety degrees offset from the direct route to the Erstallius homeworld. That course was blocked by the encroaching Polinda armada. Ten blue lines grew out of the Transport Two icon in a tight pattern that widened with distance and met the Polinda Armada near the transponder drone. The simulation recorded six hits, with two against Farquar's flagship.

"I'll take that scenario," Arlud said.

"It's only one of many," Narèndu said.

"It'll do," Eahuda said. "Let's not dally. We need to keep our distance."

"Relax," Salus said. "It's done." He pushed a button on the pedestal console and the projectiles were on their way.

On board the *Venka Kinall*, Farquar Polinda leaned forward in the dim light from the C.I.C. holomap and activated a holoscreen to speak with Jegen Marlow. He squinted from the sudden glare of light when the holoscreen appeared above his control console.

Marlow was surprised by the Patriarch's call. "Yes, sir?"

"So, it's a drone."

"Uh—yes, sir. We are bringing it aboard to examine."

Farquar leaned back. "Are you sure that's wise?"

"Oh, yes, sir. We've scanned it thoroughly. It is no threat."

"You mistook it for a transport. How can you be so sure of its contents?"

Marlow disliked that assessment but knew the High Regent's sarcasm was justified. "Our sensors are limited at that distance. The ping was a transport ident. We were deceived."

"Yes," Farquar said.

"The transmission from the Erstallius was no doubt recorded and sent from the drone. I am sure we will discover the drone's origin point from the internal guidance control system."

"I am sure you will. Order the fleet to return to GSW-183—after you have examined the drone."

"Yes, sir."

Warning klaxons blared throughout the ship.

Farquar shifted his attention to the holomap. The two icons that represented the Polinda frigates orbiting GSW-183 had vanished, and the planet shifted from the standard light blue to a deep red color. "What's happening?"

Marlow turned away from the holoscreen and accepted something from a staff officer.

The klaxons went silent.

"We just received telemetry," Marlow said, again facing the holoscreen. "Our ships at GSW-183 have gone offline."

Farquar frowned. "What's that mean?"

"There were massive energy signatures," Marlow said. "We believe they were attacked by the Aku. I have ordered all ships to advance toward the planet, weapons free."

Farquar gripped the arms of his chair. *The Erstallius have out maneuvered us*, he thought. Then the old legends about the Aku surfaced to the forefront of his mind. "Hold, Jegen," he ordered. "We need to move slower here. We have been fooled and outflanked."

Jegen Marlow disagreed. "The faster we move, the faster—"

The klaxons blared again.

Farquar was furious. "Now what!?"

Red markers appeared in the holomap, overlaying five of the armada's ships.

"Magar projectiles," Marlow said. "Minor damage."

The trajectories of the projectiles were traced by yellow lines in the holomap and showed an origin point about seventy-five thousand kilometers distant from the *Venka Kinall*, eighty-five degrees off her starboard side, about twenty degrees south of the system equator.

Marlow read an updated message from a staff officer. "Based on speed of impact, they were probably fired about an hour ago."

Farquar lowered his head. "So the ship that fired them will no longer be there."

"Yes, sir," Marlow said. "They are playing with us. They can't defeat us, so they harass us."

"Can't defeat us? We've already lost two frigates. Find them, Jegen!"

Marlow nodded, then took another message. "Look at the holomap, sir."

Farquar shifted his gaze back to the luminous globe. "What am I seeing?"

"Follow the magar trajectory toward the heliosphere."

At the system boundary, a large vortex-shaped disruption in the magnetic field flow was highlighted green.

"The Erstallius left the system," Marlow said. "They crossed into hyperspace."

Farquar fingered his control console and enlarged the disruption. It filled the entire holomap area.

"There is no way to know for sure where they went," Marlow said.

"They shot at us and ran away?"

"Yes."

Farquar examined the enlarged area, then reduced the view and changed his viewing angle to look down the axis of the warped magnetic field. He entered commands into the map control panel, and all the Alliance colonies within ten degrees of the view axis appeared in the map.

"Fifteen possibilities," Marlow said, "and none of them may be the right one."

Farquar saw it. He remembered what he had learned on Alpha Cephei Four. The Erstallius move made perfect sense. He had left to collect that Colli sapi. "U'galem," he said.

"Why U'galem?"

"That's where Erstallius will unite with the conspirator."

"Conspirator?"

"The one responsible," Farquar said. "The bitch who destroyed my mine!"

That statement caught Marlow off-guard, and he found no words to reply.

"All ships to U'galem," Farquar said.

"What about GSW-183?"

"Leave it to the Cormeds. All ships to U'galem, now!"

Marlow nodded. "Yes, sir."

CLAN ERSTALLIUS: WITNESS

Jens Orr relaxed in his pilot seat aboard the Erstallius shuttle. The interior cabin lights were off, and the blast shutters covered the cockpit windows. The only illumination in the cockpit came from the two active systems: the LSC control panel and the sensor palette. He had powered down all other systems to help avoid detection from the approaching Polinda fleet. He had sent a brief message to his comrades in Kuliq'Quad after the Guild comdrone had passed through the system, revealing the Polinda armada. Since then, he had sent only two narrow band, encoded messages about Polinda ship positions. Staying within the rubble cloud concealed the shuttle, but also limited his ability to communicate with the ground. Because of the orbital dynamics, he only had a few minutes during each orbit to transmit data without being detected.

He leaned forward and activated the transmitter to send another report to the surface.

Danik floated into the cockpit from the darkened main cabin. "What's happening?"

"Sending position data," Orr said. He pushed a button on the console and the transmission was sent.

Danik focused on the sensor palette data display. "Where are they?"

"Looks like Polinda took the bait. The bulk of his armada is following the Regent's signal. Two frigates just entered low orbit."

"How low?"

"About six hundred kilometers. What's Bril doing?"

"Sleeping. You think the frigates will attack the surface?"

Orr shook his head. "There just staking a claim. They won't do anything else without a dreadnought behind them." He turned and looked into the dark cabin. "Get some rest. We might be up here for a while."

Danik paused a moment and looked like he wanted to say something but nodded instead and retreated into the main cabin.

"You can spell me in a few hours," Orr said.

"OK. I'll set an alarm."

Orr checked the LSC panel. They had enough air for five more days. If they limited their talking and moving, they might stretch that to six days. He leaned back into his seat, turned his head toward the sensor palette, and watched new data stream in across the dim monitor. For the next two hours their orbit within the debris field blocked direct observation of the planet, so Orr focused on debris clusters and large bulkhead fragments that threatened to strike the shuttle. He fired the guns via the remote console twice to push away the encroaching material. If the Polindas were observing the wreckage, they would assume sudden changes in the debris cloud were because of the impacts that occur in large rubble fields, unless they did a detailed survey. Orr doubted the frigates below them would take the time to do an intense investigation, now that their comrades were rushing to catch the Erstallius regent.

When the debris rotation enabled direct observation of the planet again, he saw on the sensor monitor the Aku had launched two transports.

Orr opened the window shutters to get a direct view of GSW-183 and its surroundings, then activated an alarm to wake up Danik and Bril.

The three Erstallius clanmen huddled together in the cockpit with long range cameras to record what was about to happen. The blue, cloud mottled crescent of GSW-183 dominated their view. Two spherical Aku transports reflected harsh sunlight near the terminator about three hundred kilometers above the planet. They moved eastward out of the sun and faded into the black.

"That was Transport One and Three," Orr said.

The Polinda frigates appeared, two sleek silver arrows that glinted against the black above GSW-183's crescent.

The Aku transports changed course by igniting plasma thrusters and creating brief, dazzling jets of gas. One transport rushed to a higher equatorial position, and the other moved away into a southern polar orbit.

The Polinda ships noticed the brilliant flashes and separated to confront the unknown vessels.

Orr checked the sensor monitor. Transport One was the ship that climbed to a higher orbit. She settled into a two thousand kilometer orbit and waited for the Polinda frigate bearing down on her to come within range.

"She hasn't got a chance."

"No one's fired yet," Danik said.

Bril agreed with Orr. "All she's got are those old magar-cannons. They'll bounce off the frigate's hull plating like rubber balls."

"Not like rubber balls," Danik said. "They'll leave a dent."

Orr chuckled. "They need them to leave more than that if they hope to win."

The Polinda frigates were five times larger than the small Aku spheres. Their cargo holds could carry two transports and still have room for cargo. They were sleek, well-armed, and could turn the small transports into charred hulks in minutes with their plasma burst emitters or phase induction torpedoes.

Transport One altered her relative position and rotated to aim her top end at the approaching frigate.

"Their aligning their cannons toward the frigate," Orr said.

"They can fire all of them at once, but that won't make a difference," Bril muttered.

When the frigate came within five-hundred meters, Transport One fired her primary weapon. The initial discharge was a wispy, rippling green fog that surrounded the entire transport, then it swelled in density in an eye-blink and glowed with a multi-colored intensity that caused the clanmen to squint. The glowing halo shifted to brilliant white, then rushed forward and hit the approaching frigate.

The frigate turned white hot where the halo of energy struck her hull near the forward engine section.

Another blast of white energy shot from the transport and hit the frigate's mid-section.

Two plasma cannons on the frigate returned fire, but the next halo of energy from the transport engulfed the plasma bursts and struck the frigate's hull near the cannon pods.

In stunned silence, the Erstallius clanmen watched five more blasts from the Aku ship's primary weapon hit the frigate, then the brilliant halo around the sphere faded, and the wisps of glowing green fog vanished.

The frigate drifted away, a charred hulk.

Orr saw fire-rimmed cracks in the frigate's central hull, and then the forward engine section exploded with a blinding flash of light.

Farther away, high above GSW-183's south pole, the Erstallius clanmen noticed another series of energy blasts, followed by another brilliant flash of light.

Orr remembered a song he had learned as a child, and he sang the lyrics for Danik and Bril.

Clan Tuma chased them,
Into the void they ran.
Their flight was for freedom,
Into the void they ran.
A secure abode they found,
And Clan Tuma halted.
The Aku fought back,
And Clan Tuma halted.
The battle raged,
And the Aku had them.
Clan Tuma faltered,
And the Aku devoured them.

PROGRESSION

PART TWO

Scoundrels rise and greet the day on a world they know only by a number. Their hearts are empty. Their occupation sees not the beauty, only an opportunity.

— From *Conversations at Kuliq'Quad*
By Petra Sitlyn

U'GALEM: HIGH REGENT

Thirty-one hyper-hours after leaving Ni'apinu, the Aku transport dropped out of hyperspace and entered the PDN163 system. In standard time, almost four days had passed. That difference in time would help Arlud succeed, because if Polinda followed him here after the magar projectiles hit his armada, he could not arrive for at least twelve standard hours.

Because U'galem was the main trading port in this region, Clan Dejoria had created hundreds of security stations throughout the inner system to monitor and regulate all visitors and restrict smuggling of commodities via the Guild. That massive effort to control the system had resulted in Clan Dejoria having one of the largest system-bound fleets in the Alliance. Official estimates had their strength listed higher than all but three clans—a major factor in Arlud's decision to come here.

Arlud peered out the small window next to his table in the mess hall and watched the distant gas giant called *Numa Kru* retreat as the transport headed toward the inner planets. *Numa Kru* was the largest planet in this system, a gold and red banded globe, her apparent size through the window just a fraction smaller than Arlud's thumbnail. Her rings were a thin line angled at about thirty degrees and flanked on each end by small moons.

"We'll be safe here," Arlud said. "I told you I would lead Polinda into a fleet. Polinda will hit a wall of resistance equal to a response from our fleet."

Gustav Eahuda was at the far end of the table, focused on devouring one of the packaged meals the Aku had supplied. "I agree," he said, with his mouth full of pristal-berry. "As long as we stay in this system. Clan Dejoria will not venture beyond their own territory."

Salus entered the room. "We need you to send the Alliance codes."

Arlud nodded and followed Salus back to the bridge.

Once contact was made with the nearest Dejoria security station, and Arlud identified the Aku ship as an Erstallius transport, access was granted to the port city, Kythria, with a specific orbit entry path and instructions regarding speed and entry angles.

After they entered orbit of U′galem, Arlud sent a message he wanted to meet with the High Regent if he was available. U′galem was not the clan's homeworld, but Jhared spent half of each year at the clan's compound north of Kythria. When the response came over the comm channel he was surprised to see Jhared's face on the holoscreen.

"High Regent," Arlud said, "good to see you again."

Jhared Dejoria was a plump man, short of stature but large of appetite, and hairless. He looked almost too soft to be the leader of one of the most powerful clans in the Alliance. His physical appearance had fooled many among the clans who sought to take advantage, only to realize too late just how formidable he could be.

"Arlud—excuse me—*Regent*, Arlud Erstallius," Jhared said. "You have grown a bit since we last met. What brings you to U′galem? Is your father with you? And your mother?"

"I come alone with my clanmen for refuge from a tyrant, and to seek help with other matters."

"Tyrant? You must mean Polinda."

"Yes. We believe he is on our tail and will arrive in a few hours."

Jhared raised a hand, which brought the conversation to an end.

"Speak no further. We can discuss this more at length when you arrive. I will have my people send you coordinates for my private landing field. Peace be with you."

The holoscreen went black.

"That was easy," Salus said.

Arlud turned in his seat. "It helps to have connections."

Two hours later the Aku transport arrived in glaring mid-day sunlight at Jhared's private landing field. Arlud, Eahuda, and Salus stepped into the hot summer air from the transport's lower cargo lift. They were escorted by Dejoria guards across the tarmac to the main entry of the adjacent residence.

The Dejoria home was a palatial building, designed as a vacation retreat by Jhared's great-grandfather. The ancient stone walls that lined the path to the main entry radiated a coolness that was a welcome surprise for visitors during the days of oppressive heat and was an introduction to the climate-controlled environment preferred by the High Regent.

House guards led Arlud's group across the entry threshold into the vestibule, then retreated without a word and shut the entry doors.

The vestibule was an eight-sided room, with vaulted corridors left and right of the entry. Between the corridors, across from the entry, three wall panels made of duraplex allowed guests a view of the home's central atrium.

Arlud was struck by the immediate coolness of the room, but his attention was pulled to the floor by the dark and light wooden tiles that formed a spiral pattern that radiated from the center. The ceiling held a round, opaque white diffusion screen, created to block the harsh midday sun but still brighten the interior. "This is a fine home."

Eahuda agreed. "Very nice."

"I'm glad you approve," Jhared said, as he padded into the room from the left corridor. The High Regent preferred bare feet over shoes, and covered his ample proportions with a light blue, ankle-length tunic.

Jhared's personal aide stopped an arm's length behind his right shoulder. She was a small, thin woman, plain in appearance, clothed in a gray pant suit and casual, slip-on shoes. Her red hair was pulled back into a tight bun.

Arlud had expected more security personnel, and realized this was Jhared's way of saying, "I trust you." That was a sign of respect rare among the clans, even between those engaged in partnerships. He appreciated the sentiment but also knew an overwhelming security response was only a hand gesture away, hidden perhaps behind wall panels, doors, or even in the scrawny woman at Jhared's side.

"Thank you for seeing us on short notice," Arlud said.

"My pleasure," Jhared replied. "Follow me." He turned around and led everyone down the corridor. "I enjoyed my stay with your family, young Erstallius. I hope one day I will return to Baleiou. Those were two of the best weeks I've had in the last two years."

"We enjoyed having you with us. We were sorry to see you go."

Jhared smiled and pushed open the double doors that led into his private office. "Please, make yourselves comfortable."

Arlud, Eahuda and Salus reclined on the cushioned couches that surrounded a low table made of gray marble. Jhared planted himself across from Arlud, and his personal aide sat on a cushioned stool behind the couch to his left.

Arlud wasted no time getting to the point: "Polinda is coming to destroy us. About two weeks ago his clanmen attacked us at GSW-183 as a reprisal for the destruction of his mine on Alpha Cephei Four. Only nine of us survived the attack."

"Did you attack his mine?"

"No. Farquar's animosity for Clan Erstallius blinds him from reality."

"Uah'eki," Salus said.

Jhared turned his head to face Salus. "What?"

"Uah'eki," Salus repeated. "An imagining of the mind that subverts logical thought."

"Polinda's insane," Arlud said.

Jhared leaned back on the couch and crossed his bare feet on the table. "Yes, well, I agree with that. Polinda will be stopped. That pompous ass will learn his place. If his armada advances past the orbit of *Numa Kru*, my forces will destroy him."

"Then I hope he ignores your warning," Arlud said.

Jhared chuckled. "I am sure he will keep his distance."

"He could plead his right to retrieve," Eahuda said.

Salus furrowed his brow. "Retrieve?"

"Gus is right," Arlud said. "Clan Cormed brought survivors from the mine here. Polinda might seek his right to reclaim them."

"Yes, he could," Jhared said. "He can claim who he wants, but his fleet will not pass *Numa Kru*."

Arlud sat up straight. "We need to find the survivors before Polinda finds them."

Jhared heard renewed intensity behind Arlud's words. "Why?"

Arlud withdrew a memory chip from his coat pocket and placed it on the table. "Everything you need to know is on this chip."

An hour later, after Jhared had reviewed the material related to the unknown attacker, and the recorded interviews about the dreams that plagued some survivors, he joined his guests in the atrium.

The smell of roseweed filled the garden and reminded Arlud of the gardens his mother managed back home. The multi-colored flowers populated beds around the perimeter. Stone paths from the encircling residence converged at a large round bed of velvet grass, from which an overarching pepper tree had grown to a height of ten meters.

"This scent reminds me of Baleiou," Arlud said, and his thoughts drifted to home, and the comfort he had with his family.

"My wives loved this garden," Jhared said. "I find comfort in the memories this place brings me. That's why I spend most of my time here."

Salus was examining the pepper tree when he overheard Jhared's remarks. "You had wives?"

"Yes," Jhared said. "They are both buried at your feet."

Salus jumped back onto the stone path and examined the velvet grass.

"I could not imagine having them anywhere else," Jhared said. "They loved this garden."

Arlud found it odd there were no markers to identify the graves. "But this is not their memorial?"

"No, no, no," Jhared said. "They have their plaques and statues on the clan homeworld where our citizens can honor them. This garden is for them. This is our quiet place."

Arlud watched Jhared drift into deep memory for a few heartbeats, then in a blink he was back in the present.

"Your chip," Jhared said. "Thank you, young Erstallius. This needs to be in every clan's database. This could stop Polinda in his tracks."

"I would like to believe it would, but he's a determined scoundrel."

"With your permission, I would like to broadcast this information to all the clans."

"Do it."

Jhared flicked a hand signal to his ever-present aide, and she fingered her compad.

"Now," Jhared said, as he passed the chip back to Arlud, "how can I help you?"

"Keep Polinda at bay until we can find the mine survivors."

"Done."

"Allow us to gather spare parts for our transport."

"Spare parts? Well, it's an old ship, but I'll have my master engineer see what he can find. They may be expensive."

"Price isn't a concern, but wholesale would be appreciated."

Jhared grinned. "He'll get you a good deal, if he can find what you need."

Salus passed a small piece of paper with a list of the needed parts to Arlud.

Jhared accepted the list from Arlud, and passed it back to his aide, who began jotting down the info on her pad.

The High Regent grinned and stepped in front of Salus. "So, you are Aku?"

Salus nodded.

"And you have partnered with the Erstallius?"

Salus nodded again.

"Clan Tuma will cringe when they hear that news."

"Good," Salus said.

Jhared laughed. He extended his right hand. "Nice to meet you."

Salus gripped the small, fat hand. "May you prove to have as much honor as the Erstallius."

Jhared took that statement two ways: as a wish for future success, and as a declaration that Aku friendship was conditional. He tightened his grip.

"May we all prove honorable," he said, then released his hand.

"Jhared," Arlud said, as he moved closer to get the old man's attention, "what can we do for you?"

This young man expects to earn my favors by reciprocating them back to me, Jhared thought. *What humility!*

"What I want," he said, his voice filled with intensity, "is for you to succeed. Find the survivors. Find the bastards who attacked the mine and the Alliance frigates. The future of the Alliance may depend on it."

Arlud took a step back during Jhared's statement. He'd never witnessed the old patriarch that forceful about anything. "Well," he said, "we will do our best."

Jhared grinned. "Of course you will." He turned and retreated down a path that led back into his residence. "Come along everyone," he said with a sweeping hand gesture. "I've instructed my staff to give you a clean set of clothes." He stopped at the doorway and turned to face his three guests. "You'll want to change clothes to protect your identity while on U'galem. Polinda will have spies searching for you. And I've ordered the baths prepared. No offense, but you all carry the smell of travel and haste filled days."

Arlud exchanged glances with Eahuda and Salus, and they all agreed they needed a bath.

Jhared released a quiet chuckle. "Come along," he said, and he entered his residence with his aide following close behind him.

CLAN ERSTALLIUS: EMBASSY

The Cormed embassy guards stopped the van carrying Arlud and Eahuda at the entry gate, even though the Dejoria clan crest was emblazoned on the doors.

Arlud displayed his Grant-of-Authority papers signed by the High Regent, and the guards waved them through the entry. The clothes Jhared had given them removed all indications that Eahuda was an Erstallius Degen-of-the-Corp. They looked like typical government lackeys on a quest to fulfill clan business.

Upon entering the main lobby, Arlud noticed a thin, ebony-skinned woman in a green skirt suit standing to the right of the reception counter. Her worried expression pulled him toward her.

"I'm Karisa Marsh," the woman said. "You are from the High Regent?"

Arlud nodded.

"The High Regent's aide informed us you were coming. I understand you are looking for the Polinda mine survivors?"

"Yes," Arlud said. "We would—"

"They are no longer here."

"Oh—I see."

Gustav Eahuda took a step forward. "Would it be possible to acquire their present locations?"

Marsh shifted her gaze to Eahuda. "I suppose. I can have a list made for you, but it will not be complete. Are you intending to retrieve?"

"No," Arlud said.

"Very well then," Marsh said, and she turned to leave. "I'll get that list for you."

Arlud called out: "Why an incomplete list?"

Marsh stopped and faced Arlud. "They may have already moved on to other places. By law all contract labor must be returned to their home of origin when an employer does not fulfill their part of a contract, but after they arrive and check in with the local labor board, they can go anywhere.

We most likely do not have access to any additional locations. You will need to go to each labor board to discover that."

"Is Milos Fore here?"

"No," Marsh said, surprised by the change of subject. "He returned to Roth-513 last week. I'll get the list."

Eahuda moved close to Arlud as Marsh left the lobby. "Should have brought Pallis Nin," he said in an undertone. "Our reception might have been warmer."

"We're doing fine. They're cooperating."

Karisa Marsh returned an hour later with the list.

Arlud and Eahuda unfolded from the lobby chairs as Marsh approached.

"Here you are," Marsh said.

Arlud took the paper list and scanned it. Five small pictures with names and locations. "There's one missing."

"Those are the names," Marsh said.

Arlud passed the list to Eahuda. "Miss Marsh, we need all the names and locations. We are not retrievers from Polinda. All we want is to talk to the survivors about what they experienced after the attack. We need to see all of them."

"Those are the names."

"No," Arlud insisted. "Bev Colli is not on the list."

Marsh flinched—a small jerk in her eye movement that betrayed her lie.

Arlud pressed further: "Milos Fore delivered to me the news about Alpha Cephei Four, and he mentioned Miss Colli specifically. We need to talk to her."

"And who are you?"

"Arlud Reynaldo Erstallius, Regent of GSW-183."

"Prove it."

Arlud extended his right arm and pulled back his sleeve to expose his wrist.

Marsh grabbed a portable ident reader from the reception desk and scanned Arlud's wrist. Upon seeing the results, she relaxed her posture, an outward sign of relief knowing this son of the Erstallius patriarch was telling the truth. "Bev was my friend, or at least she became my friend while she was here. I promised to protect her identity. She disappeared two weeks ago."

"Disappeared?"

"She walked out of the embassy and vanished. We searched for days, monitored all hospital and justice admissions, but never found her."

"Could she have gotten off planet?"

"I doubt it. She had started a legal claim for her contract and the arbitrator loaned her some credit, but that wasn't nearly enough to pay for passage off planet, and the account hasn't been touched since the day she disappeared."

"Do you have her arbitrator's name?"

"Ozwald Rugeri. He doesn't know where she is, I've already contacted him."

"Maybe he does," Eahuda said, "and he is just not telling."

"No," Marsh said. "He received a message from her the day she left telling him she was in fear of Polinda and included a Transfer of Authority form so he could handle her case without her being present."

"Damn," Arlud said. A search could take weeks without a good lead, and they did not have time to waste.

"We have this list," Eahuda said. "Five out of six is better than none."

"Right," Arlud said. "Thank you, Miss Marsh. You have been very helpful." He turned and headed for the exit.

"Wait," Marsh said. "Don't leave yet." She moved to the reception desk, nudged the girl on duty aside and commandeered her station.

Arlud and Eahuda paused in the center of the lobby.

Once she had what she needed, Marsh walked over to Arlud. "All Polinda sapi have a mark to identify them and their term of contract. It's like a personal ident but it leaves a mark on the skin. Bev's mark is under her left eye." She handed a small picture of Bev to Arlud. "She began hiding it with cosmetics the day she disappeared."

"Thank you," Arlud said. "We'll keep that in mind."

As their van drove away from the embassy, Arlud relaxed in the back seat next to Eahuda and examined Bev Colli's picture. The mark under her eye was a reddish-brown stain, like a henna tattoo. "Why would Polinda go to this extreme?"

Eahuda had been thinking about the names on the list. "What?"

"Why would Polinda use a mark like this to label his workers?"

"He wants his sapi to know he owns them. It's his way of broadcasting they're his property."

"There's got to be more to it than that. Why would everyone in his mine need an outward mark of identification?"

"I've heard marks like that fade over time, based on the length of contract."

"But would that make them necessary?"

Eahuda found the discussion redundant. "It's just a way for Polinda to affirm his hold on someone."

Arlud shook his head. "No. Marsh said it was like a personal ident." Then he realized: "Tracking!"

"What?"

Arlud focused on Bev Colli's picture. "The marks are tracking devices."

"How do you figure?"

"If one of your contract laborers decides they made a bad decision and abandons their job, how do you track them? Marsh was concerned about Polinda retrievers. The fastest way to track someone is to implant a beacon on them. I think these marks are ident transponders that fade with time. Once the contract expires, so does the beacon."

"I imagine it's difficult to get off Alpha Cephei Four with or without a mark. They would be of little use on that rock."

"Well, it may be a custom developed elsewhere, but the marks would still be useful. A great way to see who is on shift and where they are at in the mine."

"You may have something there, lad."

"All we need to do is find the right frequency."

"Once we're back at the residence, we should check the comnet for info about that."

"The first thing on my list," Arlud said. He focused again on the picture. Bev Colli was younger than he had imagined, and he found her appearance intriguing. Almond-shaped green eyes, and smooth, light brown skin. "First time I've seen someone with crimson hair."

Eahuda glanced over at the image. "It has a strange appeal." He noticed Arlud's fascination, and that worried him. "Steady, lad. Focus on the mission."

Arlud smirked and slipped the picture into his coat.

CLAN POLINDA: OPPOSITION

The *Venka Kinall* slipped out of hyperspace into the outer boundary of the PDN163 system. She detected the destroyer and two frigates from the Polinda armada that had proceeded her. The ships were blocked from entering deeper into the system by twenty ships from Clan Dejoria's fleet.

A message came over the comm system and was relayed to Farquar via his C.I.C. station.

"By order of the High Regent of U'galem you are not granted passage into our system."

Farquar activated a holoscreen and hailed Jegen Marlow.

"Yes, sir?"

"Can we negotiate through this mess?"

"Unlikely, sir. They have too much firepower. We are grossly outnumbered."

"When the rest of our armada arrives, disperse for our best defense."

"Yes, sir."

"Contact the High Regent and pass him through to me."

"Yes, sir."

The holoscreen went black.

Farquar called up the holomap of the PDN163 system. There were too many ships in too many places to slip through this blockade. He would need to use diplomacy. He hated that.

Marlow reappeared on the holoscreen.

"Sir, the High Regent is unavailable. Shall I contact someone else?"

"No. Let's just wait a bit. They'll get tired of having us sit here. In the meantime, devise a way to send retrievers for our missing sapi."

"Yes, sir."

Farquar shut off the holoscreen and leaned back in his chair. He gazed at the glowing holomap and the shifting ship positions amid the orbiting planets and moons. He knew this holdup was because of the Erstallius, he could feel it in his bones. *The insolent scoundrel has persuaded Dejoria to be his protector,* he thought. *That will not deter me, you Erstallius prig! I will breach this barricade and rush forward to end your life.*

U'GALEM: DISCOVERED

After leaving Jhared's residence, Salus returned to the transport to confer with the Dejoria Master Engineer about the request for spare parts. By the following morning most of the orders had been fulfilled.

"They are delivering the fuses now," Salus said. He spoke to Arlud via transceiver from the transport's lower cargo bay. "They gave us two hundred to the exact specifications. That's enough for five ships if we replace all of them in each ship."

"That's good news," Arlud said. "I knew Jhared would come through for us."

"The Kottrel Spheres we need are rare. I was told two might be available because of the out-of-date design. We won't know for sure until later today."

"OK. Thank you, Salus. Keep me posted."

Arlud turned off his transceiver and shoved it into his rear trouser pocket.

The street before him was a broad avenue that led south into the industrial section of the city. A gray panorama of manufacturing complexes, storage facilities, and aircraft repair shops. Vehicles sped along the paved highway at random intervals, but the air traffic was a steady roar as shuttles descended toward the spaceport nestled along the coast less than a kilometer away. The few pedestrians who traversed the walkways next to the street would soon disappear as the sun rose higher and brought with it another day of oppressive heat.

"This city is too hot and crowded for me," Eahuda said. He stood next to Arlud and looked down at a small metallic device in his left hand. "About five hundred meters due west."

Arlud turned and looked down the narrow cross street that was flanked by squat, flat-roofed buildings. Beyond an intervening street, at the distance indicated by the homing signal, a green, three-story building rose above the surrounding structures. "She won't recognize us and seeing two men approach might startle her. We should split-up."

"I agree," Eahuda said. "We'll have a better chance of spotting her that way."

Arlud felt like one of those dreaded retrievers Karisa Marsh had mentioned. Bev Colli would assume he was one. The key to success was to subdue that reaction in her as soon as possible. The only problem was not knowing the best way to do that fast enough to prevent her from fleeing. They had no information about her surroundings—if she would be alone, with a crowd of people, or in a vehicle. "We need to do this carefully," he said. "Engage her in a conversation that can lower her guard and then ease into the real issue."

"Do that and we'll probably have a foot race to catch her," Eahuda said. "She's a smart girl, lad. If you want to get her attention and keep it, be direct. Steady and direct." He patted Arlud on the shoulder, then walked away toward the nearest southern cross street and disappeared around the corner.

Arlud paused a moment to relish his solitude and let himself relax. He had been through a lot since the shuttle crash. He had gained new friends and buried old ones, found company in pirates, and injustice where only rightness should be. He had fled like a coward from tyranny, and in doing so may have saved a planet and an entire people. He held no shame for his actions, only regret that he could not do more to protect his friends.

An acrid scent reached him from one of the manufacturing centers down the main boulevard that jolted him back to the present. He felt the magar-pistol under his tunic and hoped he would not need to use it to restrain Bev Colli. *She's a survivor,* he thought. *She hates Polinda as much as I do.*

Eahuda's words echoed in his mind: "Steady and direct."

By the time Arlud reached the entrance to the warehouse office the sun had crept over the eastern buildings and pushed away the cool morning air. A white rectangular sign board above the entrance had "KASIMIR STORAGE" written in red letters. He peered through the duraplex door and saw the light green customer lobby was empty. He entered the lobby, bristled at the rancid odor of a dead animal, propped the door open to help evacuate the smell, then stood at the marble-topped counter and examined the room. The wall behind the counter had posters with fees based on cubic meters and length of time in storage. Rustling sounds came through an open doorway to his left.

"Anyone here?"

With no answer, Arlud moved down the counter to peer through the open doorway. A small fan was ruffling a stack of papers in an open folder on a desk across from the doorway.

"Anyone here?"

The lack of response, combined with the stench, told Arlud the staff were probably removing the carcass of whatever had died. He lifted the hinged section of the counter and moved into the adjacent room.

Another desk along the back wall also had a fan that was aimed at an open window. Through the window, Arlud saw two men carrying a bulging cloth sack stained with blood toward a metal trash container.

He examined the room and found the source of the odor along the wall to the right of the desk with the rippling papers. A large rodent trap sat at an angle to the wall in a pool of blood mixed with gray fur.

"Who are you? What are you doing in here?"

Arlud turned toward the voice. Standing in the side doorway that led to the main warehouse, a tall, white-haired man clothed in dirty gray coveralls held a bucket in one hand and a crumpled rag in the other.

"Pardon me," Arlud said. "No one answered, and I was curious about the smell."

"Rats," the man said. "We get them in here once in a while. Big hairy ones. They come in to escape the heat but are mostly drawn by the smell of the produce we store. We're a central distributor for several grocery outlets in the area. Not all the produce is frozen."

"Oh."

The man brushed passed Arlud to clean the floor behind the desk. "How can we help you?"

"I was hoping to store some equipment here. Just temporary while our transport is repaired."

The man wiped the floor clean and dumped the blood-soaked rag into the bucket. "I'll get the manager."

Arlud moved back into the lobby and a few minutes later the obese warehouse manager appeared behind the counter. "Thanks for propping that door open. We don't get many walk-in customers."

"I like to meet the people with whom I do business."

"So, how much stuff do you need to store?"

"Two hundred conduit fuses and two Kottrel spheres," Arlud said. That was a lie, a deceitful strategy he disliked, but necessary to gain access to the warehouse.

"What's a Kottrel sphere?"

"The main power furnace for an old Mayfair-Courkos transport."

The manager furrowed his brow. "That means they'll be big and heavy. We may not have the proper equipment to move something like that."

"They're about one-hundred and fifty cubic meters."

"That's not too big. Let me see what we have available." The manager withdrew a data pad from under the counter and searched the warehouse schedule. "Your fuses come in crates?"

"I believe they do."

The manager fingered his data pad. "Yep. Twelve per case. That means they'll take up about two-hundred and fifty cubic meters of space." He fingered the pad again. "The power furnaces will fit if we can handle them. Looks like we'll have room in two days. How long do you need to store the stuff?"

"At least two weeks."

"We can handle that," the manager said. He punched in some data on his pad. "Cost will be five thousand with two-thousand additional for special handling."

Arlud nodded. "OK. Can I see where our stuff will be stored?"

The old man balked.

"My employer is very picky," Arlud said. "He'll expect a clean, secure area, free of rats."

The manager chuckled at the mention of rats. "Rats don't eat metal. Your stuff will be fine." He moved down the counter and lifted the hinged top. "Come with me and I'll show you the area."

Arlud followed the manager through the fan-rattled office into the main warehouse. Harsh sunlight poured into the massive enclosure through an open doorway to his immediate right and created a bright rectangle on the concrete floor. That doorway led to the trash bins where the rat had been dumped. The storage shelves began about ten meters further into the building. High intensity lights hung from alsteel rafters between the shelves and cast dull reflections on the concrete floor, and filled the ground level with soft, neutral illumination. Beyond the shelves, along the opposite wall, more sunlight streamed through five loading bays. From his vantage point, Arlud could see trucks parked in two of the bays. Most of the workers were in that area.

"This will be faster than walking," the manager said.

Arlud turned and watched the overweight manager slide into the driver's seat of a small white utility cart. He walked over and sat on the passenger seat and noticed the smell of garlic. He had missed that smell because of the dead rat, and he wondered if the man was aware of his own stench.

The manager drove the cart to isle four.

As they advanced deeper between the shelves, Arlud searched for Bev Colli. The stacked crates blocked most of his view, and he only saw two male workers before the cart stopped.

"Here we are," the manager said. "Row eight, section nine."

Arlud jumped out of the car, walked over to the shelves and inspected the metal crates. "Are these durillium?"

"Durillium composite," the manager said from the cart. "Strongest stuff available. The locks are unbreakable. Your stuff will be very secure. This is where the fuses will be. We'll keep the power furnaces down the next isle over."

"OK," Arlud said. He walked to the passenger side of the car and was stopped by a distant yell and a sudden boom that echoed through the building.

The brief silence that followed was broken by the sound of footfalls as workers scrambled to the source of the disturbance.

Arlud jogged into row nine and stopped in isle three when he saw Bev Colli. She stood, legs apart, arms outstretched in front of her, holding a pistol with both hands. The pistol was aimed at a man lying on the floor.

The confused workers formed a loose group on the other side of the injured man, silent from the shock of what they were witnessing. No one came closer than five meters to Bev Colli. Then someone called out for a med kit. Two men ignored the gun and broke from the group to help the injured man.

Arlud's first thought was about Eahuda, but as he drew closer, he saw the man on the floor was not his faithful Degen-of-the-Corp.

Bev swiveled at Arlud's approach. "No further!"

Arlud stopped and raised both palms as a gesture of peace.

Bev kept the gun pointed at Arlud and glanced down at the injured man as the med kit arrived.

"She shot him in the shoulder," the man with the med kit said.

The manager stopped his cart a few meters behind Arlud and called emergency services on his compad.

Eahuda shouldered through the line of workers and was relieved to see Arlud standing on the other side of the injured man. He glanced at Bev Colli, then knelt alongside the men dressing the wounded man's right shoulder. "Good job, lads, he might have bled to death."

The injured man gasped for breath and tried to speak, but his voice box wouldn't work. He reached into his coat with his left hand and gave Eahuda a small scroll.

Bev swung the pistol toward Eahuda as he stood to face Arlud. "You see what she did, lad? She crushed his windpipe. He can barely breathe. I'll wager that's his pistol."

Bev shifted her gaze between Arlud and Eahuda.

Eahuda read Bev's intentions. She was sizing up her chances of taking out both Arlud and himself. "You're safe now, Miss Colli," Eahuda said in a soft, comforting tone. Then he spoke so everyone close by could hear: "This man is working for Clan Polinda." He held out the small scroll so Bev and Arlud could see it. "This is his writ for retrieval. It is illegal per the High Regent's decree."

Bev was surprised by Eahuda's announcement but kept the gun ready.

"You can lower the weapon," Eahuda said, as he stuffed the scroll into his tunic pocket. "You won't need it anymore."

Arlud lowered his hands but kept his distance from Bev. "My friend and I are from the High Regent. We are here to protect you from men like him. I apologize for not getting here sooner."

"Protect me?"

Arlud nodded.

Commotion erupted at one of the loading bay doors as security forces arrived with a medical team.

Eahuda turned to face the advancing EMT unit and waved them toward the injured man. As the gurney rolled past him, he stepped to his left and blocked the uniformed security officer from reaching Bev. "Situation under control," he said, and he presented his *Grant-of-Authority* papers to the officer.

Bev lowered the pistol to her waist and stepped back toward the open aisle behind her.

"You're all right," Arlud said. "Just lower the weapon and stand at ease."

Bev wanted to bolt, but something about Arlud's attitude held her in place. "I'm keeping the gun."

"Fine," Arlud said. "Just stop pointing it at people and put on the safety."

Bev examined the pistol.

"It's usually where you place your thumb," Arlud said.

Bev flicked a glance at Arlud. He seemed too calm for the average person in this situation, and that perked her curiosity. She examined the gun again. She found the safety and clicked it on. "Thanks."

"Wouldn't want you to shoot yourself."

Bev looked at Arlud again. He was about her age and small for a man assigned to a security detail, but she could see strength in his build by the way he stood and the set of his shoulders. Then she noticed the bulge of a handgun under his tunic. *He's armed but has left it in the holster*, she thought. She glanced over at the man he called, "friend," who was speaking with the security officer. *They want to protect me.*

The warehouse manager stepped up behind Arlud. "She should be arrested."

The crowd that remained parted to clear a space so the EMT's could wheel the injured man to their evac shuttle.

Eahuda broke from conversation with the security officer and walked over to the manager. "The man who was shot was breaking the law. The girl was only protecting herself."

The manager fumed. "She shot him! She's dangerous! I want her out of here!"

Eahuda turned and saw the uniformed officer was questioning the loitering workers and ignoring the manager's demands. The *Grant-of-Authority* had worked. He faced Bev. "Polinda will send more retrievers when he discovers what you did. You should come with us."

Arlud displayed his *Grant-of-Authority* papers to Bev. "We'll keep you safe."

Bev peered at Arlud's papers. "Why does the High Regent of U'galem want to protect me?"

Arlud stuffed his papers into his tunic. "You're a survivor. An eyewitness to things that are very important."

The manager sat in his cart. "You weaseled your way in here, weasel your way out, and take her with you. I want her out of here!" He pulled the brake off, turned the small vehicle and drove back down the aisle toward his office.

Bev watched the fat old man retreat. Her employment here was over. She scolded herself for acting so rash. *I shouldn't have pulled the trigger*, she thought. *Things happen too fast sometimes, and there is no way to take it back.* She had no regret about injuring the retriever, she just hated losing control. "Where will you take me?"

"The High Regent's residence."

"You can't be serious."

Arlud nodded. "Very serious."

Eahuda took a step backward and gestured for Bev to join them. "It's the safest place on-planet."

"I'm keeping this gun."

"That's fine," Arlud said. "Let's go." He turned and headed toward the office.

Bev shoved the pistol into her pants and followed Arlud.

Eahuda fell in step behind Bev. *Fiery little thing*, he thought. *Blink with this girl and you might regret it.*

Arlud stepped into the hot sun outside the warehouse customer lobby and raised his transceiver to his mouth. "We're at Kasimir Storage, customer entry."

Bev stopped beside him. "Who are you calling?"

"Our car."

"How did you find me?"

Arlud pulled out the picture Karisa Marsh had given him and handed it to Bev. "That mark is more than just a clan symbol. It's a transponder. That's how the retriever could find you so fast."

Bev touched the spot under her left eye and rubbed off the cosmetic camouflage. She had never known about the tracking element. No one in the mine had a clue it was Polinda's way to keep tabs on everyone. "Does it fade with the mark?"

"Probably."

"Where did you get this picture?"

"Karisa Marsh. She's worried about you. So is Ozwald Rugeri."

"They're good people. I never meant to hurt them. I just had to disappear."

"Well, you won't need to disappear anymore."

"Who are you?"

"We're from the High Regent."

"No, what's your name?"

"Arlud."

"Arlud?" Bev smirked. "Never heard that name."

"His name is Gustav," Arlud said, as Eahuda stood behind them.

Bev turned to face the old Degen. "I'll bet they call you, Gus."

Eahuda grinned. "Some do."

Bev turned back to Arlud. "Why me?"

"Not just you," Arlud said. "You're just the first. The other survivors all left for their home cities. You were the closest to us. The High Regent has sent teams to find the others."

"More questions? I already told that fat little Cormed envoy everything I saw."

"Did you tell him about your dreams?"

Bev stiffened. *How does he know about that!?*

The van pulled up and the side door with the Dejoria house crest slid open.

Eahuda brushed past Arlud and entered the vehicle.

Arlud stepped back and gestured for Bev to follow Eahuda.

Bev hesitated. "After I finish answering your questions, I'll be free to go?"

"Anywhere you want."

Bev fingered the pistol stuffed in her pants. "Can you stop by my apartment so I can get my things?"

"Yes."

"Turn right at the next block. It's three blocks down on the left."

Arlud nodded and Bev climbed into the van.

BEV COLLI: MAD JAPER

Bev Colli entered the oval bedroom, and dropped her backpack on the white satin bed cover. The walls were softened with tapestries that depicted scenes from an ancient mythology unknown to her. The large single window was framed with white satin drapes and covered with sheer white curtains. The curved top of the white dresser was cluttered with jars and bottles filled with perfumed ointments, creams and grooming implements she had no clue how to use. She pulled the pistol out of her pants and sat on the edge of the bed. The mattress was softer than she liked. Nothing in the room appealed to her.

She laid the pistol next to her on the bed and opened her backpack. Each piece of clothing was rolled up, so she laid each garment out flat and stacked the pants and shirts in separate piles on the bed. She tossed her extra pair of shoes onto the floor.

Someone knocked on the open door.

Bev looked up and smiled at the High Regent's female aide. "Hi."

"Everything okay here?"

"A little too frilly, but it'll do. Thanks."

The older woman smiled. "Good. If you need anything, just press the call box on the nightstand."

Bev looked around and spied the metal box next to the small glowball. "Okay," she said. "Thanks."

The aide turned with a smile and was gone.

Bev looked in her backpack and withdrew the last item, her compad. She activated the small device and searched for news about the shooting at the warehouse. She scrolled through the latest reports and found no mention of the retriever or the shooting.

That's odd, she thought.

She switched channels to see the latest interstellar news and for the first time found four reports about Alpha Cephei Four. It had taken almost three standard weeks for the news to reach the old worlds, and another three weeks for the reports to populate the comnet here on U'galem. She focused on the most recent report from the "Old Worlds Post" out of Makenzie:

Sabotage Leads to Escalation of Old Feud

Posted 160.5.16

> "It was announced today that sabotage seems to be the cause of the mine disaster on Alpha Cephei Four. Investigators believe the attack was conducted to stop all mining operations. This has led Clan Polinda to accuse Clan Erstallius of planning the attack to stifle competition . . ."

That's ridiculous, Bev thought. There was no sabotage. She scrolled to the next report from "News of the Worlds" out of Thrum Dau:

Trouble Brewing Among Clans

Posted 160.5.11

> "Factions are forming among the Clans as each house reviews the official report from Alpha Cephei Four. Now that a natural cause for the disaster has been questioned, the clans with holdings in the district are reassessing their defensive capabilities. "Clan Polinda has implied that Clan Erstallius, the newest clan to colonize in the district, was most likely responsible for the attack . . ."

Bev closed her eyes and recalled the fear that gripped her when she saw the cyan light rising as the evac lift pulled her up the shaft. *Yeah*, she thought, *that wasn't natural.* She navigated to the next report from "The Vestlok Chronicle" out of Vestlok Prime:

A Guild Resurgence?

Posted 160.4.23

> "Yesterday a report from Clan Cormed's Security Intelligence Bureau was sent across the comnet that suggested the Alpha Cephei Four incident was related to revived Guild belligerence, and could signal a new campaign against all outlying colonies . . ."

They're guessing, Bev thought. She flipped to the oldest report from the "Alliance Register" out of Wan'tei:

> **Mine Disaster on Alpha Cephei Four**
> Posted 160.4.18
>
> "Clans have rallied to help the survivors of the mine disaster on Alpha Cephei Four. Early reports specify the western side of the mine was destroyed. No cause has yet been determined, and the casualty count is very high. Clan Cormed and Clan Sabballi are spearheading the effort to help rescue survivors . . ."

Bev turned off her pad. *The oldest report just related the facts. Every post after that is filled with speculation.*

The reports confirmed what she had recognized about the news services since her rescue from the mine. They existed only to issue propaganda. *They muddle the truth, unless the truth advances the right agenda. That's why there were no reports about the warehouse. The High Regent wants knowledge of the Polinda retriever kept from the public.*

She stuffed her pad into her shirt pocket, then tossed her empty backpack across the room toward the chair by the doorway. It hit the left arm and dropped onto the seat.

"Good shot," Arlud said. He stood in the doorway with Gustav Eahuda standing close behind him.

Bev looked at the two men and stifled the reflex to stand. *My protectors,* she thought. These men were a bright spark of encouragement amid all the chaos. She hoped she could continue to trust them. She could sense earnestness in the younger man. The older man was a fighter who she believed would defend her, although why he would do so was a puzzle. *Am I really that important?*

"If you're settled in," Arlud said, "we would like you to come with us now."

"Where to?"

"The main house."

"Why?"

"We need you to see something."

Bev grabbed the pistol and stood. She raised the left side of her shirt and stuffed the barrel of the small weapon into her pants, so the hand grip pointed to her navel. She lowered her shirt and straightened the fabric over the gun.

"You won't need that," Arlud said.

"Then it will stay in my pants."

Bev followed her protectors out of the guest quarters, into the hot midday sun, and down the stone path that cut through the landscaped courtyard north of the main house. She noticed the top of a spherical transport beyond the four-meter-high stone wall that encircled the compound. "Is that the High Regent's ship?"

Arlud turned and looked at the gray metal dome. "No. That's our ship."

Bev didn't expect that answer. It implied these men were independent of the High Regent, which contradicted their earlier statements. "I thought you said you were from the High Regent?"

"Yes, I did," Arlud said. "We were sent with his authorization, which was given to supersede any other authority who might want to prevent us from protecting you. Like the security officer at the warehouse."

"Where are you from?"

"I was born on Baleiou. Gus is from Thrum Dau."

Arlud and Eahuda stopped at the end of the path and held open the double doors so Bev could enter the main house.

Bev hesitated as more questions revolved in her mind about these two men and their intentions, but then she locked eyes with Arlud and saw no deception in him. She stepped across the threshold into the cool air of the rear foyer and heard a click as Arlud and Eahuda entered behind her and shut the doors.

"Welcome, welcome, welcome," Jhared said.

Bev turned to face the approaching patriarch. His plump proportions jiggled beneath his ankle-length, gold-trimmed, white tunic, and she flinched at the sight. *No one in the mine ever got that big*, she thought. *The warehouse manager was fat, but this man is huge!*

"Good to meet you, Bev Colli," Jhared said, as he extended a hand. "I am Jhared Dejoria, High Regent of Clan Dejoria, and your resident host."

Bev shook the fat hand, hoping her startled reaction wasn't noticed. She detected the scent of roseweed near the High Regent. She withdrew her hand and took a step back from the strong aroma. His hairless skin and rotund appearance reminded her of an infant. "I am honored to meet you, sir."

Jhared appreciated Bev's polite response. Her surprise at his size did not go unnoticed. He got that reaction from almost everyone upon first meeting. *She hasn't yet learned to hide*, he thought, and he found her openness refreshing. "I understand you were a mad japer."

Bev was surprised to hear sapi slang from the High Regent. "Yeah."

"How are you finding life here on U′galem?"

Bev took a deep breath. She was standing before the most powerful man on the planet, the man who owned U′galem. The last thing she wanted to do was insult him, but he seemed pleasant enough so she answered: "Hotter the last few weeks than I expected it would be—too hot for my liking, but much better than the mine. Hot air is better than no air."

"This is our summer season."

"If you've read the Cormed report, I don't know what else I can tell you about the mine."

Jhared tilted his head at that statement. He scrutinized Bev's posture. The placement of her feet below her hips, with toes pointing straight, and the balanced set of her shoulders told him she had martial training. He saw impatience behind her vibrant green eyes. *She dislikes the politeness of small talk*, he thought. The bulge from the pistol under her shirt was obvious, and he was intrigued that she did not try to conceal it. *She has a bravado I have rarely seen in women. No doubt the product of her time in the mine.*

"Sometimes, my dear," Jhared said with a smile, "we know more than we think we know." He stepped aside and gestured for Bev to enter the vaulted passage to the left of the entry. As they walked side by side, with Arlud and Eahuda close behind, Jhared said: "We are not so interested in the mine, as we are about what transpired after you reached the surface."

Once seated in Jhared's private office, Bev reviewed the data given to Arlud by Erlis Pardee on a large holoscreen that floated above the low marble table. She reclined on the cushioned couch and watched the data stream for an hour without a hint of reaction. Even the occasional explanations offered by Arlud that added depth to the information elicited no response from her.

And then the presentation was over and the holoscreen blinked off.

Bev reclined in silence for a few minutes, as she sorted the information she had witnessed. She looked to her right at Arlud and Eahuda, who sat on the couch that paralleled the right edge of the table, and asked: "So you think the same thing that attacked the Cormeds attacked the mine?"

Arlud sat up on the couch. "Yes."

"And whatever attacked us is trying to communicate through dreams?"

"Yes."

"Has anyone ever done that before?"

"Not that we know."

Bev thought about that answer for a few heartbeats, then pulled the gun out of her pants so she could sit up without the barrel poking her hip bone. "Well, that's interesting," she said. She scooted to the edge of the couch and laid the gun on her lap. "Why would anyone with that much power want to communicate with me?"

"That's what we are trying to find out," Jhared said.

Bev looked at the High Regent. He reclined across from her with his bare feet propped up on the marble table. She was impressed at his lack of concern for her gun. *He's not the least bit worried*, she thought. *His security response must be flawless.*

"When I was laying in the dirt," Bev said, "close to death, watching the mine being destroyed, I never imagined I would meet the ones responsible. Then, as the plasma wisps streamed away from the surface, one came back and floated above us—above my dying comrades and me—a glowing, pale blue fog with twisting bolts like lightning. I thought I could sense something living in that cloud."

Jhared's mouth dropped open.

Arlud and Eahuda exchanged a quick glance. None of the survivors interviewed had mentioned anything close to what Bev had just revealed.

"I didn't realize it then," Bev said. "It was only later, once I came here to U'galem, that I understood what I had felt, and that was because of my mental state after having one of those dreams." She exhaled and looked at Arlud. "Deep inside I know I'm right, but for the life of me I can't understand why they would want to destroy the mine."

Arlud shrugged. "It seems they're trying to communicate with anyone who will listen. Maybe they're trying to tell us why."

"Well," Bev said, "they're not doing a very good job." She recalled what she had seen in her dreams and the overwhelming feelings of regret and pain they left in her. "The dreams are depressing. That woman screaming, pleading for help." She leaned forward and rested her head in her hands. "It gets harder to watch every time I see it."

Eahuda leaned back on the couch. "Do the dreams change?"

Bev looked up at Eahuda. "They're slightly different each time."

"How different?"

Bev sat up and placed both of her hands over the gun on her lap. "At first I just saw the woman, but then I saw she was in the cave, and then I saw the land outside the cave."

"What kind of land?"

"Jagged gray rock, red hills, white sand."

Arlud leaned forward and sat on the edge of the couch. "So, like the others you see more information each time you have a dream. Do you ever drift into the dreams when you're not sleeping?"

"You mean like daydreams?"

"Yes."

Bev shook her head. "Not like that. Sometimes I think about them, but nothing new happens until I go to sleep."

"Would you allow us to induce sleep so we can monitor your dreams?"

"No."

"The more you dream," Jhared said, "the more we will learn."

Bev understood the imperative behind the request. The source of the dreams was a threat, a threat the Alliance could not defend against, but she had no desire to be poked and prodded like a lab rat. "I've learned enough already."

Jhared dropped his feet to the floor and sat up straight. "What have you learned?"

Bev pulled her compad out of her shirt pocket and placed it on the marble table. "At first I just wanted the dreams to stop. Then, as they revealed more, I jotted down notes about what happened. I thought if I analyzed what they meant they would eventually stop, but they didn't stop, they only got more intense." She turned on her pad. "Can I link this to your holoscreen?"

Jhared reached under the table and withdrew a thin, black, rectangular device as wide as his palm and as long as his forearm. He placed it on the table and slid it toward Bev. "Place your pad on this."

Once Bev's compad touched the black device, the holoscreen reappeared above the table with the content index from her pad displayed on the left side of the screen.

"At first the woman was just an anonymous terror," Bev said, "As more detail was revealed I got the impression the dreams were a memory of a real event. I searched for reports of cave disasters that killed or injured a woman. Nothing was available from current records, so I broadened my search to historical accounts."

Bev fingered through the index on her compad and the holoscreen displayed a hand-written document from her search. "This is a report that was filed forty-seven years ago by the prime investigator for the Department of Planetary Settlement." She rotated the holoscreen so the others could read the content. "John Avrim Parker was the head of the Judge Advocate for Planetary Settlement office for Clan Sabballi."

MERCHANT ALLIANCE OF GREAT CLANS
DEPARTMENT OF PLANETARY SETTLEMENT

Investigation: *#1798*
Date: *113·11·8*
Holding: *Arrilen Po*
Primary: *PDN1527 (Trigelles' Star)*
Subject: *Clan Halva's Withdrawal*
Investigator: *John Avrim Parker, Degen, HSab, JAPS*

Charges: *Twenty-three negligent homicides· Eighteen critical injuries because of improper safety precautions· See record 1001-1798 for casualty list and incident details·*

Comments: *Twenty-three people died because of a total lack of preparation· They should never have attempted colonization· Arrilen Po is a dangerous world· Large expanses of land are devoid of any surface water and are battered by winds that have been clocked at 600 kph· Lightning storms strike 40 percent of the land area every day· The initial surveyor's reports were negligent· Proper establishment of the erratic peculiarities in the planet's weather would have occurred if a more detailed and lengthy surveillance of the planet had been conducted· Clan Halva's guilt lies in their failure to carry out a proper analysis before the first planet-fall·*

Recommendation: *Arrilen Po should no longer be considered for habitation· Clan Halva should be stripped of all rights concerning the planet· Any equipment left within the orbital boundary of the PDN1527 system belonging to Clan Halva, should be seized by the nearest Alliance authority· Veto status for Clan Halva should be removed· No further issuance of Acquisition Certification should be considered for Clan Halva, until adequate measures have been taken to correct areas of improper performance·*

Note: *One crewman of the evacuation team (Ludi Prell, Nared-Major), has been declared dead· His death was reported as accidental (his body was not recovered)· Cynth Halva, who last saw Mr· Prell, has been charged with criminal negligence in relation to*

> *Mr. Prell's disappearance. Further investigation should be vigorously pursued.*

Arlud finished reading the report and leaned back on the couch. "What does this have to do with your dreams?"

"Cynth Halva," Bev said. She replaced the report on the screen with a highlighted section from record 1001-1798:

> **Halva, Cynth:**
> **Injuries:** *Both legs and left arm lost because of severe burns and compression of the bone.*
> **Status:** *Critical.*

"She survived," Bev said.

"That's interesting," Jhared said, "but that happened a long time ago. How does it fit into your dreams?"

"She was found in a cave, barely alive. She lost both of her legs and an arm."

Arlud leaned forward. "You've seen her injuries in your dreams?"

"No," Bev said. "I see her half buried in the ground. I feel her agony, and I saw her face." She replaced the record on the holoscreen with an ident image of Cynth Halva from the report. She was thirty standard years when the incident occurred; a slim brunette with the high cheek bones typical of the Halva family. Her deep blue eyes were like glittering jewels.

Jhared turned the screen for a better view and enlarged the picture. "Nice looking woman. You're sure she's the woman in your dreams?"

"Not one-hundred percent sure," Bev said, "but she resembles her, and she was found nearly dead in a cave. I see that black rock every time I have one of those dreams."

Jhared rotated the screen so Bev could see the correct orientation. "That incident nearly destroyed Clan Halva," he said. "They lost most of their holdings paying off the debt they incurred because of it."

"She's still alive," Bev said. "She entered her seventy-seventh year two months ago."

"You're quite the sleuth, young miss," Eahuda said. "Let's suppose she's the one. How is that event connected to Alpha Cephei Four and the attack on the Cormeds?"

"And the Sabballi ships," Arlud said. "They still haven't been found."

"We need to ask Cynth Halva," Jhared said.

Arlud looked at Bev. She had been through more than most people experience in a lifetime. *A brave girl*, he thought. *Tough and smart.* "Bev," he said, "would you be willing to go to Cestratha?"

"Cestratha?"

"Clan Halva's homeworld."

"No."

"If Cynth Halva is the woman in your dreams, only you can tell us that."

"You have my info and my statements. You don't need me. Tell her about what's happened. Tell her about the dreams. She'll know if she's the one. I want the dreams to stop. If I go there, I know they will just get worse."

"How?"

Jhared's aide burst into the office. "Excuse me." She rushed up to Jhared and gave him a data pad.

"One moment," Jhared said to those seated. He reviewed the information on the pad and whispered instructions to his aide, who then hurried out of the room.

"Pardon the interruption," Jhared said, "but it seems Polinda has ignored my decree once again." He pulled the black device on the table toward him and fingered the buttons along the shorter edge.

The holoscreen refreshed with a live image from an aerial drone of a security incident on the outskirts of Kythria. Two blocks beyond the river that cut through the western suburbs, a thin pillar of black smoke ascended from the wreckage of a two-seat flyer that had crashed into the side of a gable-roofed house.

"Seems we've caught a retriever who had a Polinda sapi with him," Jhared said.

The view shifted as Jhared switched to a ground camera carried by a security officer recording the wreckage. The nose of the two-seat flyer was buried in the building wall. The near side of the cockpit was riddled with small projectile craters, and the side windscreen was cracked. Hazard containment officers swarmed around the vehicle from each side of the screen as the security officer backed away to allow them free access to the wreck. As the camera view retreated from the crash site, two EMT gurneys could be seen to the right of the house in the near distance with blanket-covered bodies on them.

"The retriever refused to stop," Jhared said. "He opened fire on the security team. Not a wise move. The report says both the pilot and the passenger were killed."

Bev was astounded. "Why would a retriever risk his life for a sapi?"

"Retrievers take their assignments seriously," Jhared said. "Polinda pays well for success."

Bev shook her head in disgust.

Jhared stood. He kept his eyes on the holoscreen and said, "We must continue this discussion later, my friends. Polinda needs to feel my wrath. I suggest you prepare your ship gentlemen. This may be the best time for your departure. Miss Colli, you may stay in the guest house for as long as needed. Please leave me now to my business."

Arlud and Eahuda rose from the couch in unison and gestured for Bev to join their exit from the office.

Bev grabbed her compad, stood, shoved the gun into her pants, then turned and headed for the doorway. As she crossed the office threshold, she turned and caught sight of five blue-uniformed clanmen standing with Jhared around the gray marble table. The display on the holoscreen changed to a schematic that looked like a planetary system, and then the doors closed.

"Come along, Bev."

Bev turned and saw Arlud waiting a few paces away. Eahuda was gone. "What's happening?"

"Polinda followed us here," Arlud said. He headed down the vaulted passage toward the exit that led to the rear courtyard.

Bev kept pace alongside Arlud. "He followed you?"

"Farquar was hoping to destroy me, but Jhared blocked his entrance to this system. With that quest stalled, he contacted allies on-planet and sent retrievers to collect his workers, like the one you shot at the warehouse."

"Destroy you? What do you mean, destroy you?"

"My clan has been feuding with the Polindas for decades. Farquar seeks to kill me. They attacked us at GSW-183. I came here because I knew they would follow me."

"You knew they would follow you?"

"Yes, and I knew Jhared would protect us."

"Why would you do that?"

"To save GSW-183."

Bev's mind whirled with questions. On one hand, she wanted to slap Arlud in the face for leading Polinda here. On the other hand, she was awed by his bravery. *He made himself a decoy to attract Polinda. He sacrificed himself to save those he left behind.* She stepped into Arlud's path, causing him to stop short. "Who are you?"

Arlud took a half step backward. This confused, angry young woman mesmerized him with her crimson hair and those bright green eyes set amid her smooth tawny complexion. The increased space between them helped him fight the urge to reach out and caress her. He took a breath and steadied his mind. "I am Arlud Reynaldo Erstallius. Regent of GSW-183, the protector of Ni'apinu, and son of Armand Erstallius, High Regent of Clan Erstallius."

Bev flinched, stepped back, and placed her hands on her hips. She sensed the truth in Arlud's words and found his revelation intriguing, although she still wanted to hit him. "Really? You're a Regent?"

Arlud nodded.

"A bit young for that, aren't you?"

"Old enough."

"Am I supposed to bow or something?"

"No," Arlud said. He sidestepped Bev to continue down the hallway.

Bev kept pace as they headed for the courtyard exit. "If you're a Regent, why did you come for me yourself?"

"Is that not allowed?"

"Don't regents have other people do their work?"

"How many regents do you know?"

"It just seems odd to me."

"I came for you because we needed to find you. Milos Fore told me about you. He mentioned you by name. When the opportunity came to find you, we took it. My position gave us access to the Cormed embassy that most others don't have. If someone else had been sent, they may not have found you. We almost missed you ourselves."

"Oh."

Bev let that explanation simmer while they stepped onto the courtyard path and walked again through the midday heat. "Where did your friend go?"

"Back to the ship."

"Is he a regent too?"

"He's Degen-of-the-Corp, my personal guard, and an old family friend."

"Clanman first, friend second?"

"Degen is his profession. His friendship is forever."

Bev let that answer roll around in her mental stew of new understanding as they entered the guest house, crossed the foyer, and turned into the hall that led to her room. "So what happens now?"

"Not sure."

Bev entered her room and picked her backpack off the chair by the door, pulled the gun out of her pants, and slouched on the edge of the bed.

Arlud hovered in the doorway.

Bev appreciated Arlud's politeness, but that didn't erase her disappointment that he had led Polinda here. She placed the gun in her backpack and said, "I came here to get out of my contract. To get away from Clan Polinda for good. Why did you have to bring him here?"

Arlud leaned against the door jamb. "To save my friends."

Bev looked up and saw unselfish commitment in Arlud's eyes. The longer she looked, the more self-centered she felt. She lowered her eyes. "I didn't come here to be part of an investigation."

"I understand," Arlud said. "The decision is yours. I just hope you'll think about what it could mean if you met Cynth Halva face to face."

"It will mean nothing."

Arlud frowned at that remark.

Bev focused on Arlud again. "Look, I'm just a mad japer who ran to save my life. I'm a selfish survivor. Everyone in the mine did what they did to save their own butts. Which is probably why so many died." She hugged her backpack. "I'm just a selfish bitch who wants to be left alone."

"You're not a selfish bitch."

"Yes, I am!" She tightened her arms around the backpack and lowered her head to hide her face.

Arlud heard Bev sniffle and held his voice. What she had gone through he could never relate to, so he gave her a moment of silence to gather herself.

A flash of light blazed outside the window like the eruption of a second sun.

Arlud rushed to the window and pulled aside the left sheer curtain. East of the compound he glimpsed the fading remnant of a white fireball high in the blue sky.

Bev brushed next to Arlud and pulled the right sheer curtain aside. "What was that?"

Arlud's transceiver buzzed for attention, and he pulled it out of his back pocket. Eahuda was hailing him. "Arlud here."

"Did you see that, lad?"

"Yes. Where are you?"

"I'm on the transport. Polinda tried an end run around the blockade. That flash was one of his ships exploding in orbit. Jhared's clanmen saw the feint and hit him hard."

Arlud froze for a moment. If Farquar was on that ship the future of Clan Polinda had just changed. "Was Farquar on that ship?"

"Unlikely," Eahuda said. "From what we can tell from our telemetry, Jhared's fleet has the bulk of Polinda's armada trapped near *Numa Kru*."

Bev heard Eahuda's words and was thrilled Polinda had been hit. "I hope they turn his ships to rubble."

"What was that?" Eahuda asked.

"That was Bev," Arlud said. He glanced down at her and noticed her cheeks were still wet from her tears. Their eyes met for a heartbeat. He turned away and moved toward the doorway. "She hates Polinda as much as we do."

Bev peered out the window and wiped the wetness from her face.

"Lad," Eahuda said, "this may not be good for us. Jhared may have trapped Polinda for now, but he will have much to consider. Killing a High Regent is not something the Alliance will look upon with favor. He may be forced to just evict him from this system. If that happens there will be nothing to stop Polinda from returning to GSW-183."

"There never was."

"Yes, but the possibility of eliminating you kept him here, along with the need to retrieve his workers. Jhared has just nullified Polinda's ability to accomplish either of those things."

"I understand."

"Narèndu wants to return to Ni′apinu as soon as possible. Our window for that is closing fast. All incoming flights have been stopped by Jhared's fleet, and all public flights from the spaceport have been grounded until this situation is over."

Arlud understood Narèndu's decision. The supplies they had acquired needed to get to Ni′apinu so the Aku could activate more of their ships. Doing that before Polinda returned was the only course for success because there was no way to know if the Erstallius reinforcements had arrived. *I cannot leave the Aku to meet Polinda's armada with only two transports.* He glanced at Bev. She stood silhouetted against the window with the sheer curtains billowing around her. "I'll be right there," he said. He shut off his transceiver and shoved it into his rear pant pocket.

Bev stepped out of the curtains. "You're leaving?"

"Yes."

"Will you be back?"

Arlud saw a glimmer of hope in Bev's eyes. "You'll be safe here," he said. He turned and rushed out the doorway.

Bev slumped on the edge of the bed. For the past six years she had only felt close to one person, and he died in the mine. Josh Gridle had been like a father to her. He had protected her. The trust between them had formed during her first year in the mine. Josh had said she reminded him of his daughter. She had felt a similar trust in Arlud, and his departure left a gaping hole inside of her.

She felt tears roll down her cheeks again.

This is ridiculous, she thought, and she wiped her face with her hands.

She contemplated what Arlud and his friends had done for her, and although she knew their motive was more about what they could gain, she had also seen in Arlud something more personal. *His concern for me is genuine. Just like Josh.*

She pushed off the bed and headed for the exit.

Hot wind enveloped her as she left the guest house and stepped onto the stone path that cut through the courtyard. Her advance toward the main house was stopped by rumbling from the spherical transport on the other side of the wall. She turned to see the metallic gray vessel rise, pushed upward by the four plasma thrusters protruding from the equatorial ring. When the ship became visible above the wall, the landing gear retracted into the hull and the compression drive activated. The sphere was enveloped for a few seconds in a white halo. Then in a blink the ship vaulted into the sky and disappeared in the clouds.

Bev's heart sank. "Eetah!"

She turned toward the guest house, her hope deflated.

The walk back to her room was filled with thoughts about Arlud and the information he had shown her. By the time she entered her room and dropped onto the bed, she knew her dreams would stop once she knew their meaning, but that would not happen if she was left to find the answers on her own. She curled up in a fetal position with her back to the door.

I should have said yes!

The hall outside her room was filled with commotion.

Bev rolled over to see two Dejoria house guards standing in her room in front of the doorway. They were dressed in their gold trimmed, blue armor, each holding a combat staff..

"Bev Colli," the lead guard said.

"Yeah?"

"The High Regent requests your presence."

"Why?"

The guard looked down at Bev with derision. "We must not keep the High Regent waiting."

"OK," Bev said. She pushed up to a seated position and flung her legs over the edge of the bed.

Arlud appeared in the doorway. "We should hurry."

Bev jumped to her feet. “I thought you left!”

“Let’s go, the High Regent is waiting.”

Eahuda appeared in the doorway behind Arlud. “What’s taking so long?”

Arlud turned and followed Eahuda down the hall. Bev kept pace behind Arlud, and the two guards followed in her wake.

U'GALEM: DIFFERENT PATHS

The vaulted hallway to Jhared Dejoria's private office was blocked by a house guard.

Gustav Eahuda stopped a few paces away from the armor-clad sentry and turned to face Arlud. "You know what's going on here?"

Arlud halted his advance. "No."

Bev stayed a few paces behind her two protectors. Their confusion raised a caution flag inside of her, and she regretted leaving the retriever's gun in her backpack. One guard behind Bev took a station in front of Eahuda and gestured down the hall to their left.

"This way," the guard said. He led the group through the hall, beyond a set of double doors held open by two more guards, down a flight of stairs, and into a narrow, stone-lined passage.

By the light of dim glowballs hanging from the ceiling, they advanced through the narrow tunnel that curved to the left about ten meters beyond the entry.

The dank air inside the passage brought a chill to Bev's exposed skin. "Where are we going?"

"Keep moving," the guard behind her said.

After the curve, the passage headed straight for fifty meters and ended at another flight of stairs. At the top of the stairs, a large metal door blocked the exit.

The leading guard pulled back the lock bolt, grabbed the handle and swung the door open. He gestured for the others to enter the bright room that lay beyond the threshold.

Eahuda, Arlud, and Bev passed through the doorway. The guard closed the metal door behind them, and they heard the lock bolt slide back into place.

The white room was about ten meters square, with large metal cabinets to either side of the entry. The wall opposite the doorway was smooth white metal.

"OK," Eahuda said, "where are we?"

The metal wall parted, and a hot wind rushed into the room.

Jhared Dejoria, clothed in his gold-trimmed, white tunic, stood about ten meters from the opening surrounded by four clanmen in black battle dress. He turned toward his approaching guests. "Good, you're finally here."

Arlud followed Eahuda toward the High Regent and was surprised to discover they were in the rear area of the shuttle hanger at Jhared's private landing field. Hot air flowed into the building through a narrow gap between the hanger doors. Maintenance crews hustled around four shuttles—sleek, low-profile transports, covered with low-reflectance, black hull plating. They were like the shuttles used by Arlud's clan, but they not only had magar cannons jutting out of their rear hull panels, they also had turret-mounted cannons beneath their noses.

Bev hovered behind Arlud's left shoulder as Jhared met them inside the rear safety zone marked by diagonal yellow stripes on the smooth concrete floor.

"The bi-weekly comdrone from the Old Worlds passed through this system about an hour ago," Jhared said. "It broadcast an encrypted report about the reaction to the Alpha Cephei Four incident. The Clans are in turmoil. Polinda's forces engaged Clan Erstallius at Thrum Dau. There were heavy casualties on both sides, but the Erstallius held."

"As usual," Arlud said. The news didn't surprise him, and neither did the outcome. The Erstallius always held. They had never secured a decisive victory against Clan Polinda. *That needs to change*, he thought. "Any word about my father?"

"No," Jhared said. "He was not mentioned as being present during the battle. We should know more when the next scheduled comdrone arrives."

Arlud drifted into deep reflection as he considered the possibility that his home on Baleiou had also been hit by Polinda forces.

Eahuda pressed closer to the old patriarch. "What else?"

Jhared continued: "Clan Tuma and Clan Emlito have created blockades against the other clans around their joint holdings in the Colliri-3 system, and at Glasel-221. The Alliance has split apart."

Bev stepped around Arlud to face Jhared. "All that because of the mine?"

"This has been simmering for many years," Jhared said. "The mine incident was just the spark that set things in motion."

"What does that mean?"

Jhared replied to Bev's apprehension with a stoic response: "Chaos. I fear the Alliance will fade away." He faced Arlud and Eahuda. "But before that happens you need to get out of this system, my Erstallius friends."

Arlud pulled himself out of his well of contemplation. "Farquar wasn't just trying to clean-up what his forces had started at GSW-183. He planned his attack to coincide with his strike on Thrum Dau, and he had to plan that before he left his homeworld. He probably also sent an armada to Baleiou."

"We are at war," Eahuda said. "We must kill them all this time. No other outcome will do."

"But you won't do that from here," Jhared said. "I have Farquar trapped five million kilometers from *Numa Kru*. I have neutralized him for now, but he could still pose a genuine threat to U'galem. My forces will evict him soon, which means you need to leave now, while he's still trapped. I've ordered one of my frigates to take you to Cestratha."

Jhared turned to Bev. "You, my dear, should go with them. You know the reasons. The three other miners we found are waiting for you aboard my frigate. But if you wish, you are welcome to stay."

Bev noticed a hint of affection behind Jhared's words. His attraction to her was unexpected, and as she looked at his overstuffed physique, she realized how lonely he must be, now that his wives were gone. She flashed a brief smile. "I'm going."

"Then be urgent about it," Jhared said. He stepped aside and gestured to his shuttles.

Farquar Polinda leaned back in his chair, as Jhared Dejoria's round face appeared on the holoscreen floating above his console in the Command Intelligence Center on board the *Venka Kinall.*

"Mister Polinda," Jhared said. "That was quite a loss you suffered. Haven't you lost enough?"

"My dear Mister Dejoria," Farquar said, "I am prepared to lose much more."

"Why?"

"I will sacrifice all I have to defeat my enemies."

Jhared pinched his fat lips together. "We just received word about your attack against Clan Erstallius at Thrum Dau. The Alliance is falling apart."

Farquar leaned forward in his chair. "You can blame that on the Erstallius. They destroyed my mine."

"You old fool. You know the investigation could not substantiate that claim. I've sent you data that proves something else is at play here."

"The only thing at play is an Erstallius conspiracy."

"What conspiracy?"

"They trained an insurgent to attack the mine from within."

"What's your evidence?"

"That Colli sapi you're protecting. She was present when the first explosion occurred. We have a recording from her suit camera."

"Rubbish! You can't convict someone just because they were present. She's just an excuse for you to vent your belligerence at the Erstallius."

"Then why did that Erstallius prick come here? That Colli sapi wasn't from U'galem. She should never have come here."

"The Erstallius came here for my protection. Miss Colli was trying to get out of her contract. Coming here was her best option. If the Cormeds had taken survivors to Oikía, she would have gone there instead. Your argument is full of too many holes."

Farquar glanced up at the glowing holomap. His armada was surrounded. "You have many ships, Mister Dejoria. What do you plan on doing?"

"Well, since the Alliance is crumbling, the governmental limits on my choices no longer apply."

Farquar gulped a breath. The real-time updates in the holomap showed Jhared's ships had maneuvered into a strike position. Tightness gripped Farquar's shoulders and his chest throbbed. For the first time during this foray to kill the Erstallius survivors, fear seized him.

"Since our clans have been mutually respectful of each other in the past," Jhared said, "I will not obliterate you as we speak. You have five minutes to retreat from my system."

The holoscreen blinked off.

Farquar pushed a comm button. "Get us out of here, Jegen!"

Bev stared out the window in the frigate's rear observation deck and watched the cloud-covered crescent that was U'galem retreat as the ship rushed out of orbit. She turned and looked up at Arlud.

"Why didn't you leave on your ship?"

Arlud kept his gaze on the shrinking planet. "It wasn't my ship."

"What? I thought you said—"

"It's complicated."

Bev heard the impatience in Arlud's words. She knew the High Regent would not help him get to Cestratha unless the reason was sound. The arguments against going had lost their force, but a new concern rose inside her and found her voice: "If the Alliance is in chaos, won't Cestratha be in chaos too?"

"Based on Clan Halva's history, I don't think they'll be affected much by what's happening among the Old Worlds."

"So it will be safer?"

Arlud nodded.

"Are you sure Polinda won't follow us?"

"As far as he is aware, we're still on U'galem," Arlud said. He gestured to the shrinking planet outside the window. "The planet is eclipsing our frigate from Polinda's view. She'll stay between us until we get well beyond the heliosphere. He'll never detect our passage. He'll retreat toward GSW-183. That's his best option."

"But won't that put your friends in jeopardy?"

"Yes, it will."

"Then I don't understand—"

"It's complicated."

"Will you quit saying that! What's the big secret?"

Arlud looked down at Bev. She could be the key to solving all this mess. None of the other miners on board had the dreams. He wanted her to be free of anything that could bias her impressions. She was a book with blank pages, and he feared too much information about other matters would muddle her potential to discover the truth. "I have obligations I must fulfill."

That answer only made Bev more curious and inflamed her annoyance at Arlud's evasive answers. Her eyes narrowed, and she crossed her arms. "Fine," she said, "it's none of my business anyway."

Arlud leaned away from Bev's anger. "That was the only option I had."

Bev turned away from the window and headed toward the exit. "I'll be in my bunk."

Arlud watched her leave the observation deck as U'galem became lost in the sea of stars outside the window.

Farquar Polinda watched the changing ship positions in the holomap as his armada fled the Dejoria battle fleet. The frigates at the rear of the retreating ships felt the impacts of plasma bursts from the pursing dreadnoughts, and their icons changed from blue to red as the repetitive bursts made contact. The twinkling colors told Farquar the pursuit was strong enough to push them out of the system, but not powerful enough to destroy them.

Jhared fears Clan reprisal, he thought. *Killing a patriarch is not a thing that should happen, least Jhared suffers the same action against himself. His caution will come back to haunt him one day.*

Farquar turned toward the holoscreen above his console. "Set course for the rally point."

Jegen Marlow blinked on the screen. "Yes, sir. What about GSW-183?"

Farquar leaned back in his chair. "By now the Erstallius reinforcements have probably arrived. Our frigates disappeared from orbit before we left, which means the Aku probably have the upper hand there. We need to regroup with the Sabballi fleet as planned. This battle has become a war."

Marlow nodded. "It has always been a war, sir. Only now the battles will be bigger and the stakes much higher."

Farquar pursed his lips. Marlow's admission did not surprise him, but it pushed his thinking onto a different path. Polinda holdings across the Alliance had been ordered to prepare defenses for Erstallius attacks. If the assaults against Erstallius interests on Thrum Dau and Baleiou had gone as planned, the Old Worlds were now engulfed in chaos. *Shatter their serenity and fill them with dread*, Farquar thought. *Confusion is the friend of rebellion and a helper to the one causing terror.*

"The stakes have always been high," Farquar said. "Once we eradicate the Erstallius filth, you will witness what unbridled power can do for us, and how the Clans will weep as they willingly deliver their sovereignty to me."

Marlow tipped his head, and the holoscreen winked off.

THE GUILD: HOME

Shanna Sy hugged her mother's left arm as Wellen leaned against her for support. They stood at the window in the forward observation room on board Erlis Pardee's freighter. They had been granted an express orbital pathway through the traffic pressing toward Wald-415 and had seen more ships while on approach to the planet than they had ever seen at Al-phaq. Shanna counted thirty-two freighters and twelve smaller vessels from the system's outer boundary to the orbital path of Wald-415's largest moon.

Their destination was four-hundred thousand kilometers away from the moon, a thin crescent aglow from the sunlight scattering through the rich atmosphere. As they crossed the void and dropped into a three-hundred-kilometer orbit above the night side of the planet, Shanna spied twenty more ships along the way, illuminated by their running lights, holding station within dedicated orbital paths to allow Pardee's freighter unrestricted access to the planet.

"The entire Guild must be here."

"Yes," Wellen said. "Your father tricked us."

Shanna had imagined a wilderness world, free of human intrusion. The perfect place for her to experience open air for the first time. But her first time had happened on GSW-183, and Wald-415 was no longer a wilderness. "No," she said. "He let you pick this world for our new home. It's just like him to surprise us that way."

They left the planet's night side and were greeted by a brilliant dawn above an ocean covered by a spattering of thin clouds. Wald-415 had shallow seas, and Shanna noticed how much more aqua-blue the water looked than the deep blue oceans of GSW-183. The continents she could see below the wisps of white cloud were narrow bands of green and tan. "It looks warm down there."

"That's why I picked it," Wellen said. "The average temp is twenty-six degrees Celsius at the equator, where our lodging will be. It is very different from Al-phaq."

"How's your leg holding up? Would you like to sit down?"

"I'm fine with you here to support me."

Shanna closed her eyes; thankful they were here. During the Cormed rebellion, Wellen had fled her cabin and her right kneecap was struck by a projectile as she turned into the alcove that led to the corridor stairwell. Shanna rubbed her mother's shoulder. It was a gesture of assurance and gratitude. The horrible events of that day were far behind them. *We survived.*

"Will Father join us here, or will he wait for us to planet-fall?"

"He's waiting in our new home."

Now in their prime orbit, the other ships were high above them, illuminated by the sun. Shanna saw a ship she had never seen before rise above the planet's limb. It looked like two spheres connected by a band of hexagonal framework. "What is that?"

Wellen turned her head to see the new vessel. "Well, I never—"

"What?"

"That's a dreadnought, my dear. A Guild dreadnought."

"I didn't know we had those."

Three more dreadnoughts appeared high over the horizon, and then a large grid-like structure came into view in an orbit closer to Pardee's freighter.

"My, my," Wellen said. "You see that large thing over there?"

Shanna watched the white and blue construction grow larger as Pardee's freighter drew closer. "Is it a space station?"

"A shipyard," Wellen said. "See the unfinished hull deep inside the grid?"

Shanna released her mother's arm, leaned into the window, and watched the shipyard pass their starboard bow. "Oh, Father has been busy."

"Yes, my dear. He has been very busy."

The Guild shuttle landed on the circular pad next to the Director's residence under a steel blue sky. Once the vessel's air-fins retracted, a cloth-covered boarding tunnel extended from the adjacent building like the bellows of an accordion. The beige-colored fabric fluttered from light gusts of wind as the ribbed sections extended. Cushions encasing the end of the tunnel pressed against the shuttle's hull and enveloped the port side hatchway.

The port hatch dropped open and Shanna Sy walked down the boarding ramp into the filtered daylight inside the fabric tunnel. She took a deep breath. The air was thinner than she had experienced in the keep on Al-phaq, and much dryer than the moist air of GSW-183. She felt an immediate dryness in her nose. She turned to help her mother down the ramp.

Wellen waived Shanna away. "I'm fine." Her knee was covered with the medical device she had worn since the injury, but the limited movement it created was not debilitating. She hobbled down the ramp and followed Shanna through the fabric tunnel.

The door at the end of the tunnel slid open to reveal Wolfram Sy standing just beyond the threshold.

Shanna rushed forward and wrapped her arms around her father in a tight hug. "I'm so happy to see you again."

Wolfram held Shanna tight, then pulled away and looked down at her smiling face. "You had me worried. Welcome home." He looked up as Wellen approached.

Shanna moved aside and allowed Wolfram direct access to his injured wife, and he embraced Wellen without a word. Wellen buried her head in Wolfram's chest and Shanna retreated into the adjoining hallway.

Two hours after arriving, when the greetings of the house staff and the brief tour of their dwelling had been completed, Shanna settled onto the soft cushions in the bay window in the lounging room, wearing the white, floor length dress the Aku had given her. The view outside was dreary. A dry dirt field abutted the stone walkway that surrounded the building and stretched to a fence of metal and wire fifty meters away. Beyond the fence, dark green shrubs and brown skeleton grass covered the ground to the rolling hills along the horizon. *A bleak place to build a home,* she thought. *How could Father choose such a place?*

And then she remembered her mother had been the one to choose.

She placed a cushion against the wall behind her, leaned back, and rested her bare feet on the cushions at the opposite end of the window seat. So much had happened since leaving Al-phaq. Her mind was in a constant whirlwind, and she wondered if she would ever find inner peace again. She was glad to be with her family, safe and secure, but something gnawed deep inside of her she could not explain in words. She tilted her head back and focused on the wisps of cloud high in the steel blue sky. Their meandering motion, combined with the radiant heat from the windows, caused a sudden heaviness to her eyes. She scooted into a more reclined position, so her head rested on the cushion and drifted into sleep.

Visions erupted in her mind of the painful hours as a captive of the Cormeds. Grom Anen's foul breath caused her to flinch away from his swagger-fueled raving, and then her pain diminished as Anen's face was replaced by the calm appearance of Arlud Erstallius. The Erstallius Regent impressed her with his humble devotion to truth and rightness. Without his help, she would still be stranded on Ni'apinu. Arlud's face drew close to hers and she relived her kiss, but in her dream the kiss lingered, and his arms wrapped around her.

"Shanna?"

The voice intruded into her dream and Arlud disappeared.

Shanna whirled from her reverie and was jolted back to the reality of the window seat. She felt the soft support of the cushions, and a warm pressure along her left calf. She opened her eyes to see Wolfram seated on the edge of the bench next to her legs. She pulled her knees up to give him more room. "I must have fallen asleep."

"You've had a busy day. It usually takes me a good day or two to recover from a long trip."

"Where's mother?"

"She's resting. That injury."

"Did you want something?"

"Just to know you're OK, and to tell you the kitchen staff prepared your dinner."

"Oh. I'm fine. I'm not hungry."

"Well, I would like to have our first meal on this new world together, at table, like a real family."

Shanna heard the regret in her father's words. So much had kept Wolfram occupied elsewhere his family had become disconnected. "You're right." She smiled at him. "We should."

Wolfram wrapped an arm around Shanna's raised knees. "Then shake the sleep out of your pretty head and get moving." He stood and turned to leave.

"Wait," Shanna said. "I need to ask you something and I'd prefer mother not hear it."

"Keeping secrets from your mother?"

Shanna smirked. "Not secrets."

Wolfram raised an eyebrow at his daughter's candid admission. He pulled a chair over to the window seat, sat and waited for Shanna to continue.

"The conditions here are rather spartan," Shanna said. "Why would mother choose a place like this? Was the other world worse?"

"The options I gave your mother were the best two worlds we have surveyed during the last five years. This one has benefits the other one does not have. They are both superior choices, but it will take time to build all the infrastructure."

"It's just so—" Shanna searched in her mind for a tactful word and found the perfect adjective: "Rustic."

Wolfram chuckled to himself. "You need to see the bigger picture, my dear. Al-phaq was doomed. The advancing clans were becoming an unbearable threat. You have firsthand knowledge of how belligerent the Alliance can be. This world will be our new home because it offers more than Al-Phaq ever could. When our keep is completed, you will see just how magnificent this world will be."

Shanna thought through Wolfram's explanation. "I don't mean to sound ungrateful—it's just so barren here."

"I know. You deserve much better than this. Be patient."

Shanna flashed a thin smile. "I know you are doing what is best for us, and for the Guild. I promise not to be a nag."

Wolfram leaned back in the chair. "Never think of yourself as a nag. You have a right to have your questions answered. Just remember, though, the answers may not always be what you want to hear."

Shanna nodded acceptance of Wolfram's admonition, then sat up on the window bench. "Not all the clans are enemies."

Wolfram tilted his head at the conviction in Shanna's words. "Some are more reasonable than others, but all of them bow to the decrees of the Supreme Council."

"Not all of them."

Wolfram knew where this conversation was going. "Pardee informed me of all that transpired on GSW-183. The Erstallius are an honorable people, but they are still members of the Alliance."

"The Alliance is falling apart like leaves falling from a tree. The fallen leaves are worthless, good only for the fire. The leaves that remain desperately cling to the branches because they have nowhere else to go. Give them someplace else to go."

"And when did you become such a fountain of wisdom?"

"You mock me?"

"No, my dear. I am astounded by you."

"Arlud helped us. Even when his own people were threatened, he helped us."

“Yes, he did,” Wolfram said. “And I will not forget that.”

“Thank you. I hope you can meet someday.”

Wolfram leaned forward and gripped the arms of the chair. “Cordova told me you were enamored with that Erstallius fellow. Don’t worry, my dear, he’s not on my hit list.” He smiled and stood. “Now, let’s eat.”

Shanna nodded and watched her father exit the room.

“Don’t dawdle now,” Wolfram called back to her. “The food will get cold.”

CLAN ERSTALLIUS: CESTRATHA

The Dejoria frigate reached Cestratha after five days of hyperspace travel and ignited the Halva fleet into frenzied activity. Two sleek Halva destroyers guided the frigate into the orbital zone reserved for all unscheduled arrivals, between Cestratha's third and fourth moons.

Sixteen hours after entering orbit, a reply from the Halva directorate granted permission for Arlud Erstallius and his aides to planet-fall. A shuttle was sent to pick up the visitors because Clan Halva prohibited planet-fall for all military vessels belonging to off-world clans.

Arlud watched the shuttle enter the frigate's docking bay through the window in the staging room. She was an old Zavos passenger carrier. The compact model that had eight seats in the passenger cabin. She looked battered and bruised. Her patched hull was evidence she had been repaired multiple times.

"Look at it," Arlud said. "Do we really need to use that to planet-fall?"

The carrier dropped into the docking clamps, and the pilot waved to the pressure-suited docking crew.

"Looks like they pulled her out of a junkyard," Eahuda said, "but they wouldn't send her if she couldn't make the trip."

"Looks fine to me," Bev said. She waited apart from her two protectors at the opposite end of the window. "Some clans don't have the best stuff."

Bev's words forced Arlud to recognize his own bias, and he berated himself for his crass remark. "You're right," he said. "Not all clans are equal. Especially Clan Halva."

Once the bay was pressurized, Arlud led the way into the shuttle. He entered the passenger cabin, ignored the rear-facing couches closest to the cockpit, moved toward the rear, forward-facing couches, and sat on the port-side aisle seat. The thick padding formed to his body as he leaned back. "Nice," he said in an undertone. He secured himself into the safety harness. "Maybe this ship isn't so bad."

Gustav Eahuda sat on the couch that faced Arlud and fought the safety harness for more slack. He gave up after a brief struggle and moved to the window seat. The harness there was a better fit.

Bev sat across the aisle from Arlud, next to the starboard window. "Smells old in here."

Thirty minutes later they were dropping into atmosphere.

Light turbulence rattled the shuttle.

Arlud looked across the aisle at Bev. She had propped the seat cushion from the adjacent seat against the curved bulkhead to use as a pillow. Her eyes were fixed on the streaming plasma outside the window. Every time he looked at her, he found himself enthralled by her appearance. She wasn't the most beautiful woman he had seen, but she was the most intriguing. They had spoken little during the past two days. She had become withdrawn the closer they got to Cestratha. He assumed she was nervous about meeting Cynth Halva.

The glow outside increased, and the shuttle jerked sideways.

Bev glanced around the cabin as it creaked and groaned and noticed Arlud staring at her. "What?"

"You OK?"

"Yeah, why wouldn't I be?"

Bev pushed the loose cushion back into the adjacent seat and tightened her safety harness.

Arlud shifted his gaze out the port-side window. The plasma flares subsided, and the black outside had shifted to pale blue as they dropped into thicker atmosphere.

The shuttle continued to rattle and sway as the pilot adjusted their flight path.

Arlud reviewed what he knew of Clan Halva: After losing their colony on Arrilen Po, the restrictions imposed by the Supreme Council had planet-bound the clan's influence. They had become the only Great Clan confined to one holding. Forced to live on the resources of one world, they had retreated from all off-planet relationships. Only the annual meeting of the Great Clans on Makenzie pulled the Halva High Regent off-planet to fulfill his Alliance obligations.

Arlud expected a cool reception from Cynth Halva but shrugged aside thoughts of her expected indifference. He was not here to confront the past. He was here to change the future.

"What's wrong, lad?"

Arlud glanced up at Eahuda. The old Degen could always tell when he was troubled. "Wondering about the barrier we're about to break."

Eahuda contemplated the wall of isolation Clan Halva had erected between themselves and the other clans. He saw a crack in the mortar. "She accepted your request to meet. That's a good start."

"I just hope her invitation was sincere, and not a ploy to fling insults."

Eahuda held onto the shoulder straps of his harness as the shuttle bounced and jerked. "It's a good start, lad. Remember, steady and direct."

Bev followed Arlud and Eahuda into the round reception room. The main source of illumination was through a small circular opening at the apex of the domed ceiling. The small aperture confined the light to the center of the room and highlighted the inward faces of the smooth columns arrayed in a circle about five meters from the exterior wall. Everything between the columns and the wall was cloaked in shadow. Below the opening, the crest of Clan Halva was emblazoned on the floor. The design held a gray dire wolf in profile below three golden disks. The wolf and the disks were within a black circle. The black circle was centered upon a silver shield.

Arlud and Eahuda stopped between the two columns in front of the entry, which caused Bev to come to an abrupt halt about an arm's length from Arlud's left side.

The gray-haired official who had greeted them outside walked to the center of the room. His light footfalls rebounded off the marble floor. He turned when he reached the crest and said, "I will announce you. Please wait here." He then disappeared into the shadow on the opposite side of the room.

Bev had an empty feeling in the pit of her stomach. She hadn't been this nervous since her first days in the mine. The sparse lighting in the room heightened her anxiety, and the expression on Arlud's face did nothing to reassure her. "Should I be worried?"

Arlud glanced down at Bev. "No."

"You look worried."

"He always looks like that," Eahuda said. "It's not worry, it's self-ridicule."

"Ridicule?"

"Don't listen to him," Arlud said. "Sometimes my face doesn't match my mood, and he exaggerates."

"Well," Bev said, "whoever comes out of that shadow better see a friendly face or this trip will be for nothing. I'm nervous enough worrying about myself, I don't need to worry about you too."

Eahuda grinned.

Arlud stared back at Bev, not sure how to take her rebuke.

The sound of a door bolt echoed from the shadows.

The edge of a door frame became visible in the wall behind the columns to Bev's left, highlighted by the light in the adjoining room.

A cloaked figure moved through the doorway into the shadow behind the columns with heavy footfalls that clacked like metal slapping stone.

Two male servants carried a padded bench into the reception room, placed it on top of the clan crest, then hurried away through the open doorway.

The door closed with a click.

A few more metallic footfalls echoed through the room, and the cloaked figure appeared next to a column behind the padded bench. "I am Cynth Halva." Her voice had a smooth, youthful quality, but she raised her right hand and pulled back the gray hood to reveal a gaunt face, lined from age, rimmed with hair like matted spider-webs. "You are the Erstallius?"

"I am Arlud Erstallius, Regent of GSW-183."

Cynth moved to the bench. Her cloak reached the floor and hid her clacking feet from her guests. She sat down with her arms folded in front of her, hidden under her cloak's long sleeves. "And who are these others?"

Arlud gestured to his right. "Gustav Eahuda, Degen of the Corp, and my personal guard."

"Your guard?"

Cynth inspected Eahuda and saw his balanced posture and the angled stance that belied his martial training, the firm set of his jaw, and his gray eyes that analyzed her as she scrutinized him. She shifted her gaze back to Arlud. "Are you always this insecure?"

"I adhere to custom. It has served me well. Gus is an old friend, and a welcome voice when matters need reviewing."

Cynth pondered Arlud's answer for a few heartbeats, then turned her attention to Bev. "And you are?"

Bev felt her heart pounding and gulped a breath. "Bev Colli."

"And what is a Bev Colli?"

Bev dropped her gaze to the floor. She could feel the condescending tone behind the old woman's question and felt if she answered truthfully, she would be removed from this meeting. She was a sapi, born into the Drupal Caste System—sapi were not allowed to speak to clan hierarchy.

"She's a survivor," Arlud said.

Cynth looked at Arlud.

Arlud continued: "Do the weekly comdrones still arrive with reports from the Old Worlds?"

Cynth tilted her head, curious about Arlud's redirection. "Yes."

"Then you know about Alpha Cephei Four."

"I do not waste my time with off-world matters."

"Off-world matters are why we are here."

"Then you should have requested an audience with my brother."

"We've sent the High Regent a detailed report of our concerns, but you're the one with whom we need to speak."

Cynth blinked and returned her gaze to Bev. "And what is a Bev Colli?"

Bev looked into Cynth's pale blue eyes. The old woman's quizzical stare demanded an answer.

"I was deep in the rock on Alpha Cephei Four," Bev said, "twenty-two levels down, when an eruption began. I escaped by hanging from the undercarriage of the evac lift. As I rose above level eighteen the blast wave hit the shaft. The tunnels should have collapsed, but the blast wave rose upward, keeping pace with the lift. I knew then the eruption wasn't natural. Once I got to the surface, I could see the entire complex in the valley below me. Only the abandoned eastern section of the mine was still intact. Cyan-colored streams of plasma rose into the airless sky from the wreckage. As I lay close to death a small part of the plasma broke away from the main stream, dropped back toward the mine, and floated above me for a few minutes before disappearing."

"So you are a survivor," Cynth said. "You seem no worse for it."

"After I was rescued, I began having odd dreams about a young woman in a cave. I believe that young woman was you."

"And why do you believe that?"

"You were injured on Arrilen Po. You were found in a cave. Your pictures from that time resemble the woman in my dreams."

Cynth looked down and frowned. "That is not something I wish to discuss with you." She rose off the bench. "Please leave."

"It wasn't a random, natural event," Bev said. "Whoever caused the eruption on Alpha Cephei Four made a conscious decision to return and review the survivors. They were inside that plasma. And I dreamed about you. Every night I dream about you. Over and over again."

Cynth turned to leave. "That's ridiculous, Child."

"Other people dream about you."

Cynth stopped and turned back toward Bev.

"Other people?"

Arlud took the next ten minutes to explain to Cynth the details about the Cormed frigates and the survivors who experienced the same dreams.

Cynth sat back down. "You imply that I am connected to this Alpha Cephei Four incident, and the attack on Alliance frigates?"

Arlud took a step forward. "No. We're implying the cause of those events is the same as the force behind the disaster on Arrilen Po. That cause is intelligent and has made a connection with the survivors through dreams about you. Whatever happened on Arrilen Po is the key to unlocking this mystery. We were hoping you could tell us more about it."

"I'm as ignorant as you. You've come a long way for nothing."

Bev stepped forward. "I don't believe you."

Cynth sighed. "It has been a long time since anyone questioned my honesty."

"I don't question your honesty."

Arlud placed a hand on Bev's right arm and whispered: "That's enough."

Bev flicked a glance at Arlud and pulled her arm away from his touch. "No, it's not."

Cynth rose off the bench.

"I don't question your honesty," Bev said, "I question your willingness to remember."

Cynth faced Bev. "Remember? Child, I remember every day."

With one graceful movement, Cynth flung off her cloak, letting the garment drape over the bench behind her. She stood upon metal legs connected to her at mid-thigh. Her left artificial arm hung at her side—a robust metal construction similar in style to the legs. Her human hand rested on her hip. What remained of her body was clothed in a tight-fitting leotard with a padded, rust-colored yoke and silver torso.

Bev gasped at the sight of Cynth's injuries.

"You may leave now," Cynth said.

Arlud touched Bev's arm again.

Bev shrugged off Arlud's gesture and rushed up to Cynth. "I feel your pain every night. I see your anguish every night. I feel it every night—that cloud was alive!"

Arlud held Bev's shoulders from behind and pulled her backward. "That's enough. Let's go."

Bev whirled and broke Arlud's grip with her right arm. "Leave me alone!" She pushed him aside and headed toward the entrance.

Cynth closed her eyes as Bev's words echoed inside of her and drew out visions of Arrilen Po from the depths of her memory.

That cloud was alive!

Cynth opened her eyes and saw Bev retreating toward the entrance. "Stop!"

Bev ignored Cynth's command.

Cynth bent her metal legs and jumped into a high arc. Her momentum carried her over Arlud and Eahuda, and the three-point stabilizers on her metal feet slammed against the marble floor less than half a meter in front of Bev.

Bev flinched back as the din from Cynth's precision landing echoed through the room. "Whoa."

"What do you want?" Cynth asked.

Bev took another step back. She saw the old woman as a threat now and scanned the room for her best options.

Cynth looked at Arlud and Eahuda. The old Degen had his hand on a pistol at his hip. The Erstallius Regent looked dumbfounded. She wondered why her security people had missed the weapon but knew the old warrior wouldn't use it. *He's just being defensive.* "Relax. I'm no threat to you." She turned toward Bev. "Or to you, Child."

Arlud regained his composure. "That was amazing what you just did."

Cynth asked again, "What do you want?"

"The Alliance is crumbling," Eahuda said. "Finding the attacker will bring a swift end to all the chaos and could restore your clan's reputation."

"Our reputation?"

"Being a victim of disaster," Eahuda said, "is different from being the cause."

Cynth faced Bev and noticed she had relaxed a bit. "I apologize if my leap startled you. I take my abilities for granted and forget the impact they can have on strangers."

Bev accepted Cynth's apology with a nod. "It was startling."

Cynth moved closer to Bev and their eyes locked. "I don't know who's responsible for your chaos, but I can tell you what happened on Arrilen Po." She reached out and placed her human hand on Bev's shoulder. "I can feel your sincerity, Child. I don't understand what's been happening to you, but I will try to believe you as best I can."

CLAN HALVA: STATION 38

Cynth Halva's review of Arrilen Po's colonization was nearing the one-hour mark. She had presented aerial survey maps, global weather tracking data, ground-level geologic survey information, and population data charts on the holomitter in her sitting room. Portions of the data had never been seen by anyone outside the original survey team. "Up to this point," she said, "all the data we collected gave us a positive impression of colony potential."

"Very thorough," Arlud said. He reclined in one of the cushioned chairs to the left of the small couch where Cynth controlled the data stream to the holomitter. "If I'd been with your team, I would have voted for planet-fall."

Cynth felt a measure of satisfaction in Arlud's response. "That was the typical reaction among the team members. We were given the OK to proceed by the D.P.S., and by the end of the following month two-hundred colonists were on-planet."

Bev was curled up in one of the cushioned chairs to the right of Cynth's couch. She turned her head toward Cynth. "You sent autonomous orbital probes, ground-based probes, and eventually manned teams, and nothing unusual was detected?"

"After thirty-one years of analysis," Cynth said, "nothing unusual was recorded."

"And they still claimed your clan was incompetent?"

"Not at that point."

Cynth brought up a weather map of Arrilen Po's southern hemisphere on the holoscreen. "This data was captured eight days after the last load of colonists arrived. Notice the spiral cloud patterns over this desert region. Standard meteorological forces should not have produced those storms. This was the first sign that something unusual was influencing the weather patterns."

Cynth replaced the southern map with a time-lapse weather map of a region in the northern hemisphere. As the time code played in the lower right corner, a long, sweeping storm front traveled eastward, splintered into five distinct spirals, and sent lightning storms in five different directions, two of which reversed their motion and headed west.

"If I hadn't seen this, I would never have believed it," Cynth said, as the time-lapse recording repeated. "By the end of our first month on planet we had one-hundred and fifty weather stations recording data. We also added two satellites to map weather patterns, so we had real-time forecasting from three orbitals."

Arlud asked: "You reported this to the D.P.S.?"

"We sent regular reports every ten days, per protocol."

"How did they react?"

"They recommended we set-up more ground stations."

Cynth scrolled through more images from the weather satellites and stopped on one that was taken over the main colony. "This was captured the day the evacuation began."

Bev sat on the edge of her chair and examined the kilometer-wide swath of shredded buildings north of the main water reservoir. "What are those rectangular things around the remaining buildings to the east?"

"Stone slabs," Cynth said. She zoomed into the scene and focused on one building. The rectangular slabs were arranged so their edges overlapped and formed a jagged circle around the building, with a gap in two areas wide enough for a person to walk through. "Each slab you see here is about three meters long and a meter thick, but they are also five meters tall." She changed the viewing angle, and the scene shifted to a ground-level perspective. "They're set in a foundation five meters below ground."

Bev stood and stepped toward the holoscreen. "To protect you from the wind?"

"Yes, windbreaks," Cynth said. "Our normal building materials could not withstand the winds. Gusts of three-hundred and fifty kilometers per hour were recorded at the colony. Six-hundred kilometers per hour in other areas. The colony elders came up with this solution. We became megalith builders. We used the work pods and beam cutters. Every able person helped with the construction, and we protected ten buildings before the winds returned."

Cynth backed out of the ground-level view and hovered over the eastern section of the settlement where only a few of the dwellings remained. "We considered encircling the entire settlement, but that wasn't practical."

Eahuda was confused. "Why didn't you just leave?"

"At first, we thought the storms were like storms on any other Class One planet. By the time we realized the danger, both of our shuttles were destroyed, and the orbiting cargo ship was in hibernation mode with no one on board to fall to our rescue."

Arlud shifted in his seat. "You were lucky everyone wasn't killed."

"We sent a command to revive the cargo ship," Cynth said. "The engineers programmed two comdrones onboard the ship from the surface, and they launched successfully. Four weeks later the Sabballi transport arrived."

Bev returned to her seat. "Well, there was no way you could have known how dangerous that place is. Why did the Alliance revoke your certification?"

Cynth looked at Bev. She enjoyed the young woman's naïve honesty. A quality that had somehow survived the hardship of the mine. "Government decisions are often based on more than facts. There have always been underlying tensions among the clans. Clan Sabballi rescued us, but that rescue did not end well."

Cynth flipped through images on the holoscreen, and stopped at a recording labeled, *Station 38*. "On the day we were to leave I made my last trip to station thirty-eight. The station is one-hundred and forty kilometers from the settlement and has a drill assembly for deep core sampling." She activated the recording. "This is from my body cam."

Cynth trudged over rough, red rock toward the granite walls of the station. To her immediate left, a steep ridge rose above the basin floor to a height of thirty meters. To her right, another ridge about five-hundred meters distant defined the northern boundary of the basin. She negotiated the narrow opening at one corner of the station and entered the drill assembly area. The precision-cut slabs had endured the battering winds, but the drill tower supported by the walls had suffered repeated strikes by lightning. The main spindle hung within its twisted framework, leaning off axis, bent away from the sensor pallet attached to the base of the wall.

Cynth eased around the bent girders and stopped at the canvas drape that covered the sensor monitors. She knelt, loosened the canvas ties, and threw back the covering. All the instruments were still online and she withdrew her data pad from her jumper and began entering the sensor readings.

"You're wasting your time, Miss Halva."

Startled by the voice, Cynth whirled, rising to a firm stance.

The man was tall and robust, clad in a tan work uniform with a bulging pack at his left hip. His chiseled features were close shaven.

Cynth demanded: "Who are you?"

"Nared-major, Ludi Prell," the man said as he stepped closer. "I came to retrieve you. We entered orbit about an hour ago."

Cynth relaxed a bit. "I have work to finish."

"You can load your rover onto my shuttle. We'll return to the transport from here. The settlement is being evacuated."

"I didn't see your shuttle on the way here."

"I landed beyond the ridge to the north. The ground's more level there."

"I'll need a few minutes. I've got to record these readings."

Ludi nodded and looked around the station. "Too bad it didn't work—the colony, I mean."

"Yes," Cynth said. She knelt again and continued recording data.

"This entire endeavor has been a disaster from the start," Ludi said. "The Alliance will dispute this affair for years to come. A worthless holding."

"Not worthless," Cynth said. She turned to face her rescuer. "Just misunderstood."

Ludi chuckled. "Right," he muttered, and strolled to the ruined drill assembly. He bent and peered down the empty shaft.

Cynth moved to another monitor. "We weren't prepared for the radical changes in climate. We—"

"How deep is this?"

Cynth looked at Ludi, disgruntled at being ignored. "Five hundred meters the last time I checked."

"Anything valuable down there?"

"There's always something valuable," Cynth said. She pulled the canvas over the monitors. "It just depends on your point of view."

"Like I said, worthless."

Cynth fastened the canvas ties, fingered her data pad, and stuffed it into her jumper. "This land still holds promise. We just need to learn more about it."

"Well, I can't foresee a viable colony here no matter how much information you collect."

Cynth stood. "We'll be back one day."

"I doubt it."

"Follow me. I'll show you something." She led the transport crewman through the gap between the stone walls, westward over the red rock, then down onto dark brown soil of a small, furrowed field. She squatted, gestured to the tiny green shoots growing in the furrows, and grabbed a handful of the moist earth. "This is why we'll be back," she said. "Despite the horrible weather of the last few months, we've accomplished this."

"Impressive," Ludi said. "But a three-meter garden won't support a colony of two hundred."

"One day this world will be a paradise."

"You'll first need to combat that." Ludi pointed to the northern horizon. A black, swirling wall moved across the desert. Another terrible storm rolling east from the prairie. Lightning flashed upward from the turbulent mass, stabbing the silver sky and sending a visible shiver of caution up Ludi's spine. "We should leave."

Cynth brushed her hands together to remove the soil. "Unless it turns, we're safe enough. No thunder means it's too far to matter."

"Whatever possessed you people to come here?"

Cynth stood next to Ludi, her body camera focused on the distant storm. "The surveys must have taken place during a calm in the weather cycle. There is nothing to account for this in the initial reports. A meteorological nightmare."

"We should go," Ludi said. "The transport is waiting."

Cynth turned toward the station. "Right."

Ludi followed Cynth across the rough red terrain. "In fifty days, you'll be back on Cestratha. All this will be just a bad memory."

A hard, cold wind hit them, and a threatening rumble stifled their movement.

Cynth turned and looked behind her. Another storm front billowed over the jagged ridge to the southwest.

"Not again!"

Caught once before in the open she had waited for a generous break in the weather before coming here, hoping the calm would last. The storm threat had always existed though—a nagging reality that could not be ignored, and now loomed over the ridge. She grabbed Ludi's arm and urged him to retreat. "Run!"

Lightning flashed behind them and the crack of thunder quickened their pace.

The roar and hiss of the cyclonic winds pressed closer.

Cynth rushed into the station and skidded to a halt at the sight of black clouds rushing overhead. "We won't make it to your shuttle."

"We can't stay here."

The drill assembly shuddered, and the framework creaked under the strain of the battering winds.

"Follow me," Cynth said. She turned and bounded out of the station. Heading east, she raced over the red rock, pushed by the belligerent wind.

Lightning hit the drill. The brilliant blast exploded over the station, throwing out sparks that lit up the ridge.

Waves of rain showered the area.

Cynth paused in the pelting downpour. "There!" She scrambled up the granite slope on the southern side of the basin and dove into an opening in the rock. She crawled into the cool blackness, away from the wet and thundering storm. She looked back and watched Ludi's silhouette lunge inside and settle against the opposite wall.

Ludi groaned. "And you want to come back here?"

Cynth ignored the sarcasm, combed her wet hair with her fingers, and leaned back against the cave wall.

Ludi watched sheets of rain pound the rock outside the cave. "How long will this last?"

"A few hours if it doesn't stall. It's more wind than rain."

"Miserable place," Ludi said. He ignited a palm-sized glowball he had taken from his pack, and its amber light pushed back the darkness. "How many times have you been in here?"

"Once last week."

"Any creatures I should be worried about?"

Cynth giggled. "You're a brave one."

Ludi examined the angled rock above his head in the warm light. "Small things can produce big problems. Ever meet a Jai'raanian bore worm?"

"We're safe in here," Cynth said. "There are no *bore worms* on Arrile."

Ludi thought about the word, Arrile. It meant Land of Promise. "I think you mean *Arrilen Po. The Land of Promises Lost.*" He placed the glowball on the flat rock to his right and withdrew a small transceiver from his hip pouch.

"That won't work," Cynth said.

"Why?"

"Magnetic field distortion."

Ludi adjusted his position and dialed through static-charged frequencies. "I wasn't told about this."

"It comes and goes with the storms."

"Always this intense?"

Cynth nodded and hugged her knees in the chill air.

Ludi reached into his pack and exchanged his transceiver for a finger-sized scanner. He waved it in front of him, then turned and aimed it toward the rear of the cave. "Heat."

Cynth faced the deep blackness of the narrow tunnel. "Are you sure?"

"It's warmer back there by fifteen degrees. You're sure there are no creatures in here?"

"Yes."

"Damn peculiar."

"What else do you read?"

Ludi reset the scanner. "Magnetic waves at 4.98 Gauss." He adjusted the scanner for high-band frequencies and faced Cynth. "Have you explored back there?"

"No."

Ludi picked up the glowball. "I'll take a look. You can stay here." He rose and advanced into the darkness.

"Do you think that's wise?"

Ludi paused and looked back at Cynth's wet, huddled form. "This needs investigating. I won't go too far."

Cynth unfolded from the floor and followed Ludi's receding back, his hunched movement outlined by the halo of amber light from the glowball. "Don't do anything stupid."

Ludi chuckled. "Don't worry." They progressed about thirty meters at a steady decline of eight degrees per meter and stopped when a fissure in the rock beneath their feet became wide enough to be hazardous. "Watch your footing," Ludi said.

Cynth focused on the gap between her feet. "We're losing the floor."

"Yeah, looks like the split continues to widen. Look up."

Cynth turned her body camera to focus on the cave ceiling. Both sides of the tunnel rose out of range of the glowball's amber light and disappeared into blackness.

"This is a fissure," Ludi said. "From the look of the surface, I would guess a pressure crack."

"Pressure crack? Are you a geologist?"

"Hold this."

Cynth focused on the glowball in Ludi's outstretched hand. She took the light and watched Ludi pull a small metallic sphere from his hip pack. He pushed a lever and four panels on top of the sphere flipped open and revealed a circular bracket that grew to twice the original diameter. He retrieved another glowball from his pack and placed it inside the circular bracket, which then shrunk to secure the light to the top of the sphere. With the flick of another switch, the metallic sphere sprouted four appendages that produced a green aura that pushed the device off Ludi's hand and kept it suspended in the air.

"That's convenient," Cynth said.

"Self-powered probes are standard issue for Sabballi clanmen in the field," Ludi explained. "I never leave home without one."

He touched the bracelet on his right wrist and a small holoscreen appeared with controls for the probe. He ignited the glowball and guided the probe deeper into the cave. As the probe advanced the amber light revealed a narrow fissure that continued downward for three-hundred meters, then twisted to the left.

"Wow," Cynth said. "I didn't expect it would be that deep."

"It probably goes much deeper."

"Does that thing have sensors?"

"Yeah," Ludi said. He examined the holoscreen. "Same temperature. Same magnetics." The probe's visible light camera was limited to the short range of the glowball's dim light, but the probe also had infrared and echo location capabilities. He entered instructions to guide the probe around the bend in the cave and to continue until it met another obstacle. "That should do it."

Cynth turned and watched the distant amber glow vanish as the probe moved behind the bend in the tunnel. Ludi tracked the probe's progress for another two-hundred meters, a steady downward motion through the meandering fissure, and then it stopped when the sensors detected a void.

Cynth leaned closer to view the small holoscreen. "What's wrong?"

The holoscreen displayed a static-filled view of the black void.

"A big chasm from the look of it. Can't see the far side."

"That glowball's not very bright."

Ludi entered more instructions via the holoscreen, and the view shifted to infrared. He raised his wrist so Cynth could get a better view. "Look."

The small screen displayed a dim reddish mass, and at the bottom right corner of the screen a dark circle was visible.

"What's that?"

"The red area is the heat I've been detecting," Ludi said. "The circle is an area that lacks heat."

"What does it look like in visible light?"

Ludi switched the display, and it turned black. "It's too far outside the range of the glowball."

"Move in closer."

After fifteen minutes of maneuvering, a detailed picture of the chasm had been recorded by the probe that revealed a spherical chamber twenty meters in diameter with two circular tunnels on the southern side.

"That's not natural," Cynth said. "Those openings aren't cracks. Get the probe closer to the rock."

Ludi guided the probe up to the smooth, curved surface of the chamber.

"It looks glazed," Cynth said, "like it was melted."

"Volcanic activity."

"No. You said it yourself—this is a fissure cave, not a lava tube. Someone cut this out of the existing rock."

"Who? You were the first ones here."

"Apparently not," Cynth said, and she was struck with the terrible realization they may have trespassed beyond allowable limits. "We're done here. Let's go."

"This needs to be investigated."

"Not by us. We're leaving. Remember?"

"I'll file a request."

"Good luck with that."

Cynth leaned back against the rock. "Retrieve the probe and let's go."

"Wait," Ludi said, "something's happening." He turned toward the rear of the cave, intrigued by a sudden peak in high-band emissions.

A faint thud sounded in the cave.

Cynth stood erect. "What was that?"

Another thud.

Ludi focused on the holoscreen. "Wow!"

"What?"

"Temp just rose one-hundred degrees."

"What? How?"

"Look at that." The holoscreen data blinked and displayed an ambient temperature above five-hundred degrees.

A hot wind rushed through the cave and pelted Ludi and Cynth with dust and small pebbles.

Cynth turned and rushed across the cracked rock floor toward the entrance.

Ludi focused on the small holoscreen. The data flow from the probe stopped. He turned to follow Cynth.

Cynth looked behind her to see Ludi swallowed by a blazing surge of cyan-colored plasma. She stumbled as a burning pressure wave hit her back and she fell to her knees. She pushed up and tried to scramble over the cracked rock for the exit, but another pressure wave knocked her down. Her skin prickled from the heat, and she covered her eyes from the blazing cyan light as shock waves pulsed through her. She cried from the pain of charred flesh, of muscle burnt to the bone.

The holoscreen went black.

Cynth surveyed her guests. They sat in silent shock. "And that was the end of my stay on Arrilen Po."

Bev swiveled in her chair to face Cynth. "How did they find you?"

"My transponder. That's how Ludi found me."

Arlud stood and walked over to the clear duraplex doorway that led to the sitting room balcony. He could see the sculpted landscape of the Halva compound beyond the railing and the distant green hills. "Who else has seen your recording?"

"Just my family."

"The D.P.S. didn't take it into account?"

"My father felt the truth would lead to more complications for our Clan, and especially for me because Ludi died, so he hid this from the investigation team and agreed to the demands of the council. We never used this evidence."

Eahuda faced Cynth. "But this proves your innocence regarding Ludi's death."

"No," Cynth said. "This is evidence of our failure. The holding was already inhabited by someone. The chamber and tunnels are proof of that. The council would have seen this as a violation. Our right to planet-fall would have been declared premature and without legal right, and our punishment would have been much greater."

Arlud folded his arms across his chest. "Who got there first?"

Cynth met Arlud's quizzical gaze and shrugged. "As far as I know, no one has been on Arrilen Po since the day we left. Too dangerous."

Eahuda was angered by Clan Halva's lack of responsibility. "Why didn't you return to investigate what happened in the tunnel?"

"I was in no condition to do anything."

"Didn't the rescue team survey the area to find what killed Ludi?"

"Ludi was gone. I was the only one they found. They took advantage of the break in the weather to retrieve me, but the threat of more storms in the area cut short the investigation. I woke up a week later en route to Cestratha and discovered they never searched for Ludi."

Bev let the images she had just seen revolve in her memory, and she found a connection to Alpha Cephei Four. "In the mine we were warned about E.M. bursts. We were told the durillium veins amplified all E.M. frequencies. There were periodic bursts of energy that disabled equipment. Right before the eruption my drill died from an E.M. burst."

"That's interesting," Cynth said. "Was your weather also affected?"

"There's no weather on Alpha Cephei Four. It's an airless rock."

Arlud paced back to his chair but resisted the urge to sit down. He looked at Cynth, the dying woman found in a cave. "The connection is in the rock."

Eahuda almost laughed. "The rock?"

"Bev escaped from a mine. Cynth was almost killed in a cave. Whatever is at play here can be found in the rock. Ludi's probe discovered evidence of an intelligent presence deep underground. Bev experienced an intelligent presence both in the mine and on the surface."

Cynth turned off the holoscreen. "It seems I have only confounded your mystery."

"No," Arlud said. "You have shown us where we need to go."

BEV COLLI: COMATOSE

Black rock crumbled to reveal a narrow crevice that opened up to a desert of white sand dunes. The flinty smell in the rock followed Bev as she rushed out of the crevice and hovered above the dunes.

She looked back—the crevice was sealed by a landslide of gray boulders. Below her, a gaping black hole opened in the dunes. A spot of brilliant white light appeared in the hole and morphed into a vortex of cyan-colored plasma that rushed upward and enveloped her.

Her skin prickled from the heat and a crushing pressure held her body rigid.

She screamed.

The pain jolted Bev out of the dream, and she sprang up on her bunk.

This was the first time a dream intruded while she was just resting. She was still clothed and laying on top of the bed quilt. She looked over at the chronometer in the bulkhead next to her bunk. She had been in her cabin for thirty-five minutes.

The stifling grip on her body was gone, but she could still feel tingling from the burning plasma. She examined her hands and arms.

No visible damage.

She propped her pillow up against the bulkhead, scooted to a sitting position and leaned back against the pillow. *It's getting worse*, she thought. *I should have stayed on Cestratha.*

She and her protectors had boarded this Halva cruiser after a long debate about returning to Arrilen Po. Lady Halva was hesitant at first, but after four hours of intense deliberation, Arlud's logic convinced the old matriarch the expedition was the right thing to do. And the Dejoria frigate that had brought Bev and her protectors to Cestratha left orbit after Arlud notified the Commander-in-Charge he could return to U'galem.

Why am I here?

Bev saw no benefit for herself in this endeavor. All she had wanted to do was get out of her Polinda contract and find a quiet, secure place to live her life. But here she was, stowed away on this old Halva cruiser, heading to one of the most dangerous places known to man.

Arlud had a very convincing way about him. "You're a conduit," he had said. "You've seen more in your dreams than anyone we've interviewed from the mine. That's significant. You could be the key we need to unravel this mystery."

She had been flattered by that idea, and before she realized it, she had agreed to join the expedition.

He knew what to say to keep me here, she thought, and she scolded herself for giving in to his reasoning.

At the sound of the door buzzer, Bev hit the door lock switch on the wall panel next to her bed.

Cynth Halva clacked through the open doorway and stopped upon seeing Bev dressed and sitting on her bunk. "Am I disturbing you?"

Bev hugged her knees. "No."

Cynth looked around the narrow, gray cabin. The floor space was equal to the width of the bunk and just slightly deeper. She gestured to the short bench folded into the starboard bulkhead opposite the bunk. "May I sit?"

Bev nodded her approval.

Cynth pushed a lever on the wall with her cybernetic hand and the bench unfolded. She settled onto the metal seat—her legs angled to one side. Her dark green jumper covered most of her body, but her lower legs and feet were exposed metal. "I hope you don't mind these sparse accommodations. This is typical for our fleet."

"The Dejoria frigate wasn't much better. This is fine."

Cynth smiled. "Clanmen are trained for this, but it's a bit too spartan for most non-military people."

"You should see the mine I lived in. This is a palace compared to that place."

Cynth lowered her eyes. She and Bev had nothing in common, and she hoped that would not hinder her effort. She raised her eyes. "Are you still having the dreams?"

Bev nodded.

"Do you feel anything alive in the cave during your dreams?"

"Not like I did on Alpha Cephei Four."

Cynth let her shoulders slump. She had hoped for a different answer. "What happens in your dreams after you see me?"

"I first thought I saw you half buried in the ground, but now I know that was because your legs were gone. The dreams ended at that point until about a month ago. I found if I fought against the anguish, and the pain, I would rush through the tunnel toward a point of light. I usually come out over sandstone terrain under gray clouds, with flashes of lightning. Then I'm surrounded by stars, and then I'm back on Alpha Cephei Four."

"So there is a connection."

Bev thought about that assertion. "Yeah. I've been seeing that stuff since before we left U'galem."

"You said, 'usually.' What are the differences?"

"Sometimes they end while I'm still inside the cave. Sometimes I see different places. I just saw one that was new."

"What happened?"

Bev retreated into her memory of the vision. "Heat and pain above a massive hole in the sand outside the cave. You weren't there."

Cynth contemplated that new information.

"Your connection is evolving. You said during our first meeting, 'that cloud was alive.' What did you mean by that?"

"The plasma that came out of the mine. I could feel something there. Something alive, looking at me."

"But nothing alive in the cave?"

"No."

Cynth lowered her eyes again and drifted into thought.

"Your pain is so intense," Bev said. "Maybe that's why I can't feel anything else?"

Cynth looked up. "Just before I passed out, I thought I felt something there. It was just a wisp of a feeling. I don't have dreams about it. Never have."

Bev saw the old woman's disappointment and thought about her terrible pain of losing both legs and an arm. "How did they find you?"

Cynth tilted her head. "I told you, Child. My transponder." She displayed her right wrist to show Bev the small circular mark that identified the implanted beacon.

"In your body camera recording you get about ten meters through the tunnel before you're knocked down for good. That's a long way from the exit. Wouldn't the rock block your transponder?"

Cynth searched her memory. "They found me about five meters inside the entrance."

"But you didn't get that far before the recording ended. Did you get back up after that?"

Cynth recalled the moment of intense pain and pressure as she was forced to the ground. "I don't remember what happened after I was hit the second time."

"Your legs were gone. You couldn't have moved."

"The med report said—"

"You should have died deep in the tunnel."

"They said my wounds were cauterized, which kept me from bleeding out."

"But how did you get closer to the entrance? Did you crawl?"

"I can't remember."

Bev saw the confusion in Cynth's slack expression and assumed her advanced age had clogged her memory. "You don't need to remember. You survived. That's enough evidence for me."

Cynth had often wondered why she was still alive. Bev's reasoning confirmed her suspicions. "I was saved by something alive in that cave."

Bev nodded. "And we were both almost killed by something alive."

That paradox whirled in Cynth's mind. "What do you think we'll find on Arrilen Po?"

"I hope it's the thing that saved you, and not the thing that almost killed you."

Cynth was cautious about returning to Arrilen Po but knew there was no other way to restore her family name. "This time we're prepared."

This time five cruisers were making the journey to Arrilen Po. They were prepped for battle but hope prevailed for a peaceful encounter.

Bev glanced at the chronometer. The trip from Cestratha to Arrilen Po was a seven-day journey through hyperspace, and that was about twenty standard days on-planet. They had plenty of time to change course. "We can always turn around and go back."

"I'll have none of that, Child. We must do this. We must be brave."

"I do not understand why I agreed to come with you. You don't need me."

Cynth looked at Bev in silence for a few heartbeats. She saw the fear in her. "I'm afraid too," she said. "Difficult times are always fearful. We must cloak our fear with determination."

"Easier said than done."

"It is never easy."

"But you still don't need me."

"Yes, we do. I thought the Erstallius made that clear?"

Bev smirked at the mention of Arlud's persuasive logic.

Cynth disliked Bev's condescending attitude but spoke with the same soothing tone she had used since entering the cabin: "You're having second thoughts. That's normal."

"I think Arlud sees more in me than is actually there."

"He sees what I see."

"What?"

"A brave young woman who may hold the key to this mystery."

Bev lowered her head, brought her right hand to her forehead and rested her elbow on her knee. She could not bring herself to believe Cynth's assertion.

"Arlud cares about you," Cynth said. "He wouldn't ask you to do something you couldn't do."

Bev glanced up. "I know he cares. I've sensed that from him and I appreciate that, but his motive is based on what he can gain."

"There's more to him than that. You may have the capacity to unravel this mystery more than anyone else, but even if you don't, he'll still care about you."

"He cares about unraveling who attacked the mine. If that wasn't his motive, I'd still be working in the warehouse."

"Based on what I've heard, you'd probably be in the custody of a retriever on your way back to Pigrell."

Bev knew that was only part of the alternative reality. "Yeah," she said, "or locked up for shooting that guy in the warehouse." She leaned back and crossed her legs.

"Perhaps you should stop fretting over what we want you to do. Focus on what you should do for everyone's good. There comes a time when the needs of others are more important than our own needs."

"In the mine we were taught to focus on what we needed to do, before considering what others needed to do. If you didn't approach each shift like that, that's when mistakes happened, and mistakes in an airless mine can be deadly."

"Then tell me," Cynth said, "what must you do now to avoid a mistake?"

"Go back to Cestratha."

Cynth kept her disappointment in check. She knew Bev was being difficult because she did not believe in herself. "Would that solve our problems?"

"It would solve mine."

Cynth took a deep breath. "No, Child. Avoiding the solution only allows the problem to grow larger. We must be brave. We are all in this together. We have your back."

Bev leaned forward, brought her knees to her chest, and wrapped her arms around her legs. "There is no way we can be prepared for what waits on Arrilen Po."

Cynth responded with the clack of one foot as she turned toward the cabin doorway.

"The Cormed frigates could do nothing to stop what's out there," Bev said. "How do you expect us to not end up like they did?"

Cynth's pale blue eyes focused on Bev's huddled form. "I expect us to succeed because you are here. Without you—"

"That's crazy."

"No, Child. It's reality."

Bev leaned back against her pillow. "Crazy."

"I was saved," Cynth said. "That implies compassion. You and many others have been touched by dreams. That implies a desire to communicate. We may find our return to Arrilen Po a welcome one. That is my hope. With you there, the odds of that happening are greater."

Bev rolled her eyes.

Cynth stood and looked down at the discordant young woman. She wanted to say more to Bev but let the argument rest, for now. "They'll be serving dinner in about an hour. I'll see you in the mess?"

"Yeah."

Cynth smiled, then turned and left the cabin.

Bev stared at the cabin door. *Crazy*, she thought. But deep inside of her she sensed truth in what Cynth had said. She didn't understand how it was possible, but she had a connection with something in her dreams. Something that would not let go. Something that needed to communicate. The visions were the key, just as Arlud had said. Somehow, she had become linked to the force that destroyed the mine, attacked the Cormed frigates, and forty-seven years earlier had almost killed Cynth Halva. The realization flooded her mind, and she was thrust into another dream of billowing, cyan-colored clouds. She dropped her face into her hands to hide from the vision, but the dream pushed her into black rock, and she sped through layers of crumbling strata, downward, toward the center of the world.

Arlud entered the infirmary and peered through the observation window at Bev's clothed body lying on the flat exam table. Her right forearm was held in a metallic bracelet that transmitted her vitals to a holoscreen above her head. She had been in this condition since discovered comatose in her cabin a few hours after the dinner service in the mess. Cynth went to her cabin and found her unconscious in a fetal position on her bunk.

Arlud turned toward the med-tech sitting at the small desk to his right. "How's she doing?"

The young woman looked up. "No change."

"May I go in?"

The med-tech nodded.

Arlud slid open the duraplex doorway into the examination room and was struck by the cool temperature and the sound of orchestral music. He took a step toward the exam table as the door slid shut behind him. He reviewed the holoscreen above Bev's head. The brain wave pattern was like the graphs Pardee had shown him. He gestured to the med-tech on the other side of the observation window.

The young woman rose from her desk and stepped through the doorway. "Yes?"

Arlud pointed to the holoscreen. "The interference patterns in her brain wave activity, have you been able to isolate them?"

"No."

"Have you tried to block them?"

"No. Blocking those wavelengths could disrupt her brain function and cause harm. We've no way to isolate her from the effects."

"What can we do?"

"Keep her healthy until she wakes up."

"That's it?"

"There is no trauma, or underlying physical condition that caused her coma. At least none that we can determine."

"Look at her brain waves."

"We know, but we don't know what's causing them, or how to stop them."

Arlud stifled his criticism. The med-tech was doing the best she could. "Does it need to be this cold in here?"

"Reducing body temperature can have a positive effect on a coma patient's recovery."

"And the music?"

"Constant aural stimulant can help pull her back to consciousness."

Arlud looked down at the calm expression on Bev's face, then glanced back up at the holoscreen. "She is conscious," he said, "she's just somewhere else."

The med-tech reviewed the brain wave monitor. "There is a lot going on in there."

"There's got to be something you can do?"

"If there's no change by tomorrow, we'll set her up in a bio-containment chamber."

Arlud turned back toward Bev. The bio-containment chamber would give her body all the nutrients she needed, stimulate her muscles to slow down atrophy, and remove the need to change her position to prevent bedsores. He moved closer to the table and held Bev's limp right hand. It was cool to the touch because of the low temperature in the room.

The med-tech went back to her desk.

"I know you're in there," Arlud said. "We're all here waiting for you."

He stroked Bev's cheek with his left thumb, glanced up at the brain wave monitor and saw a brief spike.

She felt that!

He brushed hair away from Bev's forehead and her limp fingers tightened around his palm.

The monitor showed her pulse rise and her brain waves spiked.

Arlud leaned closer to her face. He saw eye movement under her lids. "Come on, Bev. Wake up!"

Bev's eye movement stopped, and her pulse dropped to its previous level.

Arlud stood erect. He felt Bev's fingers go limp again, and he let her hand slip out of his grip. She had warned him back on U'galem that her dreams would get worse if she came to Cestratha. Now that they were heading to Arrilen Po, her mind had slipped deeper into another reality and there was no way to bring her back.

Cynth Halva appeared in the doorway to the exam room. "How is she?"

"Not good."

"I hope this won't impact the mission."

That statement forced Arlud onto a different mental path and he was caught without an immediate response.

Cynth stepped into the exam room. "We're so close I would hate to abandon our effort."

Arlud focused his thoughts. "She told me this would happen back on U'galem, and I didn't listen."

"Her dreams brought you this far," Cynth said. "The closer we get, the stronger her connection becomes, and the closer we are to an answer. Turning back might break her connection for good."

"You have no proof of that."

"The proof is right in front of us."

Cynth clacked forward and stood next to the exam table. She reviewed the bio charts on the holoscreen.

"I fear for her," Arlud said. "We have no control over this."

"Yes, we do. We can allow it to continue."

"Then we risk her life."

Cynth looked at Arlud. "No. Look at the activity on the monitor. She's in no physical danger. I believe she may come out of this with all the answers we need."

Arlud saw the potential in Cynth's assessment, but he also saw the danger for Bev. "If she's not awake by the time we reach Arrilen Po, we should reevaluate."

"Agreed," Cynth said, and she hoped her assumptions were correct.

CLAN HALVA: ARRILEN PO

Arrilen Po appeared on the holoscreen above the navigation pedestal in the Command Intelligence Center aboard the flagship of the Halva task force. The planet was a mottled globe, with wide basins of blue sea that split the land area into five distinct continents. White cloud covered the poles, and the equator was obscured by white wisps of moisture that branched off a spiral storm over the largest sea.

Looks like it did the first time I saw it, Cynth thought. She stood at the navigation pedestal with Arlud, Eahuda, and the cruiser's executive officers.

The probe that relayed the image of the planet was seventy-thousand kilometers from the surface, and two hours ahead of the task force. The command crew in the C.I.C. were busy analyzing data from the probe at their stations encircling the room.

Green ellipses appeared around the planet, outlining the orbital paths of the three weather satellites placed in orbit by the first Halva settlers. Identifier labels for each satellite appeared at the bottom of the display:

Global Mapper 1   Global Mapper 2   Global Mapper 3

The Commander-in-Charge flicked a hand signal to a crewman behind him, and an inset image of the satellite closest to the probe appeared next to the labels. It was Global Mapper 2. Half of the satellite was a black lump of melted metal. One antenna array remained attached to the intact section, giving the object an unbalanced appearance as it rotated.

"That's not good," Arlud muttered. The other satellites were out of visible range on the other side of the planet.

"Hold course," the Commander-in-Charge said.

Thirty minutes later the probe circled around the planet as it descended to a geosynchronous orbit and transmitted images of the other satellites. Global Mapper 1 and Global Mapper 3 appeared undamaged but would not respond to the probe's transmission of the standard hail. A few minutes after reaching its optimal orbit, the probe found something unexpected.

"Zoom in on that object," the Commander-in-Charge said.

Orbiting about five-thousand kilometers above the sun-facing side of the planet, the charred hull of a medium-sized vessel spun around her long axis amid a tenuous debris field.

Arlud flicked a glance at Cynth. "Is that one of yours?"

"No."

After a brief examination of the derelict ship, the probe transmitted data that scrolled across the bottom edge of the holoscreen:

> Length: 365 meters . . . Estimated weight: 700,000 metric tons . . . Engine status: null . . . Hull integrity: null . . . Comm status: null . . .

Eahuda thought he recognized the class of vessel. "Even with that melted stern, she looks like a modern frigate."

"Yes, she does," the Commander-in-Charge said. He spoke to a subordinate, and the probe's view of the derelict ship changed to a close-up image of the blackened hull. Over the next few minutes, the probe panned across the vessel's revolving profile until it came upon the burnt remnant of her registry code near the starboard bow section.

"It's a Sabballi ship," the Commander-in-Charge said. He looked at Cynth. "Did they lay claim to this place after you left?"

Cynth raised her eyebrows and brought her human hand to her chest. "Not to my knowledge. This entire system was declared off-limits."

"You can't restrict access without guards," Eahuda said. "She must have been policing the system. Search the DPS database for her registry code."

The Commander-in-Charge signaled his comm officer to do the search.

Cynth felt betrayed. "We should have been told about this."

"Only the Sabballi needed to know," the Commander-in-Charge said. "The Alliance is not required to inform all clans of its policing strategies."

The comm officer turned toward his commander. "There are no listings for that ship in the database, sir."

"Probably restricted," the Commander-in-Charge replied. "We don't have access to the central data hub out here." He turned toward his duty officer. "Prepare a team to board her."

The duty officer snapped to attention. "Aye, sir," he said. Then he turned and headed for the Crew Operations Center.

Cynth was confused. "Is that necessary?"

"Yes," the Commander-in-Charge said. "We need her navigation data."

"How will that help us?"

"It will help us understand what happened to her."

"We know what happened to her. Just look at her."

"Yes," the Commander-in-Charge said, "we see what's left of her. We need to know the why and when of the event that destroyed her."

Cynth understood what the Commander wanted, but she wanted definitive answers about Arrilen Po, not a derelict Sabballi frigate. *What a waste of energy*, she thought. She glanced around the room. The crew were huddled at their stations, doing the work they were trained to do. She would never understand half of what they were engaged in, but she knew what was important and what was frivolous. "We should focus on the surface."

The Commander-in-Charge turned toward his matriarch. "We need to approach this with caution, my lady. Our duty demands we unravel this one layer at a time, least we miss something. This is the first layer."

Cynth pondered the Commander's logic. She had chosen him to lead this expedition because of his reputation for accomplishing difficult missions. The memory of his service record quashed her objection, and she acquiesced. "As you see best, Commander."

Arlud wasn't surprised by the Commander's approach. It was the correct mind-set under the circumstances. He understood Lady Halva's perspective, but knew a protracted, careful beginning to this investigation would not only prevent mistakes, but it would also give Bev time to recover. She was still in bio-containment and had shown no signs of awakening. His agreement with Cynth to reevaluate their position based on Bev's condition could still impact the mission, but the immediate focus was on making orbit and searching the dead vessel. He noticed Eahuda was engaged in the proceedings. He patted the old Degen on the shoulder and whispered: "Call me if anything important happens."

Eahuda wasn't surprised by Arlud's decision to leave and nodded his agreement.

Arlud slipped out of the C.I.C. and headed for the infirmary.

Bev opened her eyes to a blurry view of the inside of the bio-containment chamber. She blinked a few times and her vision cleared. The duraplex window above her head was obscured by reflections from the interior glow strips along the seam of the chamber hatch. Her right forearm was held in a metallic bracelet, and her torso was covered with a thin, thigh-length gown. She felt a restraint around her hips and saw her legs and feet, covered with white compression stockings, floating in the zero gravity inside the chamber.

I'm back.

The shape of someone's head appeared behind the window reflections, and a contralto voice sounded inside the chamber: "Lay still. We need to get your tubes out."

Bev reached up with her left hand and felt the feeding tube in her nose.

Door latches clicked and the brief hiss of escaping air caused Bev to lower her hand and focus on the chamber hatch.

The hatch rose off its seals and swung away to the right.

The female med-tech reached into the chamber and pushed a switch on Bev's forearm bracelet. "Don't move yet. We need to disconnect you first—welcome back."

By the time Arlud arrived in the infirmary, Bev was on the exam table with the back raised so she could relax in a sitting position. A light blue blanket covered her legs, and she held a cup of ice water below her chin with both hands.

Arlud stopped inside the doorway. "Welcome back."

Bev returned a blank stare and sipped her cup of water.

The med-tech stood behind Bev at an instrument panel on the bulkhead and turned two switches. A holoscreen ignited above Bev's head and displayed her heart, blood pressure, and brain wave monitors.

Arlud focused on the brain wave graph. The interference patterns were gone.

The med-tech glanced up at the holoscreen, then leaned over and flicked a pen light into Bev's eyes to check her response. "Good," she said. "How do you feel?"

"Fine."

Arlud moved closer to the exam table as the med-tech left the room. "We were all worried about you."

Bev swallowed another sip and locked eyes with Arlud. "Are we there yet?"

"Almost. We've entered the system and sent a probe ahead to reconnoiter."

"To what?"

"Reconnoiter," Arlud repeated. "To investigate what's there."

"Oh."

Bev placed the cup of ice water on the tray next to the exam table and lowered her head as she recalled the dreams that held her captive. "I couldn't get away," she said. "They wouldn't let me go."

Arlud leaned closer. “Who wouldn’t let you go?”

Bev thought for a moment, then shrugged. “I don’t know. It’s confusing.” She looked up at Arlud with tears in her eyes. “Everything was jumbled. Events shuffled back and forth around me. I’m not sure what to make of it all.”

Arlud reached out and placed a hand on Bev’s shoulder. “Your back now,” he said. He rubbed her shoulder and could feel the tightness of her muscles through the thin infirmary gown. “We can analyze your dreams once you’ve fully recovered.”

Bev reached up and held Arlud’s hand on her shoulder. She smiled at him, a thin, brief expression that morphed into a frown. “I just hope they leave me alone long enough so I can make sense of it.”

The Halva cruisers arrived at their designated positions around Arrilen Po. Two cruisers entered geosynchronous orbits on opposite sides of the planet where they could each monitor an entire hemisphere. The flagship fell into a high orbit three-hundred and twenty-thousand kilometers from Arrilen Po, five hundred kilometers beyond the track of the second moon. That far position was meant to protect Lady Halva from a possible assault. The remaining two cruisers fell into polar orbits about two-thousand kilometers from the surface. Their mission was to sweep the planet with all of their instruments to create high resolution data maps.

Now that the cruisers were in place, Cynth’s focus shifted to Bev. She had noticed Arlud’s absence in the C.I.C. before they made orbit and understood why he left. Bev Colli’s condition could handicap the mission. “Well done, Commander,” she said. “I’ll be in the infirmary if you need me.”

The Commander-in-Charge tipped his head.

Cynth was greeted by a sign on the infirmary hatch that read, “In Rehab.” She continued down the narrow corridor until she reached the open hatch to the rehab bay. She was surprised to see Bev beyond the interior observation window, dressed in her gray pants and blue pullover, walking between two support bars while holding onto the bars with her hands. The med-tech waited at the end of the bars, watching Bev advance toward her.

Cynth entered the small rehab lounge and faced Arlud as he unfolded from a chair to her right. “Why wasn’t I told about this?”

"Sorry about that," Arlud said. "She woke minutes before I reached the infirmary. Notifying you didn't enter my mind."

Cynth saw the sincerity in Arlud's answer. *He cares about the girl*, she thought. "How's she doing?"

Arlud turned his attention toward Bev. "Good. Normal rehab after being weightless for seven days."

"And her dreams?"

Arlud looked back at Cynth. "We haven't discussed specifics. I told her we'd wait until she's fully recovered."

"We're in orbit. Do we have time to wait?"

"She's confused, physically weak, and a little frightened right now. Forcing her to delve back into all that mess too soon might cause her to retreat from it completely. She needs to regain her strength."

Cynth held back her protest. She understood Arlud's concern, and as she watched Bev turn around at the end of the bars to walk in the opposite direction, she saw the weakness in her. "How long will she need to recover?"

"The med-tech said one day of recovery for every three days in bio-containment's micro gravity, but she should start feeling more normal by tomorrow."

"Then we'll question her tomorrow."

"That'll depend on her."

"She's been trying to avoid this confrontation since we left Cestratha. Her attitude should not dictate how we move forward."

"We have little choice."

"Maybe if you talk to her alone?"

"Me?"

"She's comfortable with you."

"She thinks I'm using her."

"You are. She needs to see that's not the limit of your concern. She needs to feel connected."

Arlud recognized the truth in Cynth's observation. Bev had been on her own since she was taken from Pigrell. Her service in the mine forced her to focus on surviving, not just the airless environment, but her daily interactions with the other miners. She was thrust into a life that pushed away genuine friendship and replaced it with situational camaraderie. Her trust in others wilted away, and she relied on herself to survive during her first year inside the mine. Josh Gridle helped her trust return as the years passed, but only to a limited degree.

"She doesn't have the strength to confront this unknown on her own," Cynth said. "She needs to know she can trust you. She needs to know she can trust all of us."

Bev and Arlud sat apart about an arm's length on the cushioned bench in front of the panoramic window in the port observation bay. Arrilen Po was a wanning crescent outside the window, framed by a spattering of stars, with the disk of the milky way slicing through the view behind the shadowed side of the planet. The first and second moons were visible to the left of the crescent. The first moon was a brilliant speck near the curve of Arrilen Po's blue limb. The second moon was a thinner crescent near the left edge of the window frame, about the size of Arlud's fist.

"It's beautiful," Bev said. She leaned forward and crossed her arms on the metal hand railing that protruded along the bottom edge of the window. "Where are the other cruisers?"

"From this distance they're difficult to see without magnification."

Arlud punched the small control pad with his finger and the window was overlaid with a green schematic showing the position of the other Halva cruisers.

"Wow," Bev said. "When will we planet-fall?"

"That hasn't been decided yet."

"Still waiting on me?"

"Knowing what you saw would be helpful."

"It's complicated."

"In what way?"

Bev frowned and focused on the window. "Can you turn off that grid? The view's better without it."

Arlud punched the control pad, and the schematic disappeared.

Bev lowered her head. "I was thrown down a deep hole in the rock and found myself inside a dark cavern that erupted into a blazing vortex of energy like the one that killed Ludi Prell. I was tossed upward and found myself inside the mine, surrounded by that blue plasma. I saw a Cormed frigate burn. I saw the colony on Arrilen Po ripped to shreds by the winds Cynth told us about." She looked at Arlud. "I saw destruction everywhere, and then I was floating in the dark."

"They put you through that for seven days?"

Bev gripped the hand railing and leaned back on the bench to stretch her arms. "It was exhausting," she said. She sat up straight and released her grip. "I was oblivious of the time. Most of the visions repeated, but near the end all I was shown was the vortex in the cavern and the eruption on Alpha Cephei Four. Those two scenes repeated over and over again until I opened my eyes in bio-containment."

"Did anyone speak to you?"

Bev closed her eyes and smiled. "I heard you once. You held my hand." She opened her eyes and looked at Arlud. "No other voices."

Arlud diverted his gaze to the scene outside the window. "So just the visions then?"

"Also heat and burning pain—like the earlier dreams."

"Nothing else?"

Bev folded her arms across her chest and retreated into her memory. "Panic, surprise, regret, sadness." She looked up at Arrilen Po. "There's something about the rock that was constant. Before the visions changed, I was always thrust back into that cavern. That was the starting point for everything."

"What do you think it means?"

Bev lowered her head and tried to recall something that would spark a deeper understanding. "The starting point," she said. "Everything begins in the rock."

"If that's true, how did they get there?"

Bev's mind whirled. The image of the vortex surged to the forefront of her memory. "It's a doorway."

"A doorway?"

"Yeah," Bev said. She turned toward Arlud. "I'm no scientist. I know nothing about what makes the universe work the way it does, but I get a very strong impression that the vortex opens a doorway from another place. It's how they appear in the rock."

"They?"

"The aliens."

Arlud drew back from that statement. That reality had revolved around the periphery of every report he had read about this situation. Only Degen Turl had been willing to embrace that idea with confidence. "Aliens. From where?"

"Not here."

"What do you mean?"

"I get the impression they're from outside our universe."

"Outside?" Arlud thought of the possibilities. "From another dimension?"

Bev shrugged. "I don't know, just not from here."

She looked out the window and crossed her arms on the hand railing. "I think they came to Arrilen Po after the colony was established, based on what Cynth told us. I think they caused the bad weather. I think they had no idea our colony was here until Ludi got hit by that plasma surge and they ran into Cynth."

"How would that be possible?"

"They're not human."

Arlud pondered Bev's theory. Based on all the reports from survivors, and the limited physical evidence, he had to agree. "They're so different from us they didn't recognize us?"

"Yeah," Bev said. "We didn't even register as something to investigate. I think that's what caused that cloud to split away from the main plasma stream on Alpha Cephei Four. I think they only recognized the damage they caused when they spotted the survivors on the hill."

"If that's true, it raises more questions. If destroying the colony and the mine were mistakes, why did they attack the Cormeds?"

"Yeah," Bev said. She leaned forward and rested her forehead on her arms. "I'm probably wrong."

Arlud scooted closer to Bev and rubbed her back. "You could also be right."

"I'm not sure what I know," Bev admitted. Arlud's reassuring touch was a comfort, but she still felt inadequate. "I guess I'm not much help."

Arlud slid closer and hugged Bev's shoulders. "No," he said, "you've been very helpful. We'll figure this out."

Bev raised her head, leaned into Arlud's hug, and looked up at Arrilen Po. "We need to get to the surface." Arlud looked down at Bev as she gazed out the window. He was struck by the sureness of her last statement, by how much it conflicted with her previous uncertainty. It revealed the disarray of her mental state, and he wondered how much influence the aliens had over her thoughts. "We'll get there," he said. Her warmth felt good against his body, and he held her close.

After three days of data collection, the executive officers in the Halva task force agreed Arrilen Po was safe for planet-fall. Data from the orbitals indicated the weather had returned to normal. The only storm that posed any potential danger was a tropical hurricane over the eastern sea, and that was three-thousand kilometers away from the abandoned settlement.

Information retrieved from the derelict Sabballi frigate was sparse and lacked data regarding how she was attacked. Her presence in orbit was no threat to the survey team, so the Commander-in-Charge ordered the investigation of her systems to continue, until they had explored all avenues to uncover the facts of her demise.

"Station 38 is the focal point of Bev's dreams," Cynth said. "That's where I'd like to go."

Arlud nodded to Cynth's plan as he followed her into the crowded staging room next to the shuttle bay. "I agree, as long as we have a swift means of escape."

Cynth stopped behind the clanmen waiting in front of the bay doors. She spun around to face the young Erstallius regent and reviewed his mission attire. Each member of the survey team wore the tactical environment suit of the Halva militia. It was a light garment, not as form fitting as older versions, but with the accouterments needed in a hostile environment. It could recycle body waste, protect the wearer from temperatures below freezing or above the boiling point of water, supply enough oxygen to survive four hours in an airless environment, and the duranide weave could stop a magar projectile from ripping a hole in the wearer. The streamlined helmet contained a multi-band transceiver, and a heads-up holoscreen that was fed data from the sensor array built into the outer shell. Arlud wore his suit like a professional soldier, pant legs tucked inside boots, sleeves tucked inside gloves, belt kit set high on the hip. The only thing that deviated from typical clanmen deportment was his lack of a weapon.

"You almost look like you belong in that outfit," Cynth said.

"I went through tactical training before I left Baleiou."

"That explains it then."

Cynth's suit lacked boots, and the pants only reached a few centimeters below what was left of her human thighs, but fit snug against her cybernetic legs. Her tunic contained all the benefits of the standard suit, save for the lack of a left arm sleeve, which wasn't needed. Her cyber-limbs didn't need the same level of protection as her human half, and that was fine with her.

"I don't intend to be trapped in another cave," Cynth said. "We'll send a drone in first."

"Good," Arlud said. He turned and watched Bev enter the staging room. Her expression told him how uncomfortable she was in her suit. "You OK?"

Bev flexed her shoulders. "A little tight. Reminds me of the suit I wore in the mine."

Eahuda entered the staging room with two clanmen and the entrance closed behind them.

The green boarding light flashed and the doors to the shuttle bay opened.

The survey team moved into the bay and dispersed to their assigned transports.

Three bulging cargo shuttles, each customized to carry five team members and the equipment necessary to survey the abandoned settlement, waited in line with two advanced tactical shuttles that carried fore-and-aft magar-cannons and two clusters of phase-induction missiles.

Cynth, Bev, and Arlud would planet-fall last, which was a safety protocol mandated by the Commander-in-Charge, so they entered the last cargo shuttle to their left. Eahuda joined the advance team in the lead tactical shuttle to the right.

The shuttle bay decompressed, the exit doors slid open, and the docking clamps released. The shuttles sped out of the bay one at a time, from right to left, and headed to their insertion points for descent.

Cynth Halva walked down the boarding ramp beneath the forward crew cabin. Her first view of the memorial from ground level brought tears to her eyes. On the slope of a low dirt hill to the west of the landing field, twenty-three rectangular stone markers, each engraved with the name of one casualty from the first settlement, formed three rows of half-circles. Seven stones formed the bottom arc, seven were in the middle arc, and nine made up the top arc.

We lost so much here, she thought.

She stepped out from under the shade of the crew cabin into the bright morning sunlight and surveyed the surrounding landscape. The intervening years had deposited a layer of dust over the tarmac that obscured the painted lines that marked the landing lanes and parking areas. Her shuttle sat near the southern edge of the field, about fifty meters from where the other two cargo shuttles were parked, near the rubble that was once the maintenance hangers. To the east, shattered remains of the settlement were scattered around the megalithic stones that protruded above the horizon. To the north and west, low, rocky hills led to bare granite mountains, and to the south more shredded buildings and megaliths obscured the view of snow-capped peaks in the distance.

She took in a deep breath of the crisp, clean air and walked toward the memorial hill, but grief that had never been resolved stopped her from entering the small dirt cemetery. She noticed the stones were weathered, but in better shape than she had imagined they would be. Two of the small granite slabs were tilted forward by an erosion stream that meandered down the hill.

Arlud stepped beside Cynth and pointed to one of the team members near the center of the tarmac. "What's he doing?"

Cynth wiped the wetness from her old eyes and followed Arlud's gesture until she spied the team member blasting the tarmac clean with a burst of compressed air from a blower strapped to his right forearm. "He's looking for a survey marker. See the holo-recorder he's holding in his other hand?"

"Yes."

"Once he finds the marker, he'll deploy the recorder. It attaches to the marker via an extended pole. Then he'll begin recording data. We'll compare the current data with the images we took before we left. That'll tell us how much the weather affected the area, and it'll be merged with the orbital data to create holo-images like the ones you saw in my sitting room."

"Markers are throughout the settlement?"

"Yes. Solid reference points for that type of recording. Most of them are covered in rubble."

Arlud saw the wisdom in the well-planned effort to record the settlement. "The architects of this colony should be praised for their foresight," he said. This holo-recording was beyond anything conceived by his own clan for the creation of records regarding the establishment of their colonies. He promised himself to recommend changes once he was back on Ni'apinu. "You were very thorough here."

"Yes, we were."

A tactical shuttle approached from the west, roared overhead, and banked toward the northeast.

Arlud heard the pilot's voice in his helmet: "TAC-Two to survey team. Weather is clear to the horizon. No activity."

Cynth gestured to the west, beyond the memorial. "We'll be heading in that direction."

Arlud turned and viewed the jagged mountains. "Station 38?"

Cynth nodded. "We'll use a quadcopter. If I had flown the last time, I might have been able to escape the storm."

Bev stopped beside Arlud. "Then you wouldn't have entered the cave, and we wouldn't be here now."

Cynth spun to face Bev. "You're right. We wouldn't." And she knew that would have led to a very different future. "Ludi would probably still be alive."

A voice sounded in Cynth's helmet: "We could use some help over here."

The request came from one of their shuttle pilots, who stood under the cargo section at the bottom of the loading ramp.

Cynth turned toward the waiting clanman and waived. Under normal circumstances such a request directed at the Clan matriarch would never have happened because of the protocol of hierarchy, but she had instructed everyone to treat her just like any other member of the team. "We should get over there," she said, then she bent her cybernetic legs and jumped into the air. She reached the cargo ramp after three leaping strides across the tarmac.

"Wow," Bev said, "she could out-run the storms now."

Arlud chuckled. "Come on," he said, and gestured for Bev to follow him back to the shuttle.

Bev took a step forward and froze. A vortex of blue plasma whirled around her and held her in place. She saw nothing but the surge of blue energy and felt a light pressure around her right upper arm. She was jerked out of the vision to see Arlud's hand above her right elbow. She relaxed and held Arlud's arm with both hands. "I'm OK."

Arlud returned a quizzical stare.

"Really, I'm fine."

"Are they near?"

"They're always near."

"Stay close to me."

Bev nodded. She knew there was nothing Arlud could do if she was pulled into another dream, but she appreciated his concern, and held onto his arm as they walked back to the shuttle.

An hour later Tactical Shuttle One landed at the north end of the tarmac so Eahuda could join the trek to station 38. He disembarked and walked toward the quadcopter parked a few meters from Cargo Shuttle Three's port side.

Arlud examined the quadcopter's design. The overlapping rotors fore and aft of the crew section were based on an ancient design that increased stability. Although this technology produced a light and stable vehicle, he had never seen one in actual use. "Last time I saw one of these was in a museum."

Bev was surprised by that admission. "A museum?"

"It's an old technology. Most clans opt for more modern means of propulsion."

"But it's safe, right?"

"Yes, they're very safe, just slow compared to mag-jets."

"Why is it called a quadcopter?"

Arlud pointed to the ducted blades. "Four props. They create the lift."

"Oh."

"The name's as ancient as the vehicle. I'm not surprised you never heard of it."

Bev leaned forward into the open airframe and peered at the pilot station behind the forward windscreen. "Simple controls. Not much to it. Why are the sides open?"

"Makes it lighter so it can carry more weight," Arlud said. He gestured for Bev to sit in one of the two rear passenger seats. Bev settled into the rear starboard seat and Arlud sat next to her on the port side. "Strap in," he said.

Cynth climbed into the front passenger seat in front of Bev and turned to face Arlud. "We should be there in about forty minutes."

The pilot eased into the pilot station and activated the rotors.

Eahuda climbed into the remaining port side seat. "Thanks for waiting. I would hate to miss this."

The quadcopter lifted off the tarmac with a soft whoosh sound, clearing the tarmac of dust below the rotors, and hovered about a meter above the ground.

Bev bit down on a smile as the thrill of the moment pushed away all her other thoughts.

The pilot turned to make sure everyone was strapped in. "Here we go," he said. Then he adjusted the controls, and the vehicle leaped upward and sped toward the granite mountains.

Cynth examined the land around Station 38 as the quadcopter circled the area about two-hundred meters above the rocky terrain. The red stone that dominated the western slopes blended with the lighter gray of the rocky hills to the southeast. The granite slabs that fortified the station were still there, but the drill rig that had once towered above the smooth megaliths was now collapsed into a heap of twisted metal and obscured her view of the sensor pallet that had once collected weather data. She leaned toward the pilot. "Can you put us down over there?"

The pilot turned his head and sighted along Cynth's metal arm. He nodded and banked toward the flat area at the base of the southern slope.

Bev raised her helmet visor as the quadcopter settled onto the rocky ground and the whoosh of the rotors faded to silence. She surveyed the rough terrain that undulated toward a high ridge along the northern edge of the basin about five-hundred meters away. "Where's the cave?"

Cynth turned in her seat and gestured to the rugged hill on the port side of the passenger cabin. "Up there."

Bev looked past Arlud and bent down to see more of the hill through the cabin's port opening. "I don't see it."

"It's there."

Cynth turned and stepped down from her starboard seat onto the rocky ground. Bev bounded out of the copter and stood next to Cynth. "Was that your rover?"

Cynth turned and looked where Bev was pointing and sucked in a quiet gasp. The vehicle she had used to reach this station forty-seven years ago lay among boulders on a hill to the northeast, about twenty meters above the basin floor, a twisted, corroded remnant of what it had been. "Oh my, I believe it is." She turned with a frown and walked around the copter toward the southern slope.

Arlud stepped beside Bev and noticed her worried expression. "You OK?"

"Yeah."

"What's wrong?"

"The ground."

Arlud looked down at the rock-covered terrain. "What—"

"No sand dunes."

"Sand dunes?"

"Yeah," Bev said. "I expected sand dunes. They were in all my dreams."

Arlud heard Cynth's voice in his helmet: "Erstallius, come up here." He led Bev to the southern slope. He looked up, saw Eahuda outside the narrow cave, and flicked a glance back at Bev. "Come on," he said, and trudged up the rocky incline toward Eahuda.

"She went inside," Eahuda said.

Arlud leaned over, peered into the opening, and saw Cynth bent over near the end of the cave about six meters from the entrance. Her helmet light illuminated the back wall and revealed a narrow crack where there had once been a meter-wide crevice that led to the cavern where Ludi Prell died. "Did the Sabballi close it off?"

Cynth turned toward Arlud. "No." She turned off her helmet light and returned to the entrance.

Arlud backed away to give Cynth room to exit the cave. "What do you think happened?"

"It looks like a massive internal collapse. Just enough to seal off the interior without destroying the tunnel completely. They left this part intact for me."

Eahuda squatted down and examined the cave. "To protect you from the weather."

"Yes," Cynth said.

"Nothing here makes sense," Bev said. "There should be a massive hole in the ground where that station is, and sand dunes everywhere."

Cynth pondered Bev's observation. "Why?"

"Because that's what I see in my dreams. I saw you, so why is everything else different?"

"Maybe what you saw outside was somewhere else?"

Bev scowled and surveyed the rugged landscape. "No. It was here."

Arlud hunched down next to Eahuda. "Can we reopen the tunnel?"

Eahuda was surprised by that question. "Should we?"

Arlud nodded.

"They blocked it off for a reason, lad. Probably to keep us away from what's in there. A man died."

Cynth looked down the slope toward the quadcopter. The pilot was sitting on the edge of the port side cabin opening, with his feet resting on the landing strut. She waived at him and said, "Pilot, get out the drill."

Two hours later the laser drill had punched through three meters of rock without reaching the wider crevice.

Bev stayed away from the cave during the excavation. She wanted nothing to do with the drill. She was glad no one asked her to operate it, because that would have led to a loud argument. She sat next to Arlud on a flat boulder, a few meters from the starboard side of the quadcopter. She could see the distant plain beyond a gap in the surrounding hills. It was a barren expanse that stretched to the northwest horizon. "Aren't there any plants on this planet?"

"Of course," Arlud said. "Mostly shrubs and grasses. They're just local to other areas."

"Why?"

"Terraforming takes time. Seventy-eight standard years ago the atmosphere here would not allow unprotected planet-fall. By the time the first colonists arrived the oxygen level had increased to a breathable level. That was because of the atmocons, but Clan Halva also introduced flora around the colony site that helped increase the local O2 levels. You saw plants among the ruins."

"Yeah," Bev said. "I just wondered why it was so barren here."

"Some planets have deserts. The key for settlement is whether we can maintain a healthy atmosphere."

"So that's why we have these suits?"

"Yes. The storms destroyed much of what Clan Halva accomplished, and the O2 levels have been dropping since the evacuation. We're safe enough, but it pays to be cautious."

"U'galem has lots of plant life."

Arlud nodded. "Many holdings have their own unique flora and fauna. Hundreds of years ago some holdings had old world species introduced to their habitats to fill niches that the colonists believed would help them. Sometimes that worked and sometimes it didn't. The DPS was eventually founded not just to manage settlement but to help prevent environmental disasters."

"Well, even if we didn't introduce off-world plants and animals, wouldn't the human presence upset the balance?"

"It always does."

"Then—" Bev stifled her comment and lowered her head. She thought settling a planet where humans had not originated was self-serving, arrogant, and unfair to the native species.

Arlud nudged her with his elbow. "Exactly," he said. "Our civilization was founded on many contradictions. The one thing that's allowed our expansion to continue is the absence of other intelligent species equal to our own."

"Until now."

Arlud sat up straight and took a deep breath. "Yes, but the aliens who came here aren't terrestrial, they're other-dimensional. They upset the balance too, just look at what happened here."

"They're even more out of place than we are."

Arlud nodded.

"Then why did they appear at Alpha Cephei Four? They realized the impact on us once Ludi got sucked into that vortex and they found Cynth half dead. They regretted what happened because they saved Cynth. Why would they do it again on Alpha Cephei Four?"

"I don't know. Maybe because Alpha Cephei Four is an airless rock, they didn't expect us to be there."

Eahuda's voice sounded in Arlud's helmet: "We just broke through, lad."

Arlud turned and saw Eahuda descending the granite slope behind the pilot. Cynth stood outside the cave. "How deep did you have to go?"

"A little over three meters," Eahuda said. "We're sending in a drone."

The pilot retrieved the small spherical drone from the quadcopter and brought it to the cave. He set it on auto-remote, placed it on the rock inside the entrance, then returned to the quadcopter with Cynth.

Eahuda held the drone control pad, and the others grouped around him to watch the progress on the monitor. The angle of the drone's descent was eight point three degrees from where the drill stopped and continued for about one hundred meters before the tunnel turned left, and dropped at forty-five degrees into a dead end.

"I expected that," Cynth said. "They blocked the tunnel from both ends."

Eahuda landed the drone on the rock floor and focused on the sensor data. "It's hot in there—33 degrees Celsius."

Cynth noticed the magnetic level. "4.99 gauss. That hasn't changed much."

"They're still in there," Eahuda said.

Arlud watched the data stream across the bottom of the screen. "Maybe not. That may just be evidence that their equipment is still there."

Cynth looked at Arlud. "What equipment?"

"Whatever made those tunnels you saw and activated the vortex."

"Don't matter much," Bev said. "It's blocked, and there's no way we can get that drill down there to cut through that stone."

"She's right," Eahuda said. "We're done here."

The pilot leaned between Cynth and Arlud to review the data. "That rock is only a few meters thick. We can blast a hole through it."

Eahuda focused on the pilot. "With what?"

"A plasma cutter. I packed a few with the drill, just in case."

Arlud exchanged a skeptical look with Cynth and Eahuda. Plasma cutters used a low yield fusion reaction to produce a focused pulse of plasma that could bore through five meters of granite in about two seconds. The problem with such a device was uncontrollable variability and the potential for omni-directional pressure waves that could collapse the bore hole before the initial blast had finished. The result could make the blockage more difficult to remove. "Do we really want to do that?"

Bev recalled her last view of Josh Gridle as he lay beneath the expanding ball of brilliant cyan light that had engulfed her Drill. "I say blow it up. Blow it all up." She stood unflinching against the team's startled reaction to her suggestion. "What?"

Cynth flashed a derisive smile at Bev. "Let's see what's in there first."

Eahuda recalled the drone, and the pilot loaded a cylindrical plasma cutter to its underbelly.

"We'll only have one chance with this," Eahuda said.

Arlud patted the old Degen's back. "Then make sure you place it in the best position."

Eahuda guided the drone to the end of the tunnel and used the on-board sensors to analyze the layers of rock that blocked their progress. After a thirty-minute review of the data, he settled on the best position for the plasma cutter and activated the tripod support. The three legs unfolded from the bottom of the cylinder and made contact a few centimeters right-of-center on the largest boulder. Bolts on each leg plunged into the rock with a loud thump and secured the cutter to the stone.

Eahuda backed the drone away about a meter and centered the forward camera on the plasma cutter. "She's ready," he said, and he angled the control pad so Arlud and Cynth could review the cutter's position.

"Good," Cynth said. "Retrieve the drone."

Once the drone was secure in its storage compartment, the team boarded the quadcopter and the pilot flew them south, parallel to the slope, and landed about two-hundred meters from the cave entrance.

Cynth fingered the remote detonator and looked at the pilot. "You're sure this won't damage the cavern on the other side?"

"The cavern will be fine."

"OK," Cynth said, and she pushed the switch.

They heard a faint pop, and a dust cloud billowed from the cave.

"Wow," Bev said, "that's it?"

Eahuda unloaded the drone, and once the exterior dust cloud dispersed, he guided it back toward the end of the tunnel. The team grouped outside the quadcopter and watched the dust-filled air at the back of the tunnel restrict the camera's visible light view to less than a meter. Eahuda switched to infrared, and they saw the hole the cutter produced as soon as the drone turned into the excavated passage. "Here we go," he said, and he guided the drone into the hole.

The drone's remote link died.

"Damn it!"

Arlud noticed the blank data relay on the control pad. "What happened?"

A tremor shook the ground.

The side of the hill rippled, and an expanding shock wave knocked everyone but Cynth off their feet.

The ground undulated beneath them, and small rocks cascaded down the slope.

"Into the copter," the pilot yelled. He jumped into his seat and started the rotors. Before anyone else could climb aboard the quadcopter the shaking stopped.

The pilot shouted: "Get on!"

"It's stopped," Cynth said. She extended her metal hand to Eahuda and helped him up.

Arlud helped Bev stand. "I'm fine," she said, then she pointed to the cave. "Look!"

Arlud turned and saw the hillside around the cave crumble inward. The boom and thud of the collapsing rock was followed by the expulsion of a massive dust cloud. The ground shuddered.

The pilot shouted again: "Get on!"

Cynth and Eahuda climbed into the quadcopter as the rotors whirled up to take-off speed. Arlud grabbed the side railing to pull himself into the cabin, but stopped when he noticed Bev still standing a few meters away looking toward the expanding cavern. "Bev!"

Bev stood motionless, her posture relaxed, her head bent downward.

Streams of blue plasma poured out of the new opening in the hillside and gathered into a large swirling cloud above the basin.

Arlud jumped to the ground. *She's in a dream*, he thought, and he ran toward Bev.

A hot wind rushed down from the plasma cloud and stopped Arlud from reaching Bev. He fought against the invisible force but stumbled backward and landed hard on his back. He rolled over to see the quadcopter retreat sideways toward the northeast ridge. He looked back toward Bev and watched her limp body rise inside a whirlwind of blue plasma that carried her to the cavern and into the rock.

The revolving streams of plasma over the basin followed Bev into the hill and the pummeling winds stopped.

Arlud heard Eahuda's voice in his helmet: "You OK, lad?" He turned his head toward the sound of the approaching quadcopter. "I'm fine."

"Where's Bev?"

"They took her."

The quadcopter swooped down and Arlud jumped aboard. "Go!"

The pilot banked toward the eastern ridge.

"The wind pushed us away," Cynth said.

"Both tactical shuttles are on their way," Eahuda said. "They should be here in about ten minutes."

Arlud shot a quizzical glance at Eahuda. "To do what?"

Eahuda understood Arlud's question but didn't have an answer.

"She's gone," Arlud said, "not dead."

Cynth turned in her seat. "What do we do?"

No one offered an answer.

The quadcopter flew over the ridge line and landed out of sight of station 38.

The tactical shuttles roared overhead.

Arlud leaned toward the pilot. "Tell them to veer away."

An hour later Arlud and Eahuda were at the top of the ridge. They surveyed the basin beyond though hand-held magnifiers. The new hole in the rock was circular and about twenty meters wide at the exit point. The entry angle was horizontal but dropped to near vertical a few meters beyond the entrance.

"We'd need a GPG to get down that hole," Arlud said.

Eahuda agreed. "I'll bet they did that so we couldn't follow."

"Maybe."

"What do they want with her?"

Arlud lowered his magnifier. "They've had a mental connection with Bev for months. How they did that considering the distance involved still amazes me. I don't think they mean her harm."

"Look there, lad. Inside the tunnel."

Arlud raised his magnifier and saw a hunched shape move along the ground inside the new tunnel. He touched the side of his helmet to activate the transceiver. "Pilot, get the quadcopter up here."

A few minutes later Arlud and Eahuda were aboard the copter and speeding toward the tunnel. As they swooped down toward the cavernous opening, Bev crawled out into daylight and collapsed face down on the granite slope.

The pilot guided the quadcopter to a position a few meters below Bev.

Arlud jumped off the hovering vehicle and clambered up to Bev. He knelt, turned her over, and cradled her helmeted head in his arm. She was groggy from exhaustion. Her suit gauges indicated the medpad embedded in the torso of her suit had been activated to stabilize her blood pressure and reduce vascular constriction. He pulled her torso up and put an arm under her shoulder to support her back.

Eahuda knelt down and helped Arlud lift Bev off the rock.

CONVERGENCE

PART THREE

A cowardly act, while despised, is a normal response based on self-preservation. And that is what makes bravery so unique. Bravery is the rejection of self-preservation, and therefore the most unnatural of all human responses.

— From Conversations at Kuliq'Quad
By Petra Sitlyn

BEV COLLI: MEDIATOR

Bev heard the whoosh of the quadcopter rotors and felt the gentle caress of wind along her cheek. She peered through half-open eyelids to see the underside of Arlud's helmet. She scanned her surroundings—the rear seats had been removed and she lay on the deck plates with her head on Arlud's lap. He cradled her head in one arm and rested a hand on her hip. Her helmet was stowed under Cynth's front passenger seat.

White clouds sped past the cabin's starboard opening.

We're going back to the landing field.

She closed her eyes and focused on the gentle sway and rush of the quadcopter, the comfort of Arlud's lap, and the subtle pressure against her entire body that made her skin tingle.

The aliens are still with me.

Knowledge had rushed upon her in rapid bursts, but through the confusing visions of dark tunnels, swirling vortexes, and burning plasma, she had recognized a pattern that revealed the alien nature and the reason for all the chaos. She hoped Arlud and Cynth would understand. The proof that her knowledge was true could not be found on Arrilen Po, and she expected that would limit acceptance among the Halva clanmen. Before he would alter the planned mission, the Commander-in-Charge would want hard facts, not just the recollections of a Polinda sapi.

As she pondered her options, Arlud's voice sounded in her headset: "Once she wakes, keep your questions to yourselves. She'll need time to recover. She'll let us know what happened when she's ready."

My protector, Bev thought. Arlud's words reinforced the bond that had formed between them during the last few weeks. Despite all their differences, they had become close in a way unlike any other relationship she had ever experienced. That realization cut through all the visions, and she felt her heart pounding. She turned her head toward Arlud's chest and opened her eyes.

Arlud glanced down and focused on Bev's green eyes. He was speechless for a few seconds, then whispered, "Hi."

Bev smiled, raised her torso and pulled up her knees. Arlud moved so she could pivot on the deck plates to a sitting position next to him. She leaned back against the rear bulkhead and placed her feet against her helmet under Cynth's seat. "Without that helmet, I might not have come out of there. Shouldn't I still have it on?"

Arlud leaned against Bev's shoulder. "You only have a few minutes of air left in your suit. You would have suffocated if we left it on. Don't worry, you won't need it."

Bev lowered her head. "Thanks for coming back to get me."

"We don't abandon people."

Bev looked up to see Cynth and Eahuda turned sideways in their seats, looking at her. She returned a smile. "I'm OK."

They reached the landing field twenty minutes later without another word between them. Their quiet repose was a welcome break for Bev from all the hustle and flurry of the past few hours. And then the quadcopter landed amid a louder rush from the rotors and a billowing swirl of dust.

Bev looked out the starboard side of the cabin. The sun was overhead, and the heat reflection caused ripples in the air above the tarmac. She stepped out of the quadcopter onto the dusty pavement, then reached back and pulled her helmet out from under Cynth's seat. She turned toward the cargo shuttle, and the warm sunlight brought a brief smile to her face. Arlud stood by her side, and they crossed the tarmac, entered the shade of the shuttle's forward crew cabin and trudged up the entry ramp into the cooler environment of the aft lounge area.

Bev and Arlud sat on stools at the small table in the port side nook as Cynth came up the ramp.

"I'm glad you're OK," Cynth said. She patted Bev's shoulder and continued forward to the cockpit to contact the Commander-in-Charge.

By the time Cynth returned to the lounge, Eahuda and the quadcopter pilot had joined Arlud and Bev. A meal pack had been opened and passed around the room.

Bev bit down on a protein bar as Cynth sat on a stool across the aisle from her. The old woman wore a distressed expression and asked, "What happened to you?"

Bev finished chewing and looked around the room. Everyone was focused on her. She swallowed and placed the remaining piece of the protein bar on the table. "You were right," she said. She turned to face Arlud. "I am the key."

Arlud's subtle recoil at that revelation was not lost on Bev. *He didn't expect me to say that*, she thought, and by the look on Cynth's face it was clear she too was surprised. The pilot and Eahuda remained stoic as they munched food from the meal pack.

"They needed someone they could connect with easily," Bev continued. "There was another person. An old man. I think it was the man named Duballik that Captain Pardee told you about, but he's gone now, so they shifted their focus to me."

Eahuda leaned forward in his chair. "Why did they take you into the hill?"

"To improve our connection. It's like the difference between a pickax and a drill. They both do similar things, but one is more precise. Whatever they did worked because I think I understand them now."

Cynth rested her hands on her metal knees. "They spoke to you?"

"Sort of—they showed me visions. It was confusing at first, but as they improved the process, everything began to make sense."

Arlud crumpled the wrapper to his protein bar and dropped it into the empty meal pack. "Could you speak to them?"

"I don't know."

Cynth frowned at that admission. "Did they engage in a two-way conversation, or were they only telling you things?"

Bev took a minute to ponder what she had experienced. "They told me things. I'm not sure if they got anything from me."

"A one-sided conversation is no conversation," Eahuda said.

"They need our help," Bev said.

Arlud leaned forward in his chair. "Our help?"

Bev nodded. "It's complicated." She sat up straight. "Forty-seven years ago, they came to Arrilen Po. They were experimenting with a new technology. A system to transport them into our universe. The system opens a portal, but the portal needs to be confined within a large gravity field, otherwise it won't be stable. Their first attempts opened inside what looked like the core of a star. That was no good. They fine-tuned everything and discovered they could open a portal for a short time within a smaller mass, but long enough to transfer from their universe."

Cynth folded her arms across her chest. "Why do they need to do that?"

"They're explorers, like us. They had eight locations on Arrilen Po where they opened portals. Once they bored out of the rock, they discovered they could survive here, but they didn't realize how much their presence affected the weather until they recognized what happened to the settlement."

Cynth pondered the damage that had been done, and the deaths it had caused. "Eight active portals explain the changes to the weather system, but that doesn't explain the dead Sabballi frigate in orbit or the damaged satellite."

Bev looked up at Cynth. "That happened after you left."

Cynth turned to face Arlud. "The Commander-in-Charge just relayed to me the current findings about that frigate. It appears to have been attacked two weeks after the colony was abandoned."

Arlud shifted his attention back to Bev. "What did they say about that?"

"Once they retreated, there was a group who resisted the decision to leave. That resulted in a battle to force that group back into their own universe."

Cynth leaned toward Bev. "A battle?"

Bev nodded. "Seems they have factions in their universe like we have in ours. The Sabballi frigate was in the wrong place at the wrong time."

Eahuda cleared his throat. "What about the attack on the other frigates near Al-phaq?"

"Once they secured the portals on Arrilen Po, there were no more transfers from their universe to ours. Then, forty-seven years later, survivors of the faction who fought to stay, broke through to our universe at Alpha Cephei Four. The portal they opened there was much bigger than those they opened here. Once they crossed over, they headed for the surface. Others pursued them but lost contact with them soon after they left the planet."

Bev turned toward Arlud. "I don't know why the other ships were attacked. It must have been the fleeing aliens who did that. The visions I saw showed none of that. But based on what you've told me, I think it was a mistake, because, like what happened here, once they realized what they had done they retreated."

Eahuda leaned back. "Wow. These aliens seem to make a lot of mistakes, and people die."

"Yes, they do," Cynth said.

"Bev," Arlud said, "since contact with them is so deadly, why aren't you dead?"

Bev looked at Arlud with sullen eyes. She sensed the attitude among the others had become negative toward her message. She had hoped Arlud would stay positive, but his question amplified the doubt. "They are not of this universe. I don't understand what their universe is like, but our universe is affected in different ways by their presence. How it's affected depends on the circumstances. Moving through an atmosphere differs from traveling through hyperspace to overtake a frigate. I don't know all the specifics. I wish I did. All I know is they can control how they affect us under normal, planet-bound conditions. Otherwise, I would be dead."

"OK," Arlud said. "Why do they need our help?"

"They can't find the ones who crossed over into our universe. Our universe limits their ability to track them. They need us to find them."

"And how do we do that?"

"I'm not sure. There must be a way we can track them."

Cynth tapped the arm of her chair with her metal hand. "And why do we want to do that?"

"Because the aliens who fought to stay here still want to stay. If they stay more people could die."

"So," Cynth mused, "although they know their presence can do us harm, they want to stay. That implies they have no concern for our welfare."

Bev delved deep into her memories and retrieved a vision of the first crossing. "It's like a drug," she explained. "Once they arrive, they are overwhelmed with joy by the sensations our universe gives them. When they go back to their universe, they lose that feeling. It's a sensation they can only experience here."

"Is that the only reason?"

Bev frowned. "Probably not, but the result is the same. They upset the balance in our universe."

Eahuda asked, "So if we find them, what do we do?"

"Nothing. The aliens will do what needs to be done."

"Since the aliens are so deadly," Arlud said, "what assurance do we have we won't be harmed?"

"They see everything I see," Bev said. "They will know when to take action and when to hold back."

Arlud responded with a befuddled expression. "You're their eyes?"

"Yeah, we're connected."

"Can you see them?"

"No. I wouldn't make sense of anything on their end. They revealed their universe to me once, and I was—it was very confusing."

"How convenient," Cynth said. "This could all be a ruse to help them invade our universe."

"I knew you would think that," Bev admitted. "That's not the impression I get. They want to prevent more destruction."

"Well," Eahuda said, "with the chaos spreading among the clans, it won't be easy to track the alien refugees."

Arlud faced Eahuda. "Refugees?"

Eahuda nodded. "Sounds to me like they're fleeing a place they don't like. Only refugees do that."

Cynth tapped her chair again. "What do we do?"

Arlud faced Bev. "Anything else you can add?"

Bev dove into her memories and pulled up a vision she thought might reduce Cynth's suspicions. "Opening a portal is a complicated thing. They need just the right conditions for it to work. I don't know what the specifics are, but I know they had problems here when they first began testing. They abandoned their first few locations because of the problems. Maybe if we can discover what those problems were, we can prevent them from crossing over again."

"I'll get our engineers working on it," Cynth said. "That's good to know, Bev. The best thing you've said all day." She stood and strode into the cockpit.

Arlud locked eyes with Bev. He was worried about her connection with the aliens. There were too many questions that needed answers, and he knew they would probably never find them. "Once we get all our data compiled, we'll send a drone with the info to the clans. That may help end the wars."

"How?"

"We all have one enemy now," Arlud explained. "With the data we've collected, I don't see how anyone can deny what's been happening. Hopefully the clans will put aside old rivalries long enough to unite against this new threat."

"And if they don't?"

"Then our future will be in jeopardy."

CLAN ERSTALLIUS: NEW COURSE

The flight from Arrilen Po to the task force flagship, orbiting five-hundred kilometers off the backside of the second moon, was a quiet five-hour transfer that allowed Cynth's team time to recuperate from their mission. Both Cynth and Eahuda drifted into a sound sleep after the shuttle broke atmosphere. Arlud and Bev sat apart because Bev stretched out on two adjacent seats and joined Cynth and Eahuda in sleep, although her slumber was fitful, and caused Arlud to peer behind him on multiple occasions to watch her curled up body twitch and jerk into different positions.

Arlud tried to focus on what happened to Bev, but his thoughts drifted to the plight of his people on Ni'apinu, and the persistent threat from Farquar Polinda. By the time they reached the cruiser he was ready to dive into his bunk and get his own measure of sleep, but as he tossed his travel pack onto his bunk, the door buzzer shattered his plan for slumber. He opened the door to a Halva clanman.

"Excuse me, sir," the clanman said. "You are wanted in the C.I.C."

"Why?"

The clanman didn't expect that question. "Commander's orders, sir."

Arlud closed his eyes and leaned against the bulkhead. "OK—tell the Commander-in-Charge I'll be there as soon as possible."

The clanman stood his ground. "I'm to escort you, sir."

Arlud opened his eyes and jerked away from the wall. The tone of the clanman's voice revealed the Commander-in-Charge expected an immediate response. He took a deep breath and forced back the overwhelming need to sleep. "Lead the way."

As he stepped into the corridor Arlud noticed a clanmen standing two doors down the narrow hall to his left, outside Bev's cabin. *They put a guard on her door,* he thought, and a rush of foreboding flooded his awareness as he turned right and followed his escort to the C.I.C.

The Commander-in-Charge watched Arlud enter his command center and noticed the raggedness of his deportment and the weariness in his eyes. "You look terrible."

"Couldn't sleep during the shuttle transfer. Too many things on my mind."

"We've all got a lot on our minds these days. I'll keep this brief."

The Commander-in-Charge turned toward the navigation pedestal and activated a small holoscreen that displayed a map of the inhabited worlds. "While you were on the surface, we received a comdrone from Cestratha." He pushed a button on the console and the map was segregated by five different colored, transparent bubbles that pressed against each other and defined the areas of rebellion. "Five factions are fighting for control of the Old Worlds. Polinda has joined with Clan Sabballi, and they attacked Erstallius holdings in sector seven and ten. Your clan's forces were depleted." He pushed another button and small blue spheres identified the four Erstallius holdings that had been attacked. "Your clan held, but at a high cost. The report says Baleiou suffered massive casualties."

Arlud gripped the pedestal's hand railing to steady himself. If the report was true, that would be the second time in seventy years the Polindas attacked the Erstallius homeworld.

"There were no reports regarding your immediate family," the Commander said. "There are reports of skirmishes between other clans in sectors Two, Three, and Six. The chaos appears to be spreading to the outlying areas on the other side of the Old Worlds." He extended his hand and offered Arlud a data chip. "You can review the reports yourself."

Arlud took the chip. "You'll be returning to Cestratha?"

"Yes. If we leave within the next few days, we'll make it back in time to help prepare our defenses."

"Then you're expecting an attack?"

"We expect the wave of belligerence to turn and reach Cestratha about a month from now. It's unlikely we'll be a major target, but Clan Vestlok and Clan Emlito might try to force their hand, since they've been our staunchest competitors. Review the data and you'll get a better sense of what to expect."

Arlud looked down at the data chip in his hand. "I've felt this rebellion coming for a long time. Never thought the catalyst would be an alien."

"The reports mention three anomalies like the one in your report about the Cormed frigates."

The Commander-in-Charge adjusted the emitter controls, and two small orange spheres appeared in the holomap. "One anomaly was here, near Jai'raan. Two cargo freighters were disabled about a parsec outside the system boundary. The other incident was near a service station near Fra'tei, the fourth planet of PDN185." He adjusted the controls again and another orange sphere appeared in the holomap. "Clan Dejoria said one of their cruisers is limping to the service station after being engulfed inside a cloud of white-hot plasma and losing their compression drive."

Arlud examined the position of the orange spheres. "They're not moving in a straight line."

"There's no logic to the course they've taken."

"I don't think they have a course."

The Commander raised an eyebrow. "Why do you say that?"

Arlud pocketed the memory chip. "Bev said they can't navigate very well in our universe. They were probably just reacting to the energy signatures of the ships they attacked."

The Commander turned his attention to the map. "Lady Halva told me they also have limitations with their portals." He touched the control console, and the holomap changed to an image of Arrilen Po. "We believe we've found one of their abandoned portals here in this mountainous area." A red circle appeared over rugged terrain on the largest southern continent, near the western uplift. "There are deposits of pitchblende in that area," the Commander said. "Not sure if that's significant, but the one working portal we know of lacks that feature. We had scheduled a team to investigate this southern site further, but the comdrone reports put that on hold."

Arlud was intrigued by that discovery, but his thoughts shifted from the fissile potential of uranium to the tantrum potential of an angry Bev Colli. "Why is there a guard outside Bev Colli's cabin?"

The Commander flinched. "I don't trust her."

"She's no threat to anyone."

"But her connection to the aliens might be. She'll be confined to her cabin until we get back to Cestratha."

"What then?"

"That will depend on our situation."

Arlud saw steadfastness in the Commander's expression that told him pursuing a reprieve of Bev's quarantine would be useless. He left the C.I.C. and returned to his cabin. He collapsed on his bunk and woke six hours later to the incessant buzzing of the comm on the wall panel next to his bed. He reached up and silenced the buzzing. "Yes?"

"Cynth here. You must have been sleeping."

"I was."

"Have you reviewed the comdrone reports?"

"Not yet."

After a brief silence Cynth said, "Can we meet within the hour?"

"Yes."

"Come by my cabin when you're able."

"Will do," Arlud said. He switched off the comm and turned on the overhead light. The chronometer displayed seven-thirty-five ship time on their fourth day at Arrilen Po.

During a quick shower and shave, Arlud began listening to the comdrone reports via the audio system in his cabin using the wireless ear buds. By the time he reached Cynth's cabin, he had heard all but the last five minutes of the information. He stepped through the doorway to see Cynth sitting on her bunk. "Good morning."

Cynth gestured to the bench unfolded from the bulkhead. It was the only other place to sit. "We have much to discuss."

Arlud straddled the bench. He pulled the ear buds out and dropped them into his shirt pocket. "I've heard most of the reports."

"Good. But my main concern right now is Bev."

"What about her?"

"How do we know she's not being manipulated by the aliens?"

"Manipulated?"

"Well, they could be directing her actions. They seem to have an overwhelming grip on her consciousness."

"I doubt they will make her do something she's not willing to do."

"Perhaps, but can we be sure of that?"

"She's convinced their intent is in our best interest. She's not a threat."

"I hope that's true. Unfortunately, the Commander-in-Charge is not convinced, and keeping her locked in her cabin is no help to anyone."

Arlud sympathized with Cynth's last point. Bev would need access to the C.I.C. to help the aliens track down their rebels, but he also saw the potential benefit of keeping her in her cabin. "I've been thinking about that. Keeping her in her cabin might not be a bad thing. Isolation could help her get a better grip on her situation, help her focus on the alien intent, and remove the cloud of suspicion. By the time we reach Cestratha—"

"You won't be going to Cestratha."

"What?"

"You reviewed the comdrone reports?"

"All but the last one."

"The last one is just a repetition of the earlier reports."

Cynth placed her hands on her metallic knees and leaned toward Arlud. "You understand the present condition among the worlds?"

"My clan has suffered severe losses against Polinda. Other clans have ripped peace from fifteen other holdings, and the chaos is growing."

Cynth stated the obvious: "We have our own problems to deal with and that supersedes everything else, including the needs of aliens."

"I understand, but solving—"

"But solving this alien mess," Cynth scoffed, "could put a stop to the chaos among the clans." She had hijacked Arlud's words and ended his argument. "I want to believe that as much as you do, but I can't."

Arlud watched disgust envelope Cynth's expression, and he understood her resistance to the idea that knowledge of a common enemy could rally the clans together. All it had done up to this point was split them farther apart. "I know we shouldn't rely on that as our only hope, but we should not discount it completely."

"I don't, but right now I must focus on the immediate needs of my clan."

Arlud paused for a few heartbeats to allow the tension in the room to subside. "What will you do?"

Cynth leaned back against the bulkhead and spoke with genuine sympathy. "Your clan has suffered much, and I foresee more destruction ahead. At my request, the Commander-in-Charge has agreed to split up this task force. One cruiser will stay here, with a team on-planet to continue the survey. Two others will join this flagship and return to Cestratha. The remaining ship will take you, Degen Eahuda, and Bev, to wherever you need to go."

Arlud was stunned by that decision, but as the reality of it rolled around in his mind, he saw the underlying motive. *That'll get Bev off of this ship*, he thought, *and free Clan Halva of any responsibility regarding the alien agenda.* "Where do we go?"

"Your clan's forces are depleted. You need allies."

"I thought you were our allies?"

"We are. You need more, as many as you can get."

"That's the truth."

"You should go to the Guild."

"The Guild?"

Cynth nodded. "You helped save Wolfram's daughter. I'm sure he will be grateful."

"The Guild fled Al-phaq."

"Did Pardee tell you where he was taking Lady Sy and her daughter?"

"No, and I didn't ask. If he had wanted me to know he would have told me."

"That was wise. I'm sure he appreciated you allowing him that bit of anonymity, but no matter, I believe I know where they went."

Arlud leaned against the windowsill in the starboard observation deck and watched the Halva Flagship leave orbit of Arrilen Po. The ship followed the same path the other two cruisers had taken an hour earlier and disappeared among the stars that filled the view south of the system's ecliptic.

Gustav Eahuda stood at the window's overlay controls, fumbling with the dials and switches. "So where do we go?"

Arlud turned toward the old Degen "You want me to do that?"

"I got it."

Eahuda pushed the engage button and an overlay of two planetary systems appeared side by side in the window. On the left was PDN1592, a G-type main sequence star with six planets, ninety-eight moons and an icy rubble belt that hugged the outer rim. On the right was PDN1473, an F-type sub-giant star with twelve planets, one-hundred and eighty-five moons, and two asteroid belts.

"The one on the left." Eahuda said.

Arlud examined the data chart below the system illustration. "It's farther away. Twenty-four point fifty-nine parsecs. Maybe we could swing by the other one first, just to make sure?"

"That won't work."

"They're only seven point four parsecs from each other."

"It's not the distance that's the problem, it's the Guild. If Wolfram isn't there, we could be delayed for days."

Arlud pondered that possibility. The Halva surveillance indicated both systems were now holdings of the Guild, but there was no data to identify which one held Wolfram's new keep. "The odds are the same for either place."

"No, lad. You need to calculate the human reaction to each location along with all the other data."

"What?"

"These are not just bases to launch raids against Alliance trade routes. One of these is Clan Sy's new home. If you were Lady Sy, which one would you choose?"

A basso voice called out: "I'd choose the one on the left."

Arlud and Eahuda spun around to face the Commander of the Halva cruiser. He stood in the hatchway in his blue work uniform with his hands clasped in front of his waist.

"Excuse me, Gentlemen," the Commander said. "We should get underway."

Arlud sensed the impatience in the Commander's voice. Now that the task force had split into different groups, most of the Halva clanmen who had not elected to support the survey team, wanted to get back to Cestratha as soon as possible. The sooner he dropped off his passengers, the sooner the Commander could return his ship to her original purpose. She wasn't built to be a taxi service.

Arlud flicked a glance at Eahuda.

"Set course for Wald-415," Eahuda said. "The one on the left."

The commander nodded. "We should have you there in a little over four hyper-days," he said.

Then he turned and left the hatchway. Eahuda looked back at the schematic on the left. Wald-415 was the fourth planet in the system. A class-one planet with three moons, a temperate climate, and rich in metals. The G-type star she circled would bring warmth and comfort to Lady Sy, and those were two things she never had on Al-phaq. He faced Arlud and said, "The sub-giant system imposes too many climatic variables. Lady Sy would hate living there almost as much as she hated Al-phaq."

Arlud examined the system schematics. "You might be right, Gus. We'll find out in four days."

THE GUILD: WALD-415

Shanna Sy rushed across the wooden floor toward the closed double doors at the end of the vaulted corridor, her layered lumisilk skirt rustling with each step, shimmering in the morning sunlight that poured into the hall through the windows between the ceiling joists.

Eber Kurnes sat in the armless chair to the left of the doors and watched Shanna approach. He waved to get her attention as she neared the closed doorway and was surprised when she ignored him.

Shanna grabbed the door handles, paused for a heartbeat, then burst through the doors. She stopped ten paces into the large room. "Why didn't you tell me?"

Wolfram Sy turned in his chair from his conversation with Ross Cordova at the far end of the room. He faced Shanna with a look that was both shocked and disappointed at the same time. "Calm down, Daughter."

"No, Father. Why didn't you tell me?"

Wolfram rose out of his chair and gestured for Cordova to leave.

Cordova tipped his head as he passed Shanna on his way out. He met Eber Kurnes by the doorway, and with a gesture signaled the security minister to help close the doors. They each grabbed a door handle and sealed the room as they left.

Shanna stood defiant. "Why didn't you tell me Arlud was here?"

Wolfram loved his daughter, so he kept his temper in check. "Standard protocol."

"He's not our enemy!"

"No, he's not. But that doesn't remove our security precautions. He is on a Halva cruiser."

"Why didn't you tell me?"

"Once cleared you would have received an official notice, as you always do regarding matters that interest you."

And Wolfram wondered where the breach was that leaked news of the Halva cruiser to his daughter.

Shanna pressed: "Where were they taken?"

Wolfram heard the desperation behind Shanna's words. *Her feelings for this Erstallius fellow must be genuine*, he thought. "Calm down. They have not been harmed. They were escorted to a safe location."

"Can I see him?"

"Perhaps. That will depend on why they are here."

Shanna forced herself to relax, and the realization she had acted presumptuously washed over her. She had never questioned her father about Guild procedures before this incident. He always did what was best for her, and she felt embarrassed for barging into his meeting with Cordova. "I apologize, Father. I was disrespectful."

"Apology accepted. You must hold the Erstallius in high regard."

"I do. I'm sorry."

"Don't apologize for that. Any man who can attract so much of your attention must be worthy of it."

Shanna nodded. "He is."

"Then trust me to handle this situation in a way that is best for all of us."

Shanna moved forward, fell against Wolfram and embraced him with a tight hug.

Wolfram returned Shanna's embrace. "You know, you are just like your mother."

Shanna released her hug and stepped back. "Thank you for understanding,"

Wolfram flashed a brief smile. "Now," he said, "if you don't mind, I need to finish my meeting with Cordova."

Shanna bowed her head as a sign of respect and retreated through the doorway.

Once Cordova was back in the room, Wolfram settled into his large leather chair and called for Eber Kurnes.

Kurnes entered the room and hovered a few steps inside the doorway. "Yes, sir?"

Wolfram waved Kurnes forward. "We've had a breach, Eber. Find out who told Shanna about the Halva cruiser. That's a security priority."

"Yes, sir. And what is your order regarding the one responsible?"

"Detain for interrogation."

Kurnes offered Wolfram his folio. "The report regarding the Cormed clanmen."

Wolfram accepted the report. "How did it go?"

"They were uncooperative at first, but we pried some interesting information out of them before we were done."

Wolfram glanced down at the blue folio and began flipping through the pages. "I look forward to reading this. Thank you, Eber."

Kurnes nodded, then turned and hurried out of the room. He closed the doors as he left.

Cordova settled into the wing-backed chair on the other side of the low table from Wolfram. "Those clanmen were a gift from the Erstallius."

Wolfram stayed focused on the report. "I know," he said. "He was accommodating for an Alliance regent."

"I found him to be sincere, without deceit."

Wolfram glanced up at Cordova. "That's what Pardee tells me."

"Since he's on a Halva cruiser, I assume he needs our help."

"And why do you assume that?"

"Polinda destroyed his ships at GSW-183. There have been reports of more Polinda forces in that area, and around U'galem, which would have been his best alternative for help if Erstallius reinforcements did not arrive as he expected. If he has been blocked from U'galem by Polinda, then his best option beyond that would be the Guild."

Wolfram closed the folio and leaned back. "And why would he assume we would help him?"

"He helped save Shanna—and me, Harlon, Bern, and Donté."

"And he gave us the Cormeds."

"And the Cormeds," Cordova said.

Wolfram dropped the folio onto the low table and stood. "Contact Pardee. I want to meet this Arlud Reynaldo Erstallius myself."

Cordova stood, nodded acceptance of Wolfram's request, and strode out of the room.

The security station was built on a small icy asteroid near the outer rim of the PDN1592 system. The low natural gravity was increased by embedded GPGs, and Arlud felt heavier than normal. The drag on his movement made each step feel like he had a five-kilogram weight attached to each foot as he followed two guildmen out of the shuttle bay and down a narrow, gray corridor.

The guildmen stopped at an open hatchway and gestured for Arlud to enter the adjoining room.

Arlud was greeted by a small square table flanked on two sides by armless chairs. Beyond the table, a rectangular window revealed the icy terrain outside and the stars that filled the black sky. He saw the system's distant yellow sun glowing about ten degrees above the icy horizon.

The guildmen left the hatch open and stationed themselves in the corridor on either side of the hatchway.

About thirty minutes later, Arlud was seated in the chair that faced the hatchway when Wolfram Sy stepped into the small room. He stood to greet the Guild Director. "Mister Sy," he said, "I did not expect to see you."

"Mister Erstallius. I did not expect to see you."

Arlud extended his hand.

Wolfram balked at Arlud's gesture, then relaxed and accepted the firm, but brief handshake. "Thank you for helping my family."

"We did what we could."

That response surprised Wolfram. *He deflects the credit from himself to his clan*, he thought. *Maybe there is something special about this young man.* He pulled out the available chair and sat down. "What do you need?"

Arlud returned to his seat and folded his arms on the table. "An ally."

"Yes," Wolfram said. "I've seen the reports about the attacks on your holdings. Why should the Guild ally with Clan Erstallius?"

"We have an opportunity to stop the chaos among the clans and bring an end to the alien incursion."

Wolfram pursed his lips. "I agree this alien situation needs to be handled, but why would I want to stop the Alliance from breaking apart?"

"With the Alliance broken, the Guild will face more challenges from the isolated clans. Without the unified strength of the Alliance to ensure the safety of their trade routes, the clans will be forced to compete with the Guild on an entirely new level. You could find pirates from the clans attacking your trade routes."

Wolfram pondered that reality. Arlud was right. With the Alliance gone, each clan would be forced to secure new partnerships or fight an endless battle to keep their own resources. *When one competitor dissolves into one hundred*, he thought, *the merchant strategy must change to accommodate the new threats.* He looked at Arlud and understood his need for partnership with the Guild was because of the loss of unity among the clans, but the advantage was still unstated. "And how can Clan Erstallius prevent raids on the Guild?"

"Most will reject joining with the Guild because of old hatreds. Your holdings will be in jeopardy of attack as the clans in the outer districts expand their search for new resources. I'm sure your fleet can protect your assets, but with the proper alliance those attacks will never happen."

Wolfram replied with a hint of sarcasm: "I did not realize Clan Erstallius was so feared among the clans."

"The fear will arise because of our partnership with the Aku."

Wolfram saw the benefit of that partnership. *That's a reputation that will not be ignored.*

Arlud leaned forward. "The Aku will defend their home and partnerships with everything at their disposal."

Wolfram recalled what Shanna had said about the Aku, and how astonished she was that this boy-regent had secured their favor. "A definite advantage."

Arlud leaned back in his chair. "You had to abandon Al-phaq. I would hate to hear you had to abandon this system for similar reasons."

"Would you not be torn between two opinions? How can you partner with other clans and also with the Guild when our goals are often at odds?"

"The time has come to sever ties based on prior reasoning. Partnerships must now be based on a new perspective."

"Easier said than done."

"Not if you're committed to the right path."

Wolfram folded his arms across his chest. This boy-regent had presented a good argument, but there was one point he had not mentioned. "And I assume you speak for your father?"

That was a situation Arlud was not confident about. As a regent his authority was limited. Only the Clan Patriarch had the authority to direct a clan's course. "My father gave me authority to decide the fate of our outpost on GSW-183. That encompasses all relationships with the surrounding clans and holdings, which includes our relationship with the Guild."

"What guarantee do I have that this partnership of ours will be honored by your father?"

"My word."

Wolfram heard the sincerity in Arlud's voice and saw the commitment in his eyes. "I left the Alliance because of the trade limits imposed by the Supreme Council. Those who followed me became the Guild of Free Traders. We take that freedom seriously. As long as you remember we are partners this will work. The moment your clan assumes the position of overseer, this relationship will end."

"I understand."

Wolfram pondered a future alliance with the Erstallius and found little to sway his decision. "I'll have my people draw up a written contract with the proper points of agreement and stipulations regarding disputes and trade restrictions—all the proper protocols."

"Agreed."

Wolfram leaned forward and extended his right hand.

Arlud accepted the handshake.

Wolfram leaned back and relaxed. "Good. We should have this partnership confirmed by the end of the week."

Arlud folded his hands on the table. "Thank you, Mister Sy."

Wolfram tipped his head. "Now," he said, "what is your plan?"

"To remove the alien intruders and stop the revolt among the clans."

"And how do you accomplish that?"

"We've found the dying woman and have been to the place where she was almost killed."

Wolfram recalled what Pardee had related to him—his fears about the alien attacker and the odd dreams that had plagued Einar Duballik. He listened during the following half hour as Arlud relayed all the events that transpired on Arrilen Po.

"That explains the Halva cruiser," Wolfram said. "I wondered why you arrived with them."

"Bev Colli is with us. Her connection with the aliens has grown stronger since we left Arrilen Po. The Halva wish to return to Cestratha to secure their homeworld against the advancing rebellion. We need your help to track down the aliens causing the eruptions."

Wolfram recalled the deadly impact of the alien intrusion Pardee had shown him. "How can that little girl stop them?"

"With the alien presence flowing through her, she's not someone to take lightly. They see through her eyes. They feel through her senses. They need her to relay to them the whereabouts of the ones they seek. Once we find the intruders, they will take control of them and return them to their proper place. Bev will then be free of their influence."

"And we'll be safe?"

Arlud nodded. He assumed that was correct, based on everything Bev had told him. "I have their promise through Bev."

"That's your plan?"

"Not entirely." Arlud leaned back in his chair. "Most of the clans have ignored the alien threat because of their own immediate problems. I mean to reveal it to them. Once we have a track on the aliens, we should be able to lead them using drones—they seem to be attracted to energy signatures. At the same time, our forces will lead Polinda and his forces to the same location. Once the aliens are revealed their pursuers will capture them, and the clans in denial will be forced to accept the truth as they see the event unfold in front of them."

"And you believe that will stop the revolt?"

"That is my hope. Once they witness the real cause for all the chaos—"

"It won't work."

Arlud's expression went blank.

"I understand you've thought this through," Wolfram said, "but your hope is not based on the reality of the situation."

"How do you figure?"

"Polinda is insane. He will not stop until either your clan or his is gone."

"His partners are not insane. Once they see the truth, they will be forced to reconsider their actions."

"You really believe that?"

"When faced with the greater threat, I believe they will side with us. The human connection is greater than the political one."

Wolfram lowered his head. This boy-regent was a bright, likable fellow. He could see how Shanna had become enamored with him. But, despite his good qualities, he was still inexperienced, and that had blinded him to the flaw in his plan. "And how do you think the aliens will view a large human armada bearing down on the same location where they intend to capture their rebels?"

"Bev will explain it to them. They'll understand."

"You know that for certain?"

Arlud wasn't certain, but he hoped in Bev's ability. "If we time the event carefully, our forces will see the event from enough distance that the aliens won't suspect danger from us. It should work."

"May I review your plans?"

"Please do."

Wolfram sat up straight. *Maybe this boy-regent is more intelligent than he appears*, he thought. "How many ships do you expect we'll need?"

"Enough to counter Polinda's forces if he still insists on a battle."

"So you do plan for his insanity."

Arlud nodded. "Once we get back to GSW-183, we should have enough intel to determine the size of our force."

"When do you plan on this all taking place?"

"That will depend on when and where the aliens next appear, and on the proximity of Polinda's main forces."

"What do you intend if things don't fall into place as you'd like?"

"To do the best we can."

Wolfram dropped the argument. It was obvious the boy-regent was grasping for solutions that might never exist. *Perhaps*, he thought, *if nothing else comes of this partnership, I can teach this boy a few things his own father has neglected.*

"Tell me," Wolfram said, "What are your intentions regarding my daughter?"

Arlud flinched at that question. "Your daughter?"

"She seems rather enamored with you. I was wondering what your attitude is toward her?"

Arlud slumped in his chair and recalled his brief interactions with Shanna on Ni'apinu. "I respect her courage."

"Nothing else?"

"She is a very attractive woman," Arlud admitted. "Any man can see that." He sat up straight. "She's very intelligent. I like her, Mister Sy, but nothing more than that."

Wolfram flashed a brief grin. "She has a crush on you, Mister Erstallius."

"I suspected."

"I know you respected her honor. Have you encouraged her attention?"

"Not intentionally."

Wolfram leaned back. "Very well. I prefer she not contact you. That would encourage her fantasy, and I'll not have her hurt because of a naïve infatuation. I would appreciate your compliance in this by not accepting any communication from her. I've seen this kind of thing rip a woman's heart apart, and I do not wish to see Shanna succumb to such a vile awakening."

Arlud nodded agreement. "I understand."

"Right," Wolfram said. He pushed away from the table. "Let me meet with my master-at-arms and we'll see what we can do to help you." He stood and moved to the hatchway. "These men will see you back to your shuttle. I'll contact you tomorrow." He tipped his head, stepped through the hatchway, and was gone.

Arlud stared at the hatchway, startled by Wolfram's quick exit. He thought about Shanna, how he'd been attracted to her physical form, how he had put aside any possibility of mating with her, and he felt sorry for her. Wolfram had wrapped her in a world of extreme limitations and was more guilty than anyone for her naiveté.

He shrugged off thoughts about Shanna, stood, and looked out the window at the icy landscape. His mind whirled with new possibilities. This had been a meeting to be remembered. A partnership with the Guild was unprecedented. It would secure his clan's status in the district and help ensure the alien threat was removed forever. *And perhaps*, he thought, *could bring an end to the feud with Clan Polinda.*

Wolfram Sy paused at the top of his shuttle's boarding ramp and took in a deep breath of the cool night air. The trip back from the security station took three hours. He had spent most of that time reviewing the data recorded on Arrilen Po, and much of the historical data from the failed first settlement. The boy-regent had also transferred information about Polinda's known ship movements, but he put that aside for later. He was looking forward to a good night's sleep before rallying his advisers for the debate about their new partnership with Clan Erstallius. Then he saw Eber Kurnes at the bottom of the boarding ramp. The look on the old security minister's face was more gaunt than usual, and Wolfram wondered what dire news waited for him.

Kurnes handed Wolfram a small data pad as his patriarch stepped off the ramp.

Wolfram scanned the black screen. "What's this?"

"We found the security leak. Turn it on."

Wolfram clicked the switch and read as the data scrolled across the small screen. "Where are they?"

"Detention."

"Take me there."

Kurnes gestured for a ground car.

By the time he arrived at the detention facility, Wolfram had calmed his anger. Rage would not solve this problem. He jumped out of the ground car, entered the building, and ordered Kurnes to stay in the lobby with the guards. His footfalls echoed in the wide hall as he passed empty detention cells, and by the time he reached cell Ten at the end of the hall, the sharp impacts of his footsteps silenced the murmurs coming from that last cell.

Shanna and Wellen sat together on the cot against the back wall, both dressed in the yellow jumpsuit and white slippers of the detained. When they saw Wolfram, they lowered their eyes in silent shame.

"Well," Wolfram said, "this is interesting."

The women remained silent.

"I'm sure you have a good explanation for your actions, I'm just not sure I want to hear it right now."

Wellen raised her head as if to say something, but when her eyes met Wolfram's, she bowed her head and said nothing.

"I'm tired," Wolfram said. "I've had a busy day, so this will have to wait until morning."

He turned and strode back down the hall.

The following morning Wolfram downed his usual light breakfast, reviewed his agenda for the day, then joined his advisers for their morning meeting in the oval conference room next to his private library. A lively discussion about the Erstallius proposal, and the impact it would have on the Guild, consumed the meeting's first hour. Next a review of the planetary building projects and the status of fleet readiness took another hour. Never during those two hours did the security breach come up for discussion. Wolfram saved that topic for the very end of the meeting.

"We had a minor security breach the other day," Wolfram said. "It seems my wife can't wait for the daily reports, so she acquired the ability to eavesdrop on some of our classified communications."

Only Eber Kurnes had known of the breach. The other advisers voiced their genuine surprise.

Wolfram stopped the conversation with a wave of his hand. "Wellen and Shanna have violated protocol. My family is under the same laws that govern all in the Guild. They have been detained per law and will be punished according to the decrees of law."

A solemn mood filled the room as the advisers contemplated the reaction this incident would have throughout the Guild.

Eber Kurnes stood. "This incident should reinforce the understanding that our laws are not arbitrary edicts that can be ignored by those in positions of authority. While the infractions do not demand capital punishment, they do demand chastisement with restrictions imposed for whatever length of time is deemed worthy by the magistrate."

Wolfram gestured for Kurnes to sit, then stood himself to end the meeting. "I want to assure you all that whatever punishment is decreed; my wife and daughter will gladly suffer the consequences as faithful members of the Guild. I will have it no other way. You are dismissed."

The advisers dispersed to their scheduled duties.

Wolfram returned to the detention center and met Wellen in an interrogation room. He sat across the small table from his yellow-jumpsuit-clad wife and waited for her explanation.

"I felt betrayed," Wellen said.

Wolfram remained silent and stone-faced, waiting for more words from his guilty wife.

"After the trouble with the Cormeds," Wellen continued, with her eyes downcast, "I was relieved when Pardee informed me we were finally here. But then we saw all that had been accomplished here. All the ships and the buildings. The entire Guild seemed to have moved here. You gave us the impression this was a wilderness retreat. We were looking forward to a relaxing vacation. I felt betrayed."

"I see," Wolfram said. "I thought it best to keep our move cloaked from you as long as possible. I meant to keep you free from the worry that would surely have erupted in you, and in Shanna."

Wellen understood Wolfram's motive, and that just inflamed her anger. "You think so little of me."

"No, my dear. Just the opposite."

Wellen raised her eyes and forced herself to relax. "I was angry. Before we landed, I decided to never be surprised like that again. I did the research and found the equipment I would need."

"You were wise to avoid the more restricted information."

"I only wanted to know the general layout of events, not the intricate details."

"You realize your breach could have allowed others access to the more restricted areas."

"Impossible. I made certain that couldn't happen."

Wolfram knew that, he just needed to hear it from his wife. Her motive wasn't nefarious, it was just curious. "You should have come to me about this."

"I felt you would have ignored me. I couldn't trust you to be honest."

That statement cut through Wolfram's heart like a knife. "My motive has always been for your benefit. I see now I underestimated you."

Wellen lowered her head. "What will be done with us?"

"You, my dear, will spend the next two weeks in your cell."

Wolfram pushed away from the table and stood. "You'll also be expected to make a statement of apology, along with a donation to the security service to reimburse the cost of the investigation."

Wellen looked up with sullen eyes. "What will happen to Shanna?"

Wolfram turned, left the room, and crossed the hall to question his daughter.

Shanna sat slumped in her chair as Wolfram entered her interrogation room. She avoided eye contact as he sat down.

Wolfram leaned forward and cupped his hands on the table. "You know why you are here?"

Shanna nodded.

"I need you to tell me."

Shanna kept her head down. "I accepted restricted information."

"And why is that wrong?"

Shanna frowned. "Because—I don't have the security clearance."

"What should you have done?"

Shanna shrugged.

Wolfram noticed Shanna's embarrassment by the way she avoided eye contact.

"Punishment," he said, "is sometimes complete when the guilty party feels the pain of their mistake."

Shanna hugged her elbows. "I know what I did was wrong."

"Yes, but punishment is never complete unless the guilty understand what they should have done instead."

Shanna looked up. "I didn't know what Mother told me was—how is knowing that Arlud came here so wrong?"

"There is a process," Wolfram said. "We established it to protect us and those who interact with us. We are the Guild of Free Traders, and that freedom must be protected. Once filtered through our security protocols the information would have been freely disseminated to all who need to know."

"Mother felt you were keeping things from us unnecessarily."

"Not unnecessarily. For your protection. I hope to shield you, not just from physical harm, but also from worry."

"You made her feel betrayed."

"So I have been told, but that does not excuse your actions."

"What will be done with us?"

"You, my dear, will spend the next four days in your cell.

"What about Mother?"

Wolfram pushed away from the table. "Like you, she will be expected to make a statement of apology." He stood. "I know your motive was based on emotion and not intentionally criminal, but this must play out by law." He turned and left the room.

Arlud watched the Halva cruiser bank to her starboard side and retreat toward the system boundary. He was in the starboard observation deck on the Guild dreadnought that would return him to GSW-183 and lead the search for the aliens. Nine other Guild ships had gathered into cruise formation in preparation for the command to leave their new home.

"We did it, Gus."

Gustav Eahuda stood next to Arlud, focused on the retreating cruiser. "Now the real test begins."

"Test?"

Eahuda glanced down at Arlud. "Now we'll see if Bev is correct."

"You doubt her?"

"I always doubt that which I cannot confirm."

Arlud understood Eahuda's uncertainty. He had his own reservations about how to proceed after his discussion with Wolfram Sy, but Bev's conviction overruled his misgivings. "Well," he said, "I trust her."

"I know you do, lad. I hope she's right."

Cordova entered the observation deck and activated a holoscreen that ignited inside the rectangular window. He faced Arlud and Eahuda. "Wolfram is coming online."

The Guild crest appeared inside the window, then faded to reveal the head and shoulders of Wolfram Sy.

"Greetings," Wolfram said. "To all of you assigned to the mission to track down the alien intruder—I wish you a successful journey. To our new partners from Clan Erstallius—I hope you find peace and the end to your feud with Clan Polinda. May the strength of the Guild be with you all."

The Guild crest replaced Wolfram's face, and the holoscreen winked off.

Arlud felt a low rumbling beneath his feet as the dreadnought's compression drive system ignited and surrounded the vessel with a wispy green halo that blocked the view.

BEV COLLI: STRONGER

Bev Colli stopped inside the hatchway and looked across the crowded mess hall for Arlud. He was sitting near the back wall, at the table next to the food dispenser. Gustav Eahuda sat next to him, and they both were focused on their meals. The assembled guildmen were also hunched over their dinners. No one noticed her standing in the hatchway.

She hugged her elbows. Her skin crawled along the underside of her arms, a prickling that moved in waves from her shoulders to her fingertips. She had tried meditation to relieve the sensation, but that only made it worse. What had started as an occasional and brief irritation was now a constant annoyance. She took a step into the mess hall and balked at the muffled sounds of conversation among the crew that assaulted her ears like bellowing while submerged in water. Her connection with the aliens was changing her senses, and she feared if it continued she would go insane. Eight steps into the room and she was halfway to Arlud. She focused on his hunched form as she passed the seated guildmen and missed the approach of a well-fed engineer, who bumped into her right side and dropped his food tray.

Bev was jolted sideways but kept her balance.

The engineer rebounded from the impact. "Oh, I didn't see you there."

Bev heard the engineer's words amid the persistent echo of his meal tray hitting the metal deck and the sudden rush of movement as the guildmen seated nearby turned to witness what had caused the commotion.

Then the engineer touched her right arm.

In one sweeping motion Bev leaned into the engineer, grabbed his forearm, pivoted, and flung him across the mess hall. She watched his body hit the bulkhead and fall unconscious onto the adjoining table, knocking food plates and drinking glasses onto the floor.

The men seated at the table backed away from their fallen comrade and stood, focused on Bev.

All conversation stopped.

Arlud rushed to Bev's side and ushered her out of the mess hall.

Eahuda muttered a quick apology to the guildman then followed Arlud and Bev through the corridor and into the nearest personnel lift.

Arlud hugged Bev's shoulders to keep her close to his body as they ascended inside the lift. She found comfort in his closeness, but her eyes were focused somewhere else.

"That won't sit well with Pardee," Eahuda said.

"I know," Arlud said. He focused on Bev's blank expression. "Why did you do that?"

They reached deck five, scurried down the corridor, and entered Arlud's cabin.

Arlud sat with Bev on the low settee against the exterior bulkhead, beneath the closed rectangular window. He asked in a whisper: "You OK?"

Bev scooted close and hugged Arlud's arm but kept her eyes downcast. "I'm sorry."

Eahuda sat in the extra chair near the entry to the bunk alcove. "That, my little dear, was one grand reaction. That guildman must weigh one-hundred kilos."

"He didn't feel that heavy."

Eahuda leaned forward. "You flung him five meters. Like he was a bag of rubbish."

Bev lowered her head and hugged Arlud tighter.

The door buzzer sounded.

Arlud gestured to Eahuda, and the old Degen stood and opened the door.

Erlis Pardee waited outside the doorway with his hands clasped behind his back. "May I come in?"

Eahuda moved aside and gestured for Pardee to enter.

Pardee stepped into the room and two guildmen stationed themselves in the corridor with magar-rifles cradled in their arms.

"We can't have assaults on this ship," Pardee said. "If you needed to protect yourself from harassment, you should have come to me."

Bev glanced up and saw she was the center of attention. She focused on Pardee. "I didn't mean to do it. I know he bumped into me by accident."

Pardee tilted his head. "Then why does my engineer have a concussion?"

Bev lowered her gaze and rested her head on Arlud's shoulder. "It was a reflex action."

"She's been going through physical changes since the contact on Arrilen Po," Arlud said. "They've connected with her on a level that's beyond dreams. I think they may have sensed danger and reacted to protect her."

Pardee folded his arms across his chest. "You're telling me they took control of her body."

Arlud nodded. "Maybe."

"The Halva commander warned me about this kind of thing happening. Can you assure me it won't happen again?"

Bev heard the question, but her mind was flowing down another path as she fought to ignore the prickling sensation that had spread from her arms to the back of her legs. Holding Arlud's arm was the only thing keeping her from bouncing off the walls.

Pardee saw the internal struggle in Bev's eyes. "OK. Before this gets out of hand, we need to take her to the infirmary." He stepped aside and gestured for Arlud to lead Bev out of the cabin.

Bev clung to Arlud all the way to the medical bay on deck fifteen. Once there, the doctor sedated her and, with the help of a med tech, placed her on the exam table in the isolation room.

Arlud stood next to Pardee and watched Bev through the duraplex doorway to the isolation room. "She told me she feels like she's being tortured from the inside out."

Pardee frowned. "And she's our best chance of removing that alien menace from our universe?"

"I don't like it any more than you, but we have no other option."

The doctor stepped out of the isolation room with a holopad. "Look at this."

The holopad displayed two, three-dimensional images of brains. "This scan on the left is Bev's," the doctor said. "Notice the areas highlighted yellow and orange. Those are areas of increased activity. The scan on the right displays a brain with normal activity while at rest."

The highlighted areas in the scan on the right were small and fewer than in Bev's scan.

"Her entorhinal region is off the charts," the doctor explained. "That's the area that gives us a sense of direction."

Arlud focused on the holopad. "Is she in danger?"

"Her entire nervous system is highly active. Keeping her sedated will help her cope, but if it continues at this level, it could damage her permanently."

Pardee glanced through the transparent doorway at Bev. Her limbs twitched under the exam table restraints. "Can you stop it?"

"The sedatives will help, but no, we would need to block the source and I don't know how to do that without injuring her."

Arlud pressed his hands against the transparent doorway. "She's unconscious?"

"Yes," the doctor said.

"Can you reduce the effects and keep her awake?"

"I can try, but she would be very uncomfortable."

"Try," Arlud said. "We need her awake."

The doctor glanced at Pardee for approval.

Pardee nodded, and the doctor re-entered the isolation room.

Thirty hyper-hours later, when their journey to GSW-183 was nearing the half-way point, Bev was still sedated when Arlud entered the medical bay for the fifth time.

"How's she doing?"

The doctor turned in his chair as Arlud stopped outside the isolation room. "I had her awake about an hour ago, but she began screaming about burning along her spine, so I sedated her again."

Arlud noticed the med pad on Bev's forehead and the sensor bracelet around her left forearm. "No sign of change?"

"Yes," the doctor said. "Constant change. She's better off sedated." He activated the holoscreen above the exam table that displayed a real time scan of Bev's brain that showed her parietal cortex pulsing with yellow and red patches of color. "The largest spikes in her brain activity have been moving from one area to another." He unfolded from his chair and stood next to Arlud. "It's as if they're rewiring her brain."

"How can they do that?"

"I wish I knew. Despite the buffering from the medpad it continues without interruption."

The doctor returned to his desk.

Arlud pressed against the duraplex. He regretted encouraging Bev to leave U'galem. *I should have listened to her*, he thought. She looked so helpless lying there, and there was nothing he could do. He faced the doctor. "Call me if she wakes."

The doctor nodded.

Arlud turned and left the medical bay.

Fifteen hours later Arlud was in the C.I.C. with Eahuda and Pardee when the call came from the doctor that Bev was awake.

"Keep her there," Pardee said. "We're on our way."

By the time Arlud reached the medical bay, Bev was arguing with the doctor in his office.

"I'm fine," Bev said.

"For your safety, we need to keep you under observation for a few days—"

"Excuse me," Arlud interrupted. He stood in the doorway with his gaze focused on Bev.

Once Bev saw Arlud she rushed over to him and wrapped him in a tight hug. "I'm glad you're here."

"What's the problem?"

"She wants to leave," the doctor said, "and we need to keep her under observation for a few days. We need to determine what happened—"

"I'm fine," Bev insisted.

Arlud backed out of Bev's hug and held her in front of him. He searched her expression for any sign of a problem. "We should let the doctor do his job."

"I'm fine. Really."

Arlud looked past Bev at the doctor. "Can you observe her vitals via remote?"

The doctor hesitated, and looked past Arlud at Pardee, who waited behind Arlud in the medical bay lobby. He saw no support from Pardee. "I suppose," he said, "but that's not the same—"

"Then hook her up with a remote sensor," Arlud said.

Pardee brushed past Arlud and Bev. "Do it, Doc. We need her to be with us."

The doctor acquiesced to Pardee's order. After he secured a remote transmitter to Bev's lower back, she left the medical bay with Arlud and Eahuda.

Pardee stayed behind to consult the doctor. "What happened to her, Doc?"

"In all my years I have seen nothing like it. It was as if someone analyzed every connection in her brain and made adjustments. She's not the same person."

"What do you mean by that?"

"She's different now. She's still Bev Colli, but different."

"How different?"

The doctor shrugged. "That's why we need to observe her. I do not understand what those changes mean."

"Are the aliens in control of her?"

"I don't think so, not in the sense that she's their puppet, or anything like that. They took control of her to make the changes. They rewrote who she is, but she controls what she does. She still has free will."

"Then what was the purpose?"

The doctor sat on the edge of his desk and thought for a moment. "I think they prepared her for what's coming."

"What?"

"She's a conduit. Your own analysis of the situation implies that. I think they upgraded her abilities to help them find what they've been searching for, but only time will tell if that's the reason."

"Is she a danger to the crew?"

"I don't think so."

Pardee pondered everything he had learned about the aliens and the survivors who had dreams. If Bev's upgrade was to help the aliens find their rebels, that would ensure the safety of his crew. If there were ulterior motives behind the change, Bev Colli would find her future limited.

Arlud sat across from Bev in the mess hall while she nibbled a vegetable casserole. They were the only two people in the hall because the normal dinner time for the crew had expired, and Pardee had mandated Bev could not dine with the crew.

"I'm confused," Arlud said.

Bev stayed focused on the casserole. "Confused about what?"

"You."

Bev looked up from her plate. "What about me?"

"Since we left U'galem you've been plagued by those persistent dreams, pushed into a coma for six days, abducted by aliens from another dimension, had your brain re-wired according to the Guild physician, and you sit here eating like nothing has happened."

"Not like nothing has happened."

"Then you're very good at hiding it."

Bev slammed her fork onto the table. "What do you want me to do?"

"I don't know. Maybe open up a little."

Bev lowered her head and stared at her food. She knew Arlud was only concerned for her, but his insistence that she express some emotional hysteria was not part of her persona. As a child on Pigrell she had learned to deflect reflexive reaction with a thoughtful response, the smarter path to take for a sapi. "I don't dwell on what I can't control. Crying won't solve anything."

Arlud admired her resolve, but he had also seen her cry, and knew she needed to vent even if she refused to acknowledge it. "Talking about it will help us all understand what's going on with you. You keep it bottled up so much that—"

"I'm fine. Just leave it at that." She stuffed a fork full of casserole into her mouth.

"OK," Arlud said. He leaned back in his chair and watched her eat for a few minutes, then checked his compad. They were approaching the PDN160 system, and he was expecting Pardee to call him any minute.

Bev put down her fork and swallowed. "I know you only want to help me, and I appreciate that, but how can I explain to you something I don't understand myself?"

"That's all right. I understand how difficult this must be for you."

Bev smirked. "No, you really don't."

The look on Bev's face revealed the confusion and pain she had been going through, and Arlud had to admit there was no way he could relate to how she was feeling. "You're right," he said, "I don't."

Bev's face softened a bit, and she continued eating.

"What I would like to know," Arlud said, "is how the aliens—"

"The Rhysu."

"What?"

"I call them, Rhysu."

"That's new. Where did that come from?"

"Since we're going to Ni'apinu I started reviewing the Akün language in the ship's database. *Rhysu* means, *one who searches*. I thought it had a nice ring to it. I call the ones they're trying to find, *Shoku*. That means *one who seeks refuge*."

"Refugees?"

"That's what Gus called them. I think it fits."

"I didn't know you had a penchant for languages."

Bev paused her eating. "A what?"

"That you have an interest in languages."

"Oh. I just thought it might be good to understand the locals."

"Well, what I would like to understand is how the Rhysu can stay connected to you while we're in hyperspace, but they can't find the Shoku without our help."

Arlud's com pad beeped. "They need me in the C.I.C."

"Then go."

Arlud stood. "Come on, I'll walk you to your cabin."

"I'm not done."

"Take it with you. Pardee's orders. You're not allowed to be anywhere on your own except in your cabin."

Bev rose off her chair, dropped her food tray into the recycle bin, and followed Arlud out of the mess.

Captain Erlis Pardee stood at the railing around the course-plotting pedestal in the C.I.C. and reviewed the holomap of the PDN160 system. The advance probe had detected seven Erstallius ships by the time it reached the orbit boundary of the blue gas giant. Telemetry indicated at least ten more ships scattered among the four inner planets. "Your reinforcements have arrived."

Arlud stepped up to the holomap and watched the blue icons that represented the Erstallius fleet populate the map. He had been gone from GSW-183 for sixty standard days and had feared the possibility Polinda had returned to devastate the planet. Seeing Erstallius ships was a welcome relief.

As the probe advanced toward the inner planets, it showed the Aku had secured the area around GSW-183 with four transports. Arlud wondered if a skirmish with his Clan had pushed the Erstallius vessels toward the outer planets.

"Look there," Pardee said, "near the gas giant."

The telemetry noted an Erstallius vessel within each of the debris clouds around both wrecks from the first Polinda assault.

"Salvage operations," Arlud surmised.

"And there," Pardee said.

The entangled ships in orbit around GSW-183 also had an Erstallius salvage vessel amid the surrounding debris.

That sight relieved Arlud of his suspicion about an Erstallius skirmish with the Aku. It was normal protocol to clean up debris in close orbit of a holding to prevent collisions in orbit and impacts on-planet. The Aku had no equipment capable of such tasks. An Erstallius salvage ship within the Aku zone of defense told him the partnership was intact.

"More wreckage over there," Pardee said. He adjusted the map controls and zoomed in to another area of debris orbiting GSW-183. "That's a Polinda ship."

The charred hull rotated along its Z-axis and had multiple breaches from internal explosions.

Arlud examined the data from the dead ship. "That one must have battled with the Aku."

"There's another wreck in a polar orbit," Pardee said. He switched the view to focus on the other dead Polinda frigate.

Satisfied the area was secure, Arlud placed his compad on the control console and uploaded a recorded message to a comdrone that would announce his return and prevent action against the Guild armada. He faced Pardee. "You can send it now."

Pardee checked the course for the drone that would cause it to swing around GSW-183 and send it on a return trajectory to his ship. Satisfied, he pushed the launch switch.

Four hours later, Arlud pressed his forehead against the window next to his seat in the Guild shuttle as it descended toward the Erstallius landing field. He was surprised to see the tower construction was completed, and the service buildings had been expanded to accommodate more traffic. As the shuttle maneuvered over the tarmac, he noticed a small, circular stone construction around the grave marker next to the northern perimeter fence. *They finished the memorial.* "We were away too long, Gus."

Eahuda looked out the window next to his seat. "You got that right, lad."

The shuttle landed amid a brief swirl of dust in the orange parking circle next to the central tower.

Arlud stepped into warm midday sun as he walked down the shuttle's boarding ramp and stopped in front of the fleet commander, Jegen-Major Lon Pavan. The clanman wore the dark-blue campaign uniform that displayed small rank emblems on the collar, and his short-cropped hair style gave his head a squarish appearance. Arlud extended his hand in greeting.

From her seat inside the shuttle, Bev peered through her window and watched Arlud greet the eight other officers who accompanied the Jegen-Major, while Eahuda followed behind him with his own greetings. She had sensed an emptiness inside Arlud during the past few weeks. *Now he can be a regent again*, she thought, and she smiled. *He can fulfill his duty to his clan.* She watched the Erstallius clanmen assemble behind Arlud and Eahuda as they entered the central tower. Once they were all inside, she leaned back in her seat knowing there would be a long wait before Arlud returned. Captain Pardee had insisted she planet-fall, and she knew the incident in the mess hall was the reason. Arlud wanted to consult with his command officers before she met them, so the only option available to her was to wait inside the shuttle. *No one wants me around, but they're too afraid to get rid of me*, she thought, and that idea made her giggle. She never imagined she would end up being important to so many people. The regret she had felt on the journey to Arrilen Po was now buried beneath layers of anticipation at what lay ahead for her, and for the clans.

"Hey."

Bev looked up. The shuttle pilot had left the cockpit and was standing by the exit.

"What?"

"I need to inspect the hull," the pilot said. "You going to be OK in here by yourself?"

"I'm never by myself."

The pilot returned an incredulous stare. "Well," he said, "if you need anything, just push this green button." He gestured to the five buttons on the panel next to the cockpit hatchway. The top button was green.

"OK," Bev said. "Can I collapse these seats so I can take a nap?"

"Yeah, sure," the pilot said, and he bounded down the boarding ramp.

Bev watched the pilot through her window. He greeted an Erstallius clanmen then walked past her window toward the rear of the shuttle.

I'm never alone, she thought. The sensation of another consciousness just behind her own was intimidating and left her with the uneasy feeling she no longer had any privacy.

She stood and adjusted the seats in her row so she could lie down, then went to the storage compartments in the aft section of the cabin to find a blanket.

Flashes of light erupted in the periphery of her vision and dizziness forced her to her knees in the aisle. She bent over and collapsed on the deck as the vision of an intense, cyan-colored light appeared in front of her.

The Erstallius officers settled around the oval table in the conference room inside the central tower. After a detailed review of the battles at Thrum Dau and Baleiou, and the current status of the remaining Erstallius forces, Arlud stood to speak.

"Thank you for the detailed reports. I am very glad to hear my family survived Polinda's attacks. I am sure they rejoiced upon hearing GSW-183 also survived, and I look forward to seeing them once this conflict is finally over." He paused for a few heartbeats to gather his thoughts. "I commend all the clanmen who supported my strategy to divert Polinda despite the contrary opinions. We were pushed into a corner, and with the help of the Aku we succeeded."

The clanmen filled the room with a brief round of applause.

"I understand Nared-Major, Winstone Bittle, and Nared-Major, Petra Sitlyn are away with their crew of engineers at storage site Four helping to repair more Aku transports. I want to make it known to the fleet I have promoted them both to the rank of Segen."

Arlud faced Pavan. "Please forward my letter of promotion and make sure this happens by the end of the day."

Pavan nodded.

"I also want to commend you all for the effort to finish this outpost. It was a pleasant surprise to see this upon my return. The effort demonstrates your resolve in the face of impending conflict. You should all be very proud of your accomplishment. Those responsible for this effort can expect letters of praise and significant rewards from the cadre."

Another round of applause filled the room.

"It encouraged me to see our partnership with the Aku is still intact. I understand their plasma weapon is very effective. I'm glad we don't have to meet them in battle."

A few cautious chuckles erupted around the table.

"Unfortunately, this war with Polinda is not over, and the other threat we face could prove to be more disastrous than any battle with the clans. As we move forward, I hope the plans we are now developing prove to be as successful as our recent campaigns."

Arlud paused again and surveyed the seated clanmen. "Where are the Cormeds?"

"We took them to Roth-513," Pavan said. "The envoy, Nin, wouldn't stop badgering the Field Commander. I ordered a frigate to take them to their holding a week after we arrived."

"I see," Arlud said, and he was reminded of a story he had read about an old woman who pestered a judge until he heard her case. *Nin must have read the same story.* "Without Nin's help, our ruse would not have fooled Polinda," he said. "I want him mentioned in the morning update as a recipient of the Silver Medallion for his commitment to help our clan."

Energetic applause filled the room.

Once the reaction to Nin's award subsided, Arlud said: "Thank you all for your dedication," and he returned to his seat amid a resurgent applause.

Eahuda stood. "You have all seen the report transmitted by Jhared Dejoria about the attack on the Cormed frigates. This information was supplied to us by Guild Captain Erlis Pardee. Since that report we have acquired more intel." He pushed the activation button embedded in the table in front of his seat, and a holoscreen appeared above the center of the table. He inserted a data chip into the port next to the control buttons and navigated to an aerial view of the destroyed colony on Arrilen Po. "This could be us."

A few gasps sounded from the officers around the table.

"We have learned," Eahuda continued, "that those who caused this destruction on Arrilen Po also destroyed the mine on Alpha Cephei Four and attacked the Cormed frigates. Although the Sabballi frigates have never been found, we also believe their disappearance is related to these other events."

Eahuda flipped through ground-based images of the destroyed colony, then stopped on a still view of the basin surrounding Station 38. "What you are about to see is our mission with Clan Halva on Arrilen Po. I think you'll appreciate the implications concerning our security."

The holo-image was set in motion.

"This is a recording from the quadcopter that took us to this remote site," Eahuda said.

The recording displayed everything from the first landing alongside the slope below the cavern, to the retreat away from the cavern before the ignition of the plasma cutter.

Eahuda stopped the recording. "Before this recording continues, I want to stress we had no idea this would happen."

The recording continued with a view from the grounded quadcopter that displayed the hillside dominating the field of view on the left and the stone walls of the station in the distance. A puff of dust and debris spewed out of the cavern after the plasma cutter ignition, then Bev, Arlud, Eahuda, and Cynth could be seen in the foreground. The quake occurred, and the sound of rotors could be heard behind the call from the pilot to board the quadcopter.

"Here it comes," Eahuda said.

The hillside collapsed around the cavern and the blue plasma tornado swirled out of the hole. In the foreground Arlud was pushed to the ground and the camera view backed away from his location. As the view retreated the blue plasma whirled around Bev, lifted her into the air, carried her to the cavern, and dove into the rock. The view reversed motion and approached Arlud where he lay on the ground.

Eahuda stopped the recording as Arlud jumped aboard the copter. "And there you have it," he said. "This enemy is real and something previously unknown."

The assembled clanmen exchanged quiet musings about what they had just seen.

Eahuda turned off the holoscreen. "You'll be able to review this data in greater detail, but for now just be aware, unless we stop this thing, our existence will be in jeopardy."

Pavan leaned forward. "What happened to the girl?"

"She survived," Arlud said. He stood. "I know this is not what you expected. We need to focus on this issue at once and bring as many clans into this discussion as we can."

"That will be difficult," Pavan said. "Considering the war we're facing—"

"Yes," Arlud said, "it will be difficult. But we have a plan that, if executed successfully, could solve this problem and end our feud with Polinda once and for all."

Bev huddled beneath a blanket in her shuttle seat and watched Arlud bound inside the passenger cabin and stop outside the cockpit hatchway. She averted her eyes as he advanced down the aisle toward her.

Arlud stopped next to the row of seats where Bev sat. He could see from the ashen appearance of her face that something had happened. "Sorry I took so long," he said. "We had a lot to review."

Bev kept her gaze downcast.

Arlud sat on the edge of the aisle seat. "You OK?"

"Whatever the Rhysu did to me worked," Bev said. "I saw the Shoku."

Arlud held his reaction to an internal flinch and waited for Bev to continue.

"It was nauseating," Bev said. "I almost threw up."

"I'll take you to the physician."

"No, I'm fine now. I just need to rest."

"OK."

"It was worse than the dreams because I was awake. It was like they transported me there. I lost all reference to here."

"What did you see?"

"That damn cyan light, and then a ship. It was a boxy-looking thing. Beige colored with red stripes. Never saw one like that before."

"Boxy?"

"Yeah, not curved. It looked like large crates stacked together."

"And that was the Shoku?"

Bev frowned. "No. They were the cyan light. I was seeing what they were seeing."

"Oh." Arlud thought about the description of the ship. "Sounds like you saw a cargo ship. I'll have Gus do a search."

"They enveloped the ship."

"Like the Cormed frigates?"

"Yeah."

"Did you see anything else?"

"No. After the ship disappeared, I found myself laying in the aisle back there." She pointed to the rear of the shuttle. "How long were you gone?"

"Almost an hour. You sure you'll be OK?"

"Yeah."

Arlud stood and stepped back into the center aisle. "We've arranged a room for you in the main tower. Come on, I'll show you."

"I'd rather stay here."

"You know you can't do that. The pilot needs to get this shuttle back to Pardee's ship."

Bev drew her limbs tighter to her body. She was warm and comfortable beneath the blanket, and the thought of walking right now was not what she wanted to do. She knew seeing the Shoku wasn't the same as finding them, and after that brief encounter her confidence was gone. It frightened her, not because of the physical damage the aliens could cause, but because her connection with the Shoku had ripped into her soul, and she had no clue how to stand against that mental invasion. She needed more time to reflect on what had happened.

Arlud ignored Bev's sulky attitude, stepped into her aisle, and scooped her blanket-covered body off the seat.

Bev pouted. "The last man who tried to carry me limped away with a broken leg."

Arlud smirked. "You will not break my leg. You're going to your room."

He carried Bev's blanket-covered body down the aisle.

"I'm keeping the blanket."

"I don't think the pilot needs it."

Bev withdrew her arms out from under the blanket and clasped her hands behind Arlud's neck. "Won't he miss it?"

"If he does, we'll get him another one."

Arlud carried Bev down the boarding ramp into the cool afternoon shadows cast by the central tower.

Eahuda was waiting a few steps from the boarding ramp. His eyes widened as Arlud passed him. "Want me to get the Doc, lad?"

"No. She's fine."

Eahuda rubbed his chin and called out: "You sure?"

"I'm sure."

The sentry on duty outside the entrance to the central tower pulled the door open.

Arlud entered the building with Bev smiling in his arms.

CLAN ERSTALLIUS: TRACKING

Five days after Arlud returned to GSW-183, a comdrone sped through the PDN160 system and broadcast news that Wan'tei, the homeworld of Clan Dejoria, was under siege.

"They're surrounded," Eahuda said.

Arlud reached for the data chip in Eahuda's outstretched hand. He leaned back in his office chair and placed the chip into a port on the small control console built into his desk.

A holoscreen appeared and Arlud focused on the report. A large armada of Polinda and Sabballi ships had blockaded the planet with help from Clan Vestlok. "Do Pavan and Pardee know about this?"

"Yes, they're making plans to break the blockade as we speak."

"This is it, Gus. This is our battle."

"I was thinking the same thing, lad."

Three hours later Arlud was in the conference room engaged with Lon Pavan and Erlis Pardee via holoscreens regarding what strategy to use against their enemy.

"It's simple," Pardee said from the holoscreen at Arlud's right. "We kill them all."

"Yes," Pavan said from the screen at Arlud's left. "But we must take care to protect Wan'tei from collateral damage. There are a billion people on that planet."

"If we follow that strategy, the battle will linger and more people could die," Pardee said. "You need to think beyond your training. You Erstallius have always fought Polinda with the same tactics. You need to become an animal when you want to defeat an animal. The only focus we should have is killing the enemy. If we worry about collateral damage our focus will be divided and we won't succeed."

Pavan scowled. "We have an obligation to uphold—"

"Gentlemen," Arlud said.

Pavan held his words, and Pardee shifted his gaze to focus on the young Erstallius Regent.

This discussion was heading into an argument that Arlud hoped to avoid. He knew Pavan had his training, and his experience, but so did Pardee. They were from opposite ends of the same mold.

Our path must be united.

"I'm not a warrior," Arlud said. "My father made me a politician, but I don't need to be an expert in combat strategy to know that we must win. Polinda has allies who are powerful. Vestlok is an old clan, with many ships and many victories. We must hit them hard enough to discourage their descendants forever. We must obliterate their forces if we are to have any hope of victory. Clan Dejoria's homeworld is in jeopardy, but the future of our entire Clan, and the existence of the Guild, are also at stake here. If we lose this one, we lose everything. I'll accept collateral damage if that means ending Polinda once and for all, but if we're careful, we may accomplish our goal without collateral damage. Are we agreed?"

"Agreed," Pardee said.

Pavan hesitated to answer.

Arlud understood his fleet commander's reluctance, and under different conditions he would agree with him, but not now, not with Polinda gaining allies. "Jegen-Major," he said. "I understand your misgivings, but Pardee is correct. We must keep our intent focused, no matter the consequences."

"Clan Polinda," Pavan said, "must be annihilated. To that end, I agree."

Arlud recognized that Pavan had evaded complete agreement. *The clanmen are never obligated to agree*, he thought, *but they are expected to follow orders.* He knew Pavan would do what was demanded of him, without regard for his personal feelings. "Any news about what Clan Dejoria is doing about this situation?"

"Their comdrone should arrive within the hour," Pavan said, "but I expect Clan Dejoria to send reinforcements from U'galem. I'll forward you the reports as soon as we have them. We have heard from Clan Sorrell, and Clan Rastee. They are sending forces to rendezvous with us in five days near Wan'tei."

Arlud was glad to hear other clans had joined them, but time might not be on their side. "Can Wan'tei hold for another five days?"

Pavan accepted a compad from a crewman. He scanned the pad and looked up. "Clan Emlito and Clan Vestlok have attacked Cestratha."

Arlud leaned back in his chair and let out a guttural moan. He remembered Cynth had said Emlito and Vestlok were her clan's greatest adversaries. "Is Clan Halva holding?"

Pavan scanned the compad. "I can't tell from this. We must wait for the next comdrone."

"If there is a next comdrone."

Pavan handed the compad back to his crewman. "We'll monitor the situation and let you know as soon as we know."

"Can Wan'tei hold?"

"Yes," Pavan said. "With Vestlok split between Cestratha and Wan'tei their impact on the siege will be reduced. That's an advantage for us."

Pardee sat forward. "Can the Aku defend GSW-183 in your absence?"

Arlud recalled what he had learned about the dead frigates in orbit. "Based on what they did against Polinda—yes."

"Good," Pardee said. "I fear the siege of Wan'tei may be a ruse to weaken your strength here."

"It will stretch us to the limit," Arlud admitted, "but the Aku are well equipped to bolster our defense. And besides, Polinda may not know our reinforcements arrived. The last time he was in this system, he learned Clan Cormed was the caretaker of this holding."

"I doubt he still believes that," Pardee said.

"I'm not so sure. His blockade of Wan'tei tells me he believes Erstallius forces have been degraded enough to allow him that measure of freedom. If he thought our strength was still a threat, he wouldn't have immobilized his forces around a heavily defended holding like Wan'tei, regardless of how much he wants to retaliate against Jhared Dejoria. He's insane, but not stupid."

"I agree," Pavan said. "We have a real opportunity to catch him off guard as long as we move quickly. However, I'm concerned about the alien situation. How does that play into our strategy?"

Arlud let Pavan's question revolve in his mind. Nothing about the aliens was certain. "Bev has seen the Shoku. I'll be meeting with her later to help pinpoint their location." He leaned forward and crossed his arms on the table. "Understand, the alien agenda could have a dampening effect on the battle. It is my hope the Clans with Polinda will retreat once they witness the alien conflagration, but make no mistake, we must proceed as if this alien problem doesn't exist."

"Agreed," Pavan said.

"I understand," Pardee said.

Arlud leaned back in his chair. "Thank you, gentlemen. I trust you both will work together to secure this situation. I will leave for your flagship, Jegen-Major, within the hour."

Pavan flinched. "You're coming aboard?"

"We must access your systems if Bev is to have any hope of tracking the aliens."

"Oh, I see."

"Will that be a problem?"

"No, not at all."

"Thank you, Jegen-Major." Pavan nodded and his holoscreen blinked off.

Arlud focused on Pardee's holo-image. "Thank you, Captain."

Pardee raised his right hand in a half-salute and his holo-image winked off.

Six ciâfey circled above the Erstallius landing field like buzzards searching for a carcass.

Arlud walked to the edge of the tarmac as the soaring wings began their descent through the still afternoon air. "Do you know who's with them?"

Eahuda stopped a few paces to Arlud's right. "No. They never announced they were coming."

One by one the ciâfey touched down inside the large green landing circle at the east end of the field. Five of the pilots formed a single file behind their leader and walked toward Arlud's position.

"Salus," Arlud said. "I can tell from his gait."

The Aku pilots grouped around Arlud and Eahuda and welcomed them back to Ni'apinu with handshakes.

"When I heard you were back," Salus said, "I thought it must be a mistake."

"Jhared helped us escape," Arlud said. "Now he faces the consequences."

"Well, you have renewed our trust in your clan. The elders are elated about the repair of our ships. Winstone Bittle will never be forgotten."

Arlud chuckled inside. Bittle never did like being in the spotlight, but these people would erect a memorial to his efforts. "I'm sure he appreciates that. He definitely deserves all the praise you can give him. You should also honor his crew—without their persistent effort, your encounter with Polinda may not have turned out so well."

"Your retreat ensured our safety. The Bi'au wishes to honor you in Ji'dess."

"Thank you, my friend, but there are other matters that need my immediate attention. I'll be leaving for our flagship and may not return for weeks."

Salus frowned at that news. "The Bi'au will be disappointed."

"Now is not our time to celebrate. Our mission is not yet done."

"I understand."

Bev came out of the central tower, walked over to Arlud and stopped at his side.

"Salus," Arlud said, "this is Bev Colli. Bev, this is Salus, the Aku pilot who came with us to U'galem."

"L'dyém," Salus said.

"I saw your transport leave," Bev said. "Arlud told me about you. How you taught him to fly."

"Teaching him to fly," Salus corrected. "Ciâfey take years to master."

Bev glanced over at the parked vehicles on the tarmac. "Can you teach me?"

Salus balked at that request because Aku women do not fly.

Arlud glanced down at Bev. "We'll talk about that later."

"Why?"

Arlud turned to Salus. "Bev has had contact with the aliens I told you about. She may play an important role in our strategy against Polinda."

Salus examined Bev anew. By the way she stood and squared her shoulders, some might assume arrogance, but he saw a trained fighter, a woman who could hold her own against any man here. Her close stance beside Arlud revealed a connection between them that was also obvious by the hint of adoration in her expression. "With Arlud's permission, I will take you for a ride. After that, if you still wish to learn, I will ask my elders if they will allow it."

Bev was stuck on the word, permission.

"Maybe after our mission is done," Arlud said.

Salus nodded to Arlud's suggestion.

Bev wanted to respond but held her words. She recognized her request was beyond local custom and allowed Arlud's response to end that discussion. "I'd like to see Kuliq'Quad sometime," she said. "Arlud told me about the Mânu."

"The Mânu is empty now," Salus said. "Thanks to the Erstallius."

"Oh, well, I'd still like to see it."

"When we return," Arlud said.

A shuttle roared over the eastern tree line on a heading for the landing field.

"That's our ride," Eahuda said.

Fifteen minutes later Arlud, Bev, and Eahuda were aboard the small executive shuttle and secure in their passenger seats. The narrow cabin had only one seat on either side of the short center aisle.

Bev sat in the back row behind Arlud. Through the window she watched the ciâfey take flight one by one at the far end of the tarmac. *Like butterflies*, she thought. "I would like to learn how to do that."

Arlud leaned against the bulkhead, peered out the small window, and saw the soaring wings rise into the air and head toward the northeast. "One day you will," he said.

"How many transports do the Aku have?"

"Twenty-four."

"Are they all off-planet now?"

"No. Sixteen are still planet-bound."

"Can I see those?"

Arlud turned around in his seat to face Bev. "If you wish."

"I do."

Arlud smiled. "Then you will," he said. He sat forward in his seat to review data on his compad.

Bev leaned back and smiled. Arlud could be very accommodating when he wanted to be, but this thing about permission still bothered her. "Why are Aku women not allowed to fly?"

Arlud raised his head. "You can ask them when we get back."

Bev walked behind Arlud through a narrow corridor on the Erstallius flagship with a slow but steady gait, fueled by her lack of interest. She did not know where he was leading her and would have preferred to stay in her cabin to get some much-needed sleep, but he was insistent. So here she was, plodding along behind him. He led her through an open hatchway, and across a short catwalk that jutted about two meters into a large spherical chamber with grayish blue walls. At the end of the catwalk was a curved control console where Arlud stopped and flipped a switch that brought the console to luminous life.

Bev had never seen a room like this one. "What is this place?"

"Stellar Cartography."

"What's that?"

"A three-dimensional map."

"Where?"

"Here."

Arlud flicked another switch and the room lights dimmed. A few hundred points of light appeared in the chamber, like snowflakes frozen in time. "We'll do this slowly. Less of a shock that way."

Bev watched as the room lights grew dimmer and the points of light grew brighter and multiplied, until the room lights were off, and the chamber was filled with thousands of brilliant, miniature suns, yellow, orange, red, and white.

"These are the stars that surround our inhabited worlds," Arlud said.

The points of light expanded until only those star systems within a ten-parsec radius of the PDN160 system were visible.

"These are the stars that surround Ni'apinu."

"Beautiful," Bev said. She looked down and the sun of Ni'apinu, labeled PDN160A, floated about a meter from the console, a yellow ball of light small enough to fit in her palm. A few centimeters away, a smaller orange star labeled PDN160B floated south of PDN160A. "Ni'apinu has two suns?"

"The companion sun is distant enough to just be the brightest star in Ni'apinu's sky when it's overhead. Look out there."

Bev raised her eyes and looked where Arlud pointed. The brilliant white radiance of Alpha Cephei, labeled PDN203, floated across the chamber about six meters from the console, and just a little more than a meter from the blazing orange orb of Eta Cephei, labeled PDN198. "They look so close together. I never knew Al-phaq was that close to the mine."

"The scale can be deceiving," Arlud said, "but it is close in terms of stellar distance, just one point sixteen parsecs. Look at this." He flicked another switch and the area between the console and Alpha Cephei was dotted with seven green spheres. "These are the places where the Shoku appeared. Note that Alpha Cephei has a sphere next to it. That's the mine. And the two spheres near Eta Cephei are where the Cormeds were attacked."

"What are the others?"

"Where other ships were attacked."

"That many?"

"Yes," Arlud said. "The last known appearance is there." He pointed to the green sphere at his lower left that floated about a meter from a double yellow star labeled PDN150. "I believe what you saw was there. A Dejoria cargo ship disappeared from that location four days ago."

"They seem random. There's no logic to the sequence."

"You're right. There isn't. That's why I brought you here."

With those words from Arlud, Bev understood his motive. "I can't do this."

"Please try."

"It doesn't work that way."

"You told me you saw the Shoku attack a cargo ship, and there it is."

"I did," Bev admitted, "but I can't tell you where they were, only what they saw." She gestured to the green sphere that marked the last known location of the Dejoria cargo ship. "That could be the one I saw, or it could be something else."

"You said the Rhysu can't find the Shoku because our universe limits their ability to track them, so they need us to find them."

"Yeah, I did, but I don't know how to do it."

Arlud heard the sadness behind Bev's confusion. By the way she lowered her head and diverted her eyes, he could tell she was torn up inside about not knowing what to do. He reached out and pulled her into a tender hug. "I'm sorry. I thought this would help."

Bev wrapped her arms around Arlud's back and held him tight. She pressed her cheek against his chest and could hear his heartbeat. His presence was a comfort in more ways than she could put into words. "Don't be sorry," she said. "I just wish I knew what to do."

"Have you tried asking the Rhysu?"

"Yeah, but that hasn't helped."

Arlud raised his head and looked into the star field. He knew there had to be a way to find the Shoku. All the changes to Bev had to be part of the answer. The Shoku were popping up at random locations in deep space. To capture them, they needed to be near or on a planet because a large gravity well was necessary to transfer to and from their universe. "Once in space, the Rhysu can't track the Shoku."

"Yeah," Bev said. She leaned away from Arlud's chest and looked up into his face. "That's why they need us."

"No. That's why they need you."

"Me?"

"The Rhysu need you to lead the Shoku to them. That has to be the answer."

Bev stepped back from Arlud's embrace. "How do you figure?"

"You can see the Shoku now, and that's the difference."

"What difference?"

"The Rhysu connected with you through dreams. They connected with survivors of the Cormed frigates. Not everyone. Just a few. They connected with people who had the right physical and mental make-up to make a connection possible, but that wasn't enough. They needed someone who could be altered to connect with the Shoku, who the Shoku could also see from any distance, and from any location. They made you a lure."

"A what?"

"A lure—a device that's used to attract something so it can be caught. You're a lure to attract the Shoku."

"You're saying I'm bait? They made me bait. Bait gets eaten!"

"I don't think the Shoku will eat you."

"What then?"

"I think they will see you and connect with you like the Rhysu did. Remember, they're in a strange universe, lost in space. No matter how much of a rush they get from being here, I bet about now they're having second thoughts. Finding someone from this universe to connect to will be like a swimmer finding a lifeline."

"A swimmer?"

"Have you ever been in a pool?"

"No, I don't swim."

"Oh. In pools, which are usually a few meters in size, a swimmer can float on the water and relax — it can be a very meditative experience, bobbing gently up and down with the movement of the water. But put that same swimmer in a deep ocean, out of sight from any land, and floating becomes a way to survive — a very different mindset from the swimmer relaxing in a pool."

"Huh?"

"The Shoku are lost at sea," Arlud said. "They need to find land. You are the lifeline that can lead them there."

"Lead them to be captured."

"Not captured. Rescued."

"Does that mean we need to go back to the mine, or to Arrilen Po?"

"That's a good question. I hadn't thought of that."

"I'm not going back to that mine."

"Don't worry about that," Arlud said. He smiled to ease Bev's apprehension. "That won't happen."

"Then back to Arrilen Po?"

"Maybe not."

Arlud was groping for answers and that fed Bev's frustration. She asked, "Why don't they just connect with the people on those ships that are missing? Didn't they already do that with the Cormed survivors?"

"No. Based on what happened, I think that was the Rhysu, not the Shoku."

"What? You're not making sense."

"The Shoku erupted from the mine and headed for deep space. The Rhysu pursued them. The Cormed ships were at the edge of the Eta Cephei system when they were attacked. Einar Duballik began having dreams after the attack, after the Shoku had moved on. I think the Rhysu stopped their pursuit out of fear of being lost in space themselves and turned their attention to the survivors on the *Iron Spear*. That's like what happened to you after the Shoku left the mine. That cloud you saw was the Rhysu, not the Shoku."

Bev pondered what Arlud said. His explanation seemed to make sense, but there was one thing he did not consider. "If the Shoku were fleeing the Rhysu, why did they stop to attack the Cormeds?"

"Based on your own assessment, they're so different from us they probably didn't recognize the ships as ships."

Bev recalled discussing that with Arlud while in high orbit of Arrilen Po. "Then why did they do it?"

"Energy."

Bev turned and looked at the tiny suns floating in the chamber. The space between the stars was dark, a sea of near-vacuum emptiness that meant eventual death for anyone stranded. The Shoku were not of this universe, but they still must need energy to survive. Arlud's reasoning made sense, but there was no way to know for sure if he was correct. She hugged herself. "If you're right, then my being here places you and everyone else in danger."

"No," Arlud said. "Your being here makes us stronger."

Bev embraced Arlud with a tight hug. "Don't let them eat me."

Arlud chuckled. "Don't worry about that." He rubbed Bev's back with one hand while caressing her head with the other. "No one will eat you."

"Once everyone is in position," Arlud said, "we'll send Bev out in a shuttle and lead the Shoku to Simbic Ur."

Jegen-Major Lon Pavan leaned back in his chair. He had been in his ready room with Arlud for an hour discussing the coming mission, and this was the first issue he found to be disconcerting. "Resolving the alien issue will rest upon the actions of a sapi with no formal military training. You're comfortable with that scenario?"

"Yes."

"You're sure she'll hold up under the pressure?"

"Yes."

Arlud's nonchalant response frustrated Pavan. "She agreed to this plan?"

"Not yet."

Pavan sat up. "Not yet?"

"Once she understands what's expected, she'll agree."

"Based on your own reports, that's problematic."

"She's opened up to her role in all this. I expect no protests."

"That's good, but I'm worried about our ability to contain the situation if she fails."

"Bev won't fail because she won't be alone. The Rhysu are with her constantly. She's the bait to lure the Shoku. Once that has been accomplished the Rhysu will intervene, and her mission will be over."

Pavan ignited a small holoscreen on his desk and brought up a schematic of the PDN185 system. Wan'tei was the second planet, the only class one holding in the system. Simbic Ur was the third planet, and the location of a small ice mining operation conducted by autonomous probes. The small rocky world was far enough from Wan'tei to be out of the battle area, but close enough for Polinda's forces to notice the alien presence.

"Simbic Ur is a class four world," Pavan said. "It has a thin exosphere, with a surface of ice mixed with silicates and simple organic compounds, and no subsurface ocean."

Arlud leaned forward, rested his right arm on Pavan's desk and poked the holo-image of Simbic Ur, which made the entire map rotate. "The ice mines are clustered in the south polar region," he said, "which means over ninety percent of the surface is open range."

Pavan kept his eyes on Arlud as the holomap continued to rotate. "And why would the aliens follow the girl to that place?"

"You've read the reports. They need a large gravity well to move between our universe and theirs. Simbic Ur is a few hundred kilometers smaller than Alpha Cephei Four, but with a mass three percent larger, so the size should be acceptable."

"Could this retrieval endanger our fleet?"

"Only if we get too close."

"How will the girl escape?"

"Timing will be crucial, but I'm not concerned about that. The Rhysu will protect her."

Arlud's conviction intrigued Pavan. "What would you say the odds are that the Rhysu will succeed and retrieve the Shoku?"

"Like most things during a battle, the odds are fluid until the end. It all depends on how things fall into place. I'm more concerned about Polinda."

He hopes, Pavan thought. *He doesn't know*. And that reality pushed his thoughts back to the siege. He punched in new instructions and the small holoscreen floating above his desk displayed the area around Wan'tei occupied by Polinda's forces. "My tactics instructor at the Academy called this deployment, "Inverse Porcupine." Each ship is like the tip of a quill, all pointing inward, and a source of pain for those who dare move against them. It's like a spherical cage with movable spears that can adjust quickly to push back attempts to break through the bars."

"Their reaction time is too slow to cover the entire area. Not enough ships for that."

"True," Pavan said. "But look here." He rotated the view so Arlud could see the underlying structure of the deployment. "See this area, these small reflections?"

Arlud nodded.

"Mines," Pavan said. "They've expanded their force-coverage with mines. They don't have to move far to confront multiple attacks. They can focus their forward deployments on the major trade routes and let their rear-guard mop-up the few who break through the mined areas."

"Inverse Porcupine," Arlud said. "That's the weakness. If we can attack their backs while those inside the siege boundary attack from the other direction, they'll be trapped between us, and their own mines will limit their routes of escape."

"Exactly," Pavan said. "We've identified who to contact on Wan'tei to plan a simultaneous surge."

"How much did Clan Dejoria lose to allow Polinda to create his cage?"

"Unknown. That depends on how fast Polinda setup the blockade. If they battled long, then both sides may have lost critical numbers, but if the deployment was rapid, there may not have been much of a battle at all. The data you see here is old, and we'll have a clearer picture once we get closer, but with the addition of Clan Sorrell and Clan Rastee, and whatever Dejoria sends from U'galem, the odds for us are high."

"Very good," Arlud said. "I'm encouraged by this, Jegen-Major. My father would be impressed with the way you've handled this situation."

"I trust the High Regent would have the Guild as allies. That's made the transition easier."

Arlud caught the implication in Pavan's admission. *If he did not believe my father would approve, Pavan would have balked at an alliance with the Guild.* And that told Arlud where Pavan's loyalties started and ended. *He honors my father, but not me. To him I'm just like any other Colony Regent, a diplomat loyal to the clan, bound to the laws of the clan, and obligated to obey the High Regent's commands.*

"You'll discover," Arlud said, "loyalty among guildmen is like the loyalty among our clanmen. We all support each other for the good of the clan.

Wolfram Sy personifies what makes a true clanmen. Duty, honor, sacrifice. These things will always lead to victory, and the most difficult victory to be had isn't against brigands like Polinda, it's the victory over our own hearts, over our own weaknesses. Those who lose that battle end up like Polinda, constantly striving for what they think will sustain them, but are never able to attain it. The victory over our internal contradictions is the only triumph that has lasting value. It's that victory that impels us onward, that keeps our clan together, that will unite us with the Guild, and will fortify us for the victory at the battle for Wan'tei."

Pavan was impressed by Arlud's enthusiasm, and agreed with his discourse about victory, but he wondered if the young regent had failed to see the flaw in his plan for Bev Colli because of inexperience, or if he had intentionally ignored the obvious potential for disaster. "Victory over Polinda is in sight," he said, "but we've as much control over the aliens as an ant controls the motion of stars through space. You'll be putting that girl in jeopardy."

"I know it may appear that way, but you haven't experienced what Bev has been through. She'll be fine."

"For her sake, I hope you're right."

BEV COLLI: LURE

Bev lay under the blanket on her bunk, illuminated by the small holoscreen floating above her chest. She had been reviewing the locations of Wan'tei, Arrilen Po, and Alpha Cephei Four, along with their relative distances from each other, for over an hour. Her goal was to embed each location so deep in her memory that the Rhysu would understand where she was going, and in knowing, help her fulfill her purpose.

She yawned and glanced over at the chronometer on the bulkhead. The Erstallius armada was due to arrive at PDN185 in six hours. She shut off the holoscreen, and the cabin went dark.

Time to sleep, she thought, and she wondered if her effort to educate the Rhysu was successful. She turned on her side and pulled the covers over her shoulders.

Glaring blue light burst into Bev's mind and pushed the drowsiness out of her. She sat up on her bunk and hugged her knees beneath the covers.

The Shoku are back.

She closed her eyes as the light enveloped her consciousness and blocked out all other sensory input except rhythmic waves of heat that blasted her body.

She screamed: "Stop it!"

The pounding heat continued.

She refused to give in to the mind rape and focused on what appeared to be the center of the brilliant light and screamed again: "Stop it!"

The pounding waves pulled back, the glaring light faded, and she was surrounded by swirling gusts of cyan plasma that still radiated enough heat to prickle her skin.

They heard me, she thought. *Finally!*

She opened her eyes and through the mind haze that obscured her vision she could make out the rumpled covers on her bunk, but the walls of her cabin were barely visible, a ghostly representation of the steel-gray bulkhead.

"Can you see me?"

The swirling plasma gave no response.

"I can see you."

Still no response.

They don't understand me.

Bev closed her eyes and focused her mind on the swirling plasma.

You're getting closer.

Their presence was more defined, less like a dream, but even so the sense of closeness was more a feeling than an absolute knowledge.

"Are you getting closer?"

The heat dissipated and the whirling blue clouds faded away.

Bev slumped under her covers in the dark. She did not understand how this would work. She couldn't communicate with the Shoku, and they never responded to her. *I'm the one lost at sea*, she thought. "Why can't someone throw me a lifeline?"

The door buzzer shattered the silence inside the cabin.

Bev reached over and flicked the intercom switch on the bulkhead next to her bunk. "Who is it?"

"Crewman Nolan," a deep male voice said. "Heard a scream. Are you OK?"

"Bad dream," Bev said. "Thanks for asking." She flicked off the intercom.

Although the blinding light was gone from her consciousness, the slight pressure against her shoulders was always there, the constant touch of the Rhysu that told her she was never alone. Their presence was subtle, not as intrusive as the Shoku, and she wondered if that was because the gossip was true—she was a puppet and the Rhysu her masters.

She thought about the Guild engineer she had flung across the mess hall.

Did you make me do that?

The shuttle bay was bustling with activity as crewmen prepared a row of ten black assault vehicles for deployment.

Arlud led Bev into the bay and stopped a few paces beyond the hatchway.

Bev asked, "Who's Nolan?"

"Who?"

"Crewman Nolan. He buzzed my cabin last night. He heard me scream at the Shoku."

"Oh, he must have been on watch."

"On watch?"

Arlud had wanted to avoid this conversation, but that was impossible now. "Pavan ordered you placed under guard while in your cabin."

"He doesn't trust me either?"

"It's not a matter of trust."

"Then what?"

"Safety precaution."

"Safety for who?"

"You."

"Me?"

Arlud turned toward Bev and held her shoulders with a gentle touch that conveyed his concern. "You know we're in unfamiliar territory with the Shoku."

Bev nodded.

"You've still got that remote stuck to your back so the doctors can monitor you?"

"Yeah."

"The crewman was there in case you needed immediate help. If you didn't respond, he would have entered your cabin and called for help."

"Oh." Bev frowned and turned away from Arlud's grasp. *Nolan was my lifeline*, she thought. She looked up at the row of black assault vehicles. "Which one of those will I be in?"

"None of those. Those are for combat."

Bev noticed each vehicle had nose guns and clusters of cylinders attached to short, horizontal wings. "What are those things on the wings?"

"Phase Induction Torpedoes."

"What do they do?"

"They kill the enemy."

Bev had known since before leaving Ni'apinu this day of battle would arrive, but seeing the weapons up close brought that reality to the forefront of her thoughts for the first time. "Will I be in danger?"

"No," Arlud said. "We talked about that, remember? You'll be in the shuttle far from the battle."

"Regent," Jens Orr said. He stood at attention a few paces from Arlud.

Arlud turned to face the young clanman. "Good to see you again, Mister Orr. Bev, this is Jens Orr, he'll be your pilot."

Bev nodded to Orr. She asked Arlud, "What will we do once we get there?"

"Your mission is to lead the Shoku to Simbic Ur. Once that's done, you'll get out of there as fast as you can."

"What if we can't?"

"Don't worry about that," Orr said. "I'll get us back safe."

Bev looked over at the brash young pilot. He was confident, but unrealistic. "Do you know what you're flying into?"

"The exosphere of Simbic Ur."

Bev flicked a disdainful glance at Arlud. "You told him, right?"

"He knows what's expected."

Bev faced the pilot. "Do you?"

Orr nodded. "I know the Shoku attacked two Cormed frigates and left them for dead. I know what happened on Arrilen Po and what you've been through. My briefing was very thorough."

"And you still volunteered?"

"I am honored to be your pilot."

Orr's conviction impressed Bev, but deep inside she still questioned if this plan would work. She looked up at Arlud. "You're sure about this?"

"It must be done."

"What if we fail?"

"Whatever happens," Arlud said, "you'll get back safe. I'm sure of that. The Rhysu won't let anything happen to you."

"How do you know that?"

"Because you survived Arrilen Po."

"And yet you put a guard outside my door?"

"That wasn't because of the Rhysu, it was because of the Shoku."

"So I am in danger!"

"There are risks," Arlud admitted, "but I have to believe your safety is secure because the Rhysu contacted you for this mission by intruding into your dreams. You're here because of them."

"They'll protect me from the Shoku?"

"Yes."

Bev lowered her head and considered the possibilities. No one could predict what the Shoku would do, and that meant the odds for success were beyond knowing. "I know you depend on this mission to succeed. What will we do if it fails?"

"The best we can."

Orr led Arlud and Bev to the cargo shuttle scheduled for the mission to Simbic Ur. The small black vessel was parked in the prep area of the launch corridor that had a large number one painted on the closed exit. The transport was a hybrid model of the standard class three cargo shuttle that had a detachable hold. The black hull plating had been added for this mission.

"Once we're in orbit," Orr said, "we'll jettison the cargo hold and head to the rally point."

Bev examined the aft section of the fuselage—it was three times as long as the forward section and a few meters wider. "Why detach it?"

"It contains the generator."

"Huh?"

Arlud put an arm around Bev's shoulders. "It's the lure that will lead the Shoku to the surface."

"I thought I was the lure."

"You're the first one they'll follow, but we don't want them to catch you. The generator will mimic the energy signature of a larger vessel, like the Cormed frigates. Once they detect it, the hope is they will follow it instead of you."

"What if they don't?"

Orr stepped closer and spoke to Bev: "Based on all the reports, they will. They have an attraction for energy signatures like the one this will produce."

Bev leaned into Arlud's hug. "That lure will lead them to the surface and the Rhysu will capture them."

"Right," Orr said.

Arlud looked down at Bev. "If our assessment is correct, once they near the planet they'll rush toward it. Remember, they're lost in space right now. Simbic Ur will become their rescue point. The generator is just an added incentive for them to planet-fall."

Arlud's explanation made sense, but Bev still had nagging doubts.

"We're about an hour away from launch time," Orr said. "We need to get suited up."

Arlud gave Bev a farewell hug that ended sooner than he wanted. He watched her follow Orr through a nearby hatch that led to the dressing room, then he turned and headed for the C.I.C.

Once secure in their environment suits Bev followed Orr back to the cargo shuttle. The bay had been purged of atmosphere and their launch corridor was open to space. Their suits carried enough air for three hours, so crossing the deck to the shuttle was easy enough, but Bev thought it odd the bay was already vented. Then she noticed five assault ships were gone. "Why are they launching so far from Wan'tei?"

Orr glanced over at the remaining assault vehicles. "Stealth sometimes requires an early start," he said. He entered the shuttle and veered toward the cargo hold.

Bev climbed aboard and turned the lever to seal the hatch. The utility cabin behind the cockpit was a narrow space that housed the port and starboard entry hatches and would be the only area large enough to stretch out in after they jettisoned the hold. Once the hatch closed and the green safety light came on, she settled into the copilot seat. "Will we have gravity after we separate?"

Orr slid into the pilot seat. "Won't have gravity at all after we launch." He gestured to the small umbilical hose next to the right side of Bev's seat. "Pull that hose out and plug it into the blue connector under your right arm. That'll switch your air supply and you'll save the air in your suit tanks."

Bev looked down, pulled out the hose and connected it to her suit. "Why can't we pressurize the cabin?"

"We will, once we separate."

"Why wait?"

"If I need to go back into the cargo hold, I don't want to fill up that area and waste the air."

"Oh. Why no gravity?"

"Uses too much energy. Remember, we want to hide from the Shoku after we separate."

"They'll still see me."

Orr nodded. "But by then you won't be the biggest attraction."

Bev leaned back in her seat. The cockpit controls looked simple enough. They reminded her of the controls in the drill except for the avionics section and the TAC panel. "Is this easy to pilot?"

"Once the course is programmed, it flies autonomously. I'm here to navigate the unexpected."

"Oh, and the course is all set?"

"All set."

Bev considered her options. The one possibility for success was to do nothing, the other option was crazy, and might jeopardize everything. Arlud would be furious, and that realization pushed her thoughts back to the more reasonable path.

Then Orr grabbed the safety bar above his head and pulled himself out of his seat. "I left something in the cargo hold. I'll be right back." He paused and leaned back toward Bev. "See, this is why cabin pressure can wait."

Bev watched Orr retreat into the utility cabin and once he was out of sight she reconsidered her choice. She unhooked her air supply hose, grabbed her safety bar, and pulled herself up.

Orr stepped through the access hatch from the cargo compartment on his way back to the cockpit and noticed the port side hatch was open. He wondered if Bev had left and moved to peer out the opening. "Miss Colli?"

Although her environment suit limited her movement, Bev struck with a rapidity that caught Orr off guard and flung him out the hatchway. He tumbled to the deck and looked up to see Bev standing in the hatchway as it closed and sealed him outside.

Once in the pilot seat Bev released the moorings and powered up the engines.

Orr's voice bellowed in her helmet: "Miss Colli, open the hatch!"

"Sorry, Mister Orr. I can't allow you to endanger yourself."

"What? You can't go by yourself. You aren't trained—"

"Don't you know," Bev said, "I'm a mad japer. I can handle anything."

"What?"

Bev turned the lever that opened the safety panels covering the engines and pushed the thrust throttle forward. Orr backed away from the shuttle as it lifted off the deck and moved toward the exit. He tapped the comm switch beneath his helmet. "Control, Bev Colli has commandeered shuttle 873 and is heading for the launch corridor. There is no pilot on board."

Red emergency lights flashed on either side of the launch corridor and the leaves of the exit door began to close.

Bev saw her escape path shrinking, so she pointed the nose of the shuttle toward the center of the exit hole and pushed the throttle to full thrust.

The cargo transport sped through the launch corridor toward the shrinking exit.

Bev fingered the reaction stabilizer controls to keep the cargo transport centered in the corridor, but the TAC antennas scraped the doors and were bent backward from the impact as the transport emerged from the flagship.

She pulled back the throttle to one-quarter thrust, glanced at a red warning light on the comm panel, then focused on the course tracking monitor and turned eighteen degrees to her starboard side and pitched downward seventeen degrees to match the programmed trajectory. Once aligned with the plotted course, she switched the controls to auto and pushed the button below the warning light to shut it off.

⟡ ⟡ ⟡

Arlud shoved his compad into his rear pant pocket as he entered the flagship's C.I.C. and headed for the chart pedestal. Eahuda had called and told him what Bev had done. "Where is she?"

Jegen-Major Lon Pavan turned toward his advancing Regent and gestured to the holomaps floating above the pedestal. "On course."

One map tracked the cargo transport heading toward Simbic Ur. The other map displayed the warships advancing toward Wan'tei. The Simbic Ur holomap displayed the transport's position with a red pyramid icon. The planned course was a blue line that led from the launch point to the future position of Simbic Ur.

"The pilot entered the course prior to launch," Eahuda said. He moved next to Arlud and gripped the hand railing with both hands. "She'll be fine if there are no disruptions."

"Where's Orr?"

"On his way here."

Arlud examined the holomaps. The attack force made up of Guild, Erstallius, Sorrell, and Rastee warships was moving into position to attack the siege deployment around Wan'tei. The cargo shuttle was only a few minutes behind schedule, but within acceptable limits. "Will the generator jettison when planned?"

"That was pre-programmed, like the course," Eahuda said.

Jens Orr entered the C.I.C. still wearing his environment suit, with his helmet tucked under his left arm. He stood at attention a few paces from Pavan. "Jens Orr, reporting as ordered, sir."

Arlud faced the young pilot. "What happened?"

Orr spoke with a matter-of-fact tone: "I went to the rear to retrieve the remote for the generator. On my way back to the cockpit I noticed the port hatch was open. Thinking Miss Colli had left, I moved to the hatch. She assaulted me and I found myself on the deck outside the shuttle. She sealed the hatch and launched."

"Can she make it back on her own?"

Orr nodded. "If there are no complications, her course should take her to the rally point as planned. I'm more worried about this." He raised his right hand and displayed the remote control he had retrieved from the cargo hold. "Without this, she won't be able to engage the generator."

"Can't she start it manually?"

"If she does that, she'll die."

"What?"

"We set the generator to emit an unshielded energy signature to ensure it attracts the aliens. It'll burn itself out within thirty minutes, but Bev's suit won't protect her from the radiation output. If she starts it, she'll burn before she releases the lever. Within an hour she'll be dead."

Arlud gripped the hand railing and lowered his head. If Bev died, he would never forgive himself.

"The plan was to activate it after separation," Orr explained. "I was to handle that, so I never explained the procedure to her."

"Then we need to contact her," Arlud said. He regained his composure and stood up straight. "We need to contact her right now."

Orr faced Pavan. "Give me a ship, sir, and I'll go get her."

Pavan turned toward his comm officer. "Prepare a direct-link TAC, Mister Ginis."

"Yes, sir," the comm officer replied.

Pavan returned his attention to Arlud and Orr. "The fleet is in stealth mode, running silent to prevent detection as long as possible. A retrieval mission could jeopardize our secrecy, but we can try a TAC link. If she recognizes the indicator light and activates her TAC, we'll get through to her." He stepped toward Orr. "I need you to stay in the C.I.C., Mister Orr. You're now our dedicated comm officer for the shuttle."

"Yes, sir."

Bev reviewed the system status monitor. She was on course and within the scheduled timeline. The long blast from the main engines to get the transport up to the nominal velocity occurred when the angle of the transport blocked the view of the thrusters from Wan'tei and the surrounding siege ships. From their perspective, the vessel would appear to be a small, dark rock rushing in from the outer reaches of the system that would skim past Simbic Ur in five hours. Jens Orr had programmed the perfect course.

Thank you, Mister Orr.

Once the main engines shut off and the acceleration force that had pressed her into her seat faded, Bev closed her eyes and floated under the restraint of her seat harness. She didn't know if the Shoku would appear but was determined to make that happen. She focused on her breathing to help rid her mind of all other distractions. When relaxed, she brought up in her mind the image of the cyan plasma that had surrounded her aboard the flagship.

Can you see me?

Her ever-present connection with the Rhysu pushed her awareness into a white wall of light that ripped the image of the cyan plasma out of her mind's vision.

They're blocking me.

That had never happened. The Rhysu intruded, but never blocked. And then Bev realized they were not blocking her; they were blocking the Shoku.

They see me, they see you. Is that it?

Bev opened her eyes to see a white haze obscure her view of the cockpit. She blinked a few times, thinking the haze would go away, but it remained.

Is that you?

The white haze vanished, and the weight against her shoulders lifted. Her mind raced with the realization the Rhysu were gone.

"You're just going to leave me here?"

Through the cockpit windows she saw a thin, tan crescent rise into view amid the background stars.

Simbic Ur.

The planet was an hour away, but she could see the mottled, crater-scarred surface along the lighted limb. She checked her course. *Perfect.* She scanned the control panel for generator controls and saw nothing that looked dedicated to that cargo. The timer above the mission sequence list on the mission status monitor was five minutes away from cargo separation.

Guess I need to go back there and fire it up myself, she thought. She unhooked her air hose and unbuckled her safety harness. Unconstrained because of the lack of gravity, she twisted out of her seat and pushed against the safety bar to propel herself out of the cockpit.

The transport pitched downward, and Bev slammed against the ceiling of the utility cabin.

She grabbed hold of a power conduit and twisted to look into the cockpit. The control panel had red lights flashing on the NAV panel, and Simbic Ur rushed upward and out of her field of view.

The transport's tumbling.

Bev used the power conduit to pull herself toward the cockpit, but before she reached the entry, the transport shuddered, and brilliant white light burst through the windows.

Bev recoiled from the sudden flare and turned her face away from the light as her helmet visor darkened to protect her vision.

The transport jerked upward, and Bev's legs were flung toward the deck. She released her grip on the ceiling conduit and pushed off the deck with her feet to send herself toward the cargo hatch. She grabbed the handle on the hatch, glanced back, and saw cyan streams of plasma fill the cockpit windows.

And she knew she could not lead the Shoku to Simbic Ur.

They've come for me.

The transport shuddered and began to break apart.

PDN185: BATTLE

Bev curled up into a fetal position while she watched the transport's bulkhead disintegrate around her.

Filaments of cyan plasma burst through the collapsing framework and pressed inward, forming an encasing sphere.

Pressure against her body held Bev still amid the whirling cyan energy, and she could see glimpses of Simbic Ur through the transparent filaments that twisted in their rotation around her. Her inner vision erupted with an image of a dark void filled with brilliant flashes of light. She closed her eyes to focus and deep within the darkness she could feel anger, disgust, and fear.

Vertigo hit her hard and her mind tumbled backward as filaments of the cyan energy encasing her wrapped around her environment suit.

There were no voices, only the visions and the surge of emotion, and her mind whirled with confirmation.

Arlud was wrong.

Bev opened her eyes and through the haze of her inner vision she saw Simbic Ur rush toward her as she tumbled in the grip of the Shoku along the course set by Jens Orr.

Farquar Polinda relaxed in his ready room chair on board the dreadnought, *Venka Kinall*, and reviewed the siege deployments around Wan'tei.

The holomap floating before him displayed the combined forces of Clan Polinda, Clan Vestlok and Clan Sabballi as small green icons in a grid pattern five-hundred thousand kilometers from the surface. The ships formed a sphere with the largest concentration of warships along the four main trade routes, with two dreadnought-led strike groups around each of the two moons. The mined areas were identified by yellow hash marks and encompassed the largest sections of the siege deployment. The *Venka Kinall* held a position along the south-eastern trade route with five frigates and two destroyers. Farquar had insisted that his dreadnought be placed in a forward position.

"We've been here for two weeks," Farquar said. He turned to face the holoscreen to his right that displayed the calm face of Jegen Marlow. "The envoys have debated long enough. How much longer do we need to wait before pressing forward? Dejoria will never surrender."

Jegen Marlow nodded. "A successful siege is time dependent. I would expect submission to take at least four weeks. Dejoria is stubborn."

Farquar understood the advantages of a successful siege. *Doubt will play as much of a role as physical combat in securing the victory,* he thought. *Doubt will creep into the Dejoria mindset the longer they are caged and push the hierarchy to submit.* That would lead to fewer Polinda losses and ensure the holding remained in a productive state, but he had no worries about losing ships or damaging the planet's resources, because the longer the siege, the higher the risk Clan Dejoria would receive assistance from other clans. "I understand the strategy, Mister Marlow. My patience won't endure that long."

"Well," Marlow said, "to test their response, we can send a small—"

Marlow turned his head to focus on something in the command center and moved out of range of the holoscreen.

The *Venka Kinall* shuddered.

Farquar shifted his attention to the holomap. At six areas around the siege grid, his ships were now red.

They're attacking.

Farquar's siege group and two others near Wan'tei's south-eastern trade route were being bombarded from the rear. Three other siege groups around the northwestern trade route were being hit by focused planetary defenses. That strategy was meant to split his forces and weaken the siege grid.

The *Venka Kinall* pitched and rolled against the bombardment, and Farquar could hear the impacts as they came more frequent and their concussions more powerful.

"Status," Farquar demanded.

Jegen Marlow reappeared in the holoscreen. He glanced to his left. "It's the Erstallius with Clan Rastee. We've lost two frigates, and their attack is growing with the arrival of more ships. We can't stay here and survive this."

Farquar reviewed the holomap. "Can we lower our orbit and form a defensive line with—"

The *Venka Kinall* rolled to her port side and shuddered after a heavy bombardment.

"We need to collapse the siege grid," Marlow said, "and regroup near the second moon. Dejoria is attacking with more ships from low orbit. We'll be surrounded in minutes."

Farquar analyzed his armada's position in the holomap. "Send word, all ships break grid and form up at second moon." He looked over at Marlow. "If we run through the edge of the minefield to our starboard, we'll break through their lines."

Marlow saw that route was closing fast and was their only hope to break free. "Engaging now."

Farquar braced himself against increased bombardment and watched the icons for his group in the holomap shift position and head closer to the minefield. He was certain they would escape through the mines, and once his forces regrouped around the second moon, they could turn back this assault. He brought up another holoscreen to analyze the attack against his siege group. Nine blue icons populated the display and were identified as Erstallius and Rastee. Fifty-two other vessels were identified as either Sorrell, Rastee, or Erstallius at the other attack points, along with ten Guild ships.

The Guild!

Farquar had not considered a Guild alliance with the Erstallius, but the reality of it made sense, and he laughed as the Guild ship identities populated the list. The bombardment eased up, and he looked over at the holomap. The pursuing ships had pulled back to avoid the mines.

"We'll be through the mines in five minutes," Marlow said.

Farquar glanced over at Marlow's fatigued face. "Good work, Mister Marlow."

"Our forces are fending off attacks and regroup—"

A new report distracted Marlow, and Farquar turned his attention back to the holomap.

Eighteen Dejoria cruisers appeared outside the minefield and blocked the remaining ships in Farquar's attack group from continuing toward the second moon.

"Where did they come from?"

Marlow ignored Farquar's question and focused instead on the terrible realization that their course through the minefield had them trapped.

Farquar leaned back in his couch and analyzed the holomap. The siege grid had collapsed. His fleet was in disarray and clustered into six separate groups. His dreadnought-led strike groups were boxed in around the two moons. The surviving ships in the other four siege groups were outgunned and trapped with no open route of escape. He witnessed the vanishing of three green icons representing Clan Sabballi ships orbiting the first moon. He faced the holoscreen that displayed Marlow's face. "Attack with everything! All ships weapons free!"

Marlow nodded.

The space surrounding the *Venka Kinall* became crowded with the launch of all her assault fighters. The two-hundred small, black vehicles sped ahead of the dreadnought, merged into formation with assault vehicles from the other ships in the group, and rushed toward the waiting Dejoria cruisers.

Bev hurled toward Simbic Ur wrapped in the energy filaments produced by the Shoku. Their intrusion into her mind was a revolving flood of images she could not understand. The abstract views of their other-dimensional existence blocked the vision of her own reality.

She tried to focus on her own thoughts, but the Shoku held her mind in their grip and wouldn't let go, filling her with their desperation and the stifling impact of acute sadness. Tears flowed from her and floated around her head inside her helmet.

Beneath the emotional turmoil implanted inside of her from the Shoku, a spark of realization burst to the surface of her consciousness, and she knew the Rhysu were the enemy.

The cyan energy bubble slammed into a white wall of light.

Bev jerked from the impact and the grip of the Shoku was gone. She opened her eyes to see the energy filaments around her collapse.

Arlud held onto the hand railing around the chart pedestal in his flagship's C.I.C. and watched the battle maneuvers as they populated the main holomap. The forward assault groups had surprised the Polinda forces and were breaking up the siege grid. Fifteen enemy ships were disabled and Farquar's dreadnought was pinned inside the perimeter of a minefield.

Eahuda walked over from an adjacent sensor station. "The moons are ours, lad. The siege is broken. Polinda is trapped."

"Yeah, but the battle isn't over yet."

Arlud focused on the second holomap. The TAC link had failed to contact Bev, and now the transport's location beacon had disappeared from the map. "Where's Bev?"

Eahuda fingered the pedestal controls and brought up a blank holoscreen. "The drone should be within scanning distance in a few minutes."

Jens Orr stood next to Arlud. "Her course has taken her behind the planet. She should be back in view in about ten minutes."

Arlud checked the pedestal chronometer. The rally point was twenty minutes away. *I never should have asked Bev to go.*

"Look here," Eahuda said.

Simbic Ur appeared on the holoscreen as a small gray half-circle amid a black background.

"Because of the drone's angle of approach," Eahuda said, "she'll see the transport before we do. This is via TAC link, so the delay is only a few seconds."

In the holoscreen, a brilliant ball of white light appeared over the limb of Simbic Ur.

Arlud leaned toward the holoscreen. "What's that?"

Eahuda zoomed in the view. "A ball of plasma. Almost two kilometers in diameter."

"Could the transport be inside of it?"

Eahuda examined the data stream from the probe. "It's descending to the surface. No telemetry from the transport."

Jegen-Major Pavan crowded next to Eahuda to examine the holoscreen. "Looks like the same thing that hit the Cormeds."

"Yes, it does," Eahuda agreed. He faced Arlud. "Not what we expected."

Orr pointed to the holoscreen. "Look!"

The ball of light crossed the planet's terminator and began to shrink.

Eahuda transferred the drone's data to the chart pedestal and replaced the holomap of the transport's course around Simbic Ur with the real-time imagery.

The ball of light winked out on the dark side of the planet.

"Still no sign of the transport," Eahuda said.

Where the ball of light had disappeared, a spot of cyan colored light appeared.

"Getting odd fluctuations in the magnetic field pattern around the planet," Eahuda said.

Cyan filaments of energy grew out of the cyan light, and within a few heartbeats they wrapped the entire planet in undulating energy streams.

"That's new," Pavan said.

"Send this transmission to Wan'tei," Arlud said. "I want everyone to see this."

Eahuda fingered the control panel and broadcast the drone's transmission via TAC. "If they miss this TAC, they'll be able to see it in about fifteen minutes via standard telemetry. Every ship in the battle should detect the event by then."

Arlud nodded. He wasn't sure if Simbic Ur was visible during the night on Wan'tei this time of year, but the warships fighting above her would see the alien light for sure. He had achieved his goal. "Where's Bev?"

Eahuda fingered the control panel and balked once he reviewed the current data feed.

Arlud pressed close. "What?"

"She's gone, lad. Metal debris along the plotted course. Looks like the transport broke apart."

Arlud tightened his grip around the hand railing and closed his eyes as the plasmatic filaments around Simbic Ur increased in brightness and produced a white halo around the planet.

"Wow," Orr said.

Simbic Ur disappeared behind a white ball of light as bright as the sun.

Arlud opened tear-stained eyes to see the light blink out.

Simbic Ur was gone.

CLAN ERSTALLIUS: AFTERMATH

"All hostilities have stopped," Eahuda said.

Arlud stared into the main holomap. He noticed via the data overlay that the disappearance of Simbic Ur produced ripples in the fabric of space-time throughout the PDN185 system. While the full impact of the new orbital dynamics on the planets that remained would take millions of years to resolve, the impact on the feuding clans had been immediate. His hope for a pause in the battle was fulfilled.

Jegen-Major Pavan noticed the outlying Vestlok and Sabballi ships had begun to retreat from the areas of conflict. He shot a quizzical glance at Arlud.

Arlud caught Pavan's silent inquiry and focused on the Polinda ship positions. All commanders had agreed, if Polinda retreated once the aliens appeared, then all hostilities would end. As the holomap updated it was obvious Farquar had no intention of quitting. "At your will, Jegen-Major."

Pavan nodded and turned to his comm officer to relay new orders for the fleet.

Arlud turned toward the smaller holomap that displayed the space where Simbic Ur had been. "Any sign of Bev?"

Eahuda reviewed the incoming data from the drone and shook his head.

"I'll be in my cabin," Arlud said. "Let me know when it's over."

Eahuda nodded and watched Arlud walk out of the command center. He had never seen him so distraught. He took a step to follow him, then thought better of it, and turned back to the holomap.

All around Wan'tei the Erstallius led coalition took advantage of the brief pause in the battle and maneuvered into a better position. They were joined by fifty more Dejoria ships from U'galem and twenty more ships from the Guild. Before Arlud reached his cabin, half of Polinda's ships were spewing atmosphere and dead in space. By the time he stepped through his cabin hatchway, the fleeing Vestlok and Sabballi ships had been contained within the system by the reinforcements from the Guild, who unleashed a fiery death upon them.

Farquar's persistence doomed everyone in his company. *The only way to stop a madman*, Arlud thought, *is to end him, and all his minions with him.*

That was a harsh reality, but one proven throughout history to be the simplest path to freedom. Any other choice would perpetuate the underlying cause for belligerence and would allow the madman to rise again.

Violence always begets more violence, unless there is no one left to fight.

Arlud had expected this outcome for Polinda—the old man's insanity was predictable. He had not expected Bev would be among the dead. *She trusted me*, he thought, *and because of that she died.*

He stood in his bunk alcove, and the terrible understanding that he had caused Bev's death transformed his remorse into a burning anger. He struck out with his fists, and there was no piece of furniture, or object secured to the bulkhead, that survived his blind rage.

Two hours after the disappearance of Simbic Ur, Gustav Eahuda paused outside Arlud's cabin. He knew Arlud would need time alone to mourn Bev, but some things couldn't wait. He reached out and pushed the door buzzer.

There was no response, so he pushed the buzzer again.

Still no response.

Eahuda waited for a long minute, then withdrew his compad. *He'll not ignore this*, he thought. Before he could enter Arlud's call number, the cabin hatch clicked. He pushed the hatch open and entered the cabin. The only light came from a small lamp in the kitchen area pointed toward the floor, and in the dim light he noticed the settee had been tipped over. The bunk alcove was dark, but he spotted Arlud sitting on the deck against the rear bulkhead. He reached over to the wall switch and turned on the overhead light.

The mattress was upturned and angled across the bunk frame. The bedding was heaped in a pile on the floor. The mirror above the wash basin was smeared with blood. Arlud sat next to the bunk frame, head down, with his right arm resting across his raised knee. There was a red stain across his swollen knuckles.

"You should have the physician look at that," Eahuda said. It was obvious Arlud had hit the mirror with his fist. Impacting bone and flesh against the thin duraplex sheet might have been a misguided effort to strike himself, but duraplex never surrendered to such foolish outrage.

"Bev died because of me," Arlud said. "I deserve the pain."

Eahuda grabbed the leg of a tipped-over chair, up righted it, and sat facing Arlud. "That wasn't your fault."

Arlud raised his head. "Don't tell me it wasn't my fault. It was my fault!"

"She understood the dangers."

"She trusted me. How could I have been such a fool?"

Eahuda held his words—now was not the time to debate past decisions.

"Pavan tried to warn me," Arlud said, and he lowered his head. "Even Sy had doubts. I was a fool!"

Eahuda contemplated a variety of sarcastic responses but knew that would only inflame an already bad situation, so he shifted to the matters that had brought him here. "Polinda is done."

Arlud looked up. The old Degen's dry statement pushed his thoughts into a new arena. "Do we have his body?"

"Pavan sent a crew to retrieve it. The *Venka Kinall* suffered heavy damage so he may not be in one piece."

"As long as we have his head."

Alliance protocol demanded that a defeated patriarch be returned to his homeworld for burial. That event would seal Clan Erstallius as the victor and relinquish all Polinda holdings to Erstallius control.

Eahuda scooted to the edge of his chair. "The Dejoria brought news. Your father has led a strike against Pigrell."

"I expected that."

Arlud retreated for a moment into his thoughts. Pigrell was defended well, but he knew his father would have attacked the Polinda homeworld with a massive armada so the odds for success would be high. That his father would even consider such a feat told him the Erstallius fleet was in good shape, and they had support from other clans.

Eahuda said, "Pavan's in council with Rastee and Sorrell to send a task force to Cestratha."

"Good. Cynth deserves our support."

"They'll most likely leave within the hour. Clan Dejoria has things well in-hand here."

"Good."

Eahuda leaned back in his chair. "Pavan sent three science shuttles to gather more info about the disappearance of Simbic Ur. We should know more in a few hours."

"What's the status of the fleet?"

"We lost five frigates and two destroyers. The Guild lost three ships. Rastee and Sorrell both lost five. Dejoria lost ten. Polinda lost everything. Sabballi is limping away with two frigates, and the one remaining Vestlok ship won't make it out of the system."

Arlud lowered his head and his thoughts drifted back to Bev. "I want a memorial built in honor of Bev. She sacrificed herself for us. That needs remembering."

"Right, lad. I'll get Bril on it as soon as we get back."

"I want one on Pigrell—that's her homeworld. I want one on Cestratha—she helped restore Clan Halva's name. I want one on Baleiou—our homeworld needs to know how much she served our clan. And I want one on Ni'apinu so those who serve there know how her sacrifice helped us prove our innocence and defeat Polinda."

Eahuda withdrew his compad from his shirt pocket and entered Arlud's request.

"I want her back, Gus."

Eahuda paused and looked at his young regent. "I know you do, lad." He had seen Arlud grow closer to Bev during the past two months, and he could not recall another woman who had so much impact on him. *Who would have guessed*, he thought, *that a sapi from Pigrell would attract the attention of the heir to Clan Erstallius?* There had been flirty girls and seductive girls who had tried to woo their way into Arlud's heart, but he had seen through their motives and dismissed them all. And Eahuda realized what made Bev so different—her motives toward Arlud were pure, uncluttered with hidden agendas.

"What do you want to do, lad?"

Arlud looked at his old Degen-of-the-Corp with a blank expression. "I can't have what I want. Not anymore."

Eahuda frowned and focused again on his compad.

Arlud leaned his head back against the bulkhead. "Once we have Polinda's body, I want to head back to Ni'apinu. Pavan can continue on to Pigrell without me."

Eahuda stifled the urge to protest—Arlud's depression had confused his thinking. "OK," he said. "Pavan will wonder why. Usually, the victorious regent returns the vanquished to his homeworld."

"Pavan can do it," Arlud said. "The result will be the same."

Not really, Eahuda thought. "In the eyes of those on Pigrell, Pavan would be the conquering hero."

"Let him pound his chest and prance up the Grand Highway with Polinda's head under his arm. He'll meet my father outside the Great Hall, and the spectacle will be over."

"But—"

"It'll be a good test of Pavan's loyalty. He's a good clanman. He won't let a little pomp go to his head."

"As you wish," Eahuda said. He stood and moved to the comm panel on the wall outside the bunk alcove and pushed the button marked with a medical icon.

"Infirmary," a female voice said.

"Send a medic to cabin 308."

"You must come down here. We're in triage mode, waiting for battle casualties."

The medical channel blinked off.

"That's all right," Arlud said. "I can wait."

Eahuda disagreed and pushed the button again.

"Infirmary," the female voice said.

"Send a medic to cabin 308, and I recommend you check the registry before you hang up again."

After a brief pause, the female voice said, "I'll send a medic right away."

"You shouldn't have done that," Arlud said.

"Do you really want the clanmen to see the only injury suffered during the battle by clan hierarchy was self-inflicted?"

Arlud considered the gossip that would ensue after that news spread. "I've been the object of disparaging words before. Nothing new."

"Well," Eahuda said, "I'll not have your reputation smeared because of this." He gestured to the overturned furniture. "You may be entitled to a tantrum, but the clanmen don't need to know about it."

By the time the medic arrived at Arlud's cabin, Eahuda had restored the furniture to the proper placement, and Arlud sat on the settee as the old Degen tucked in the bed covers for a proper appearance.

NI'APINU: CENOTAPH

The cenotaph for Bev was completed two weeks after Arlud returned to Ni'apinu. It was a simple memorial made of polished red granite and was placed next to the existing memorial inside the perimeter fence, along the northern edge of the Erstallius landing field. An etching of Bev's face on the chamfered front surface of the central pillar was a good likeness that Arlud insisted not show her Polinda stain. Around the central pillar the angled top surface of a flattened torus was etched with Englo'ni text that described her brief history, and how she had helped Clan Erstallius find the aliens who destroyed Polinda's mine.

The official dedication ceremony was brief, but long enough for Arlud to explain the cenotaph was established as recognition of Bev's bravery and her faithfulness to the clan. He ordered the holo-recording to be broadcast throughout the inhabited worlds.

Arlud lingered with Salus and Eahuda after the media crew retreated toward the service buildings. They were bundled in their long coats against a cold breeze from the east.

Salus took a step closer to the memorial. "Who did the etching?"

"Yancy Bril," Eahuda said. "He's good with a cutter."

"Yes, he is."

Salus looked at Arlud standing a few paces away. The young Erstallius regent had been lost in thought since the end of the dedication—his downcast eyes were focused on the image of Bev.

Salus walked up to Arlud's side and placed a hand on his shoulder. "You should come with me to Kuliq'Quad this afternoon," he said. "Grénu has planned to reveal the memorial for your clanmen at the Mânu."

Arlud flicked a glance at Salus and nodded, then returned his attention to Bev's cenotaph.

Salus patted Arlud's shoulder and walked away toward the central tower.

Eahuda watched Salus retreat. The Aku partnership with Clan Erstallius was a good one and would raise Arlud's status among the cadre.

The young lad did well, he thought. He sympathized with Arlud's grief—losing Bev stung the heart of everyone who knew her. *Only time will heal that wound.* And he hoped what Arlud had accomplished would one day supplant his anguish and allow him to revel in the victory over Polinda, and a future united with the Aku.

Arlud stepped out of the two-seat ground car onto fresh snow that crunched beneath each step. The first snow of the year covered Kuliq'Quad basin. This trip had been through a chill wind, and a light spattering of snowflakes. He followed Salus up a shallow hill, past the abandoned stone dwellings of the First People, and stopped at the base of snow-covered stone steps that led up to the entrance of Seelay's memorial. A small gray obelisk stood at the apex of the hill, surrounded by a circular colonnade that was capped with a narrow, snow-covered roof.

"In the spring there are flowers around the base," Salus said. "During that time the colonnade is usually filled with visitors."

Salus pulled a cylindrical heat-emitter from his coat and aimed it at the snowy steps. The focused blast of heat melted the ice covering the lower step. Ten minutes later all twenty steps were free of snow, and he stood with Arlud between the columns of the colonnade.

The granite obelisk at the center of the memorial was three-meters high and contained an epitaph written in Akün.

Salus approached the monument. "This was written by Seelay's own hand."

Arlud tromped across the snowy ground to examine the writing. "He's buried beneath this?"

"Yes."

"What does it say?"

Salus translated the words from memory:

> "Freedom is not a gift. It is the right of all people.
> "But the Free must be worthy of their Freedom.
> "Let us be viewed by our actions, by constancy and virtue, by fidelity and confidence.
> "Let all those who would revoke our freedom remember what we sacrificed to attain it, and how our enemies fell before us.

> "Freedom is not a gift. It is the reward that comes when tyranny is defeated.
> "Continue the fight when necessary, pursue peace when possible."

Arlud had expected something more, but the words fit the circumstances that brought the Aku to Ni'apinu. "An epitaph well written."

"It's impossible," Salus said, "to sum up the impact of Seelay's life in a few short sentences, but these words ring true in the heart of every Aku. These words keep him alive in our hearts, just as Bev Colli's cenotaph will keep her alive in yours. She'll never be gone because she's still inside of you."

Arlud nodded. *There's the reason Salus brought me here*, he thought. *He wants to console me.* He appreciated the effort and understood the intent. "I know."

"There's a time to mourn and a time to rejoice," Salus said, "but within each of us some mourning will always be there, no matter how much we rejoice, and that is the real memorial to those we have lost."

Arlud patted Salus' shoulder and turned to retrace his steps through the snow.

A stiff wind hit the colonnade behind Arlud and pushed snow off the encircling roof.

Arlud turned to see the snow fall as hot wind hit his back.

Salus moved to Arlud's side and yelled over a thunderous roar that followed the wind, "Follow me!"

A battle had been won, but the clans were still at war. Arlud rushed after Salus, thinking they were under attack.

They bounded down the dry steps and ran through the snow toward one of the nearby dwellings.

Salus reached the wooden doorway, turned the latch, gave a shove, and the door creaked open.

Arlud entered the dark interior behind Salus as the pressure wave from another deafening roar shook him to his core. He slammed the door shut against the hot wind and threw the bolt to lock it.

A burst of hot cyan light poured through gaps in the door jamb.

Something scraped the roof and a faint hiss traveled around the dwelling.

Water began seeping under the door.

The cyan light faded, and the pounding wind receded.

Arlud listened for the crunch of boots on snow but heard nothing. He inched toward the door and withdrew his magar-pistol from his belt holster.

"Careful," Salus whispered.

Arlud waited, expecting to hear movement outside. "They may have flown beyond us."

"Listen," Salus said. "We should hear cannon fire."

The absence of an Aku response against an intruder into the basin eased Arlud's apprehension.

Salus gestured toward the door.

Arlud pulled back the bolt and flung the door open. A cascade of droplets greeted him, and a swirling mist obscured his view. The immediate press of heat made him flinch. He stepped out into a slush of mud and ice.

A cyan glow lit up the surrounding terrain. All the stone dwellings were dripping from the sudden heat and shrouded by fog.

In the mist above the hill Arlud saw the source of the strange glow—a brilliant spot of cyan light, iridescent, pulsing. He gestured for Salus to join him outside and pointed to the ball of light.

Salus stepped across the slushy ground and stopped next to Arlud. "What's that?"

"The Rhysu, or maybe the Shoku," Arlud said. "Either way, this isn't good." He holstered his pistol and turned toward the ground car. A blast of wind pushed him to the wet ground. Air rushed around him, a hot vortex that rippled his coat. Memories from Arrilen Po revolved in his mind and out of that whirlwind an image of Bev rushed up before him, then faded as the hot wind receded.

Arlud lay in the muddy slush of melting snow as the cyan light dropped out of the sky and floated four meters above him. He squinted from the brilliant glare as wisps of cyan energy extended from the light. The plasmatic tendrils twitched and flicked around him. In his mind he heard Bev call: *Remember me?*

"Bev?"

The filaments of energy leaped upon Arlud and wrapped him in their intense heat. He felt a mild electric twinge as he was lifted off the ground and went limp in the energetic embrace.

I'm here, Bev said.

And Arlud knew Bev had somehow joined with the Rhysu. She was now a creature of another dimension. His mind raced with questions, and the image of Bev standing before him in Jhared's house, defiant, looking up at him with her captivating green eyes, filled his inner vision, and he was mesmerized by her beauty.

His feet touched the ground and the wisps of energy pulled away and coalesced above him. Within the surrounding glare of cyan light, he saw her.

"Bev?"

I'm OK. I'll be fine.

"What happened?"

Don't worry, everything will be OK.

The image of Bev faded and the flaming cyan ball rose into the fog and disappeared.

Cold wind flowed back into the basin and snowflakes began falling again.

Overwhelmed by the encounter, Arlud dropped to his knees. He searched the sky, but Bev was gone.

Salus rushed to Arlud's side. He noticed charred stripes on Arlud's coat where the energy tendrils had gripped him. "You OK?"

Arlud hugged himself and focused on the cold ground. The sight of Bev in the light was a vision he would never forget, and as the wonder of her transformation revolved in his mind, he felt a tear roll down his cheek.

-End-

APPENDIXES

The following information is supplied to enhance the reader's understanding of various terms and phrases contained in the chronicles.

EXCERPTS FROM CATALOG OF HOLDINGS

ALPHA CEPHEI FOUR: Fourth planet of PDN203 (Alpha Cephei). Abundant metals attracted Clan Polinda to this barren world where they established a successful mining operation. A source of pure durillium.

AL-PHAQ: Fifth planet of PDN198 (Eta Cephei). A fortress of the Guild of Free Traders. Colonized by Wolfram Sy in 3502.

ANDERS PRIME: Second planet of PDN220 (Epsilon Eridani). Homeworld of Clan Bree.

ARRILÆN PO: Fourth planet of PDN1527 (Trigelle's Star). An attempt at colonization by Clan Halva failed and the world was abandoned in 3478.

BALEIOU: Fourth planet of PDN306 (Pi-3 Orionis). Adopted homeworld of Clan Erstallius. Old World designation: Pi-3 Alpha.

BODEN: Fourth planet of PDN133 (Eta Cassiopae A). A holding-complete of Clan Sabballi.

CESTRATHA: Third planet of PDN169 (Lambda Serpentis). Homeworld of Clan Halva.

COLLIRI-3: Third Planet of PDN201 (61 Cygni A). A Joint Holding of Clan Tuma and Clan Emlito.

GLASEL-221: Fifth planet of PDN607. A Joint Holding of Clan Tuma and Clan Emlito.

GSW-34: Fourth planet of PDN145 (Tau Ceti). Homeworld of Clan Brandi. Old World designation from Guide to Surveyed Worlds, first edition, published in 3278.

GSW-183: Second planet of PDN160A (26 Draconis A). Independent Holding of the Aku people. Old World designation from Guide to Surveyed Worlds, first edition, published in 3278.

JAI'RAAN: Second moon of Wald-181 (The third planet of PDN150B [Zeta Herculis B]). A holding withdrawn from Clan Halva in 3478. Noted for its exotic mineral deposits and hot springs.

KAINOGAE: Fifth planet of PDN158 (Zeta Tucanae). Adopted homeworld of Clan Tuma. An agricultural holding. The Kainogae School is the major school of agronomy in the Alliance. Where K. H.

Epstein developed his Gamma-2 strain of Pennisetum glaucum (millet). Old World designation: ZT5.

KEAEH: Third planet of PDN136 (Nu-2 Lupi). Adopted homeworld of Clan Cormed.

MAKENZIE: Second planet of PDN209 (Epsilon Indi). A holding-complete of Clan Vestlok. The location of the annual Conference of Great Clans. The original homeworld of Clan Sy, which was forfeited after the First Rebellion when the Clan was removed from partnership in the Merchant Alliance of Great Clans.

OIKÍA: Third planet of PDN165 (70 Ophiuchi A). Homeworld of Clan Sabballi.

PIGRELL: Fourth planet of PDN103 (Surphra). Homeworld of Clan Polinda.

ROTH-513: Third planet of PDN193. A holding-complete of Clan Cormed. A micro-bionics research and development center.

SIMBIC UR: Third planet of PDN185 (Sigma Draconis). A holding-complete of Clan Dejoria. Mined for water.

TERRA PRIME: Third planet of PDN100 (Helios). Considered the homeworld of all mankind. Old World designation: Earth.

THRUM DAU: Second planet of PDN438 (Alpha Mensae). A holding-complete of Clan Erstallius. Believed to be the original homeworld of both Clan Erstallius and Clan Tuma. Old World designation: Mensae Two.

U'GALEM: Fourth planet of PDN163 (Chi Herculis). A holding-complete of Clan Dejoria.

WALD-415: Fourth planet of PDN1592. Unclaimed world. Surveys are scheduled to begin in 3530. No sanctioned settlement.

WAN'TEI: Second planet of PDN185 (Sigma Draconis). Homeworld of Clan Dejoria. Old World designation: Sigma Prime.

AKÜN VOCABULARY

AHKHÉ: A shrub native to GSW-183. A sour spice used to flavor food. Used as a natural barrier against insects.

AKÜN: The original language of the Aku people, and the predecessor of various dialects persistent on Kainogae and Jai'raan, that stems from an undetermined root whose origin among the Old Worlds is not certain.

BI'AU: The mediator. A central figure of Aku government.

CIÂFEY: A two-man, winged aircraft. Developed by the Aku after their arrival on GSW-183.

GÁSAH KAHÁFA: Name given to an astronomical event seen in the skies of Ni'apinu in 138 A. E.

IPÀG: A large avian native to GSW-183. Wingspan averages 2 meters for adult females and 1.5 meters for adult males.

JI'DESS: Largest settlement on GSW-183, located on the north-eastern coast of the Wardu Sea. Population: 1,200.

KLÂWPA: a small, carnivorous scavenger of GSW-183. It is characterized by its muscular build, black fur, pungent odor, keen sense of smell, and ferocity when feeding. Average length 90 centimeters from nose to tip of tail.

EDSUA'FAYAK: Knife of Unpleasantness. Any deliberate act of repugnance directed with a specific purpose at a specific person or persons.

KULIQ'QUAD: Place of Safety. A derivative of an old Akün expression, and the name of the first settlement established GSW-183.

L'DYÉM: A formal greeting, most often used when meeting strangers.

MÂNU: 1. A noun meaning a covered, or enclosed space. 2. A verb meaning to cover, to conceal, or to collect.

NELA'OGU: First People. The Aku who settled GSW-183.

NI'APINU: Secure Abode. Name given to GSW-183 by the first settlers.

NI'DESIAH: Leader of Twenty, Commander of the Watch.

OMÈU: A broad-trunk Pinaceae with green or yellow-green needles. Native to GSW-183. Needle length can reach 500 centimeters on the largest specimens, which have been measured up to 150 meters high.

PAUK: A legume native to GSW-183. Its green and white leaves fan out to seven points that each support needles five centimeters long. A source of gum used for tanning leather.

PRISTAL: Shrub-like plant native to GSW-183. The leaves are large, and the six-centimeter-wide lavender flowers produce a berry fruit averaging fifteen centimeters long. Height: 70 to 120 centimeters.

SIPÁ: Omnivorous mammal with gray and brown fur of the family Ursidae, bred on GSW-183 from stock originally from Wan'tei. The largest cataloged specimen was four meters in length.

SÌJ YÊBU: Akün term for the Common Language of the Alliance. A hybrid form of Englo'ni, whose origin has been traced to various language groups persistent among the Old Worlds.

SQUA PALN: Small settlement in the foothills of the Umelk Mountains. Population: 160.

UAH'EKI: 1. A pervasive, controlling force that blinds the mind to reality. **2.** The imagining of the conscious mind that subverts logical thought.

U'ALIOU: Informal greeting between friends.

WASSÚA CAPHÁGA: Valley of Streams. The rift valley between the Umelk and Dekeg Mountains that runs from the coastal plain east of Squa Paln, to the foothills south of Quel Pass and north of Kuliq'Quad basin.

MAPS

The following are maps of holdings mentioned in the chronicles, and were taken from The Planetary Database. Complied in the 160th year of the Merchant Alliance of Great Clans.

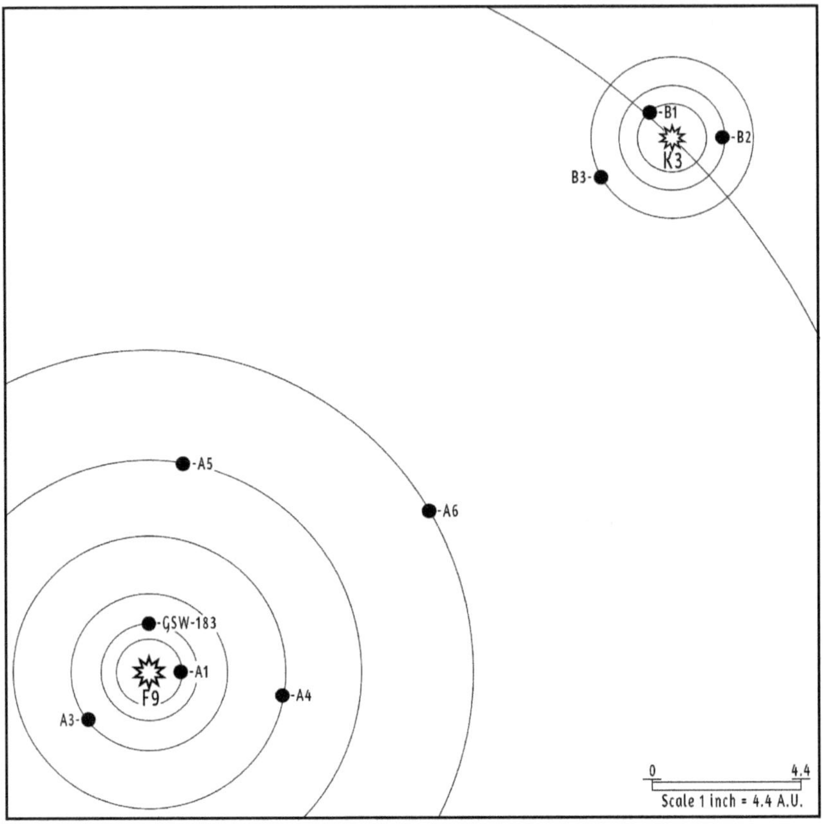
B1
B2
K3
B3
A5
A6
GSW-183
A1
F9
A4
A3
0
4.4
Scale 1 inch = 4.4 A.U.

PDN160

F and K Type Dwarf Multiple Star System

Old World Primary Name: 26 Draconis AB

ERSTALLIUS
THE NEW ALLIANCE OF GREAT CLANS

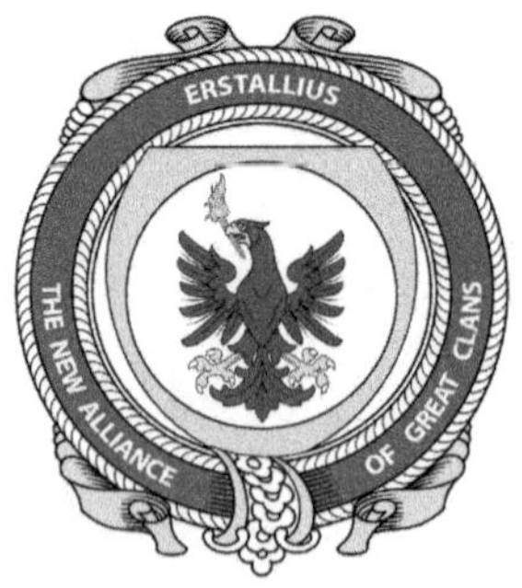

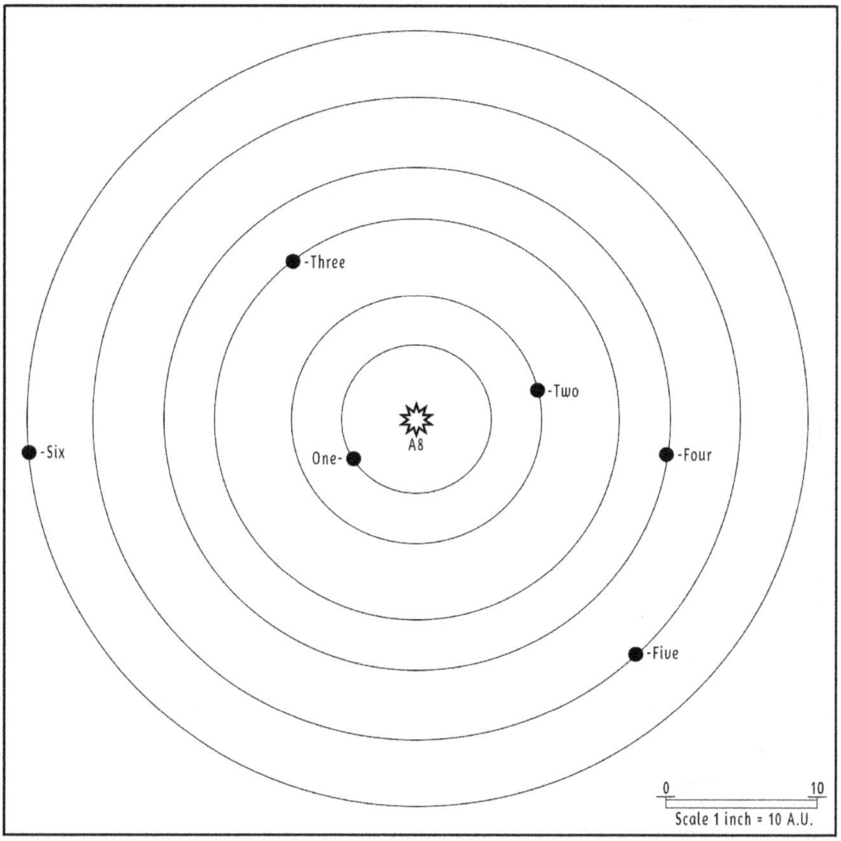

-Three

-Two

A8

-Six

One-

-Four

-Five

0 10

Scale 1 inch = 10 A.U.

PDN203

A Type Subgiant Primary

Old World Primary Name: Alpha Cephei

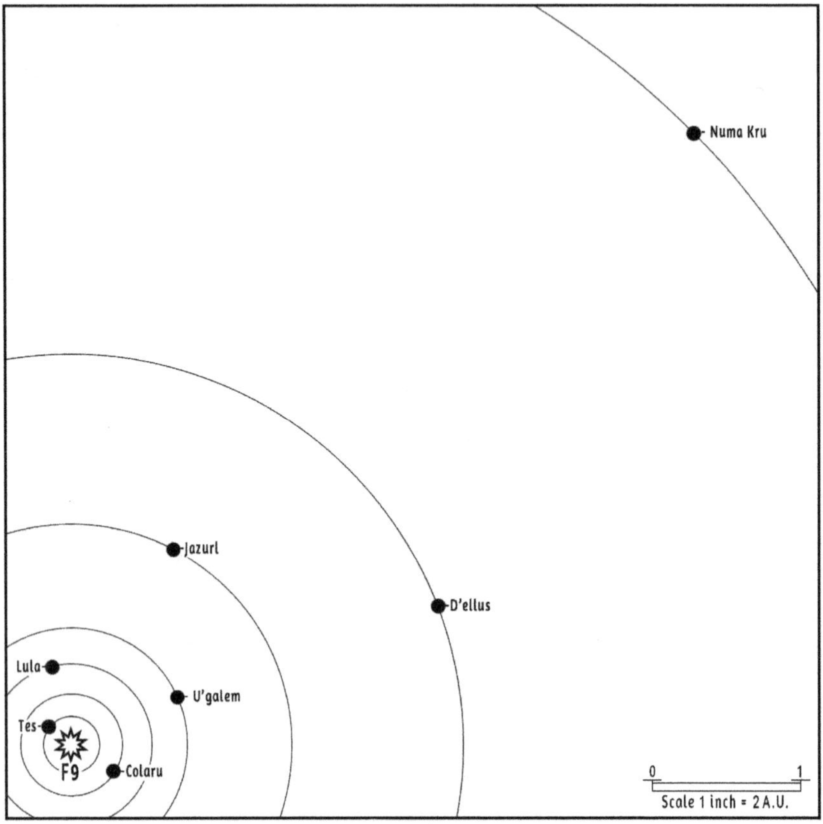

Numa Kru

Jazurl

D'ellus

Lula

U'galem

Tes

F9

Colaru

0 1

Scale 1 inch = 2 A.U.

PDN163

F9 Type Dwarf Primary

Old World Primary Name: Chi Herculis

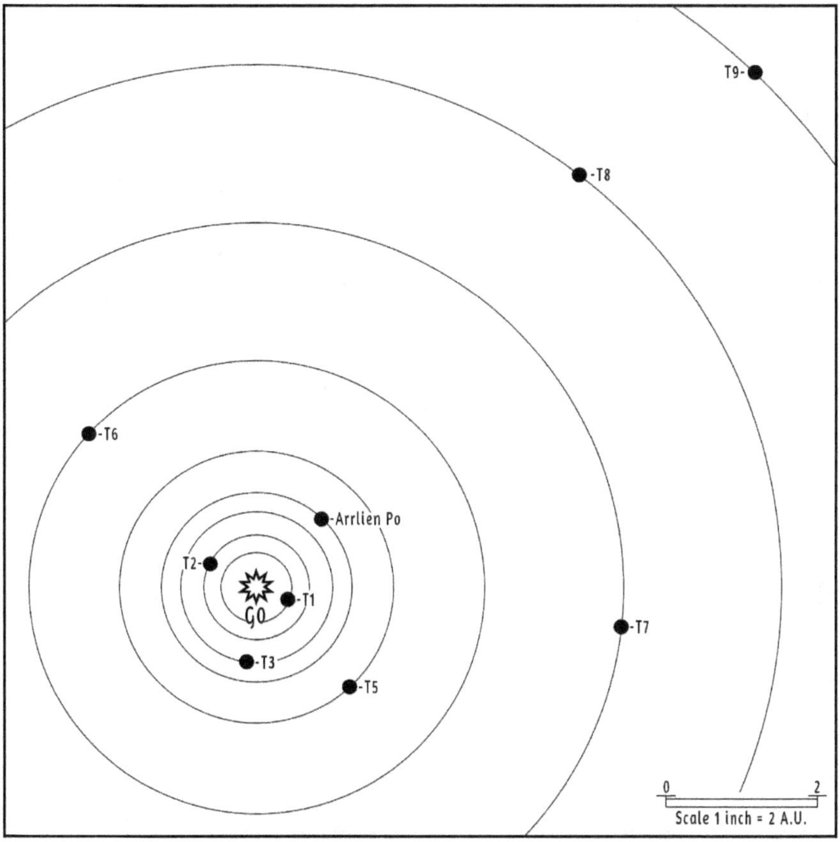

T9-
-T8
-T6
-Arrlien Po
T2-
G0
-T1
-T7
-T3
-T5
0
2
Scale 1 inch = 2 A.U.

PDN1527 - Trigelles' Star (inner system)

G Type Dwarf Primary

Old World Primary Name: HIP 82636

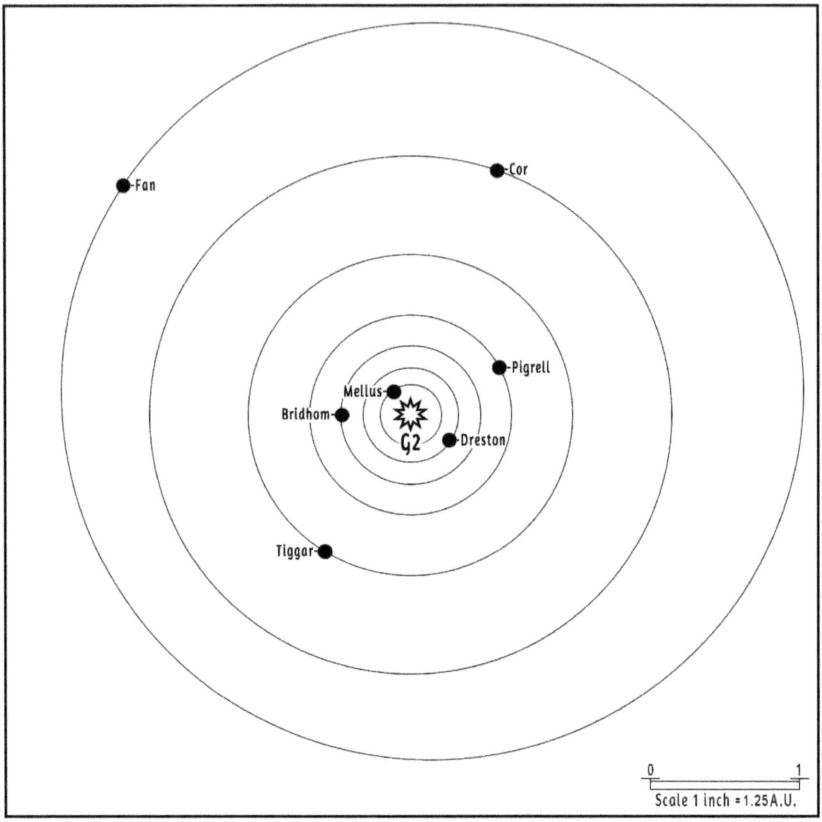

Fan
Cor
Pigrell
Mellus
Bridhom
G2
Dreston
Tiggar

0 1
Scale 1 inch = 1.25A.U.

PDN103

G2 Type Dwarf Primary

Old World Primary Name: Surphra

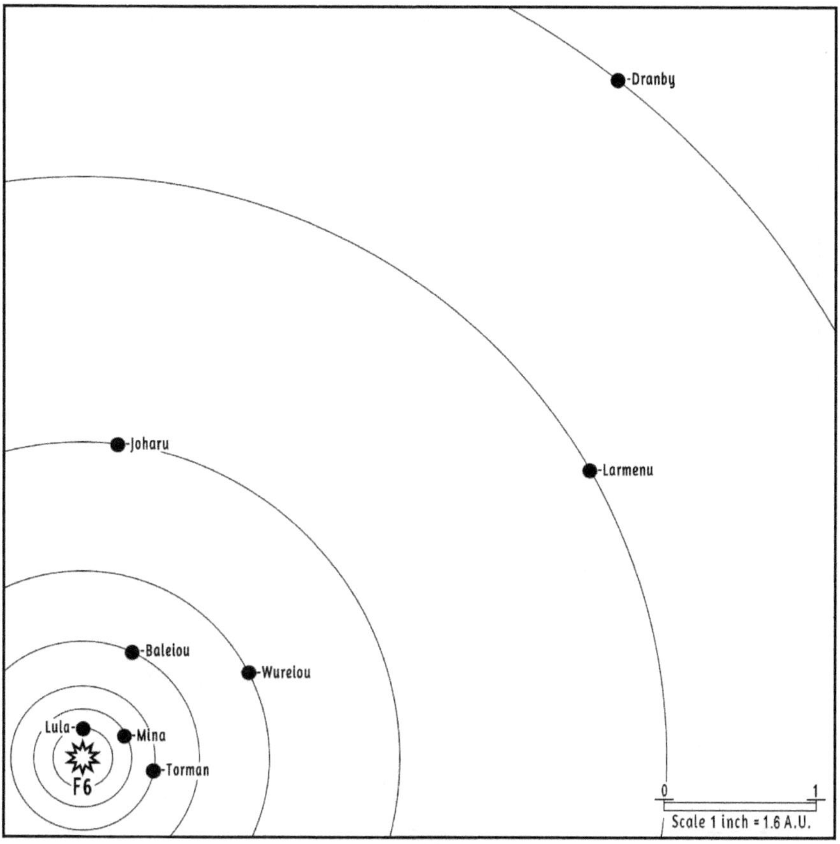

-Dranby
-Joharu
-Larmenu
-Baleiou
-Wureiou
Lula-
-Mina
F6
-Torman

0 1
Scale 1 inch = 1.6 A.U.

PDN306

F6 Type Dwarf Primary

Old World Primary Name: Pi-3 Orionis

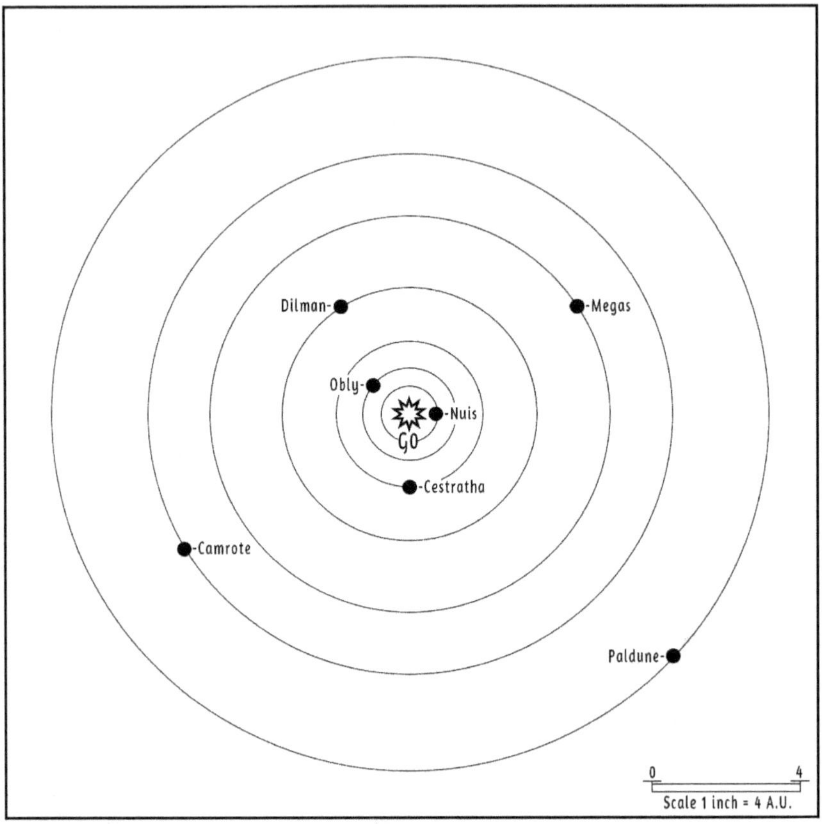

Dilman-
-Megas
Obly-
-Nuis
G0
-Cestratha
-Camrote
Paldune-
0 4
Scale 1 inch = 4 A.U.

PDN169

G Type Dwarf Primary

Old World Primary Name: Lambda Serpentis

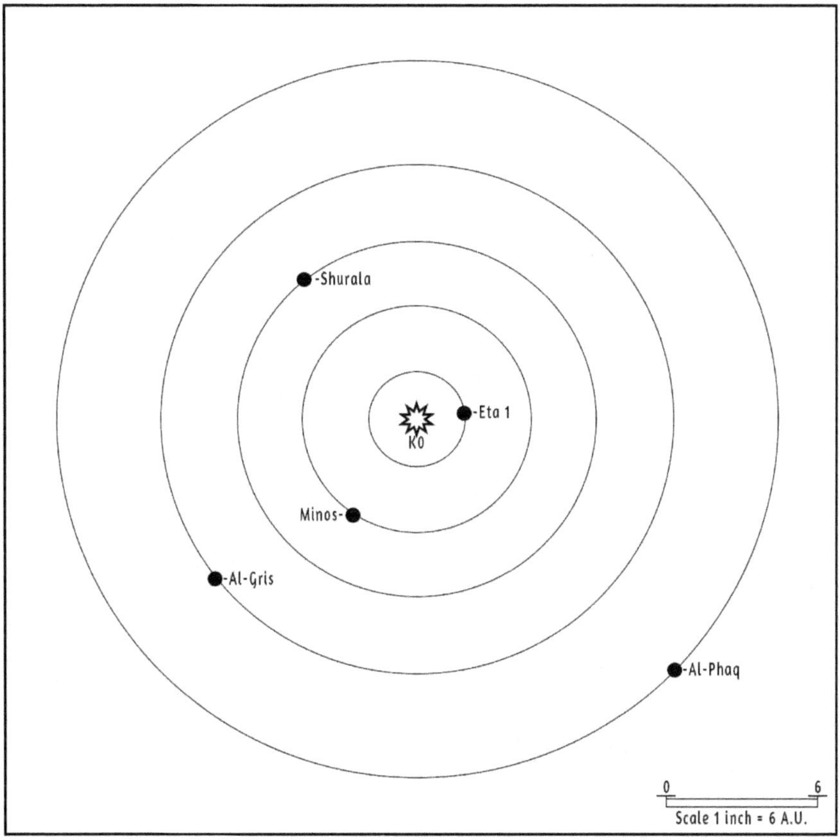

-Shurala

K0

-Eta 1

Minos-

-Al-Gris

-Al-Phaq

0 6

Scale 1 inch = 6 A.U.

PDN198

K Type Subgiant Primary

Old World Primary Name: Eta Cephei

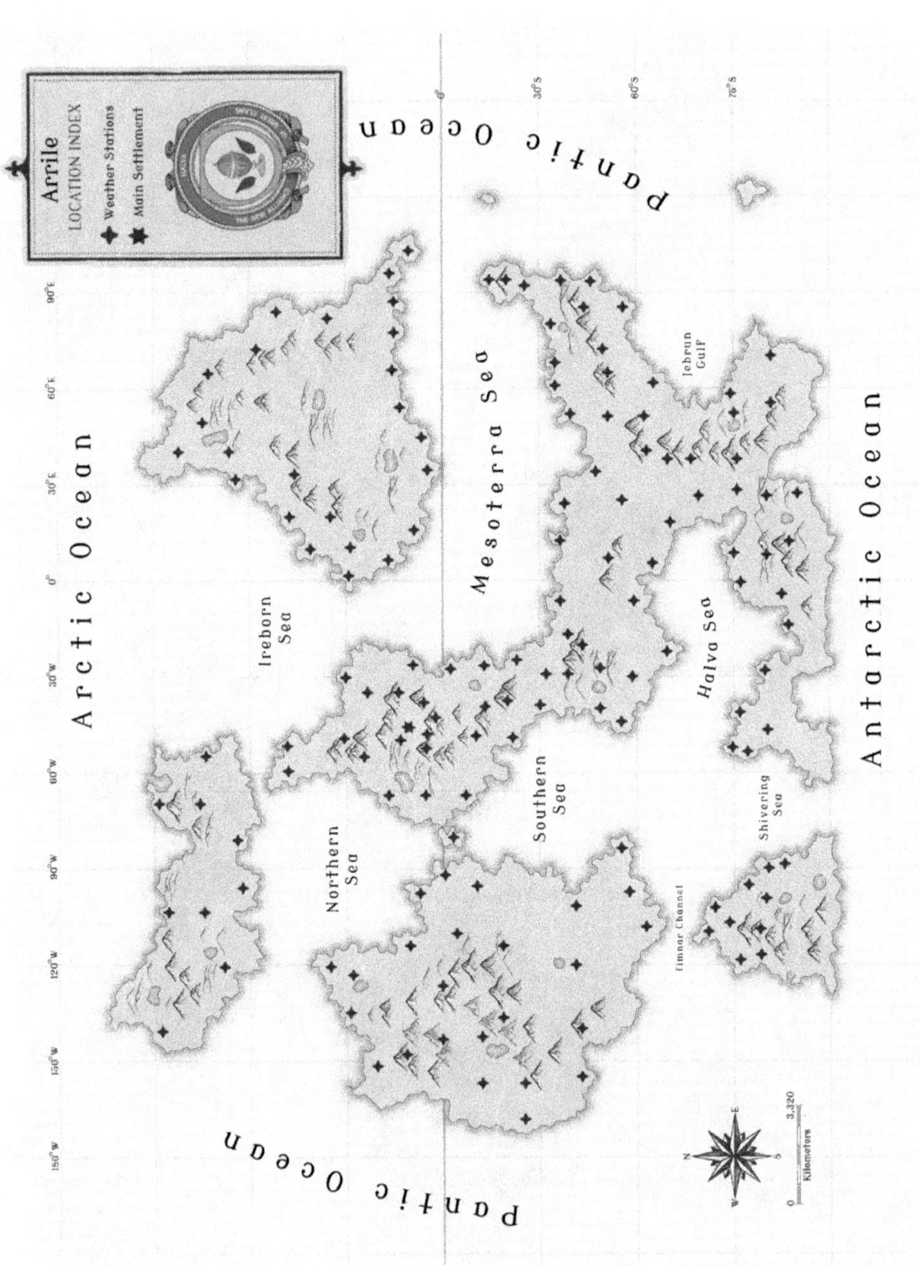
Arrile
LOCATION INDEX
Weather Stations
Main Settlement
Arctic Ocean
Pantic Ocean
Mesoterra Sea
Ireborn Sea
Northern Sea
Southern Sea
Halva Sea
Jebrun Gulf
Shivering Sea
Antarctic Ocean
Pantic Ocean
0
3,320
Kilometers

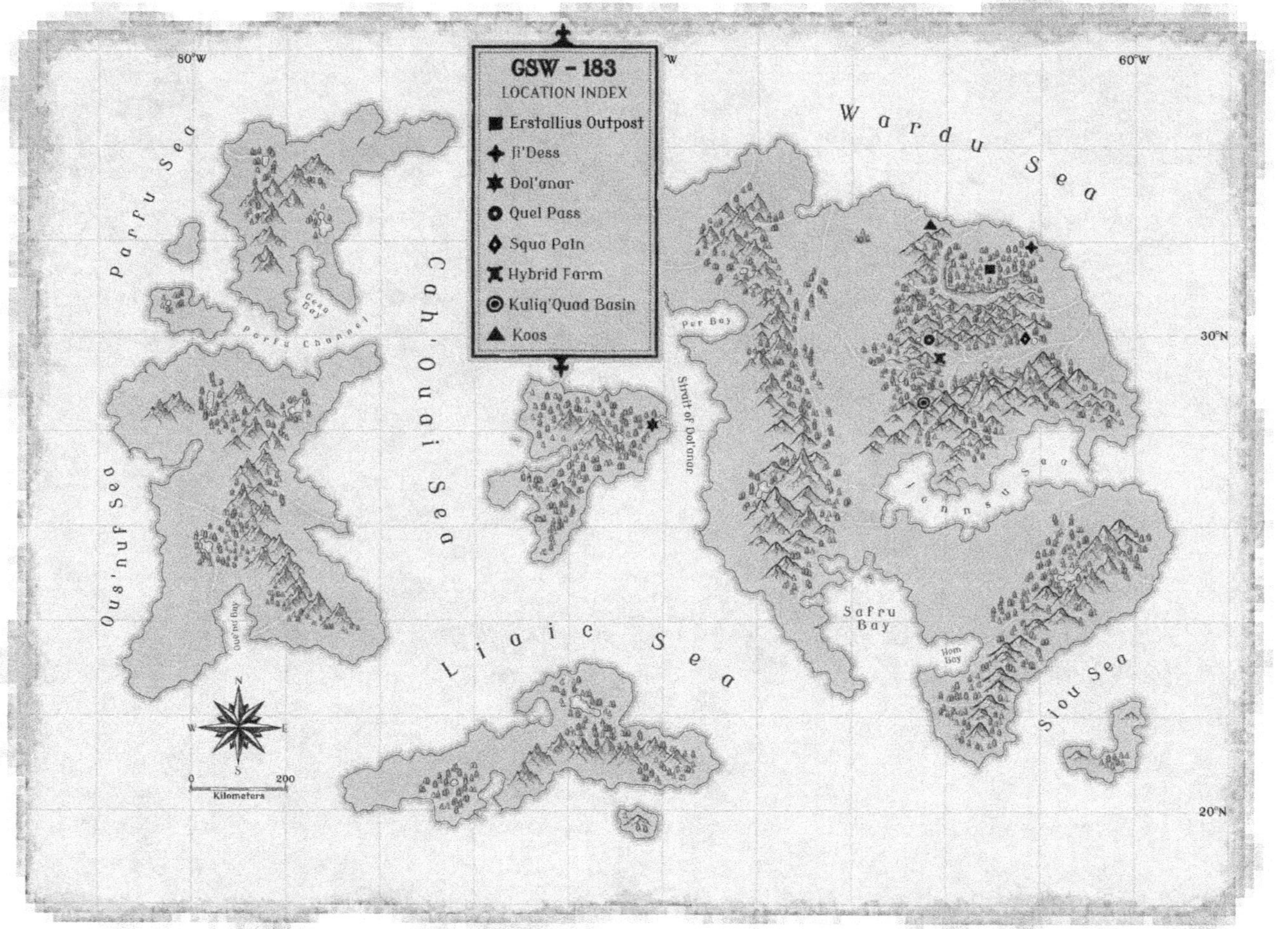
GSW – 183
LOCATION INDEX
Erstallius Outpost
Ji'Dess
Dol'anar
Quel Pass
Squa Pain
Hybrid Farm
Kuliq'Quad Basin
Koos
80°W
60°W
30°N
20°N
Wardu Sea
Parfu Sea
Parfu Channel
Ceaa Bay
Cah'Ouai Sea
Ous'nuf Sea
Que'nu Bay
Per Bay
Strait of Dol'anar
Liaic Sea
Safru Bay
Hom Bay
Siou Sea
N
S
W
E
0
200
Kilometers

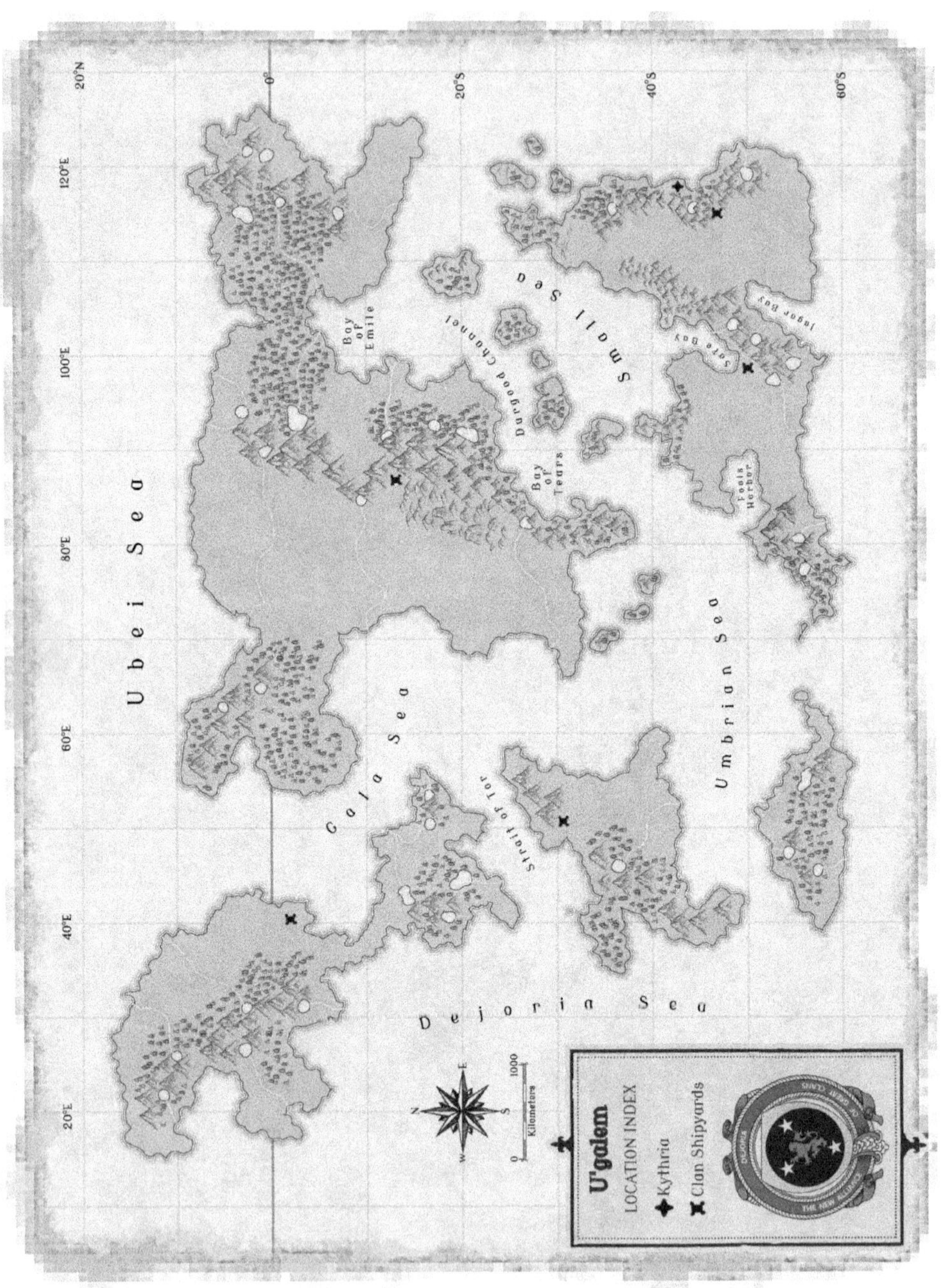

Ubei Sea
Gala Sea
Small Sea
Dejoria Sea
Umbrian Sea
Bay of Emile
Durgood Channel
Bay of Tears
Strait of Tor
Fools Harbor
Sate Bay
Jagor Bay
20°N
0°
20°S
40°S
60°S
20°E
40°E
60°E
80°E
100°E
120°E
N
S
E
W
0
1000
Kilometers
U'golem
LOCATION INDEX
Kythria
Clan Shipyards

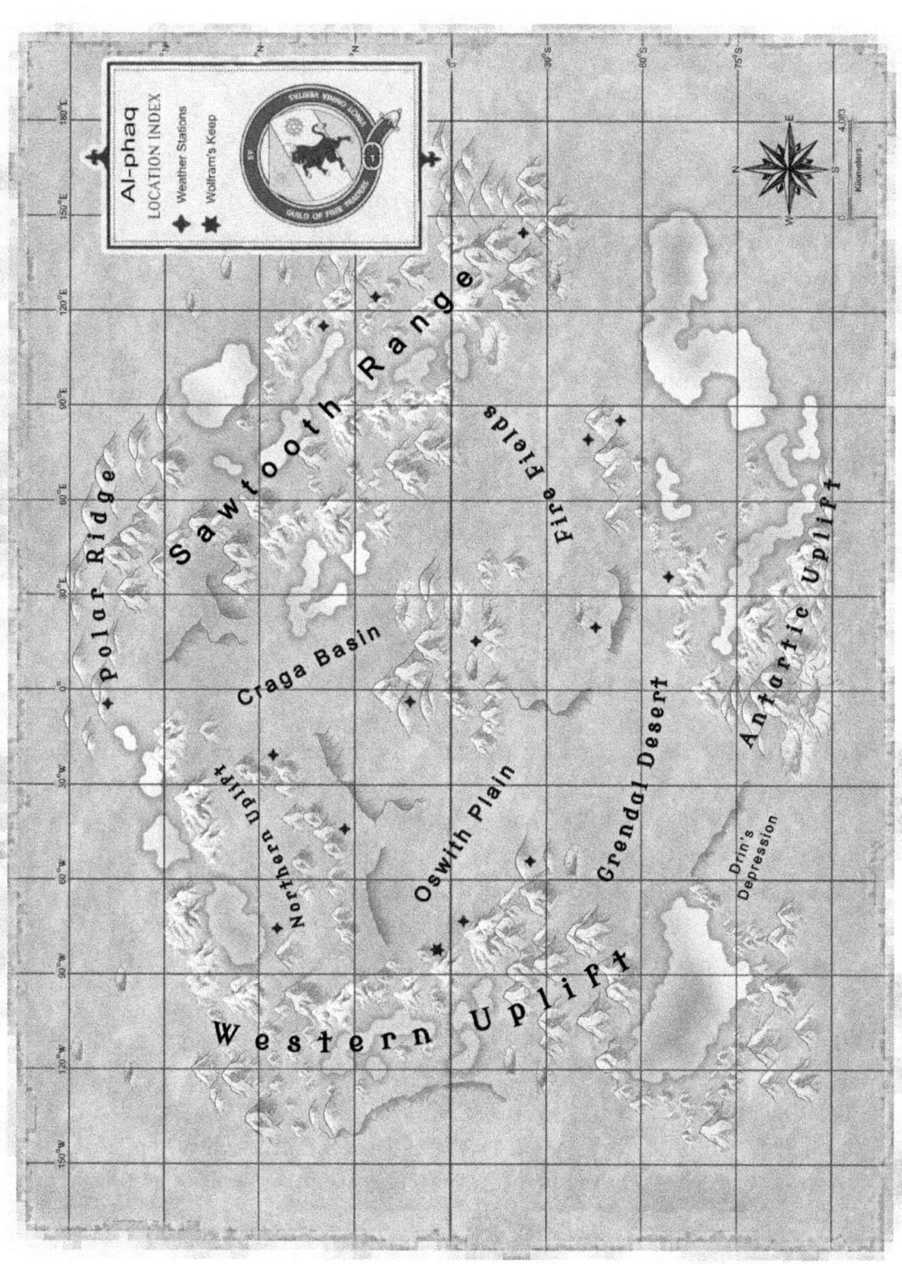
Al-phaq
LOCATION INDEX
Weather Stations
Wolfram's Keep
GUILD OF FREE TRADERS
Polar Ridge
Sawtooth Range
Craga Basin
Fire Fields
Northern Uplift
Oswith Plain
Grendal Desert
Antartic Uplift
Drin's Depression
Western Uplift
Kilometers

GLOSSARY OF CHARACTERS

The Aku

Grénu: Overseer of the Mânu at Kuliq'Quad.
Kudu: The searcher who found the survivors of the shuttle crash in the Yoslyn mountains.
Naréndu: Commander-in-Charge of the first Aku transport to leave GSW-183.
Nujo: Elder from Ji'dess.
Paaq: The Bi'au, the one who mediates.
Salus: Ni'desiah, Commander of Twenty and ciâfey pilot.

Clan Cormed

Jasur Plucket: Degen, and Chief Engineer assigned to the frigate, *Iron Spear.*
Duncun Turl: Degen, and First Officer of the frigate, *Javelin.*
Ethan Grant: Jegen, and Commander of the frigate, *Javelin.*
Eve-Ann Corbas: Prime Director of Security assigned to the frigate, *Javelin.*
Grom Anen: Degen, and First Officer of the frigate, *Iron Spear.*
Jarred Molska: Physician assigned to the frigate, *Iron Spear.*
Milos Fore: Envoy and Regional Director of Clan Affairs.
Pallis Nin: Envoy assigned to the frigate, *Iron Spear.*
Zebulan Farvic: Jegen, and Commander of the frigate, *Iron Spear.*

Clan Dejoria

Jhared Dejoria: Patriarch of his Clan.
Karisa Marsh: Clerk assigned to the Cormed embassy on U'galem.
Oswald Rugeri: Arbitrator in the city Kythria on U'galem.

Clan Erstallius

Arlud Reynaldo Erstallius: Regent of GSW-183 and son of Armand.
Armand Erstallius: High Regent and Patriarch of his Clan.
Yancy Bril: Diwa, and Junior Grade Engineer.
Sal Danik: Diwa-Major, and Senior Grade Engineer.
Dirk Sieger: Diwa-Major, and Senior Grade Engineer.
Gustav Eahuda: Degen-of-the-Corp, and Commander of Erstallius Security on GSW-183.
Haden Pyle: Nared, and Senior Construction Engineer.
Jens Orr: Nared, and Senior Shuttle Pilot.
Lon Pavan: Jegen-Major, and Commander-in Charge of the Erstallius Fleet at GSW-183.
Petra Sityln: Nared-Major, and Lead Construction Engineer on GSW-183.
Winstone Bittle: Nared-Major and Lead Aircraft Engineer on GSW-183.

The Guild of Free Traders

Bern Pryce: Pilot assigned to Freighter 107.
Donté Cegla: Marine assigned to Shanna Sy's Security Group.
Eber Kurnes: Security Minister for the Guild.
Einar Duballik: Member of the Guild Council, and Captain of Freighter 102.
Erlis Pardee: Captain of freighter 107.
Harlon Sater: Pilot assigned to Freighter 107.
Ross Cordova: Marine, and Head of Shanna Sy's Security Group.
Shanna Sy: Daughter of Wolfram and Wellen Sy.
Wellen Talillia Sy: Wife of Wolfram Sy.
Wolfram Sy: Patriarch of the Guild of Free Traders who led the First Rebellion.

Clan Halva

Cynth Halva: Matriarch of Clan Halva, sister of Gustus.
Gustus Halva: High Regent and Patriarch of the Clan.

Clan Polinda

Bev Colli: Sapi, and Mad Japer assigned to the mine on Alpha Cephei Four.
Farquar Polinda: High Regent and Patriarch of his Clan.
Josh Gridle: Sapi, and Foreman in the mine on Alpha Cephei Four.
Burgess Marlow: Jegen, Commander-in-Charge of the dreadnought, *Venka Kinall.*

Clan Sabballi

Artemis Parker: Judge Advocate assigned to the Alpha Cephei Four investigation.
John Avrim Parker: Degen and Investigator of incident No. 1798 on Arrilen Po.
Ludi Prell: Nared-Major and Pilot assigned to the evacuation team sent to Arrilen Po.
Tylo Singh: Judge Advocate assigned to the Alpha Cephei Four Investigation

ABOUT THE AUTHOR

P.D. Blackwell is a lifelong student who began studying theology, religion, and physics in 1980. He practices the guitar and piano everyday, and enjoys a good game of chess.

www.pdblackwell.com

BOOKS IN THIS SERIES

Chaos Rising:
The Erstallius Chronicles, Volume One
https://www.amazon.com/dp/B08W9RJ6K6

The Rhysu Alternative,
The Erstallius Chronicles, Volume Two
https://www.amazon.com/dp/B08W8QTC9

OTHER BOOKS BY P. D. BLACKWELL

Lawless Tradition:
God's Victory Despite Christendom's Failure
https://www.amazon.com/dp/1736609637

PRAISE FOR CHAOS RISING

"A compelling, complex, and cinematic work of science fiction with plenty of chilling psychological undertones and all-out action scenes."
— K.C. Finn, *Reader's Favorite.*

"If you enjoy complex, well-developed science fiction novels, you'll want to check out Blackwell's book. I loved how this adventure takes the reader to many new destinations full of diverse cultures, vivid landscapes, and honored pasts."
— Erin Dydek, *Online Book Club. Org.*

"Blackwell excels at characterization and vivid portrayals of each scene. Chaos Rising is edgy, clever, and layered. It kept me glued to its pages."
— Lit Amiri, *Reader's Favorite.*

PRAISE FOR THE RHYSU ALTERNATIVE

"I already had high expectations before starting The Rhysu Alternative. I was expecting the same level of intricate plot, smart characters, and impressive narrative. I was completely surprised when P.D. Blackwell exceeded all of my expectations and gave me a lot more."
— Rabia Tanveer, *Reader's Favorite.*

"Author P. D. Blackwell presents a worthy sequel after the excellent worldbuilding and complex emotional dynamics of the first foray into this incredible universe. After what Bev went through in the opening novel, I thought it would be hard to top, but her journey of empowerment in her new situation was really inspiring."
— K.C. Finn, *Reader's Favorite.*

"Blackwell creates conflict at multiple levels without taking away from the story the balance it deserves. The crisp prose is enriched by the engaging dialogues, but the strength of the narrative lies in the author's expert handling of plot points and the conflict which escalates to an explosive climax."
— Romuald Dzemo, *Reader's Favorite*

PRAISE FOR LAWLESS TRADITION

"Lawless Tradition is a tour de force with an engaging literary style that educates the reader along the journey."

— Kimberly Vargas, *Award Wining Author*

"Lawless Tradition is a book of divine wisdom, understanding, and discovery. A guide to help true Christians better understand God."

— Anthionette Ejimofor, *Goodreads.com*

"The amount of study and preparation put into this work is evident and instills in the reader a fair amount of confidence in the authenticity of this book. Nothing is pulled out of thin air; everything is backed up with evidence."

— Nzube Chizoba Okeke, *Online Book Club .Org*

This is a solid book with so much scriptural backing and commentary from theologians to support its interpretations that it cannot be reasonably ignored. Very highly recommended.

— Asher Syed, *Reader's Favorite*

P. D. Blackwell takes a deep dive into word meanings and cultural context . . . Explaining in easy-to-understand terms how to develop a first century understanding, Blackwell leads to a logical conclusion.

— Philip Van Heusen, *Reader's Favorite*

www.ingramcontent.com/pod-product-compliance
Lightning Source LLC
LaVergne TN
LVHW020522100826
845148LV00010B/1315

* 9 7 8 1 7 3 6 6 0 9 6 4 4 *